TALES OF THE
SHADOWMEN

Volume 15: Trompe l'Oeil

also from Black Coat Press

Tales of the Shadowmen 1: The Modern Babylon (2004)
Tales of the Shadowmen 2: Gentlemen of the Night (2005)
Tales of the Shadowmen 3: Danse Macabre (2006)
Tales of the Shadowmen 4: Lords of Terror (2007)
Tales of the Shadowmen 5: The Vampires of Paris (2008)
Tales of the Shadowmen 6: Grand Guignol (2009)
Tales of the Shadowmen 7: Femmes Fatales (2010)
Tales of the Shadowmen 8: Agents Provocateurs (2011)
Tales of the Shadowmen 9: La Vie en Noir (2012)
Tales of the Shadowmen 10: Esprit de Corps (2013)
Tales of the Shadowmen 11: Force Majeure (2014)
Tales of the Shadowmen 12: Carte Blanche (2015)
Tales of the Shadowmen 13: Sang Froid (2016)
Tales of the Shadowmen 14: Coup de Grâce (2017)

Shadowmen: Heroes and Villains of French Pulp Fiction (non-fiction) *(2003)*
Shadowmen 2: Heroes and Villains of French Comics (non-fiction) *(2004)*

TALES OF THE
SHADOWMEN

Volume 15: Trompe l'Oeil

edited by
Jean-Marc & Randy Lofficier

stories by
**Daniel Alhadeff, Matthew Baugh, Adam Mudman Bezecny,
Thierry Bosch, Matthew Dennion, David Friend,
Brian Gallagher, Martin Gately, Travis Hiltz, Paul Hugli,
Gulzar Joby, Vincent Jounieaux, Jean-Guillaume Lanuque,
Jean-Marc Lofficier, Nigel Malcolm, Christofer Nigro, John
Peel, Frank Schildiner, Michel Stéphan** and **David L. Vineyard**

translations by
J.-M. & Randy Lofficier & Michael Shreve

cover by
Stephan Martiniere

A Black Coat Press Book

Visit our website at www.blackcoatpress.com

ISBN 978-1-61227-813-1. First Printing. December 2018. Published by Black Coat Press, an imprint of Hollywood Comics.com, LLC, P.O. Box 17270, Encino, CA 91416. All rights reserved. Except for review purposes, no part of this book may be reproduced or transmitted in any form or by any means, electronic or mechanical, including photocopying, recording or by any information storage and retrieval system, without permission in writing from the publisher. The stories and characters depicted in this anthology are entirely fictional. Printed in the United States of America.

Table of Contents

This surreal tale, the mood of which evokes the New Wave cinema of the 1960s, stars none other than Isidore Beautrelet, the young college student who thwarted Arsène Lupin in The Hollow Needle, *and who was clearly created by Maurice Leblanc as a homage to Gaston Leroux's youthful detective, Joseph Rouletabille. Daniel Alhadeff, a Swiss writer, whose first appearance in* Tales of the Shadowmen *this is, takes on a strange journey in...*

Daniel Alhadeff: *The Vertigo*

Isidore Beautrelet opened his eyes and sat up. He immediately regretted it because the white room began a double rotation. The tiled floor suddenly appeared to be above him, while, through the open window, the trees fell up into the sky. The young man closed his eyes and leaned back to give the vertigo time to ebb away. When again he tried opening his eyes, the ceiling had resumed its normal position and the garden its immobility. Long before the nurse crossed the threshold, Beautrelet had identified the scenery around him. It had to be Dr. Morel's private clinic. He was reassured to find that he was still capable of reasoning and reassured to know that he was still in Cap d'Antibes. When the nurse, surprised to find him awake, called the doctor, he closed his eyes and tried to collect the scattered pieces of his consciousness in order to reconstruct his memories...

Knossos 1911

The Hotel Minos had opened two years earlier, with a degree of comfort and luxuriousness that were inappropriate in view of the chaotic political situation of the island. It had seen the Cretans rise against the Ottoman Empire on two occasions and, each time, it had ended in blood. The situation had been more stable since 1898, but the natives were still licking their wounds.

The uniformed doorman opened the gilded glass door to make way for one of the few foreigners who lived in the hotel. Isidore Beautrelet was a cosmopolitan gentleman of many talents. Dressed in a smart jacket, he carried a pummeled cane and wore a top hat with casual elegance. His hair was cut short and his bright eyes displayed a heightened sensitivity. He adjusted his bow tie and walked briskly towards the archaeological site of the royal palace.

At this early hour, nature itself was struggling to wake up. The site was deserted. Had another strike hit the cyclopean excavation, or had work not yet begun? While strolling among the ruins of one of the greatest architectural wonders ever built by man, Beautrelet wondered when the man he was looking for would show up, since he knew him to be whimsical and jocular. He was surprised therefore to find him sitting on a rock in a contemplative pose.

"Professor Woland!"

The other man stood up and raised his arms to the Heavens in an odd gesture of welcome.

"Ah, my young friend, how nice to see you!"

He spoke French with an Italian accent, which only added to the mystery of his origins, because no one knew if he was German or Russian. Woland was medium-sized, and wore baggy clothes that did not restrain his embonpoint; he had unruly gray hair and a tousled beard. His brown eyes sparkled and he limped, sometimes with the left leg, other times with the right.

"I tell you, all this will end badly," he said, with a big smile displaying several gold teeth.

"What are you talking about?" asked Beautrelet.

"I'm talking about humanity! That's my only concern!"

He pointed to the melancholy ruins around them.

"Come. Let us walk a little. My legs hurt."

This apparently did not prevent him from leaping like a goat over some boulders strewn around the site.

"Look at how the beautiful Minoan empire collapsed upon itself. It was once the pinnacle of civilization. Running water on every floor, wonderful craftsmen, an unimaginable fleet of warships... It could have ruled the world. And then... crash!"

"They blame the explosion of a volcano," said Beautrelet smiling, because he liked listening to the flights of imagination of the polyglot scholar.

"The volcano didn't help, but the decline was inevitable."

From where they stood, they could admire an enchanting view of the coastline. A few white sails dotted the endless sea and, in the distance, a plume of smoke heralded the arrival of a ship.

Woland, suddenly turning conspiratorial, leaned toward the young man as if to reveal a great secret.

"Progress... that is the poison that leads man to ruin."

Once again, Beautrelet did not know whether he should laugh or take his teacher seriously.

"It speaks only of steam, speed and efficiency," Woland continued. "Submarines, airships, underground trains, automobiles, scientific wonders... What a joke! All these infernal machines will only precipitate the fall!"

After this tirade, Woland took a long breath.

"Do you think that Man, caught in the grasp of industrial frenzy, will lose his values?" asked Beautrelet.

The professor nodded, seriously.

"But scientific advances are not necessarily in contradiction with social progress," objected the young man.

8

"Obviously not. The two go hand in hand for a time, the second trying to balance the first. But ultimately, mankind will lose, as outdistanced as the horse that lost to the locomotive, and everything will collapse—again."

They had reached the limits of the site, bordered by an olive grove. They were able to take shelter in its shadows as the heat of the rising sun gained in power. Since his friend now seemed lost in his thoughts, Beautrelet saw fit to revive their conversation.

"But you, Professor, you're a scientist..."

In fact, he was not sure of Woland's area of expertise. The scientist was a master in the art of dodging questions about himself and left many things unsaid.

"I am a historian and an adept in black magic."

Beautrelet hadn't been expecting that.

Woland continued, pointing at the archaeological site.

"I find that this place, with all its legends, offers a tremendous metaphor for my thesis. You are presumably familiar the myth that arose at the royal palace of Knossos?"

"Do you mean, the labyrinth?"

"I always thought that Minos had rendered a notable service to those he ruled by building it. To me, the Minotaur represents the savage instincts of man channeled into the winding maze of reason. Do you know that our brain is like a maze? And I think that the learned Daedalus locked himself up voluntarily in order to avoid succumbing to the lure of progress."

While speaking, he drew a maze on the ground with his cane, one with many twists and turns.

"That is interesting," said Beautrelet. "How do you then explain the myth of Icarus?"

"In the same fashion. He represents Man getting too close to ultimate knowledge and falling."

"A new version of the Forbidden Fruit of the Tree of Knowledge, then?"

"Indeed. It is always such a pleasure to converse with you!"

They allowed themselves a moment of silence while strolling around. A fresh breeze now tempered the heat, and the musky scent of the wild vegetation was conducive to day-dreaming.

"I keep talking but I feel there is a sadness welling up within you," said Woland. "What is it all about?"

Beautrelet was surprised that he was so transparent. He searched for the words he needed.

"I have a thirst for something, but do not know how to appease it. I have traveled, explored and experienced many dangers, yet there is still this immense void in my heart..."

"Ah, love..."

"Why do you say this?"

"You were seen in Vienn..."

The young man jumped at the mention of the Austrian capital.

"You saw me?"

"And you were not alone..."

Woland looked at him with an eye as sharp as that of a surgeon looking at the patient on his operating table.

"Yes, I met the adopted daughter of that Hungarian doctor, Kopely..." admitted Beautrelet.

Suddenly, there was a mewing sound behind them and a huge black cat leaped into Woland's arms. The professor burst into a loud laugh.

"My dear Cagliostro," he said to the cat, "I thought I'd lost you. Have you been taking advantage of your morning walk?"

The cat meowed as if answering the question.

"Good! Then I guess you are here to remind me of the fact that I have other obligations..."

Once again, the cat seemed to acquiesce. Woland let him jump down and got rid of the hairs the feline had left on his jacket.

"Well, young man, it looks like I must leave you now."

"Something to do in town?"

Beautrelet always sought to learn more about the mysterious professor.

"I must go wherever I'm needed."

"Is the market for black magic flourishing?"

"You can't imagine! Are you staying at the Hotel Minos?"

Cagliostro the cat was becoming impatient.

"Then maybe I'll see you there tonight. Did you know that they built an observatory on the roof?"

Woland tipped his hat and rushed after the cat who was running through the olive trees.

Dr. Morel himself soon showed up at Beautrelet's bedside. He took the young man's wrist, checking his pulse with a huge pocket watch. He was tall and thin, the very model of the surgeon who keeps all his emotions well under control.

"Well, well, it looks as if we're feeling better!" he said.

"I don't even know what happened to me," said Beautrelet.

"Neither do I. You were found unconscious not far from here by a crew of fishermen, who brought you to my clinic. You need rest. Spend the night here, and tomorrow you'll be in fine form!"

A sense of urgency gripped the young man, but he did not know why.

Dr. Morel didn't notice and left the room, followed by the nurse.

Beautrelet leaned against the soft pillow. He had to remember...

It was Friday, September 13; Fall had not yet impacted the colors of the lush landscapes of Cap d'Antibes. Beautrelet had rented a villa in this little frequented part of the French Riviera. Tired of big cities and all the social obligations that came with them, he had elected to go on a retreat to try to find some meaning to his life. Every evening, he enjoyed the sweetness of the fragrant air and the sound of the waves, while sitting in the shade of the pine trees. But he still had not found the answers he sought.

Since no one knew he was there, he was very surprised, one morning, to receive an envelope containing an invitation.

One of his neighbors, Dr. Schok, had arranged a tour of his mansion, turned into a science museum, and had invited him for that same evening. The reception would be accompanied by a buffet. Always driven by curiosity, the young man had decided to accept. After all, it was only a short walk along the beach to the mysterious scientist's estate. He had questioned his neighbors, but no one could tell him anything about Dr. Schok.

The museum was housed in a beautiful 18th century mansion decorated with turrets and colonnades. A vast lawn sloped gently toward the sea. As Beautrelet got closer, he saw several silhouettes on the white gravel esplanade. Soon he found himself in the presence of the other guests, who were standing by a well-stocked buffet. There were three of them. One stepped forward to greet him. Athletic and chiseled, he had slick, black hair plastered to his skull and a small mustache.

"Welcome, friend," he said, with good humor. "I'm Alexis Vorski. Who might you be?"

Beautrelet smiled, shook the hand extended to him and declined his identity.

"You are French; I am German," said Vorski "Let me introduce you to the others."

They were more reserved and did not seem comfortable with Vorski's exuberance. The German began by presenting a young red-haired woman of striking Nordic beauty.

"This is Miss Brunner, from Berlin."

The woman with overly made-up eyes and an icy smile held out her hand. Beautrelet bowed and lightly kissed it.

"*Schön, Sie kennen zu lernen.*"

The last guest was a blond giant with a square jaw and a sagacious look.

"You must be American?" guessed Beautrelet, turning away from the young woman.

"Hareton Ironcastle," said the giant, crushing his hand.

Beautrelet smiled.

"Nice to meet you."

Suddenly, there was a flutter of movement and the young man saw the eyes of the other three guests move to a point behind him.

"Isidore?" said a voice that he had thought he would never hear again.

He hesitated, his heart full of doubt, like Orpheus fearing he would lose Eurydice forever.

He turned slowly. She stood before him in the orange light of dusk; tiny, her eyes reflecting a mixture of hope and fear. The other three, aware that they were witnessing a moment of rare intensity, remained silent. Just as Miss Brunner had exuded an almost palpable sensual charm, this newcomer radiated purity and love.

"Rachael," muttered Beautrelet, incredulous.

She came up to him and hugged him, as if seeking to prove her identity without using words.

He stepped away to give her a deep look.

"I'm glad to see you," she said.

"Rachael," he repeated.

She wore a dark, conservative suit; her brunette hair, cut short, accentuated the pallor of her face.

"Rachael..." he said, for the third time.

She responded with a delicate laugh.

"Won't you introduce me to your friends?" she asked.

Beautrelet caught himself like a magician who's missed a trick.

"Yes, of course. This is Miss Brunner."

The cold woman stepped forward, almost gliding in her green evening gown.

"Delighted," she said.

She had a head on Rachael and consumed the young girl with her gaze, but Rachael stood her ground and did not lower her eyes.

"Alexis Vorski."

The German stepped close to her as if he was trying to hypnotize her; the young woman's hand could have touched his mustache,. But he, too, failed to break her composure. Rachael was not as fragile as she looked.

"And Mr. Ironcastle."

This time, the American was careful in shaking hands. He bared his perfect teeth in a beatific smile.

"It would seem that we are all here."

Miss Brunner pointed to a small table next to the buffet where five boxes had been placed, each bearing the name of one of the guests. They approached and opened the boxes; inside were odd pairs of glasses not unlike sunglasses.

"Please enter!" said a metallic voice, coming from the living room, the bay windows of which opened on to the terrace. They did so. The large room was almost empty; a large open space had been cleared, in which light projectors created an unusual flicker.

"Put on the glasses," said the disembodied voice.

They obeyed and were immediately surprised to see appear in front of them the huge face of a man they did not know. His semi-transparent mouth shook and the sound of laughter filled the room.

"Welcome to my humble abode, my dear friends!"

"Dr. Schok, I presume?" said Vorski.

The giant face floated before them, rotating to look at each of them in turn, its eyelids blinking and a faint smirk stretched over his face.

"Unfortunately, I cannot be here tonight..."

"Can you hear us?" Ironcastle asked.

"...But that should not stop you from enjoying your visit."

"He doesn't hear us," Rachael realized.

With that last word, and a small and somewhat strange laugh, the astonishing apparition disappeared. They put away the glasses, a little disturbed by the phenomenon that they had just witnessed.

"This whole thing seems rather odd," said Vorski, whose hand was exploring the empty space that Schok's head had occupied.

"Fascinating!" muttered Miss Brunner.

"I gather none of us knows Dr. Schok?" asked Ironcastle.

The others nodded in unison.

"Why invite us then?" wondered Vorski.

"Maybe we should pass on that visit," said Rachael, offering no reassurance.

"Still, a man capable of such a feat cannot be uninteresting," noted Miss Brunner.

"I must admit that this demonstration makes me want to explore his museum," said Beautrelet.

The five guests looked at each other. The unusual was their passion, danger their drug of choice. They had already seen much in their lives, yet nothing approaching the challenge that had just been thrown at them. Vorski summed up their thoughts:

"Let's go!"

There was only one door out of the room. They took it and arrived in a lobby. A monumental staircase led upstairs. They cautiously climbed it. They might have been intensely curious, but they were nonetheless on their guard. A single door opened from the landing onto a large room. Several strange machines stood inside, behind velvet ropes, with signs explaining their purpose.

"A Time Machine," said Vorski, reading the first sign.

It looked like a copper sleigh. Behind the driver's seat stood what looked like a combustion engine, but they all knew enough to realize that it wasn't one. Its most interesting feature was a blue fluorescent tube throbbing as if it were alive. Beautrelet leaned over the controls that were similarly beyond their understanding. Vorski, who stood just behind him, reached out and pushed a button.

Immediately there was a sound like a foghorn which echoed all around them. The two men hurriedly stepped back.

"What did you do, you fool!" said Ironcastle, alarmed.

The machine began fading in and out and progressively lost its substance, until it eventually vanished.

Only Miss Brunner thought this was amusing.

"Come see this!"

Vorski had already moved on. He was fidgeting around another strange invention which included a keyboard similar to that of an organ, attached to a metal coffin inside which a human could have slipped.

"Pleasure Machine," read Miss Brunner.

"I wonder how it works," whispered Vorski.

"Nobody will test it for you," said Ironcastle. "We do not touch anything more!"

The German shrugged, annoyed.

"Come away," said Ironcastle, worried that Vorski was going to trigger some kind of catastrophe.

He led the two young women to another room. When they entered, it was plunged in darkness. Beautrelet pressed a switch and the lights came on. They all fell back before the amazing sight they discovered.

The nurse stuck her head through the crack of the door.

"Are you asleep?" she inquired.

"No," replied Beautrelet, opening his eyes.

"You have a visitor."

He sat up suddenly. The nurse stepped aside to let Miss Brunner enter. Beautrelet sighed, disappointed.

"Don't look so happy," she said mockingly

"Excuse me, but I had hoped..."

"I know exactly whom you were hoping to see."

She examined him just like a doctor.

"You seem fine."

"What happened at Schok's?"

"You don't remember, or you don't want to remember?"

Suddenly a series of images assailed him. Darkness... madness... Rachael! Miss Brunner put her hand on his bare arm.

"Calm down... What do you remember exactly?"

Dr. Schok's Corridor

They all stepped back from the monster standing in the center of the room. After their first fearful reaction, they realized that it was but a sculpture. But what sick mind could have made up such a creature? It was an unlikely mix of a

14

man, an insect and a lizard. Its exoskeleton was black, oily, with plates along its spine like a dragon; its hands and feet sported terrifying claws; its long tail ended in a sharp point. Its head was oblong, misshapen, eyeless, but furnished with a double row of teeth.

Beautrelet looked at the small placard.

"An alien?"

Still shaken, they continued their visit. The next attraction was a mannequin dressed as a cowboy. But its face opened like the lid of a box and inside its head were cogs and clockwork mechanisms.

"An automaton." said Miss Brunner. "Quite sophisticated!"

"Scary," Rachael remarked, "but less than the alien."

They followed a long corridor that took them to the northern wing of the house. Suddenly they felt the ground tremble under their feet.

"Watch out!" Ironcastle shouted.

But the warning had come too late. The corridor turned into a slide and sent them into a large cavern with damp walls. They stood ready to face the new danger waiting for them.

On a dais stood what appeared to be an ordinary cane made of black lacquered wood. Its pummel was an iridescent globe that projected intermittent animated scenes on the walls of the cavern. It showed two men in bowler hats fighting with umbrellas; a short distance away, a beautiful black woman was triggering storms.

"The Vertigo," whispered Miss Brunner, impressed.

His beady eyes widened as if under the effect of some intense pleasure.

Beautrelet felt his head turn. A subtle spell was at work. Ironcastle staggered back.

"Nobody move!"

Vorski had lost his mind. His face, distorted with rage, became unrecognizable. He put his arm around Rachael's throat; his other hand was brandishing a revolver.

"Vorski, what are you doing?"asked Beautrelet.

He was terrified by the look of panic that the young woman gave him.

"Take the cane!" ordered the German.

Rachael grabbed it. Vorski began to back away, still keeping her hostage as his human shield.

"Don't do that!" said Beautrelet.

The villain disappeared through an opening in the rock. The young man glanced at the others: Ironcastle was on all fours, throwing up. Miss Brunner stood there, paralyzed.

Beautrelet rushed after Vorski. When he caught up with him, the German had just reached the outside.

When Vorski saw Beautrelet, he pushed Rachael away and grabbed the cane. He pointed it at Beautrelet as if it were a magic wand. Immediately, the young man felt himself caught up in a vortex. He was thrown to the ground violently.

When he rose, the scenery had changed. He was no longer on the French Riviera; perhaps not even on Earth. It was dark. It was not night, but heavy ash clouds filled the sky. A short distance away, a huge volcano was spewing its dark contents into the air. It smelled of carrion.

The colossal walls of an ancient fortress surrounded him. He saw a procession of nightmarish creatures marching at the bottom of a narrow gorge.

A fear unlike any he had ever felt clutched his heart—the panic one feels when confronted by the uncanny. Was he in Hell? Beautrelet had never believed in such nonsense. Suddenly, he felt a light presence. He spun around. A huge tower stood nearby, and at its tope was... What was this new nightmare? An eye—a huge eye, burning with a hatred so intense that he felt it deep within his soul.

He screamed in terror. He struggled to save his soul, to chase away this thing, this being, from his mind and his heart. But the Other resisted, chuckling.

Beautrelet thought of Rachael and redoubled his effort. He felt the black wave yield gradually. The young man stood firm. There was a tear in space and he was projected into a kaleidoscope of sounds and colors.

The Vertigo...

Beautrelet read fear in Miss Brunner's eyes. She took a few steps back to give herself some countenance.

"You know what I'm talking about, don't you?" he said.

"Yes and no," she replied cryptically.

He showed his annoyance.

"I do not know what this place is that you described," she said. "But I knew of the existence of this artifact and I had heard of its power."

She paused, confused.

"Continue," he said.

"It has many names: Cosmic Egg, Eye of the Serpent, Jewel of Judgment, or... Vertigo. It has the power to break through the walls of reality!"

Miss Brunner looked at Beautrelet to determine if he understood her words.

"Do you know the theory of parallel worlds?" she asked.

"You mean the 'multiverse' mentioned in the works of Oswald Bastable?"

"Yes. According to him, there exists an infinity of possible worlds, separated only by metaphysical veils."

The young man tried to remember what he had read.

"Universes which occupy the same space, but exist on a different wavelengths. You think Vorski threw me into one of those other worlds?"

"Oh, he didn't know what he was doing. He had hoped that you would simply disappear—and it worked, more by luck than design."

"He sent me to the Devil," whispered Beautrelet thoughtfully. "What were you and the others doing during that time?"

Miss Brunner tried to deceive him.

"I... I do not know. When I regained consciousness in the cavern, everyone was gone. I left Schok's house. As I walked by Morel's clinic, I saw a crowd. I inquired..."

"And here you are."

"We must find the Vertigo!" she stressed.

"No, we must find Rachael!" he retorted.

She brushed the objection aside.

"Please turn around," Beautrelet asked. "I'd like to get up."

She smiled mockingly.

"I've seen naked men before."

He gave her an irritated look, and she complied. But while he dressed, she looked in a well-placed mirror and missed nothing of the show.

"What do you propose?" Beautrelet finally asked, after adjusting his tie pin.

"Antibes is a small town. We'll quickly discover what means Vorski used to leave the area, and hopefully we'll also learn his destination."

"Don't you think he'll have left some false clues?"

"How do I say this? Vorski gave me the impression of a person... somewhat limited, intellectually speaking. Moreover, he wasn't the same man when he took your girlfriend hostage."

The adventurer frowned, more worried than ever.

"Do you believe he might be in the grip of another's will? Some mediumistic influence or mind-control... I know very little about all this parapsychological hodgepodge."

"We can't exclude it. I must say that I see the world in a very different light since our visit to Dr. Schok's mansion."

Nowhere Island

Everything went as planned. Although night had already fallen, they found the German's trail at the harbor where they learned that he and Rachael had taken a boat heading for Venice. They looked for another boat and found Captain Flanders who agreed to take them there aboard his ship, the *Fulmar*. The long night voyage began.

It was nearly midnight. Beautrelet couldn't sleep. He stood on the deck, leaning on the railing, watching the boring spectacle of the lights of the ship reflected in her wake on the sea. It seemed better than turning and twisting in his all too small and smelly bunk.

There was an ominous rumble ahead and the young man looked up. A bunch of strange clouds seemed to be following them. They had an evil, greenish tinge and shone softly in the night. Suddenly, a bolt of lightning flashed inside the hideous mass. Its color, too, looked unusual. Beautrelet shuddered.

Miss Brunner appeared silently at his side, pale as a vampire and as sinister as Cassandra on the walls of Troy.

"A storm is brewing," said the young man in an attempt to break the evil spell of the clouds.

"I felt it. This phenomenon often accompanies the Vertigo. This is a shadow storm that can pierce even the walls of Terra."

The woman's conversation was turning increasingly mystical. Beautrelet wondered if she wasn't going mad.

Captain Flanders came from the bridge.

"There's going to be a bad storm," he said. "Hold on tight or return to your cabins!"

They felt the ship move faster; the Belgian Captain was trying to outrun the storm. The chase began, uneven and lost in advance. It was not raining, but the wind grew fierce. The sea took on a nasty yellow tint and glow, but did not become more agitated. They felt a warm breath upon them...

Suddenly, an unnatural stillness enveloped the ship. The sea became an oil slick and the *Fulmar* was bathed in an unreal, golden atmosphere. The wind blew over; the silence was total.

"We're in the eye of the storm," said Miss Brunner, still enjoying her role as a prophetess of doom.

Then the walls of night fell apart around them and they suddenly found themselves in full daylight in the turquoise bay of a small island!

Flanders took the *Fulmar* to a jetty which extended from a natural rock platform. Beautrelet and Miss Brunner went ashore.

"You have one hour before I leave," shouted the captain from the bridge.

He did not seem overly bothered by the inexplicable phenomena they had encountered.

Beautrelet and Miss Brunner walked around. The beach was lined with a row of birch trees which they crossed. Beyond it, they discovered the charming spectacle of a small lake with clear waters. On the other side of that was a building made of white stones, clearly intended to be their destination. They knew they were the pawns of forces beyond their comprehension, which had decided on the purpose of their journey. They hastened their steps, eager to meet the occult power that had maneuvered them so far.

As they reached the villa, a man marched out to meet them.

"Vorski!" cried Beautrelet.

"In the flesh, my friend! Are you glad to see me?"

The young man sent his fist crashing into the German's nose. Shocked, the villain rolled onto the ground. Beautrelet grabbed him and held him up by the lapels of his jacket. He was going to hit him again when Miss Brunner intervened.

18

"It seems that our German friend has recovered his good sense," she said.

"Who tells me that he won't turn tail and run again?" retorted Beautrelet without letting go of the German.

"We'll keep an eye on him."

Reluctantly, Beautrelet dropped the braggart.

"You have a good right fist on you, my friend!" grumbled Vorski.

"Where is Rachael?"

"Oh, she's safe, don't worry. I would invite you to join us but..."

"What about the Vertigo?" asked Miss Brunner.

"I don't know what you mean."

"Well, take us to your leader then," ordered Beautrelet.

They entered the house and Vorski led them into a conference room. On a dais, in the shadows, were five silhouettes sitting behind a long table, with nameplates indicating their identities. Beautrelet read the following names: Professor Stangerson, Dr. Cinderella, Dr. Helfern Mr. Outremort and Dr. Kramm. No doubt it was they who were their nemesis—a conspiracy of mad scientists who had manipulated them from the very beginning.

"And notice their initials," said Vorski, with a wink. "S.C.H.O.K. Impressive, no?"

"Indeed," said Miss Brunner, sarcastic.

"We are the Supreme Scientific Tribunal," said the same metallic voice they had already heard in Antibes. "You who appear before us stand ready to hear our verdict!"

"What verdict?" said Miss Brunner. "Of what crime are we being accused?"

"Silence!" thundered the voice.

Beautrelet did not understand why the five men remained in the shadows since their identities had been revealed. He decided to check it out.

"Halt!" screamed the voice. "You do not have permission to approach the Tribunal!"

The five scientists were moving in their chairs, but that did not stop the young man who soon discovered the deception. Although they may have passed a cursory review, the five scientists were nothing but articulated mannequins. Their facial expressions, in particular, were caricatured, with reduced mobility.

"Automata," said Beautrelet to the other two who had joined him.

"This means that we still have to find the real puppeteer," hissed Miss Brunner, angry.

"He won't be too far away."

Looking around, they noticed a screen. They went behind it and found themselves facing an old man who was still hanging on to the acoustic tube he had been using to give a voice to his mechanical creations.

"Er... Good morning," he said, shyly.

"And who might you be?" Beautrelet asked.

"Gentlemen," Miss Brunner said, "may I present to you the most famous of our physicists, Professor Spallanzani, a world specialist in automatons!"

"So you're the one who's been pulling our strings!" accused Vorski.

"Not at all," replied the little scientist, defending himself. "The other five were there, but they're strong personalities. They started bickering over nothing and, in the end, they went their separate ways. They instructed me to keep their lair going, and give the illusion of their presence."

Beautrelet did not care. There was only one thing that mattered to him in the midst of all this carnival.

"I want to know where Rachael is?" he asked.

"Will you tell us who this girl is, and why she matters so much to you?" asked Muss Brunner, exasperated.

"I met her in Vienna. We spent a wonderful week together, and then, she was gone, as if he'd been erased from the face of the Earth!"

"Isidore!" said a voice he'd thought he would never hear again.

The young woman had emerged from a secret passage, and threw herself into Beautrelet's arms. They shared a long kiss while Miss Brunner rolled her eyes.

"Well," she said, "now that the two lovebirds have been reunited, it's time to get serious!"

She turned back towards Spallanzani, who had not moved.

"Where is the Vertigo, Professor?"

"That thing is dangerous," he said, after some hesitation. "You should destroy it!"

Miss Brunner changed. Her hard face became a smooth mask, and her raspy voice sweet and beguiling.

"This is exactly why we're here," she reassured him. "But in order to do it, you must take us to it."

Spallanzani did not look fooled, but the fear she inspired in him made him surrender.

He led them through winding corridors. They left the house by a back door and found themselves at the bottom of a flight of stone steps in an ancient open-air theater.

There, the scientist stopped, surprised.

"I ... I don't understand. It was here…"

He pointed to a dais similar to the one upon which the Vertigo had rested in the museum at Cap d'Antibes.

Miss Brunner examined the empty slot with a dark eye, then vented her rage. She screamed curses and stomped her foot. Spallanzani seized the opportunity to slip away. When she returned to the small group of adventurers, they were looking at her suspiciously.

"We must find who has the Vertigo," she said, ominously calm.

"Spallanzani told you: it is dangerous," replied Beautrelet. "Myself, I have experienced its power and I do not wish it upon anyone!"

Miss Brunner shook her head.

"You don't realize the power of the thing. Imagine what we could do with it. We could remake the world into a paradise...

Suddenly, a huge burst of laughter broke out, not far from them, amplified by the special acoustics of the place.

"A theater... What better place for the final scene of this tragicomedy," said a faceless voice.

"Who are you?" asked Miss Brunner, angrily. "Show yourself, you coward!"

"Hadn't you guessed? I'm so disappointed. Especially by you, my young friend..."

"Professor Woland!"

The odd-looking character stood before them, bowing comically, but as sinister as the Harlequin of the Divine Comedy. He held the Vertigo on his cane and twirled it expertly like a stage magician.

"I warned you that this would end badly!" he said.

"But you were talking about progress..."

"Yes, that's right, but what do you think the Vertigo is? In a not so distant future, fifty-seven years to be exact, a scientific organization called AIM, Advanced Idea Mechanics, will create this nightmarish artifact, the supreme technological invention. It is interesting to note that AIM is also the name of an ancient demon. You see, the Forbidden Fruit of Knowledge always comes back to haunt us!"

Do Automatons Dream?

Beautrelet faced Woland for the grand finale.

"What are you talking about?" said Miss Brunner who could no longer stay silent.

"Let me explain what just happened to you. All of you, Spallanzani, Cinderella, Kramm, Helfern, you all belong to different worlds. You were brought together here by the power of the Vertigo!"

His speech had hit the mark; now they understood what he meant.

"Do you mean...?"

Beautrelet paused. It was too big. His mind struggled to grasp the overall picture.

"Yes, I mean," said Woland like a teacher in front of a class of slow-witted children, "that the Vertigo attracted you like a magnet. That is its power. It weakens the boundaries between worlds and, creates holes in reality. It gathered six mad scientists on that accursed island, and brought you, Ironcastle, Vorski,

Rachael, and Miss Brunner to Cap d'Antibes. The museum also contained trophies gathered across the multiverse by the Vertigo."

"What about you?" asked Beautrelet, moved by a fleeting intuition.

"I am a Guardian. I exist in all realities. You just know me by different names. I'm here to balance the forces and repair the fabric of the continuum. Do not worry, I do not expect you to understand."

Vorski sighed, relieved. Miss Brunner took advantage of the distraction to attempt one last desperate action, but Woland had only to move a finger to "freeze" her in a ridiculous posture.

"What fiery nature. A little maturity and she will become a formidable opponent. Anyway, I did my job; you'll go to bed a little less ignorant tonight. Now I must ask you to say your goodbyes, because as soon as I'm gone, taking the Vertigo with me, you'll all return to your respective worlds"

Rachael moved a little closer to Beautrelet when she heard these words.

"It's impossible," cried the young man vehemently, 'we belong to the same universe!'

"When you met in Vienna," explained Woland, "you'd already crossed paths with the Vertigo, without realizing it, of course, which is why you were able to meet."

He saw the tears in the two lovers' eyes.

"I am sorry. The magic will remain for a few hours after I leave. Try to make the most of it!"

He walked away, took a few steps, then his nature reasserted itself and he turned theatrically, bowed and tipped his top hat to them.

"I have the honor of saluting you!"

Then he spoke to an invisible character:

"Are you coming, Cagliostro?"

A large black cat appeared from nowhere. He looked at the little group and a crescent-shaped smile distorted his face. He jumped on Woland's shoulders and began to disappear in bits: first, the tail; then, the body. Soon, there were only the eyes, the ears, and his strange smile left. Then, nothing. Woland shimmered like a mirage; his body was reduced to two dimensions, and the next moment, he, too, had disappeared.

Miss Brunner found her mobility returned, but felt empty.

"Where is he?" she asked.

"Gone, flew away, evaporated!"

Vorski had lost what little remained of his mind. He hopped around, whistling, picking flowers, making bird noises. The others looked at him. Perhaps he was the happiest of them all.

"What are you going to do?" Beautrelet asked Miss Brunner.

"I'll try to convince Spallanzani to work with me. Perhaps with his help, I will find the Vertigo."

The young man looked at her with compassion. She had not taken the shock well; her madness seemed to have taken a different form, more insidious, more obsessive. Unless she had always been that way?

Rachael and Beautrelet left. They wanted to return to the boat, leave this accursed island, hoping that Woland's influence would disappear and his disastrous prediction come to naught.

Miss Brunner joined forces with Spallanzani. He had no idea how to find the Vertigo, but suggested that they return to Germany. He knew a man there named Rotwang who was pursuing a worthwhile project—something named Metropolis.

The *Fulmar* sailed at good speed towards Venice. Sitting in the back, Rachael and Beautrelet remained entwined in silence. The young man threw frequent glances behind him as if he was afraid that Woland might be pursuing them. He had found a small origami unicorn in his pocket and did not know how to interpret this omen.

Could Woland make them coexist in the same universe? Would he? Could Love balance the power of the Vertigo? All these questions turned endlessly in his head. Finally, he stopped thinking and concentrated on the present. Smiling at Rachael, he tightened his arms around her.

Translation: Jean-Marc & Randy Lofficier.

This story was written by our regular contributor Matthew Baugh for a French anthology devoted to the characters from Hexagon Comics, one of the oldest French comics publishers' universes. This is its first publication in English. It features the western hero Jed Puma, who never uses guns and relies only on martial arts to defeat his foes. Jed Puma was created by Italian artist Enzo Magni in June 1965, quite a few years before David Carradine's Kwai Chang Caine from the television series, Kung Fu.

Matthew Baugh: *High Noon of the Living Dead*

Las Vegas, 1865

"What d'you reckon those two are supposed to be, Bull?" Jacky Martin said.

"Dunno," the blacksmith said, scratching his head. The man on the horse was a good-looking young cowpoke, chestnut-hair and clean-cut. He carried a lariat, but Bull saw no sign of pistol or rifle. The man on the donkey was shorter, stockier, older, and more unusual. He wore what looked like heavy white pajamas girded with a black cloth belt. What struck Bull most, though, were the man's exotic features.

Bull's heavy brows came together in a scowl and he moved toward the men. "What do you boys want?" he asked.

"We'd like to stable our mounts," the young man said, swinging down from his saddle.

"I don't usually do business with no Chinamen," the big blacksmith said.

The cowboy smiled pleasantly. "I'll make it worth your trouble," he said.

Bull frowned. "I reckon that'd be okay."

"There is also something we ask you to make for us," the Asian said.

"You've got a lot of nerve, mister," Bull said. "Just what kind of Chinaman are you, anyway?"

"The Japanese kind," the smaller man said, smiling. "I am Tashi."

"Well, we don't want your kind around here." The blacksmith put his massive hand on Tashi's chest and shoved. To his surprise, the smaller man did not resist him directly. Tashi caught Bull's wrist and spun to the side, pulling the big man off balance, then shifted his grip. The next thing Bull knew, he was landing on his back.

Jacky whooped with delight. "What happened, Bull, you trip?"

"Damned Chinaman caught me by surprise," Bull said. He drew himself up to his full, impressive height and balled his massive fists. To his surprise, the Japanese didn't look at all worried, and his young friend looked amused.

Bull swung a roundhouse right that would have taken the smaller man's head off, had it connected. Unfortunately for him, Tashi stepped inside the punch, caught his arm, and threw him neatly over his shoulder. Bull rose again and stared at Tashi in disbelief. He decided not to give the smaller man a chance to try any more of his tricks. He lowered his head and charged at him like his namesake. Again, Tashi caught the charge and, with little apparent effort, rolled the big man over his hip to slam to the ground again.

"This is a very interesting ritual your countrymen have, Jed," he said.

The young cowboy laughed. "Well, try not to hurt him. Remember, we need his help." He turned to Jacky, who was watching the strange fight wide-eyed.

"I never thought I'd see it," said the man. "Bull's about the strongest man in the New Mexico Territory."

"Yeah, but Tashi knows how to turn a fella's strength against himself," Jed said. "Listen, can I ask you a question?"

"I reckon so."

"Who would you say is the best known gunfighter in these parts?"

Jacky thought for a moment as he watched Tashi throw Bull through a wooden railing. "I guess that'd be Doc Holliday," he said.

"Where can I find him?"

"That's Doc Holliday at the poker table," the saloon girl said, before moving off to get Jed Puma a beer. It had taken him the whole afternoon to complete his simple-seeming quest. With the coming of the railroads, the little mountain town of Las Vegas had grown to rival Denver or Tucson. The burgeoning city was filled with little saloons and gambling houses, and finding the one owned by Doc Holliday had been surprisingly difficult.

Doc was easy to distinguish from the other players. He was a thin, un-healthy-looking man dressed in a dark suit. He didn't look that dangerous, but Jed knew that was deceiving. Doc had a reputation as one of the deadliest men in the west, and that made him the perfect target for the men Jed was looking for.

"Here you go, honey," the girl said, her fingers lingering on Jed's hand as she gave him the beer.

"Thanks, miss," he said, returning her smile.

"Hey!" A tough-looking cowboy stood up from the poker table. "You keep your hands off of Lily. She's my gal!"

"Easy, mister," Jed said. "I didn't mean anything."

"Yeah, Mike," the girl added. "I'm just doing my job."

"You stay out of this, whore," the big man said. "This is between me and the dude."

"Why, Mike Gordon," Doc Holliday said in a soft Georgia drawl. "Does this mean that you are forfeiting this hand? I feel so slighted."

"No, Doc," Mike said. "You just hold on. This won't take me but a minute."

"If you are leaving the table, Michael, then the pot is mine."

"What are you taking this greenhorn's side for?" Gordon asked with an angry scowl.

"For the same reason I would take your side if he challenged you to a duel of wits. My sympathies are with the party who is unarmed."

Mike's scowl deepened but he sat back down. "OK, Doc," he said. "I call."

Doc Holliday smiled and placed his cards face-down on the table.

"I fold," he said.

"You didn't have nothin'?"

"I did not. Now, rather than ruin this auspicious moment with a brawl, I suggest you take your winnings and retire."

"You're tellin' me to get out?"

"Much as I shall miss your delightful company, yes, I am."

Mike's face turned red but he took the money and left. When he was gone Jed moved to the poker table.

"Such an excitable fellow," Doc said. "I worry that I may have to kill him someday."

"Thanks for sticking up for me," Jed said. "You didn't need to do that."

"No?" Doc looked him over. "Are you hiding a firearm somewhere I cannot see?"

"I don't need one," Jed replied. "A friend taught me how to take a gun or a knife away from another man."

"Do tell?" Doc looked amused. "Perhaps I should have let you show me."

At that moment, a man dressed all in black pushed in through the door. He was tall, as lean as a rail, and even paler than Doc Holliday. Jed knew instantly that this was one of the three men he had been warned about.

"Doc Holliday," the man said, his gaze settling on the gambler. "I'm calling you out."

"And just who are you, sir?" Doc asked, turning to face him.

"My name don't mean anything now," the man said, "but by tomorrow everyone will remember Cole Thornton as the man who killed Doc Holliday in a fair fight."

"Wait a minute…" Jed said.

"Stand aside, youngster," Doc interrupted, settling into a shooting stance. Jed hesitated as the rest of the people in the room sought cover, then moved aside himself. However, he tensed his muscles for what was to come.

The two men drew. The stranger moved with reflexes that no human could have matched, but without much skill. In the fraction of a second it took him to aim, Doc Holliday shot him between the eyes. The man clutched his face with his free hand and staggered backward. Then he laughed.

"They said you was good, but I never expected you to shoot me in the face," he said. He took his hand away, allowing Jed and Doc to see the wound knit itself closed.

Holliday was stunned by the sight, but not Jed Puma. He sprang at Thornton and caught his free arm. Using the limb as a lever, he spun the man in a circle before throwing him across the bar. The gunman struck the mirror and, before he shattered it, Jed saw that he cast no reflection. He had held onto Thornton's gun and tossed it away.

Thornton was back up amazingly quickly and leaped over the bar. Doc Holliday put two bullets his chest, but the man only grinned, exposing wickedly pointed fangs.

"You can't kill a vampire, Doc," he snarled.

Jed leaped forward, thrusting the ball of his foot into Thornton's solar plexus. The blow to the normally sensitive target had no effect, and Jed followed with a flurry of hand strikes to the *atemi-waza* pressure points on the man's neck and torso.

Thornton sneered and grabbed Jed by his shirt-collar. Lifting him with unnatural strength, he hurled Jed the length of the barroom. Only the countless hours of learning to fall under Tashi's tutelage saved him from serious injury.

"Perhaps I cannot kill you," Doc said, "but I believe I can inconvenience you some." He shot Thornton once in each knee, causing the vampire to fall.

"You're just delaying it," Thornton said as his wounds began to heal. Then he made an angry noise as Jed Puma grabbed his gun-belt from behind and used the grip to throw him through the saloon doors into the street.

Jed followed, springing through the doors as Thornton started to rise. He pounced like his namesake onto the vampire's back and locked his arms around its neck in a powerful *hadaka-jime* choke. He locked his legs around the creature's waist, making the hold even harder to break.

Astonishingly, the vampire rose to its feet bearing Jed as if he weighed no more than a kitten. He caught Jed's wrist in a crushing grip and plucked him loose. "Don't work too well, trying to strangle someone who doesn't need to breathe." He seized Jed's throat in his free hand. "Too bad that ain't true of you."

Jed struck at the pressure points on the vampire's arm, but to no effect. Thornton raised him so that his feet dangled over the ground.

"That fancy fighting won't help you now," Thornton said.

Suddenly he winced as something splashed over him. Though he could barely breathe, Jed caught the aroma of lamp oil. Twisting, all he could he caught sight of Doc Holliday in the doorway of the saloon.

Thornton cast Jed off to the side and took a step toward Doc. The gambler struck a match with his thumbnail and tossed it at the vampire. Thornton screamed as he caught fire.

"Sometimes the old ways are still the most reliable," Doc Holliday said.

"So, what in Perdition is this all about?" Doc Holliday asked.

With the coming of the Las Vegas fire brigade and the town marshal, Doc and Jed had decided not to stick around. They had located Tashi and retired to Doc's dentist shop. Jed stared at the rack of what looked like implements of medieval torture while Doc poured himself a glass of whiskey. He offered some to Jed, who shook his head.

"They are called vampires," Tashi said. "Immortal monsters who feed on blood."

"I would say that such things are myth," Doc replied, "but the late Mr. Thornton has changed my mind on the matter."

"Do you know the Taos Kid?" Jed asked.

"I have not had the pleasure."

"Well, you never will. We found him dying about a day's ride out of town. He'd run across Thornton and two more just like him. He beat one of them to the draw, but his bullet didn't do any harm and the vampire gunned him down."

Doc was silent for a moment, and took a long sip of whiskey. "It seems that being a living dead man has its advantages in a gunfight," he said. "I know something about that."

"What do you mean?"

"A dead man does not fear death," Tashi said. "That makes him the perfect warrior."

"True," Doc said. "In the case of these vampires, they know bullets cannot harm them. In my case, a bullet would be preferable to the tuberculosis that is eating away my lungs."

Jed lowered his eyes. Vampires were hard enough to handle, but this talk of a man he was coming to like dying of a terrible disease was too much.

"They are seeking to gain a reputation," Tashi said. "They have come to your city to kill three of the fastest gunfighters in the Southwest. This will give them the influence they need to raise an outlaw gang and dominate the territory."

"That leaves us with something of a conundrum," Doc said. "What do these dead men fear?"

"Life," Tashi said, holding up a thick metal wand. When he closed his hand around it, an ornate knob projected from the top of his fist and another from the bottom.

"What is it?" Jed asked.

"The *konga* is a holy Buddhist symbol," Tashi replied. "It represents life energy or spiritual power."

28

"That's what you had the blacksmith make?"

"It is."

"I mean no disrespect to Buddha, but wouldn't it have been easier to borrow a holy symbol from one of the churches in town?" Doc asked.

"A Buddhist is better," Tashi said. Swinging his arm in a powerful arc, he slammed the *konga* into a wooden coffee table, shattering it to splinters.

"I suppose that is more practical than trying to pummel our foemen with a crucifix," Doc said. "Come, let us complete our arsenal. I believe I know where we can find the other two vampires."

Later that evening, two men in black rode up to the Hot Springs Hotel. One was tall and blond to the point of albinism and the other short and rotund with a satanic van dyke and tufted eyebrows. The men tied their red-eyed steeds to the hitching post and moved toward the door but hesitated when a man, nearly as pale as them and dressed in a long black duster stepped out of the shadows.

"Stand aside," the blond man said in an eerie, sepulchral voice.

"How dramatic," the stranger drawled, stepping from the shadows.

"Doc Holliday!" said the short vampire. "How...?"

"How did your friend Thornton fail to kill me?"

"It doesn't matter," the blond said. "It only means that I will claim one more victim this evening."

"Goodness, you are frightening," Doc said, producing and lighting a cigar. "I hope that I can manage to keep from falling over dead with terror."

The short vampire laughed, and spoke again in a heavy German accent. "I see we have underestimated you, Doctor Holliday," he said. "Just as well. If Thornton could be taken by a mortal--even one as skilled as you—then he did not deserve my dark gift."

"Gustav," the tall vampire said, "What are you-...?"

"The fittest will survive, Carl," the portly vampire said. "I believe that Doctor Holliday has proven he is more fit than poor Thornton to ride with us."

The vampire called Carl growled, but made no attempt to contradict the other.

"What do you say, Doctor?" Gustav continued. "If you are so deadly as a mortal, no one could stand against you as one of us. I know that you are diseased and dying; I can smell it in your blood. You are a man who knows how to seize the pleasures of life. Join us and you will have them for all eternity."

"Tempting," Doc said, "though I find the joys of life sweetened because of their brevity, not in spite of it."

A dozen feet away, Jed Puma and Tashi crouched, hidden behind a small wall. Sensing that the conversation had come to an end, Jed signaled Tashi. The two men rose and began to move on the vampires from behind.

They moved swiftly and silently, but Gustav still sensed them somehow. "Behind us, Carl!" he hissed. "I will deal with Holliday."

With reflexes no human could hope to match, the portly vampire's hand darted to his holster and the pistol cleared leather so fast that the human eye could not have tracked it. As he pointed the weapon, Gustav's eyes widened at the sight of the shotgun barrels appearing from underneath Doc's long coat. Surprise mingled with the tiniest bit of fear made him rush his shot and the bullet that should have struck Doc between the eyes only nicked his ear.

Gustav cocked the pistol again but before he could pull the trigger the shotgun belched gun smoke, fire, and small silver beads purchased from a Navajo jewelry maker. The impromptu pellets caught Gustav in the torso and he sank to his knees.

Doc tossed away the shotgun and, brandishing a silver-headed walking stick, advanced on the wounded vampire. Gustav aimed his pistol, but Doc struck the weapon away with his cane and began to rain down blows on his head and arms. After several moments, he stopped and looked down at the vampire's helpless form.

"Fool," Gustav whispered. "You cannot kill me and my body will heal even the wounds caused by silver. What do you hope to do?"

Doc laid the stick aside and produced a massive pair of dental tongs from his coat pocket.

"I plan to resort to my other profession," he said.

As this was happening, Carl drew his pistol and fired at Jed, who only managed to twist away by the smallest fraction. He tried to turn the gun on Tashi, but the Japanese fighter was already on him, and numbed his arm with a blow of his *konga*.

Carl swung a powerful backhanded blow at Tashi, which swept him away, but failed to injure him. Jed moved in, scoring a blow to the thigh with his *konga*. Carl turned to attach him, only to feel sting of Tashi's weapon between his shoulder blades.

Each time one of the *kongas* struck, there was a searing flash and the smell of scorched flesh that reminded Jed of branding a calf. He and Tashi kept up the unrelenting attack, driving the vampire back and never giving him a moment to ready a counterattack.

Then, in a desperate burst of inhuman speed, Carl shot forward. Avoiding their defenses he caught Jed's throat in his right hand and Tashi's in his left. Sensing that they were less than a second from death, the two men lashed out as one. Jed's *konga* struck the vampire on one temple as Tashi's caught him on the other. The vampire screamed as light streamed from his eyes and mouth, then it faded and Carl's body crumbled to ash.

"What in thunder is going on around here?"

Jed looked up to see two strangers standing in the doorway. The first was about thirty and close to six feet tall with a compact, solid build and short, neat hair. His companion was scruffier, about twenty, and several inches shorter with a lean build. Doc Holliday rose to greet them and Jed wondered where the vampire Doc had been fighting had gone.

"Doc Holliday?" the younger man said. "Is that you? Who's that you got with you, Doc?"

"These are my friends, Jed Puma and Tashi," Doc said.

"You runnin' around with Chinamen now?"

Doc ignored the question. "Gentlemen," he said, "this lad sometimes goes by Henry Antrim and others by William Bonney, but he always answers to Billy the Kid."

The Kid offered a cocky smile and nodded his head to Jed and Tashi.

"His friend is the infamous…"

"My name is Howard," the older man snapped. "Tom Howard."

"Of course," Doc said. "Mr. Howard is emphatically not a famous train robber from Missouri, and he has never used the name Jesse James."

"You haven't answered me, Holliday," the man who called himself Howard said. "What's happening here?"

"We just did away with a couple of *hombres* who were fixing to bushwhack you," Jed said.

"They weren't *hombres* though," Doc said. "Technically they were vampires."

"Vampires?" Billy said.

"Yes. Reanimated dead men who live on human blood."

"You sound skeptical."

"Naw," Billy replied. "It's just that this sounds like the tall stories me and Mr. Howard been telling each other tonight."

"These men," Howard said. "You ran them off."

"Assuredly so," Doc replied.

"Then there's no sense in waiting around here. I'm gonna turn in."

"Yeah," Billy said. "I should be gettin' back to my pals." Good night to you, fellas."

When they had gone, Jed turned to Doc.

"What happened to that blood-sucker you were fighting?" he asked.

"It seems that he needed these to remain corporeal," Holliday replied. He opened his hand to display two long, sharp fangs."

"Why did you do that?" Tashi asked.

"A foolish impulse," Doc replied. "The teeth seemed eager to attack me even when the vampire was incapacitated. Still, he dissolved to ash when I pulled them, which solved our problem."

"What are you gonna' do with them?" Jed asked.

"I shall keep them as a memento," Doc said. "After all they are the last teeth I think I shall ever pull. I plan to devote myself full time to gambling and gunfighting from now on. Dentistry is far too dangerous."

André Laurie's Spiridon, *the giant, intelligent ant who is the star of the epony-mous 1907 SF novel (available from Black Coat Press, ISBN 978-1-934543-61-3) has already inspired other writers; it is, after all, a fascinating and quirky character. But it seems particularly appropriate to transplant him (it?) into this rollercoaster of a prequel to the classic 1954 film,* Them! *To top herself, Adam Mudman Bezecny has also dredged up the hero from "The Ant with a Human Soul" by Bob Olsen, originally published in 1932 in* Amazing Stories...

Adam Mudman Bezecny: *A Bug's Life*

New Mexico, 1953

In the deserts out near Alamogordo, New Mexico, a figure strode across the sand. Though the heat beat down on him mercilessly, he was dressed in heavy gray robes, which concealed his form from whoever might be watching. As he walked, his head was bent low to the sand, as if he was being shepherded along by some invisible presence scurrying along the ground. That was exactly what was happening. A single ant led the figure through the desert, towards a rocky outcropping that housed the mouth of a cave. If one was close enough to this scene to see the ant, they could see that its follower was also an ant. But an ant the size of a man—and his name was Spiridon.

The ant scampering ahead of him answered to the name of Kenneth Williams. Unlike Spiridon, he ordinarily maintained an existence as a human. Near-ly twenty years ago, Williams had met Dr. Armand de Villa, a brilliant scientist who was capable of transplanting a human brain into an ant. With such a pro-cess, de Villa had used Williams to learn about ant behavior. The experiment had saved Kenneth's life. If he hadn't learned about the diversity of life by be-coming another species, he'd have killed himself long ago.

It had been many years since Kenneth Williams had felt six legs under him—since he had clicked his pincers about, and waved around his antennae. He had barely believed his eyes when Spiridon had greeted him in his apartment; his wife had fainted, at least for a few seconds, for Spiridon was undeniably gro-tesque. At first, Williams had wondered if he was like that Samsa fellow, a man turned into insect.

"Who—what are you?" he had asked.

"Do not be alarmed, Mr. Williams. My name is Spiridon, and I have come to request your assistance."

"My assistance? But... but... you're a-a giant ant! An ant-person!"

"Kenneth," Mrs. Williams had said, "you're acting as if that thing talked to you."

"It did. Can't you hear it?"

"Your previous experiences with ants have enabled you to understand the Morse-like code I use to communicate," said Spiridon. "Your wife won't be able to hear me, I'm afraid."

"Oh, God, I feel like I'm going crazy!"

"You're not, I assure you. I am surprised your time among the ants never brought you word of my island—on that island, the ants enhance the size and intelligence of their leader. I am—or was—that leader. Almost fifty years ago, I suffered an injury which took away both my kingdom and my higher functions. But I have regenerated over the decades, and now an incident is transpiring in the United States which interests me deeply. It will interest you, as well, if you have the concerns of both man and ant at heart."

"I see. You looked for me because I was once a bridge between those two worlds. What sort of menace do you mean?"

"Ken, I thought all this weirdness was over. All this ant stuff," Mrs. Williams had said.

"Tell her that I'll only need you a brief time," said Spiridon

"He'll... only... need me a brief time... I guess?" had repeated Williams.

"But in order to help me, you'll have to go through Dr. de Villa's process once more."

"You want me to become an ant again? Tell me what's going on before you ask me to consider that you can even do that. I thought the secret had vanished with de Villa."

"It nearly did, but I was able to recreate it with my own methods. In fact, I was able to improve on de Villa's shortcomings. He used a crudely-manufactured herakleophorbia analogue for the growth process, and..."

"Mr. Spiridon, what is the threat you need me for?"

Spiridon had realized that he had provoked annoyance in his unwilling host; such an emotion intrigued him, for he himself did not understand it.

"There are stories that ants have been vanishing throughout the desert, taken by a human called *the Butcher*."

"Someone is kidnapping *ants*? But why?"

"He is turning them into monsters. Giant ants, larger even than myself. These monstrous ants are likely weapons for the Butcher, for some nightmarish purpose."

"You want me to take down giant ants?"

"I will need you to infiltrate the hive the Butcher uses as an insider among the ants," had replied Spiridon. "Together, we'll discover the Butcher's identity and stop his mutant abominations."

"Well... I can't let innocent people be hurt."

"Ken, what are you saying?" had asked Mrs. Williams.

"I'm going to go with him... I trust him. It must be an ant thing."

"Ken, you can't!"

"But I have to, honey. There's sincerity in what he says..."

She had sighed, hoping only that this would be brief.

"You said that I have to become an ant again?" Williams had asked Spiridon.

"Yes. Some ants under my service have captured a single ant from the Alamogordo hive. It took the lives of hundreds of them to obtain this one ant. I have a portable version of de Villa's ray, which I can use on the specimen. From there, it will be a simple matter to perform the brain transplant."

Spiridon and de Villa had much in common, Williams had realized. They were both direct in their motions—and they had no conventional sense of ethics. It was clear to him that Spiridon was a being without emotions, at least as humans understood them.

Still, he had wanted to become an ant again. It had nonetheless been a curious sight when the trail of ants had entered in through the open door. His wife had clearly been uncomfortable with this, but he had known that Spiridon wouldn't let his "troops" pitch a permanent camp in the apartment. Almost comically, they had brought in a prisoner bound in minuscule ropes; this was to be Williams' new body—at least for a while. Spiridon was somehow going to arrange transport for himself and this ant once Williams' brain was secured.

Without a further "word," Spiridon had produced a small handgun. It fired light instead of bullets, and the bound ant had begun to grow in size. The Williams had been familiar with de Villa's process, but Mrs. Williams couldn't stay in the room when the time had come for Spiridon to remove Ken's brain. He had hardly felt a thing—and it had been quicker than with de Villa. He had briefly been aware of his nerves crossing the barrier into an enormous flailing body; then, there had been the soft sensation of shrinking as he had returned to the proper size of an ant.

The ants at Spiridon's command had released him from his body, and the old feeling of ant-consciousness, so distinct from human-consciousness, had returned to him.

"Mr. Williams, can you hear me?" Spiridon had asked.

"Yes—and clearer than I could before. Can *you* hear me?"

"Very clearly. Let's get down to the street, and I'll show you our wings."

"Wings?" Williams had paused. "Let me say goodbye to my wife first... oh! I suppose that's not possible. English is beyond my capacity now."

"I have an idea," Spiridon had said.

Mrs. Williams had still been waiting in the other room, realizing just now herself the communications predicament, but a line of ants had entered the room, much to her disgust. They had arranged themselves into columns and these columns had become letters. These letters had spelled out: "BE BACK SOON."

She had sniffed, unsure of how to respond. Without a sound, the ants had departed the apartment.

Williams had followed Spiridon outside the building and onto the street. It was early in the morning, and few people were about; Spiridon had donned his concealing robes and, as long as no one looked too closely—a good likelihood if they hadn't had their morning coffee—no one would suspect anything. And there would be few witnesses for what came next.

"You mentioned wings, Spiridon," Williams had said. "But neither of us are winged ants."

"I am now, thanks to a scientist named Francis Ardan. At least, that's what he called himself when last we met."

Williams had crawled low under Spiridon, and could now see that his gray robes concealed a heavy piece of machinery. The thruster at the bottom betrayed what it was in an instant.

"You can't be serious!" he had blurted out.

"Don't worry! I have a small box to carry you in, which will keep you quite comfortable during the journey."

"But what about the witnesses?"

"What about them?"

Williams would have sighed if ants could do such a thing.

Spiridon had produced the box for him, and he has crawled inside—Spiridon had held the box tight. With a free appendage, he had reached for the controls of his jet-pack, manufactured by a famous scientist whom Williams knew under a different name.

The ignition had been deafening, and he could still detect the cries of by-standers over it—from shock, not from injury. The walls of the container, which cushioned him perfectly, had been transparent, and he was able to see the narrow stream from the jet-pack. Spiridon had been a perfect pilot.

It hadn't been a long flight, which had impressed Williams. As it would have been too risky to land right outside the targeted hive, they had had selected this open patch of desert.

Initially, Williams had wondered if they would be searching for a single anthill in the span of the whole New Mexican desert; but that the ants were in a cave made sense. Humans had to go in, and giant ants had to go out.

There were no footprints to indicate either in the sand outside, but at once, both he and Spiridon became alert. The darkness of the cave could break at any moment to reveal danger.

"Let's get to work," Spiridon said.

He set the heavy jet-pack down at the cave entrance in case they needed a hasty retreat.

"Find a crack in the wall and hide yourself in it. Find your fellow ants. You may have noticed your host is marked with a red pigment dot on its foreleg—that's how I'll find you."

"You read Dr. de Villa's notes thoroughly," Williams said, remembering the particular problem of separating him from millions of identical insects. "What are you going to do?"

"I'm going to see what I can find taking the human entrance."

"I see. I'll meet you up ahead."

Spiridon did not reply, but Williams moved all the same—finding a crack, as Spiridon specified. Soon, he was surrounded by thick stone capillaries. His feet scanned the rock for signs of vibrations. He could already feel ants up ahead, very far ahead—probably in the same area towards which Spiridon was now headed. He regretted suddenly that they were separated; he now felt a certain anxiety, as if Spiridon was a big brother ant keeping him safe from the bully ants. It was all coming back to him now—ant-instincts. Beast-instincts. Actually, it was a strange homogenization of his experiences through ant-senses striking his human consciousness. The stimuli he felt as an ant now called to him, pushing him into the *conformity* of ant-hood, and away from the individual liberty of being human. There were so many ants, and together, they formed the one-thought of "the nest." Keeping his mind above the nest would be tough when it was so damn noisy, but he had done it before, and he could do it again.

Suddenly the tunnel yielded to a massive space, and Williams laid his faceted eyes on something that filled him with revulsion. Ordinarily, ant nests were vast systems made of tunnels such as those he now marched through, but this whole area had been hollowed out, and it was stacked from bottom to top with squirming, flailing ants. They seemed to have no reason among themselves, blindly crushing each other and themselves in the mass of squiggling appendages. Worse, some of them had become cannibals, devouring bits and pieces of the ants around them. They were probably drugged, meaning this whole environment was flooded with chemicals by the Butcher... or the builders of this nest were fugitives from his experiments. In either situation, he'd have to cross this ball of chaos to reach the other end.

If there were pheromones involved, he'd be as vulnerable as the next ant. Still, he had his human brain, and that had saved him from temptation before. Of course, it would do him no good if he was torn to pieces or eaten alive, but he still had to try. Williams thought of his wife and began his crossing.

The experience was nearly beyond human description—few humans have undergone a comparable experience and survived. The writhing battery of limbs wouldn't be comparable anyway. To a full-grown human, the sway of the myriad arms would be like the tickling of hundreds of hairs; Williams was kicked and battered this way and that way, and that was before the mouths got to him. He lost a leg, and he thanked God it wasn't the leg with the pigment-dot. He would have screamed if that was possible—and he would have just been another voice in a sea of thousands, all screaming like lunatics.

At last, Williams reached the entrance to the tunnel opposite his. Admittedly, the horde had helped him cross, as he had walked over it to reach this catacomb. Similarly, passing through that many minds had taught him much about the kind of ants the Butcher was working with. He had to find Spiridon as quickly as possible.

Spiridon found that there were only a few curves to the cave before it opened up into light. He walked into an extensive rounded half-tunnel, rather like a hangar in dimensions and construction. But instead of being filled with aircraft and other vehicles, it was a chemical production plant. It would take a detailed inspection to determine what they were making here, but Spiridon could guess it involved mutagens, possibly the same sort of growth hormones used by he and Dr. de Villa. Similarly, his chemical-conditioned body sensed possible atomic elements. For now, he looked for personnel, and saw none, despite the immensity of the chamber. He then looked at the near wall for any sign of a crack.

There was the slightest one, and now an ant with a red dot painted on his leg was staggering out.

"You've been hurt," said Spiridon.

"Yes," replied Williams. "The ants who have been brought here... who have become the dominant ants of this cave... they're dangerous. Even when they're not monsters."

"Oh?"

Williams was rather shocked by his companion's lack of concern for him, but he figured it was typical.

"They're a Brazilian breed," he continued. "The entomological research I did after my work with de Villa makes me think they're the same Brazilian ants written of by the engineer Holroyd."

"I remember the Holroyd account."

"Yeah. These ants certainly aren't passive little priests of Mye-Mye."

"Who?"

"The stories of the Mye-Mye ants are unknown to most of the Western world, but I found record of them, as Timothy Thümmel did, among the Minunians of Africa. This breed of ants have many legends. They claim all ants of the Earth are descended from an ant called Mye-Mye, their Adam and Jesus figures in one package. Some of these ants claim their ancestors grew monstrously large and found their way to the moon."

"Maybe that explains the account of Professor Cavor?"

Williams didn't ask further. There was someone coming, and they both knew it. They hid behind one of the large processing machines, even though it was only Spiridon who needed to hide.

"...wish I could get *out* of this, Fryser. I really wish I could, but *you* keep holding a gun to my head."

"It's not my gun, Hobbs. It's the doc's. I just wish you could understand his point of view."

"His point of view is monstrous... literally. Those things have enough formic acid in them now to kill twenty men. And he's making them think like us, too? What's the point in that?"

"So the doc's a little screwy—that's just how it goes sometimes. What matters is that we're getting paid to help him. At least, I am."

The man identified as Hobbs grew quiet at this, but Fryser did not shut up.

"I think that the doc really believes what he says sometimes. Sometimes, he says it so proud I believe him, too. You know, in this new decade, we really need a sort of new social order to keep another war from breaking out, and I think the doc's gonna be the one to bring it in. We're all flawed, in a Satanic sort of way, but by experimenting on beasts, he's really experimenting on how to bring us closer to God. By taking us farther away from the beasts, get it?"

"But he's making *giant mutant ants!*"

Williams and Spiridon didn't need to hear more. They started to creep away, with Spiridon keeping a line of machinery between himself and the two men. He sought the passage they came from, and Williams followed him into it. There were several doors built into the rock, which, judging from their spacing, appeared to lead into small rooms. There was one door at the very end of the hall that had a golden doorknob. Spiridon figured this was probably where they'd find the Butcher—"the doc."

He opened the door, and found that the room within was bereft of light. A dusty old desk stacked with papers was directly before them, and off to the side was a large piano, in considerably better condition than the desk. Williams couldn't see much from his height, but Spiridon's eyes locked onto a particular posting on the wall behind the paper-stacked piece of furniture: he knew from his time among the universities of man that it was a diploma. As he walked up to it, the name on it became apparent. "R.G.V. Moreau."

The lights came on. Spiridon turned around, and as the owner of this office walked into the light, Williams had to take care not to be stepped on. He was an unusual sight, even to Spiridon, this man who claimed for himself the name of Moreau. Scientists commonly wore white, in the form of lab coats, but he was dressed in white robes. He looked more like a religious leader than a scientist, and his youth perhaps explained that. An egotistical fixation on personal power fit in with the sort of inadequacies humans experienced while young. Williams knew his face, then, and he was surprised that he hadn't guessed it was him all along.

For now, however, their host was angry, even if only his face said so.

"What are you doing here?" he asked in a cool, gentle voice, carried on a surely-fake British accent.

Spiridon was in trouble, as this "Dr. Moreau" couldn't understand his Morse code. But he realized there was a certain cadence to his words: his emphasis in that sentence were on the word "you." The man had recognized Spiridon and wondered why he, specifically, was here.

But despite his strange garb, this "Moreau" was clever. In the span of a few minutes, he had assembled many of the vital details.

"Of course," he said, in that bizarre affected voice of his. "The ants told you. That would explain why they are so easy to operate on... they do possess hidden intelligence. Hidden societies. They answer to authority, even deposed authority like you, my King. You know... I only wish now that my grandfather had operated on insects. He would have made progress so much faster."

Spiridon wished he could communicate with this man, but while he couldn't quite do that, he could at least talk to Williams.

"This man calls himself Dr. Moreau," he said. "A supposed descendant of the original. But the original doctor, Alphonse Moreau, died without issue many years ago. At least, so I've been told. This man isn't his heir. His real name is Robert George van Ee. His actual father is a psychologist named Joseph van Ee. Few know that Joseph van Ee once answered to the name of Robert Parry Renault. Renault was a renegade scientist who turned animals into humans in the style of Dr. Moreau—he worked with your Dr. de Villa at least once. Robert van Ee, then, must have used what little survived of the original Moreau's notes, plus his real father's own records, to enact experiments on animals. He is the Butcher."

"Then kill him. We'll stop his ants here."

Spiridon had that very idea in mind, but he hesitated. He remembered his old days of vivisection and where it had led him. If for nothing else than a sense of self-preservation, he didn't dare lash out at the fraudulent Moreau. But in an instant, Hobbs and Fryser were at the doctor's side, and while Hobbs seemed content to lurk in the background, Moreau directed Fryser authoritatively.

"Montgomery, I need you to secure this creature. His name is Spiridon, and I've reason to believe he's come to interfere with my operations. In any case, it's time for our children to walk free—let him see what he came to stop in person." And he allowed himself a faint little chuckle. "Let him see for himself that his mission was a fool's errand!"

Moreau hadn't noticed Williams—there was no reason for him to do so. The two ants knew that that was their only way out of this.

Fryser, whose first name may or may not have truly been Montgomery, bound Spiridon in ropes, and began to walk him back out of the cave. As they walked, Moreau, pausing only occasionally to chew pensively on his lower lip, spoke to Spiridon as an equal.

"You know, sir, there are many changes that have passed in time that make my work possible, at least comparatively so, next to that of my noble grandfather. Alphonse Moreau never dreamed of nuclear power and what it can do to a life-form swollen with herakleophorbia. My surgeries on both the body and brain of the creatures, involving infusions of human tissues, have created physical and mental giants. As I said, you'll be seeing them first-hand, Mr. Spiridon—they'll be coming through those doors over there."

Neither Spiridon nor Williams had noticed the large hangar shutters which apparently contained Moreau's "physical and mental giants." Given what they both knew of the original Dr. Moreau, they were extremely doubtful that Moreau's idealistic perspective had any grounding in reality. His "enhanced" creatures were going to turn out to be monsters.

But just as that consideration passed through Spiridon's mind, Moreau said, "I think you'll be doubly proud of my freshest batch of children, Spiridon, given that you inspired me to make them."

Though unable to speak, the former king charged suddenly at the Butcher, breaking out of Fryser's grip. "Damn it, Hobbs, get him!"

Hobbs didn't move, but Spiridon didn't get far with the ropes pinning him. There was genuine fear in Moreau's eyes as he backed away, and strong relief when Fryser stopped him.

"Hobbs, you're a useless bastard..."

"No harsh words, Montgomery. We are a family here. A family of peace."

"Even when you kidnap your assistants," Hobbs put in.

Moreau didn't address his presence.

"The chemicals I use are not merely products of atomic decay, but a variety of other compounds as well. Some might refer to them as 'unstable,' Mr. Spiridon, but I've heard that you are a brilliant scientist, and perhaps you might help me with the formula."

"Read his fine print," Hobbs said.

Spiridon looked at him sympathetically.

Moreau seemed to find amusement in all of this. He led them out into the desert, and, from his pocket, produced a small remote control. He pressed a button on it, and very distantly, Williams and Spiridon detected the vibrations of the hangar doors opening back in the base. Williams dreaded the approach of the Holroyd ants, the lunatic ants, given cunning and size. He realized that Moreau must have worked with de Villa, who, after all, had been his father's colleague. De Villa could make ants grow in size, just as Moreau could. This was the legacy of his twenty year-past experience, and he wondered now if he'd escaped death during those experiments only to be killed here by some ghost of de Villa's.

The ants were coming one by one. They were slow, likely having trouble moving their own bulky mass, but it was a miracle of biology and physics that they could move at all; Moreau's compounds evidently included some extremely exotic elements. Given the patchwork blend of chemicals he was giving these poor animals it was amazing they still even faintly looked like ants. They made a high-pitched chirping sound which nearly deafened Williams; it was an ant language, but it was too loud and broad a frequency for him to understand it. They *were* intelligent, then, as well as giant... the size of elephants. Spiridon was the right size to properly study their language, but there was another barrier to him—their language seemed encrypted somehow. Then these ants had managed to come up with a language based on no other ant dialect, entirely by themselves.

These creatures would become the new masters of Earth if they didn't do something. Williams didn't need prompting to climb up Spiridon's body to get to work on his ropes—now that he knew he was one of those Brazilian ants, he had absolute faith in his teeth. But neither of them had any certainty that there was any way out of this.

"Welcome to the sun, my children," Moreau declared cheerily. "Look upon its beauty. Know its power. And built great hives to hide from it, and to build your empires in, to bring in the new era of life."

"He's crazy, Fryser—crazy," Hobbs said then. He spoke quietly, but it was clear to all, including Hobbs himself, that Moreau could hear him. "Shoot him! You've got the gun! Shoot him!"

Fryser was agitated by the giant ants, but he didn't listen to his comrade. But suddenly, he wasn't the man with the gun anymore. Spiridon was free, and the way he held the rifle once he snatched it from "Montgomery" showed he knew how to use it.

"You can't stop me here, Spiridon," Moreau laughed.

He pressed another button on his remote, and, suddenly, the stone of the cave yielded to reveal a long metal track, which extended out into the sands of the desert. There was once more the sound of heavy movement, but this time it was mechanical—a large tram came speeding down the track, carrying a load of cargo out into the day.

"My children are about to receive their next batch of mutagen. They will become even larger and even more intelligent. And then, the next phase of existence on this world will begin. There will be fire, at first... but then there will be peace."

Fryser was up by Spiridon in an instant, and he revealed now he carried a second gun, a pistol. He had it pushed into the ex-monarch's back. Williams was still clinging to Spiridon, but he slowly descended, and began to move back towards the cave.

"And most importantly, I can laugh in the face of my rivals. Claiming I never won the Nobel Prize, the fools. All of them will pay: my father, my professors—that impersonator, Dart..." But then there was a hiss. "What is that?" Moreau quipped. "It smells like... rocket fuel?"

Williams had activated the Ardan jet-pack. He was just heavy enough to press the button. The force threw him through the air and, for a moment, it looked like the end.

And not just for him. The rocket plowed straight through the crates mounted up on the tram, and there was a burst of chemicals which hissed in the air as they reacted with one another.

"Oh, no—!" Fryser roared. "No, no, no! They were meant to be introduced to the chemicals individually! These compounds should never meet!"

Spiridon bolted at that, as did Fryser and Hobbs. But Moreau insisted on staying near to his creations. There was an eruption of chemicals and both Moreau and his "children" were soaked in them. What was more was that the force now drove back along the track, and the rock of the cave vibrated uncertainly.

Far away, half-crippled and buried in the thick sand, Williams remembered that the walls of that cave were pitted with the tunnels of those drug-crazed ants. The stone was already weakened to begin with. Now the whole structure came down, and between the fingers of crumbled stone there writhed an uncountable amount of dead and dying ants.

Their gigantic cousins were also dead, but their demise had come from chemical burns. Spiridon now looked for any sign of Moreau, whom he anticipated to be similarly burnt. He found him seeking the faint shadow of what remained of the cave-mouth, and he appeared uninjured. He looked a shade paler, perhaps, but now a strange mania seized him. He raised his robe-clad arms in a desperate attempt to push away the afternoon blaze.

"Oh, I can't stand it anymore! The sun! Oh! My skin just can't tolerate the sun!"

But again, to Spiridon's trained eyes, he appeared uninjured—the chemicals had already evaporated off of him, and seemed to have the same effect on his human tissues as water.

He had to find Williams. As he moved out into the expanse of the desert, ignorant of both Hobbs and Fryser (who lay unconscious near the blast zone), he felt blisters rise on his flesh. He, too, was an ant after all, and whatever had killed those titans would burn him as well.

Williams could move just enough to send a signal along the ground, and Spiridon homed in on it. When he found Williams, he was nearly dead—Spiridon hadn't expected to locate him alive. But this was easily remedied. He still had his handheld ray, and there were plenty of other ants nearby. At least one of them had to be in good shape.

It took a bit of wrestling but eventually Williams found another host body. Dr. Moreau, left lurking pitiably in the shadows in the wake of the death of his dream, uttered some comment about the hypocrisy of Spiridon creating giant ants when he hadn't allowed him to do the same. Spiridon ignored him. In a matter of moments after the impromptu surgery, Williams was coming around again.

"Thank you," he tapped out weakly. "I thought it was the end."

"It is, for Moreau at least. If there are any survivors from his 'children,' they'll be adversely affected by the chemicals in the area. Furthermore, their breed will lose their intelligence, as I once did."

"The original Moreau learned how tricky the line between man and beast was. And while I doubt those things were anything like men... it's probably best they remain as beasts."

But Kenneth Williams forgot that his companion was not a man, nor was he ever one. Spiridon acted on his own drives. He would restore Williams to his body, but not out of any sentimentality. It was pure logic; if he left him there, then his wife would become upset, and if she was upset, she would contact the authorities, and those authorities would take away his peace. And there was a certain resonance to that peace, which no creature of pure beastliness could properly enjoy. It was never a question, though, that Spiridon was not a beast. If anything, he was too far in the other direction. A look at what mankind would be like in the future, when that resonance of peace went totally quiet and only being cold kept the pain out.

Moreau, or van Ee, or whoever this clumsy, preening maniac was, had feared the war-scarred wastes of the future, and that made him do what he did, in his own way. Kenneth Williams remembered the serums and radiations which bred the buried hordes; and he remembered that the Soviets were edging closer with every new day. Closer to what, he did not know; this new "Cold War" was so vague and slippery. He remembered all the reports already speculating on the depths his nation and theirs were willing to go to in order to defeat one another. He remembered reports coming out of Japan, of science having gone wrong there, too. It was an echo from the past, and a symbol of what was yet to come, a harbinger of death that spat out flame—no. That beast, like these, was not a child of science. Destruction was its only parent.

It only made sense to him that, when at last they would spring open the doors of Destruction it would come in serpent's scales, or crawling on six legs. The demons of Hell were real, and they carried a Cherenkov glow and the stench of acids and bases.

Thierry Bosch is a distinguished French scientist who in life looks nothing like Professor Challenger, but who could easily, at least in his own imagination, partake in the same kind of adventures. His scientific background gives this story a uniquely authentic touch...

Thierry Bosch: *A Waltz in Norbury*

London, 1928

The door opened quietly, revealing the austere face of Austin, the silent chauffeur of the famous Professor Challenger. The man was still barely likable, only talking when it was absolutely necessary and with as few words as possible, as if he was saving them for his future retirement. Tight-lipped, for real. In his defense it must be said that his work was no bed of roses, seeing that the Professor's personality could best be characterized as grumpy and this only by the most forgiving of men. To be honest most of his contemporaries considered Challenger absolutely unsociable if not downright unbearable. I happened to share this point of view sometimes, I have to admit with regret as we have been friends for many long years since.

On seeing me, Austin would just give a little groan, which I decided to translate as a polite expression like "what a pleasure to see you again, please come in" or some polite nonsense that a butler is supposed to say when a friend of the house comes to visit. That said, Austin deserved credit for staying with the master of the house while the vast majority of other servants left within a week, to the great displeasure of Jessie, the Professor's wife. For this he is and always will be excused.

What do you expect, I am naturally big-hearted.

So, I went through the porch and into the lavish house of Professor George Edward Challenger, GEC to his friends, without any unnecessary conversation but with all the assurance of someone familiar with the place. While I was heading to his workroom at the end of a long hallway, Lord John Roxton came striding out of the room.

"Hey, baby! I hope you're wearing some solid armor under that. GEC is in a particularly foul mood this morning," he said, patting me on the back. "For a few days he's been having visitors and you know how much he hates the social constraints that entails. I'd rather go head to head with a lion in the desert than stay with him when he's like this!" he shouted down the hall as he left, laughing.

So much for solidarity. Lord John, tall and thin, with dark red hair, was a real lion with a flaming mane when it came to facing danger but I still could not

44

ask him to come to my aide against the raging anger of the Professor. Not that he was scared, he simply refused to play the games imposed by GEC.

After taking a deep breath, I knocked on the door. After all, I was here at his request, which I received properly in my office as a telegram insisting that I come see him in the morning and not bother about useless details like my availability.

A sound that had nothing human about it came bellowing out of the room. Something like a roaring bull, the cry could in no way be associated with the voice of a respectable university researcher. And yet, it was without a doubt the most polite way for him to invite someone to enter his lair. When I walked in, he raised his huge, ruddy head with its startling black beard trimmed like an Assyrian and falling to the middle of his chest, in stark contrast to his purple smoking jacket. Even sitting he gave the impression of formidable power, with his barrel-shaped body and huge, hairy hands. Even though I am a former international rugby player weighing a healthy 200 pounds, I had the chance to test my strength during our first encounter that degenerated into a fistfight, pure and simple, and only ended thanks to a bored policeman who was used to this kind of thing with the volatile Professor. As strange as it might seem, after this exchange of blows we became friends.

He aimed his gray-blue eyes at me and his expression turned from the usual scorn—which he reserved for all visitors who, by definition, could only be coming to disturb his highly important work—to anger. I would have to exercise the utmost diplomacy if I did not want us to start boxing again like so many years before.

"Malone!" he roared on seeing me.

His anger, therefore, was not furious enough to keep him from pronouncing my name clearly. Maybe I had a chance of surviving this appointment even without the help of Lord John.

"How dare you publish such an article in the *Daily Gazette*! Such drivel and gibberish! You who, for a journalist of course, seemed to me to be slightly less stupid than the usual stiffs of this shameful and sinister profession!"

Okay, the root of the problem was known now. I just had to find the little detail that had offended my friend.

"Dear Professor, I don't doubt for an instant that your anger is warranted, despite the fact that I can't positively identify the reason for your outrage. It seems to me that my last article was showcasing your genius and…"

I did not have the chance to finish because GEC cut in with his baritone.

"You don't find it shocking, then, to write about, here I'll quote the text for you, 'the bold theories of Professor Challenger'?"

"Well, I thought the term was appropriate for your latest theory to date in order to highlight your visionary side for our public," I said, a little taken aback.

"By writing that, Malone, you're making your vulgar readers believe that my theory is some madcap hunch not supported by solid, scientific reasoning. And worse, you imply that I, Professor Challenger, might be wrong!"

"Dear Professor, needless to say that was not my intention and if I committed any blunder, be assured that it was purely accidental. No doubt it was due to my lack of any real journalistic talent. You are truly the shepherd leading the human flock to Knowledge."

I did my best to stay courteous, not wanting to start a fight with him. For several months I was, in fact, nursing the hope of one day finding GEC peaceful enough to talk with him about the tender feelings I had for his adorable daughter, Enid. Feelings that were mutual, I have to say. We were only waiting for the right moment to bring up the delicate subject but this was obviously not the day for it. Given GEC's strong personality, it might be a very long time before he was in a good enough mood to listen to me without falling to blows. Let's say in a little less than a century, according to my most optimistic estimate.

But GEC, in his wrath, was not even listening to me. He just got angrier. "As if I haven't proved I was right, again and again, despite all opposition!"

"Certainly, Professor, you..."

"Are you confusing me with that arrogant little detective?" he paid no attention to my attempted objection.

I admit that I was a little lost, surprised by such a question with no apparent connection to the subject at hand. What detective was he talking about and why in the world? No matter how used to GEC's sometimes very abrupt leaps, requiring mental gymnastics to follow him if you did not want to suffer his accusations of being dim-witted, here I did not understand a thing.

"What are you talking about?" I said, staring wide-eyed at him.

"Haven't you read the Memoirs of Sherlock Holmes?"

I had to agree that I had indeed but a very long time ago.

"Well, Dr. Watson confessed that his friend, despite his gifted deductive skills, committed a monumental error by simple intellectual laziness."

"Holmes was wrong? I can't believe it!"

I was stunned by this assertion. I had great admiration for this person whose faculties of observation and deduction I valued highly.

"And yet, he himself recognized his defeat and he asked Watson to remind him of the name of the city where the stinging failure occurred if he ever again let down his guard."

GEC went looking for the work in question in his vast library.

"Here, read this."

I skimmed through Dr. Watson's report about the affair of the Yellow Face. I remembered the text whose conclusion, alas, left no room for doubt. Holmes had been wrong in one of his investigations. Him, the ultimate thinking machine in criminology! I was really upset to have to remember this.

"I always thought the detective's reputation was terribly overestimated," the Professor continued in a slightly more gentle voice.

It must be said that except for basking in his own triumphs in complete immodesty, GEC loved nothing more than delighting in the failures of his contemporaries, especially those susceptible of stealing the limelight from him in the newspapers and salons. Recalling the failed investigation of Sherlock Holmes was a great help in improving his mood. To the point that he was almost friendly to me.

"Look, Malone, if ever, by some bizarre accident, I fall into such intellectual neglect, if ever I don't use the entire, immense potential of my genius to solve a problem that I alone in the world can grasp, if you notice this one day, I'm allowing you, no I'm asking you to do as Dr. Watson did immediately. You only have to say one word: Norbury! Am I understood?"

I had to promise that in a case, as highly unlikely as it might be, where GEC was slipping up and I happened to be the witness, I would pronounce the name of the small town south of London to bring him back to the full range of his capacities. But only in case of his verifiable responsibility for the negligence.

"Even though you've chosen the deplorable profession of journalism, you know that I respect you, Malone. I think you're less ignorant and greedy for gutter gossip than the rest of the contemptible mob. Since you seem honest, I'll put your last article down to lack of tact and the endemic absence of stylistic subtlety. Come on and see the fruit of my 'bold theories'. You'll have the chance to witness my genius publicly."

We left his workroom and went into a big room, painted all in white, at the back of the house. In the middle of this room stood a machine that called up bad memories, memories that were too recent and too painful. Surely the worst of our adventures together, even if it was hardly spectacular and very little known to the public.

"But that's the Nemor disintegration machine! So, you've recovered it... but how?"

My voice died under the emotional stress and I could not hold back an expression of horror on seeing the terrible Latvian's machine once again.

Of course, the chair on the zinc platform had been replaced with a steel cabinet vaguely shaped like a pear around eight feet in diameter at the base and five feet tall, pierced with windows fastened by huge gold bolts all around the upper part, maybe a foot and half more narrow. Its top consisted of a conic hood covered in copper.

But it was definitely the same infernal machine that I saw before me. I recognized the main parts around the cabin, like the transparent prism facing a magnet balancing on a pedestal and the whole thing topped with countless copper wires hooked up to some impressive central machinery covered with blinking lights and screens and switches.

Nemor once wanted to sell it to the highest bidder, thus making it possible for a foreign power to have the ultimate weapon able to disintegrate entire battalions. England would never have recovered. I was seeing GEC once again lower that rubber-coated lever, thus saving the world from the schemes of that evil scientist and spreading his atoms into the infinite cosmos with the help of his own invention. Yes, I was an accomplice to murder but a murder that had saved millions of innocent lives. And I never regretted this tragic but indispensable decision.

"Even if Nemor claimed that no one but he could understand or even copy the mechanism, I preferred not to take any risks," GEC said.

"But the foreign buyers, if they couldn't make this terrible weapon work without Nemor's help, would've left empty-handed," I said.

"Indeed!" he answered. "So, I asked my friends to help me move it here so I could study it more closely. And it was the right thing to do! Nemor overestimated it a lot, like many of his peers. His machine didn't hold up against the analysis of a top-notch physicist. And then let me introduce you to Maxime… where are you, my friend?"

A clean-shaven man, still in the prime of life and wearing a bluish-gray lab coat was busy behind the cabinet. He was working noisily on the machine and paying no attention to us.

"Let me present my colleague, Professor Maxime d'Olbans, who just came from France," GEC spoke loudly to get his attention. "He's been a big help in transforming Nemor's machine and modifying the crystalline network of our new prism. A material with unique properties and without equal in all of nature!"

The man finally realized we were there. He greeted me with a quick nod then continued working without any more acknowledgement. I saw why GEC got along with him, French to boot, and he could collaborate with him. Clearly the two scientists shared the same innate sense of sociability.

"Are we going to be ready soon?" GEC asked.

"After a few little adjustments and we can move onto our final experiment," d'Olbans answered with that dreadful French accent that the decadent people always feel they have to use when mangling the beautiful language of Shakespeare. But at least I can say that for a Frenchman he made an effort to speak in grammatically correct English, which many of his contemporaries have a very hard time doing. Only his accent tortured my ears. Of course, like all Frenchmen, he was probably arrogant but in this matter GEC would certainly be a match for him. At the very least.

After making his final checks Maxime d'Olbans walked over to us slowly, almost sliding, and held out his hand, smiling, which made him no more handsome but a little nicer anyway.

"Sorry to be so rude and not stop working but what can we do when faced with such an exciting discovery. I'm like a child in a candy store!" he made a funny face that must have been meant for an apology. "Sometimes I can even forget to eat and sleep."

"So, what exactly are you working on?" I asked, curious like any self-respecting journalist.

"Oh come on, didn't you understand the meaning of what you so badly summed up in your mediocre article?" GEC thundered, always as unforgiving of his neighbor. "It seemed to me, however, that I explained my theory clearly enough for even you to understand. Didn't I tell you about my space-time theory?"

"Of course but..."

"So you need more to see what our machine is for, good lord! You've got everything you need to play science detective, Malone."

"Well, this machine can disintegrate matter," I said cautiously.

"We've also changed it to destroy space-time!" GEC literally roared triumphantly, not leaving me time to think. "You have before you the first machine that can travel in time! Wells only dreamed of it, Challenger did it!" He puffed out his chest, very satisfied with himself. "With the valuable help of Professor d'Olbans, which goes without saying," he added, remembering the fundamental principles of politeness just in time, but noticeably late.

I silently ignored this show of pure modesty that was part of the charm of our good Professor. Maxime d'Olbans just smiled humbly. I was really starting to like him, for a Frenchman. Not being one of those chatty scientists, he spoke plainly, with no useless preambles or superfluous comments.

"We live in a three-dimensional space whose time, in reality, makes up another kind of dimension. This dimension is unfortunately singular in our space-time, which forces us to make a one-way trip, from birth to old age. We have, however, observed that with Nemor's machine, after a few minor adjustments to the crystalline properties of the prism in an electromagnetic field we can not only disintegrate matter but inverse the coordinates of space-time."

"Excuse me? I'm a little lost again."

"Well," he continued with a hint of irony in his voice, which betrayed his justifiable intellectual satisfaction, "we created a local space with three dimensions of time so we're no longer forced to follow the usual course of time but can travel it as we please. On the other hand, the space dimension is reduced to a line that prevents any displacement in space during the voyage other than in a straight line, like a train rolling down a perfectly straight track. If you've ever read the excellent work *Flatland* by Edwin Abbott you'll be able to visualize this idea of a dimensional-limited space.

"No need to go into detail, he won't get it anyway!" GEC barked, as kind as ever. "Malone doesn't have the scientific basis to understand such concepts. He's only a journalist after all! He could mistake a firefly for a shooting star! Don't expect him to show the slightest trace of scientific education or to have the necessary cerebral connections to allow him to understand even the gist of such an avant-garde theory. His pitiful article is proof enough."

GEC finished his rant with his arms raised, a sign of desperation concerning my supposedly inexistent ability to understand anything.

D'Olbans smiled an apology at me but he did not continue his explanations, as confusing as they were for my poor little brain that was, it's true, little educated in scientific matters.

"On the other hand, my friend Malone is an honest journalist, a very rare case in the annals of that cursed profession, I assure you!" GEC went on. "And brave as well, which is always appreciated."

When GEC complimented me and became so friendly, you could be sure that it was a bad omen for my physical well-being. Hadn't he already dragged me around to confront savage tribes, dinosaurs and even the anger of our beloved Earth? The worst was yet to come. I admit that I would have felt a lot better if Lord John were there because he knew how to face danger in style and inspire his comrades with courage.

"And so you intend to test this machine?" I asked nervously, hinting at the unsaid "with me inside?"

"We, my good friend, are going to test it today! It's the main reason I brought you here this morning, my dear Malone."

I held back the queasy feeling I had, not doubting for a second that this "we" meant only "me".

At this moment, a stranger entered the room after knocking quietly to signal his arrival. Well built and with piercing eyes that were different from common mortals—they seemed to see all the way down into your soul.

"Leo, you're back just in time! There's nothing more to wait for now!" GEC bellowed.

The man sprang forward, holding out his hand to me. "Leo Saint-Clair," he introduced himself with a strong grip.

"Glad to make your acquaintance. Ted, Ted Malone," I said. "I've heard of your battle against Lucifer…"

I was shaking the Nyctalope's hand, me, a lowly editor of the *Daily Gazette*!

"Let's not talk about that," he spoke gently. "We have much more exciting things to do today than revisit the actions of the past when the future is awaiting us."

He spoke like a real man of action for whom the best is always to come. In the meantime, Maxime d'Olbans was busy lowering levers and turning dials. Like during Nemor's demonstration of the disintegration machine, I was obviously one of the lab rats who would take the initial test, an honor that I would have gladly passed up. But I sensed that to live through an adventure next to the Nyctalope was well worth a few risks, as great as they might be. For, I had no doubt at all that he was going to travel with me.

50

With a wave of his right hand GEC invited me to head for the dull gray, steel cabinet. I nodded to the chief and obeyed. I entered the infernal machine and sat in the farthest of the three brown leather chairs, then buckled myself in with straps over my chest. In front of me was a huge control panel with switches and levers, silver dials indicating God knew what, various wheels and all kinds of lights blinking different colors.

The Nyctalope sprang into the middle seat before GEC took the seat by the door. The man was, without a doubt, impossible to live with but he was brave, there was no denying it.

"You're joining us?" I was surprised. "Your life is too precious to risk it so lightly, Professor."

GEC did not deign to respond. There was room enough for all three of us in the cabinet despite our more or less developed muscles that might have proved very cumbersome. On the back of our seats was a tin trunk that must have contained what we would need to face all kinds of situations, as well as an empty space to collect objects that we would surely be picking up during our exploration.

Maxime d'Olbans leaned on the door, which closed with a soft hiss. I had the feeling of sitting in a safe furnished with windows.

"Don't think that I'm trying to be over-courageous here," GEC finally said, looking me in the eyes after he finished buckling in. "I'm just sure of my theories and I have full confidence in the engineering skills of Professor d'Olbans."

My mistake. GEC was so full of himself that he could not even imagine running the slightest little risk. Quite the reverse of Leo Saint-Clair who was giving the situation a clear and severe analysis, perfectly aware of the danger but accepting the situation and ready to face anything with honor and determination. I would have loved to have half his courage at this moment. To put on a brave face I tried not to let my teeth chatter too loudly and I controlled my trembling limbs.

This was going to turn out badly. I was thoroughly convinced of it. But I did not want to show it to my two intrepid colleagues, afraid of looking like a coward in this prestigious company. I mustered my courage by thinking of the fabulous story I could tell my readers. If I survived, that is.

"Did you make any preliminary tests?" I could not help asking, trying not to let my voice crack in this pathetic effort to sound relaxed although you could see the nervousness in my eyes.

"What for?" GEC said, surprised by such a trivial question. "Professor d'Olbans and I checked our calculations both separately and together. And in the case, hypothetical of course, that we come up against a minor problem, Professor d'Olbans insisted on adjusting the emergency system to bring us back to our starting point right away," he nodded his chin at a red button in the middle of the control panel.

"Vive la France and the French!" I whispered under my breath as I gave a look of gratitude to the Professor who acknowledged me discreetly with a little nod. I still felt sweat beading on my forehead. Go figure.

Challenger started turning wheels and flipping switches, which immediately changed the readings on several screens and made a bunch of lights start blinking, especially the yellow ones. The reds stayed off, which I took as a good omen. Because I was now down to looking for positive signs like a pagan Saxon in the medieval past.

"Where are we going?" I asked flatly.

"Where? Nowhere, my friend. You should be asking when! Off to the future! Let's go visit the next century. What marvelous advances in science we'll discover." GEC was roaring with pleasure again.

By contrast, Saint-Clair's excitement, although noticeable, was controlled, disciplined, as if channeled out of the habit of facing the worst dangers. The contrast between the two men was quite striking.

I am sure that at this moment GEC, lost in his excitement, would have given me Enid's hand in marriage if I were calm enough to ask for it. No doubt he would have assented without really listening to me, and as a man of honor he could not have taken it back later. But alas! I was too busy trying to control my growing fear to think of marriage at such a time. And yet I always considered myself reasonably brave. I had volunteered to explore a lost world, probably blinded by love. I had even gone to the center of the Earth to communicate with its sensitive core out of loyalty. Dangers to face, certainly, but nothing that a good rifle, a pair of fists and a solid pair of legs could not overcome. But here, I admit that I was terribly worried. Time travel—what madness! Pure madness!

"Off to new adventures!" GEC literally screamed as he slammed down a lever with a big smile on his face.

The first result was a metallic clacking outside the cabinet, then blue flashes surrounded by smoke between the prism and the magnet, and everything smelling like burnt oil. My heart skipped a few beats. D'Olbans gave us a friendly wave, all smiles and not at all disturbed by the lightning flashes only a few feet away from him. Saint-Clair answered him with a little nod, smiling also, looking completely relaxed. The man had a heart of steel! You would think this was not his first time travel!

Obviously I was the only sane human being in the room. The only one who showed a reasonable dose of worry. The only one not smiling. An adult amidst children blinded by science without a worry in the world for the consequences.

Here we go! Alas! All that was left was to suffer the consequences.

Through the windows I saw the room and Professor d'Olbans slowly dematerialize, become blurry, then the images started trailing long colored snakes, red, green, yellow and blue, before exploding in a maelstrom of blended colors, fading away. The cabinet literally hummed now, sometimes also jolted, tossing us about and preventing us from talking. Even though we were all totally concentrated on the development of our situation and not very interested in expressing our opinions.

Then I got a weird feeling, as if I was slowly coming apart, all the way down to the molecular level, losing all feeling *in fine* of my own body. And everything suddenly became black. I lost my grip. Was I blind? Did I even have eyes to see with anymore? A wave of panic started to surge up. Help! I wanted to scream but how could I scream when I did not have a mouth? And then the feeling stopped, leaving me with an unpleasant emptiness deep down in my body.

A few pale patches of light studded the darkness. Gradually they became less blurry, got brighter, as if we were focusing a microscope on the images seen through the windows. All of a sudden, after one final jolt, the machine stopped vibrating and the humming became lower and softer before ceasing altogether.

I looked through the windows at what I supposed was our final destination.

"My God!" I spit out in terror.

GEC panted a muffled groan that had nothing reassuring about it. For, we were in the middle of nowhere, in outer space. The spots of light had turned into stars shining in the immensity of space. Already the difference in pressure was cracking the windows, the air starting to escape through the joints, whistling out violently.

One glance at Professor Challenger's gaping mouth and popping eyes confirmed my suspicion that we were in a terribly dangerous situation. Saint-Clair was already on the move. While GEC and I sat petrified, he was pushing the emergency button that would put an end to the whistling.

The machine started buzzing, shaking like never before. The feeling of atomic diffusion came back briefly, making me nauseous, as the stars slowly disappeared, replaced by new colors, mostly green and brown and gray. I was gripping the arm of my seat as if holding on for dear life might save me from any peril.

Then came a hard shock that threw us against each other, heads knocking, feet suddenly thrown up against the control panel. The straps dug hard into my chest, forcing out a painful moan. Then silence in the cabinet, broken only by drizzling rain drumming on the roof.

Stunned, my stomach still painfully sensitive, I looked through the rain-streaked window. We had landed in the middle of the English countryside. I had never found it as beautiful as now, even though the sky was covered with low clouds that let through only a feeble, gloomy light.

Our arrival had certainly disturbed a few cows that were grazing peacefully in the field in the persistent drizzle. But the brave cattle only sauntered off a few yards before going back to their ruminating without another glance at us. Luckily no one was hurt by our untimely arrival. There was no habitation nearby because in every direction we saw only green fields, tilled land and thick woods.

I took Saint-Clair's hand to thank him as warmly as my frail, trembling strength allowed. Then I turned to Professor Challenger, who was dazed and haggard, with an ugly but harmless bruise on his forehead, his mouth still hanging open.

"How could I..." he finally muttered, much more injured in his ego than in his flesh. He repeated this phrase as if to convince himself of the reality of the situation.

"Do you know what happened?" I asked in a hoarse voice.

GEC came out of his stupor, first wiping his face, then shaking his head with a brief grimace of pain. He spoke softly and for once without the slightest trace of arrogance. "It's obvious."

My lord, I have to admit that a few words of explanation would have been most welcome if GEC could have brought himself to be a little more talkative. I was still not fully recovered by my journalistic vein was already feeling the imperative need to understand, to analyze. GEC cleared his throat before speaking again, softly, a sure sign of trouble.

"We've managed to travel in time, my friend, no doubt about it. But we forgot to subdue our all too human pride. What an inexcusable error on my part!"

"Could you enlighten me, Professor?"

"But it's obvious! Although we crossed the abyss of time, we didn't move an inch in space during our experiment. I should have thought of this! I wrongly calculated with a terrestrial reference when I should have used a cosmic reference in this mono-dimensional space. The error was to think that the Earth is the center of the universe whereas we are only dust on a meteor speeding through the cosmic immensity."

"Of course... but I have to admit that I still don't understand."

Saint-Clair, our savior, who had said nothing so far, spoke up with his grave serenity in exceptional circumstances. A serenity that he had never lost during our whole voyage in time, staying concentrated to assure our survival. This man had already faced too many dangers to let himself be so easily affected.

"It's clear now. We didn't move in space while the Earth continued its rotation around the sun. We landed in space, in the same place where we started, but Earth kept moving for a century. Outside of an improbable coincidence, there could be only empty space where we were a century before."

GEC nodded in approval at this explanation that confirmed his claims. Then in a voice trembling with restrained frustration he cried out, "Wells got it all wrong! How could I not have thought of this sooner?"

"Norbury..." I muttered timidly.

The shadow of a smile appeared on his face as GEC nodded briefly without saying a word to curse me.

"After all, if the best detective in the world, the greatest deductive genius can make a mistake, who am I, the humble Professor Challenger, to pretend to be infallible?"

I sat there dumbfounded. Not at hearing his abysmal insincerity—I was long used to that—but at hearing him call himself humble. It was an historic moment.

We left the cabinet and stood gladly in the wonderful English soaking rain. I took a deep breath, inhaled the humid air with delight. The icy breeze whipping my face brought back some calm to me, helped me pull myself together after such an adventure. My nausea was fading away, replaced by a migraine that was soon chased away by the fresh air.

"How far do you think we are from your house, Professor?" Leo Saint-Clair asked, always the pragmatic.

"Hmm, I'd say you acted with exceptional speed, truly worthy of your reputation, Leo. No doubt at the right instant, maybe just a bit late. The speed of the Earth's rotation around the sun is 18 miles per second, so you see that it'll be necessary for us to get our legs moving before we see any trace of civilization."

We started our trek without saying another word, searching for the first farm to take us to a station. I was just hoping that the train would not stop in Norbury so as not to twist the knife in the gaping wound of the dear Professor's ego. The rain trickled down my neck in long, cold streams while my shoes filled up with muddy water. But I did not care. I was too happy to be alive. Even feeling this wet cold, what a pleasure!

After a short while GEC stopped walking. Pointing at me, his face turned red with mounting anger and he said, "I hope that you won't be reporting this minor, momentary weakness in that fish wrap you call a newspaper, Malone!"

This was not a question but an order that he was giving me. His ego was obviously doing much better. I reassured him, explaining the angle I was counting on giving my paper.

"I think it's better to focus on the fulfillment of your brilliant theories about the nature of space-time and to explain the purely logistical details that would prevent any concrete application in the immediate future. Does that seem appropriate to you?"

The Nyctalope smiled slyly but like a perfect gentleman said not a word. He seemed a little absent, probably already thinking about the consequences of our unfortunate experience and imagining the corrections to make to the machine.

GEC furrowed his brow in deep concentration before giving his approval. "After all, we did manage to travel in time and that alone is what really matters, Malone!"

Clearly GEC was regaining his composure just fine and back to his usual self, including his enormous self-confidence that nothing could shake up for long.

"Exactly how I see things, too, Professor. Despite the brief inconveniences, your experiment was a splendid success, which your genius alone is responsible for. In my view, you're the lighthouse of knowledge guiding all of mankind, if I can use this image."

"You can, my friend, you can," GEC said, shamelessly brimming with pride.

I was certainly not very proud of behaving like a vile bootlicker, especially with an exceptional hero like Leo Saint-Clair as witness. But perhaps I've already mentioned that I found GEC's daughter particularly charming...

Translation by Michael Shreve

As was the case with Matthew Baugh's story, this tale was also written for a French anthology devoted to the Hexagon Comics characters—with a surprise guest at the end.

Matthew Dennion: *The Crater of the Dead*

The two teenagers reclined in the bed of the pickup truck and stared up into the clear twilight sky. Rick had parked just outside the cemetery. Lori was a little uncomfortable at first, but Rick had reassured her:

"My father always said it's the safest place in town. Everyone's dead."

He smiled at her as she stared into his eyes. The look she gave Rick sent a chill through his body. He started to lean to kiss her when she suddenly sat upright and pointed to the sky:

"Rick, what's that?!"

Rick turned to see a ball of light with a tail behind it streaking through the firmament. He didn't respond, he simply wrapped Lori up in his arms and covered her, as the cemetery exploded in a cloud of smoke.

Rick stayed on top of Lori, shielding her with his body until the dust and smoke cleared. Through the ringing in his ears he did his best to mouth the words *Shooting Star*. Lori nodded as he stood up and helped his girlfriend to her feet.

The entire cemetery was reduced to a smoking crater. Pieces of shattered gravestones and caskets were strewn throughout the pit. Lori grabbed Rick's arm and directed him towards the back to the truck, but his curiosity got the better of him. He shook her off and stepped to the edge of the crater.

Rick stared down at the bodies of the deceased scattered in the crater. He shrieked in terror as the head of one of the bodies lifted itself off the ground and turned to stare back at him.

Aspen, CO – C.L.A.S.H. H.Q.[1]

The young John Douglas Emerson, a.k.a. "Jaydee," had taken on his alien salamandrite native form. He was now a 1500 pounds hulking beast. He ran his long tongue across his fangs as the androids closed in on him.

As he exhaled, a frightening smile crept across his massive jaws. The androids took their first step forward attempting to surround their opponent. Jaydee unleashed a ground shaking roar as he sprang at his antagonists. He landed in their mists like a lion attacking a herd of sheep. His claws and teeth moved in a blur, slashing and crushing the androids before they could attack.

---

[1] *Consortium for Law-enforcement action and the Security of Humanity.*

57

Two spectators watched the carnage from the observation deck above the training room. C.L.A.S.H.'s Special Agent No. 2, Sara Kissinger, a.k.a. "Miss Kiss" turned to her guest:

"He has excellent strength, speed, and agility when in his salamandrite form. He does, however, tend to show increased levels of aggression. Without employing a degree of mental self-control, he would be little more than an unstoppable killing machine."

Professor Quanter, whom the tabloids had labeled "the highest IQ on Earth," kept his eyes on the training room floor below.

"An unstoppable killing machine is exactly what I need," he stated.

Jaydee crushed the last of the android attackers and the two observers walked down the stairs to the training room floor.

When they reached the floor, Miss Kiss called out to her pupil:

"Jaydee, a visitor is here to see you. I am sure you will remember Professor Quanter?"

The juggernaut strode forward and wrapped a massive clawed hand around the shoulder of the scientist. He spoke in a deep gruff voice:

"Of course I remember the professor very well. What exactly can I do for you, prof?"

The scientist removed the large claw from his shoulder and pulled a small computer from his pocket.

"A potential Extinction Level Threat has occurred in Pennsylvania."

A 3D image of the state filled the area between the trio. Quanter adjusted it causing it to focus in on a small town.

"This is Evans City, a town roughly 40 miles outside of Philadelphia."

The image focused on an even smaller area, displaying one of the main streets in the town. Evans City appeared as if a hurricane had run through it. Store windows were shattered, cars were overturned, and people were running rampant through the town. A middle-aged woman was slowly running down the street. She appeared exhausted and out of breath. She stopped for a moment to rest on a parked car. As she leaned against the vehicle, several more people shuffled into view. They all walked slowly, many of them limped, almost as if they were all injured in whatever catastrophe had befallen the town.

Knowing what was about to happen, Quanter turned his head away from the image. Miss Kiss and Jaydee watched as the group surrounded the exhausted woman. She appeared to scream when the group fell upon her. The massed people began to tear her apart.

Miss Kiss' face turned pale as she watched one of the people begin to chew on the arm of the victim. Jaydee shook his head in confusion.

"Those people, why would they attack someone like that?"

"Their faces!" said Miss Kiss. "What was wrong with their faces? They appeared as if they were in a trance. I could swear some of them were missing skin. I thought I saw one man's exposed jaw bone as he bit into that poor woman.

Quanter turned off the display and replied:

"The creatures you saw are not people. At least they are not people anymore."

Miss Kiss pleaded with the scientist.

"If those things are not human what are they?"

Quanter shook his head.

"Horrors. They are now horrors. Animated corpses... the living dead... commonly referred to as zombies. Some manner of meteor crashed near this town. It caused the recently deceased to emerge from their graves in a five-mile radius from the crash site. These re-animated corpses appear to have an insatiable hunger for living human flesh. They have begun consuming the people of Evans City. The people devoured by the dead are the lucky ones. Reports are coming in that people who are bitten by the zombies and live are becoming zombies themselves.

"That's not the worst of the problem. The radiation waves sent out by this meteor will blanket the entire Earth within 72 hours. They will cause this scene to replay itself over and over again across the planet. My friends, if we do not stop that radiation wave, this plague will bring an end to humanity."

"What can we do?" asked Jaydee.

"I need to locate the meteor causing the phenomena and drain the radiation from it." Quanter took a deep breath. "If my research holds true, without a source to power them, all of the reanimated corpses should return to their natural state. The problem is that the area the meteor crashed is also where the largest concentration of zombies will be located. They seem to be drawn to the source of the radiation. Due to the nature of the radiation, all vehicles shut down within a half-mile from it. Thus we will need to approach the meteor and the massed zombies on foot. The zombies will attack, overwhelm, and devour me before I can siphon the radiation from the probe. That is where you come in, Jaydee. Please understand what I am asking of you. I will need you to use all of your fury and unleash it on those zombies to keep them off of me. I know you struggle with maintaining your humanity in your salamandrite form, but in this instance, I need you to let go of that humanity and become the monster. You will be facing creatures who desire nothing else but kill and eat; you must be prepared to match their brutality. You are one of the few beings on the planet with the strength and stamina to undertake this mission. Furthermore, the scans I conducted on your body indicate that your skin is thick enough to keep the zombies from penetrating it and mutating you into one of those creatures yourself."

"Why not just fire a bomb or a rocket at the meteor?" asked Miss Kiss.

"There are several problems with that solution," said Quanter, shaking his head. "The radiation would knock out the guidance system of any projectile we fired at it. Even if we were lucky enough to land an explosive near it, the meteor was able to survive reentry through the atmosphere. A substance that durable would easily withstand any conventional weapon. Most importantly, even if we could destroy the meteor, the Law of Conservation of Energy is still in effect. Simply destroying it would not remove the radiation; it would still continue to animate the corpses. The zombies will continue to march across the continent devouring everyone in their path, while the radiation wave will spread across the world causing this scene repeat itself everywhere. A small surgical attack to siphon off the energy and store it safely is the only option"

Quanter stared into Jaydee's eyes.

"In exchange for your assistance, I will also divert all of my attention and resources to helping you with metabolic issues—assuming we survive. Consider my offer carefully but quickly; each second we waste, more people are dying."

"There is nothing to consider," replied Jaydee. "I will go with you."

Quanter turned and began heading for the door.

"Excellent, come with me, we do not have a moment to waste. My high-speed plane can get us outside the target area within the hour. I have been in contact with the Governor of the state as well as the President. The military and most police forces are busy evacuating the towns and cities ahead of the zombie horde as it expands from ground zero. Satellite surveillance shows over 200 hundred zombies massed around our target. The Governor is sending a Special Tactics police team to help us reach ground zero. Their goal will be to attract the zombies' attention and draw as many of them as possible away from the meteor. From that point, it will be up to us to fight through whatever zombies are left, reach the meteor, and apply the radiation siphon."

Evans City, PA

The Police Urban Assault Vehicle plowed through the walking dead as it headed for the crash site. Jaydee still in his salamandrite form stared silently ahead as he prepared himself for the upcoming battle. Quanter armed himself with various weapons, while most of the Special Tactics team donned their armored riot gear. Quanter was impressed with their leader Sergeant Valentine. The athletic-looking young woman opted to wear a short skirt and tube top in order to maximize her speed and agility.

Sergeant Valentine stood and addressed her officers:

"Listen up. Our objective is to draw as many zombies as possible away from the crash site. Reports indicate that the only way to stop them is to destroy their brains, so don't waste time firing at their bodies; it's headshots or nothing."

The officers silently nodded as the vehicle rolled to a stop. A driver called out that power to the engine had died. Sergeant Valentine grabbed the door handle.

"All right, looks like this is the last stop. On my count!"

60

The officers stood up as their leader counted down from three and pulled the large side door open. She sprang out followed by her team while Quanter slammed the door shut behind them. The police began firing their shotguns into the mass of undead corpses. After the first volley, the police began running for the tree line at the far end of the field. From the assault vehicle, Quanter counted roughly thirty zombies that had followed them. He cursed under his breath. He was hoping more zombies would take the bait.

As the majority of the group ran for the woods, one officer was cut off from the forest by a group of zombies. Resigning himself to his fate, he decided to stand his ground in a vain attempt to buy his teammates a few extra seconds.

Quanter and Jaydee watched in disgust as the zombies surrounded the man and attacked him. The dead ripped large chunks of flesh from the still living man and devoured it. It took the horde of corpses just under a minute to kill the man, but Quanter was sure that, from the victim's perspective, the torture had felt like an eternity.

Quanter looked away from the dreadful scene and stared at Jaydee. The scientist could see that the monster was prepared for the battle. Drool poured out from between his fangs, and his face had the eager look of a starving wolf about to attack an injured deer.

"Wait a moment, Jaydee, remember the plan," he said. "When we open the door ,we will head for the meteor. It should be about a half mile from this spot at the bottom of a crater. Once we reach the crater, you keep the zombies at bay while I drain its energy."

Jaydee growled in response. Quanter took a deep breath and opened the door of the vehicle. The scene unfolding in the moonlit night before them gave even the monstrous Jaydee a pause. The field was full of zombies. From the vehicle, the duo could see hundreds of the reanimated corpses swarming across the field. At the far end of what had once been a peaceful cemetery was the smoking crater in which the meteor was embedded.

Jaydee stepped through the door and roared a challenge into the night. He looked down to see that a contingent of zombies had begun to surround the vehicle. Jaydee jumped into the line of zombies and brought his claws down on top of the lead zombie's head. The force of the blow split the dead man in half. Jaydee stood up and threw both of his claws out in opposite directions smashing the heads of two more of the foul corpses. A third zombie grabbed his arm. As it opened its mouth, the salamandrite closed his jaws around the rotting cranium of the corpse and bit its head off. Then he spit the head out, grabbed the dismembered corpse by the legs, and began to smash two more zombies into pulp with the body of his last victim.

Quanter was enthralled by the situation. He was watching a primordial battle. On one side was man reduced to his most basic need, the need to eat. Opposing was a creature reduced to his basest desire, the desire to kill. For a moment, Quanter was not sure which of the two monsters he feared the most.

Quanter pulled a long metal pole from beneath his coat and planted it into the chest of an approaching zombie. The air sizzled and the smell of burning flesh wafted into the wind as the pole electrified the zombie, frying its brain. The pole was lodged in the corpse's body, forcing the professor to release it and start running toward the crater at the far end of the field. He did his best to drown out the cries for help from the police in the forest. He reminded himself that only by stopping the radiation pulse could he save those people.

A group of a dozen or more zombies began to lumber toward Quanter. He quickly reached into his coat and threw several small balls in their direction. As the balls rolled into the crowd of corpses, a white gas emitted from the spheres. When it came into contact with the zombies, it instantaneously froze them solid. The professor continued toward the crater and saw three zombies fly past him and crash into the ground with tremendous force. He glanced to his right and saw Jaydee tossing zombies across the field as if they were rag dolls.

As Quanter approached the crater, the volume of zombies increased exponentially and he wondered if this hadn't been a suicide mission after all. He again reached into his coat and withdrew a hand full of small disks. He flung them into the mass of dead creatures blocking his way to the crater. A dozen of the zombies suddenly shot into the sky like rockets. The anti-gravity disks attached to them would carry the dead men into the vacuum of space where they would explode in the cold void.

The scientist rushed into the small opening he created in the mass of zombies. He was almost at the crater's edge when the rest of the horde began to close in around him. He pulled his last weapon from within his coat, feeling that it was in vain, when a massive figure blocked out the moon. Jaydee landed directly on top of two zombies, crushing them. He plunged his claws into the face another zombie, grabbed a third, and hurled it into a group of his fellow flesh-eaters. The zombies Jaydee threw his projectile into tumbled backwards into the crater, allowing Quanter access to it.

Quanter sprinted into the pit and ran up to the probe as the zombies poured into the crater from all sides, like water into a basin. He reached into his coat, pulled out the energy siphon, and attached it to the meteor.

A humming sound rang through the night as the siphon began to drain the meteor of the reanimating radiation. Quanter shook his head impatiently as the siphon continued its job. He turned to see zombies closing in from all sides.

The scientist took a deep breath as a roar echoed through the night sky. A mass of zombies converged on a sphere that had rolled into the pit. When the ball of death came to stop, Jaydee stood up and shook several of the zombies off of himself. Quanter looked in amazement at the savagery displayed on his friend's alien face.

"Jaydee, we just need to hold out a few more moments in order to let the siphon absorb the remaining energy. Once it does, the corpses should return to their normal state."

Quanter readied himself to fight when Jaydee spun around and grabbed him by his lapels. The salamandrite lifted the scientist and threw him out of the crater. He landed behind the horde of zombies, and watched as they continued to flood into the pit.

He could hear Jaydee roaring from inside the pit as the zombies converged on him.

Refusing to let Jaydee sacrifice himself, Quanter utilized his final weapon. He pulled out a jar with two maggots in it, opened it, and placed the maggots on the ground. He then pointed a device at the two larvae and a wide-spread beam cascaded over them. The two maggots quickly grew to the size of African Elephants. Following their natural instincts, they began to consume the decaying flesh that surrounded them. Quanter had created the first natural predator of zombies!

The scientist looked over his shoulder to see the massive maggots ingesting one zombie after another as the brainless creatures did nothing but continue to attempt to enter the crater.

Reduced to more conventional weapons Quanter grabbed his knife and drove it into the skull of a zombie lumbering toward him.

He looked at the crater and saw body parts flying as Jaydee continued to bellow his rage. The ravenous maggots had cleared most of the zombies from edge of the crater. Quanter stabbed another zombie in the head and called for his friend. Seeing his opening, the salamandrite sprang from the pit, covered in rotting flesh and entrails.

Jaydee landed next Quanter while the gigantic maggots continued to devour zombies. The salamandrite lunged at a group of zombies and began to tear them apart when they suddenly stopped. Quanter watched as the entire horde of zombies also fell to the ground limp. He breathed a sigh of relief. The siphon had done its job. He walked toward Jaydee and called to him. The salamandrite lifted his claw and growled at the scientist before regaining his composure.

"I am sorry, Professor. Sometimes I lose myself when engaged in a battle like that."

"It's OK! You did what needed to be done. We have stopped this plague from spreading across the planet. Now, let me shrink these maggots back down to size. Then, we'll see if any of those officers who helped us need medical attention."

Quanter Labs, Chicago, IL

Quanter stared at the energy siphon in front of him. The zombie plague had been stopped and no new reports had come since the meteor had been drained.

Jaydee was back in Aspen, and most of the police unit which had helped them had survived.

The issue now was the siphon, The Law of Conservation of Energy was still in effect. The radiation which had caused the plague still existed within the siphon. The Pentagon had already contacted him about confiscating the siphon. No doubt, they wanted to see if the radiation could be modified for military use. Quanter could see the military employing this weapon on one of their enemies, hoping they could contain the zombies before they spread out. The scientist knew the siphon had to be placed somewhere safe, and given the nature of the radiation, it could not be placed anywhere that contained sentient life.

Quanter had one last option. His father, Bernard Quatermass, had left him a beacon which could be activated if a situation ever arose which was beyond the capabilities of the human race to handle. He had spoken of being, a Lord of Time and Space, who traveled the cosmos addressing problems such as these. Quanter hoped that this being would be able to take the siphon to a place where the radiation it contained would never become a threat.

Until this point, Quanter had never activated the beacon. He was unsure if it would work, or what exactly to expect.

A blinding light suddenly appeared in the laboratory. He shielded his eyes and could see the form of an elderly man walking toward him.

Quanter remembered the stories his father had told him growing up, and he whispered the name: *Doctor Omega.*

Amongst our perennial favorite characters is Doctor Omega, the mysterious cosmic traveler invented by French proto-SF writer Arnould Galopin in 1906, who has since become a more than adequate substitute for the BBC's Doctor Who. Our newest contributor, David Friend, made use of this resemblance to craft a story that throws an entirely different light on one of the Doctor's archenemies...

David Friend: *Doctor Omega and the Future Museum*

Paris, 1912

Friedrich Köhler was tense, alert, and listening for footsteps that would signal an instant death. All he heard, as he shuffled through a puddle, was the tinkle of his splashes echoing softly across Montmartre hill. It would happen soon, though. He had sensed someone watching him all evening. Tightening his grubby moleskin coat around himself, he bent a balding head in the direction of the Basilica of Sacré-Coeur and his little apartment.

The door, he discovered with a stab of surprise, was already open and a pale glow reached warningly through the crack. Köhler stiffened. This, he knew instinctively, was it. His thin features set into a look of grim resignation, he stepped inside. A man was lounging contentedly in an armchair, nursing a bottle of Armagnac.

"Don't mind, do you? I was parched. You know what it's like."

Köhler squinted, confused. The stranger had boyish brown hair and a wiry body that was almost lost beneath a double-breasted sack suit, thick Raglan overcoat and striped, sponge bag trousers. He seemed to be in his middle thirties with a thin, pale face that somehow managed to be both convivial and cold, and spoke with an English accent.

"Drink with me!" he demanded and raised the bottle in the air. The little that was left slopped guiltily in the glass. "Actually, do you have anything else? I'm in the mood for a malt, for some reason."

"I don't know you," said Köhler stoutly.

The Englishman sneered and shook his head with cynical amusement. "Well, I know all about you, Friedrich Köhler. For one thing, I know that isn't your real name." With a squeak of leather upholstery, he leapt restlessly to his feet. His whole body, it seemed, surged with insuppressible energy. "You aren't German, either," he continued, "and you don't usually look this way. The real Köhler worked for the White Star Line and died on the *Titanic*. He was a second cousin to the Duke Gerhard of Württemberg. You wrote to his business secretary in Strasbourg and claimed to be Köhler, impoverished after the disaster, and asked for two thousand marks so that you might recover all you have lost. I intercepted the last of these letters and shall show it to Inspector Juve of the Sûreté, if we can't come to an arrangement of our own. I'll settle for a brandy, if that's all you've got in."

Friedrich Köhler seemed too indignant to even speak. "These—these are lies!" he blustered, trembling now.

"No," said his guest pithily, "you're an ingenious French criminal, a master of disguise, who is loyal to no one. In short, you are Fantômas."

Köhler paused, cautious and thoughtful. "I do have some malt," he allowed. His German accent had now vanished. Turning to the sideboard, he picked up a bottle of whiskey and poured a glass. A keen observer would have noticed how the narrow shoulders had folded confidently back and he was no longer trembling.

"So," said the Englishman, clapping his hands briskly together, "do I have to inform the police?"

The word was like a curt command. Fantômas whirled around and hurled the bottle into the hearth. With a dull rumble, the fire swelled angrily outwards, spitting sparks across the carpet and onto the sheepskin rug. The Englishman made to move, but a forceful shove sent him reeling backwards into the chair, upending it onto the floor.

How had this whippet of man found him? The very fact he had done so was embarrassing. Emasculating, even. Fantômas threw off his bald cap disdainfully, unsheathed his coat and knelt over his guest. A glint of silver, and he was suddenly holding a knife. "Tell me, sir," he growled, "who are you? I want to know what to carve on your grave."

The Englishman stared indulgently up at his host with eyes of dark humor and dangerous intent.

"I'm from the future," he said, and smiled.

Shoreditch, 2005

Jaz delved into the washing basket, pulled out a pair of smart trousers, and wondered if she should hang them. Since the accident, her father barely ever left the house, so it was not as though he would need them. He needed nothing, in fact, from his town council days. Jaz could hear the television from the kitchen window—*Eggheads*, as usual—and knew he was sitting sullenly in front of it.

It wasn't fair. He was still a young man, really. Other people were allowed to wander around and do whatever they liked. She stared absently into the property next door. Their old neighbor, for instance, still had the use of his legs, but what did he do with them? He watered plants and clattered noisily in the semi-abandoned hangar located at the other end of his garden, but nothing of use.

She wouldn't have noticed otherwise, but that hangar of his had been silent for half an hour. Jaz paused, her olive face crimped in confusion. Usually, her neighbor was in there, all day. She tossed a sock back into the basket and drifted

66

curiously to the fence. And that was when she saw him, through the half-opened doorway of the hangar. The old man was lying on the ground, his top half hidden from view.

Jaz moved instinctively. Gripping the fence, she hurled herself upwards and onto the other side. For months, she had dreaded something similar happening to her dad, and now all that tension was uncoiling inside her. She rolled the door aside (it was mounted on rails), stumbled, fell to her knees, and stared into her neighbor's thin, lined face.

"What the devil are you doing?" he barked.

Jaz jolted up with fright and hit the metal door behind her. It clanged hollowly. Looking about her, she realized that this was no ordinary hangar. There were tools, yes, and the windows were stained with grease and soot, and there was a bench packed with complex electronic equipment that emitted a strange hum of power—but in the center of it as occupied by a massive object that looked like a giant cannon shell, except with a door and portholes. The old man had been fiddling busily beneath it, and now she wished she hadn't disturbed him.

"Sorry," she said, suddenly breathless. "I thought you were dead!"

Her neighbor's head tilted towards her and his blue-green eyes flashed with indignation. "It will take more than a leaking carburetor to finish me, young lady."

Jaz was stung. It wasn't *her* fault the old goat was still alive. "This looks like that junk yard down the road," she said, nodding at the mess. "What is it you're doing in here, anyway?"

With a groan of effort, her neighbor leaned forward into a squatting position and Jaz had her first proper look at him. Stringy white hair curled down to his neck and the rest of his head was bare, but for a rebellious thick tuft at the front. His clothes were just as odd. He was wearing a yellow tweed waistcoat, a white-collared shirt with a black ribbon tie and a pair of grey tartan trousers and elasticized boots. Jaz had never seen anyone dress in such a way before. Not even for charity.

"I'm a scientist," he said, stretching painfully upright. He was taller than she had realized and his eyes were wide and angry and glared out of his gaunt face as though she had done something unspeakably foul. "I was just making repairs."

"To what?" asked Jaz, undeterred. "That unexploded V-2 rocket?"

The old man smarted fiercely. "Of course not! I wouldn't have any use for something so primitive. No, this is something of mine." He looked at the young woman with a new awareness, taking in her tip-tilted nose, yellow hoop earrings and untidy ponytail. "I'm Doctor Omega," he said and, interrogatively, "Who are you?"

Jaz was caught off-guard. Snapping out questions was usually something *she* did. "Jaz," she said.

"Like Glenn Miller?"

"No, just one..."

"I gave him his first trombone, you know," said the Doctor with sudden reminiscence. "He was fiddling about with a mandolin when I met him."

Jaz frowned bemusedly. The old man was clearly nuts. "Hold on, if this thing of yours needed repairs, it must've worked at some point," she reasoned, "and yet, I haven't seen it before. How did you get it inside in here?"

The Doctor snorted derisively. "You wouldn't have *seen* it," he said. "Humans aren't very observant. I've learned *that* much from being here."

"Being where?"

Perhaps, she wondered, he was from another country. Jaz had always wanted to go abroad—like Greece, or the Gulf of Honduras—but the only time she could book foreign holidays was at the travel agency where she worked and even that was for other people.

"Hopefully, I should be able to take off very soon," he was saying now.

For Jaz, the conversation was unraveling out of all comprehension. "Take off?" she said. "You mean—it can go places, then? Like a plane, or a helicopter?"

"Oh yes, but not in the way that a place or a helicopter can."

"But it could get us to town?"

His pale face creased with amusement and pride. She seemed to have calmed him a little. "It could take us a lot further than that, my dear," he assured her. "Most ships do."

"Ships?"

"That travel through time and space," he said, as though it were obvious.

Jaz lifted her hands. "I'm standing in a garden shed," she said, "which contains a spaceship?"

"Yes."

"*This*," she emphasized, pointing at the shell-like contraption, "is a ship?"

The old man seemed to take her incredulous tone as a personal affront. "Yes, and it is *mine*."

Jaz knew she should humor him. There was something, however, in his manner—that certainty, those incredulous, mocking eyes, the implication that it was *she* who was being ridiculous—which made her deeply irritated. Jasmine Driscoll could be patient and compassionate, and usually was, right up until the moment when she felt her intelligence was being underestimated.

"Explain how it works," she demanded and, even to her, this sounded like a playground dare.

The Doctor accepted this seriously. "Mainly, on Bernoulli's equation but, if you ask me, none of the Bernoulli boys really understood mathematics, though they could get a bit tetchy if you pointed it out to them." He leaned towards the door of the shell and opened it wide, inviting her to get inside. "It would be better if I showed you," he said pragmatically. "Explanations can be dull."

68

She went inside; he followed her, closing the door behind them. The lower floor of the craft was divided into two rooms, one that led to the engines, and the other a store room.

"The bridge is up there," he said, pointing to a metal ladder bolted to the wall.

Jaz went up. The middle floor was divided into three rooms, each connected to the central column by a small door. She kept climbing and reached the top floor which was clearly the bridge.

There were three chairs bolted to the floor, and six portholes. The middle chair was the pilot's chair. It sat in front of a steering wheel and a console with mysterious, yet simplistic devices that looked as if they'd been pulled out from a Lego box—or a primitive art exhibit.

The Doctor sat in the pilot's chair and, with a single flick of a switch activated one of these mysterious devices. He then looked at her with curious expectation.

"Where would you like to go?" he inquired.

Jaz smiled, confused. "Where would I like to go?"

"Hmm." He seemed to consider this a reasonable offer. "We don't have to leave Shoreditch at all, but we could go somewhere else, if you'd like. Disneyland; the time of Boadicea; Disneyland in the time of Boadicea. Perhaps even Greece or the Gulf of Honduras."

He cocked a knowing eyebrow and Jaz wondered if he was joking, but something in his thin, stern face told her that he wasn't. He seemed to believe everything he had said. With a stir of nerves, she tried to remember whether she had mentioned her travel ambitions. She hadn't, of course. And yet, somehow, he knew of them already.

"All right, then," she relented, like an exhausted parent agreeing to play another game with a child. "Let's travel through time and space."

"Excellent!"

"I'd like to see Paris," she added, still humoring him.

"Priam's son, you mean?" The old man's mouth crimped contemplatively. "Well, I'll warn you, it gets rather bloody. Last time I was there, I almost got shot with an arrow!"

Jaz shook her head briskly and her ponytail danced. "I mean Paris, the city of lights, in present times."

The Doctor shrugged. It made little difference to him. He took hold of a long, white lever and yanked it down with a stiffening squeak. Quite suddenly, Jaz heard something from outside. Somebody's lawn mower? An electric saw? Whatever it was, it seemed to be getting louder too, like a dozen air compressor pipes that were broken and blasting and out of control. She felt a primitive desire to run.

"What's going on?" she shouted.

"The engine, my dear," the Doctor called back unconcernedly.

Jaz gripped her seat's armrest. Suddenly, she wanted to get off this strange contraption. Through the portholes the interior of the hangar had gone, replaced by twirling clouds of light made of ever-changing colored stuff—a kaleidoscopic tunnel made of pure—something.

With a heavy, metal thud, the craft was suddenly still. The noise had stopped as well. Jaz felt herself swaying unsteadily in her chair.

Someone was speaking. A male voice, but not her dad's. It was older, colder, and without the concern. Jaz opened her eyes blearily. The strange little scientist was looking at her with a detached interest, as one might stare into a glass tank at a rare breed of tropical fish.

"I've met a fair few humans," he said, "and most have been cynical, unimaginative and irrationally stubborn beings. You're... slightly less so."

Jaz heard the words, but she wasn't ready to untangle them. "Thanks?" she said, not quite knowing whether this was a compliment or not.

The Doctor nodded pompously, as though he himself were receiving praise. "We're here, by the way," he added inconsequentially.

They were certainly somewhere else. Jaz did not know how she was so sure, but it was a firm, frank conviction unlike any other she had ever felt. Whistling tunelessly and without spirit, the old man went down the ladder, moved towards the door and flung it casually open. Jaz followed him, tottering forward, realizing with relief that she could still walk. At this point, she wasn't taking anything for granted.

The hangar, the garden, of course, were no longer there. Instead, a bright artificial light was beckoning them onwards. Jaz paused, unsure whether to leave or not. Finally, after a moment to prepare herself—and, indeed, after many years of wanting desperately to see something other than her local high street and the pale glow of a computer screen—she smiled.

"Well," she said, "I've a feeling we're not in Shoreditch anymore."

Anywhen

The doors opened, music blared, and the Englishman spun on the spot flamboyantly. He had always enjoyed showing off and, in his view, the best thing to show off was power. The big, loud, obvious kind that nobody could deny and everyone could envy. He strutted forward like the whole world was his own private dance floor—shameless, assured and drunk on funk. With an energetic bound, he slid across the console room and towards a vending machine.

"This song's about me!" he crowed. "I'm getting back to where I once belonged!"

Fantômas was standing off to the side, dressed resplendently in a black dinner suit and shirt, his mask draped over his hands. Despite changing into his own clothes, however, he did not feel the control he usually did. All this talk of the coming days and sailing boats to the stars—it was the sort of thing written by Jules Verne or H. G. Wells. And such strange, clattering noise, too. He gave his host a cold stare and the music was reluctantly terminated.

"That," said the Englishman with critical emphasis, "is the greatest band in history. Seriously, you have no taste."

The thief, however, wasn't in the mood for such discussions. "How did you know about the letters?"

"We're still on that?" the Englishman complained. "You end up writing a memoir and I read it. Simple."

"And this…?"

"It's a machine that can reach the sky above and the times ahead. Sorted?" The Englishman turned to the console and began tapping the keyboard keenly. "I've always had difficulty driving these things. I could do with a SatNav, really."

None of this made sense to Fantômas. "It can go places?"

His pilot paused at the keyboard. "Well, yeah," he said, "but not in the way a hansom can."

"But it could get us to town?"

The Englishman laughed. It was a stiff, unmelodious sound and strangely devoid of delight. "It can take us a *little* bit further than that," he said with scorn.

Fantômas decided to focus on matters of which he had some experience. "You want me to steal something for you?"

The Englishman bit his lip hungrily and pulled a lever down hard. A stertorous breathing surrounded them and he punched the air victoriously. "Gets me every time," he enthused, then remembered what his new friend had said. "Stealing. Yes. It shouldn't be difficult for someone like you." He pressed a button and an image sprung up on the monitors above them. It was a photograph of himself beside a thin, blonde woman with delicate features. "In 2007, I am Prime Minister of Great Britain." He bobbed his head, grinning conceitedly. "I know, right? Amazing."

"It certainly is," said Fantômas, but the other did not discern the irony.

"I enslaved the planet, reversed the economy and dismantled the technology. Usual stuff. Now, though, I must focus on bigger things, not on some stupid resistance."

"Resistance?"

"Led by a woman, would you believe? They're bringing hope to the people and are seen as heroes." The future Prime Minister smiled. "But I will put them in their place." He scratched his chin, as though he were used to having a beard there, and began to explain his plan.

It was more than the Frenchman could ever have imagined.

Afterwards, the Prime Minister's face split into a self-satisfied smile. "Come on," he said, taking the lever again, "let's break the speed limit. Live a little." And, with that, there came the crunching, confident chords of *All Right Now*.

Fantômas watched with amusement and awe as they entered into oblivion.

Paris, The Future Museum

It was, to say the least, a surprise.

The rambunctious ride in the craft—which, Jaz had learned, was called the *Cosmos*—could have been simulated somehow, but no such trick could be responsible for this. She stared with methodical concentration at her new surroundings. She had been transported, quite evidently, and in a way which was almost magical. And now, she and the strange old man were standing in an auditorium with a wide linoleum floor, high ceilings and fluorescent lights. Most obviously, there were glass display cases positioned at intervals, though Jaz did not recognize anything that had been placed inside them.

"What is this?" she said with anxious inquiry. "The Louvre?"

The Doctor seemed to enjoy her astonishment. His ashen face had crinkled into a thin smile and he was watching her with paternal indulgence. "Not quite," he said, and pointed to the wall. "Out there are the Catacombs of Paris. An underground graveyard packed with the bones of six million people. Wall to wall skulls and not for the faint-hearted. We're towards the right, beneath the sixteenth arrondissement." He tugged at his lapels grandly. "This, my dear, is the Future Museum."

Jaz looked blank. "What's that?"

She was only asking to be polite. Really, if this was Paris, she wanted to see the Eiffel Tower or the river Seine. What was the point in visiting one of the world's most beautiful cities and spending the entire trip underground? She might as well be trapped in the Channel Tunnel.

The Doctor was disgruntled. "Good gracious me!" he said, his grey brows swerving together like two beetles in a fight. "Isn't it obvious? This museum exhibits artifacts from the future instead of the past." He began moving nimbly between the exhibits. "We jumped the queue, arriving this way, and we haven't had to bother with the gift shop either. All those tea-towels, notebooks, sticks of rock…" He shook his head disapprovingly. "You pay for the name with that sort of thing."

But Jaz wasn't interested in souvenirs. She was staring, dumbstruck, at this most unconventional of museums. "How come I haven't heard of it before?" was the first thing she wanted to know. "You'd think it would be world famous."

She wondered obscurely if this was an insult, but the old scientist seemed to have expected the remark. "Those hinges," he said, lifting a finger to the tall doors, "are fitted with an Automatic Memory Mangle. When you leave, you shall think have seen only *speculative* ideas about the future. You've probably noticed your memory's a bit hazy already."

"Yeah, you're right," said Jaz, and touched her temple dubiously. "I can't... It's weird, but I can't even remember what my dad looks like."

The Doctor nodded, unsurprised. "It's a side effect," he said. "I have it too. This way, whatever invention people see cannot influence the world before it has been invented, therefore preventing paradoxes."

He spoke with such authority that Jaz trusted him implicitly. It was as if she had known him for ages. Almost like a relative. He certainly had a grandfatherly look about him—but then, she supposed, that probably came with getting old. She got the feeling he could be irritable and curmudgeonly, and had been a bit already, but wasn't that the way with all granddads?

"This," he said, leading her to a flying car from Aston Airborne, "is what inspired me to start the place. Someone told me how the modern day wasn't what they had expected. I brought this back from the future to show them and, before long, I was putting other things with it too."

Jaz noticed a television mounted on the wall. "Why is there a telly?" she asked. "We have those already."

"Ah, that's a news report announcing the result of the 2071 republican referendum. It shall spell the end of the British monarchy as we know it."

Her expression was caught, somehow, between delight and horror. "Will it hold?"

"In a manner of speaking. After forty-six years, the monarchy will return under the honors system. King- and queen-ships will be awarded to those who represent Britain in some way internationally, with each incumbent keeping the title for ten years." He suddenly looked quite wistful. "People can get rid of things a little too hastily," he said, "and it isn't long before they want them back again."

Already, Jaz was distracted, scrutinizing a leaflet she had found on the floor. "What's *Death Knell*?"

The Doctor hesitated. "Well, it looks like a metal suitcase, but it's actually a super-weapon," he said carefully. "When it was replaced, it was put on display here, too much controversy."

"I bet," she said, only half-listening. She was looking at another exhibit now and grinned with embarrassment. "A headset," she read from the object label, "which allows two people to share dreams while asleep. A bit racy!"

The Doctor didn't approve of the humor. "Psychic phenomena isn't so unusual. If a person went near his past or future self, the proximity could make their minds entwine, with one asserting itself over the other."

"The way you talk," Jaz said with ironical disbelief, "you could make time-travel boring!"

The old man's mouth set sourly, and she wondered if she had overstepped the mark.

A young voice erupted behind them. "Hey, Mrs. Carnegie," it sneered. "I think you might need this!"

The pair turned to see a short boy of around seven or eight years-old with scrupulously tidy brown hair and designer clothes. A round, middle-aged woman came up beside him. Jaz felt sorry for her. The exhibit was for a "hunger pill" which expanded in the stomach, removing any hunger pangs, and contracted a couple of hours later. It would, she read, threaten weight-loss empires, delight busy business-people and inspire corporations to eliminate lunch breaks among their labor workforces.

"We should keep moving," advised the Doctor. "There's a lot you'll want to see."

Jaz smiled. He seemed to treat these wonders with a sort of weary indifference, as one who lives beside the Statue of Liberty may become bored of the cooing tourists and flashing photographers. Did anything take him unawares? It was certainly not time-and-space machines—those domestic rockets that hurled people across temporal planes and international borders without even touching the sky. Jaz couldn't think of anything weirder than that. Maybe, she speculated, only aliens caught his attention, but did they exist? It was one of the more obvious questions to ask and she was surprised it had only just occurred to her.

"You'd like the Space Room," he said, as though she had already asked him. "It has the first extra-terrestrial ship, discovered by NASA in 2057. Most humans make a fuss of that." He smiled fondly. "Really, you are like dogs barking at your own reflection."

"I'm allowed to be a little impressed," said Jaz coolly. "Weren't you, when you first came here?"

His old face crumpled as he crossed the years. "Back then, there wasn't a museum to be seen," he recalled. "I had to have one built."

Jaz felt a giddy confusion. "Wait," she said, hands flat and fingers splayed in that way she always did when she wanted to get her facts in line. "The museum had to be here for you to have heard of it, but it couldn't be here if you hadn't built it. That's a paradox, surely?"

The Doctor looked amused, like a parent whose child had learned a new word. "No, no. Apparently, I shall live for a while in the early 1980s. Hence, in the past, my future has already happened. I will go on to build the place, but I didn't know that until after I had done it."

She considered this critically. "Sounds a bit… wibbley-wobbley," she concluded. "How long has it been here?"

"The question is," said the Doctor, "how long *will* it be here?"

Jaz made a face. She disliked it when people answered questions with more questions. It was like being criticized and corrected all at once. "Go on, then, how long?"

He was quite lofty about this. "Well, I haven't really checked, but it should be forever. In fact…" He would have continued, but a voice called out from behind him.

"Doctor!"

74

It belonged to a slim forty-something woman in a blue business suit with blonde hair pulled back into a tight bun. Jaz had the uneasy feeling that she was not to be crossed, but Omega seemed pleased to see her.

"Ah, Liz," he said. "Jasmine, this is Liz Shaw, the curator of the museum. She used to be my assistant, as it were, travelling around."

The woman was serious. "It helped," she recalled wryly, "when it came to my Futurism degree." She eyed Jaz with a curious aspect but, irritatingly, did not speak to her directly. "Your friend, I trust, is from the past, Doctor?"

"2005," he said with a knowing smile. "Still keen for visitors from all eras, Miss Shaw?"

"Temporal diversity is very important," she said stiffly.

The Doctor shook his head with something like disgust. "Political correctness gone mad…"

A radio buzzed. "Excuse me," said Miss Shaw and took it from her pocket. Jaz didn't catch the message, but it was obviously not good news. The curator's face tightened anxiously, like an actor who had forgotten her lines on opening night.

She turned, faltering, to the room at large. "Could I have everyone's attention, please?" she called. "You must all remain in this room until further notice. We are in lock-down."

Doctor Omega was frowning. "What is it, Liz?" he asked, but there was no time to help. No time, it seemed, for anything at all.

With a groan of resignation, the lights above them flickered once before plunging into an empty darkness.

The curator's voice came through coldly. "There's a robbery in progress, Doctor."

Things were going well.

The security guard had been too busy fetching coffee to witness their stylish arrival, and he only noticed something was wrong when his monitor snowballed. Now, the Prime Minister had rerouted all close circuit footage to his ship and was checking to see how many visitors were in the museum.

He had seen the place before—indeed, had life membership and was eligible for free parking and the quarterly magazine—but this was the first time he had tried to rob it, and he felt an almost sensual stir of excitement. A good thief, he had stolen everything from a nerve gas missile to the bodies of living people, but he had trouble accessing vaults—and that was where Fantômas came in.

The criminal himself was at the door and getting restless. "I always act fast," he said with professional pride. The mask cloaked his face—only his eyes were visible—and reached heavily over his neck. "Is our time now?"

"Indeed, it is," said his new partner smoothly. "Let's see if you really are the best cracksman in European history. I shall join you in twenty minutes and help you carry it back here."

The criminal nodded. "And then, Mr. Norman—or whatever your name is—I will expect my letter. You had better not cheat me; I have quite an *appétit* for revenge."

"Oh, I'm aware of that, believe me, though I don't intend to betray you." The Englishman smiled with a sickening sincerity, and Fantômas decided that he must be a politician after all.

The Prime Minister sensed movement on the monitor and turned. The Doctor, he noticed, had slid into view. He had recognized him at once, but only intuitively. It had been many years, and time had certainly changed both their appearances. But then, of course, it changed everything.

"This has just become a little more interesting," he said.

"How?" asked Fantômas. "Who is he?"

"Just an old friend," said the Prime Minister reflectively, and scratched his chin again. "Well, best friend. We even vowed to visit every star in the galaxy together. But you know how it is. You lose touch. Meet new people. Start wars." Brisk again, he tapped at the console busily. "Let's get the security boys back online. Least we can do is give the Doctor half a chance." His fingers finished with a flourish and he turned to Fantômas with new purpose. "The plan is changing slightly."

The thief looked startled. "No!" he protested fiercely. "Who is this... this Doctor, you speak of? Is he a physician? Does he save lives?"

"Sometimes," said the Englishman lightly. "But today he's about to lose a few."

A faint hum, and the back-up generator summoned some light. It wasn't much. Just a few small bulbs glimmering shyly. A birthday cake would have been brighter. But it was better than nothing, Jaz decided, and at least they were able to see one another.

"What now?" she asked. As was usually the case, she was eager to do something, but wasn't sure what that something would be.

Miss Shaw held up her smartphone. "Our cameras are back on now and they just caught this." It was an image of a man in black. "I will run it through the transparency scanner."

Jaz was not sure she could tolerate any more technology. "What's one of them?" she asked, suddenly out of her depth. This, she supposed, was how old people must feel in an age of e-mails, text messages and online banking. Even her dad had struggled with it at first, but he had lately taken to ordering groceries over the internet whenever she couldn't do the late night shop. It was the first sign he was becoming reclusive; something which concerned her still.

"A transparency scanner is a computer software program which scans an image and strips it of fabric, allowing us to see underneath," the Doctor explained. "But it isn't necessary. I recognize the black attire." His flinty eyes tightened distastefully, as though he had just sampled a plate of spoiled fish.

"It's Fantômas. A famously ruthless criminal of early twentieth century origin."
He harrumphed with frustration. "This is what happens when you hire humans
instead of mechonoids as guards."

Miss Shaw was clearly embarrassed. "We do have one, but it's… an exhibit. People stand next to it and get their photograph taken."

With a hiss of static, there came a small, faraway voice of little confidence:
"Dr. Shaw? I've tried calling it in, but I can't get through. I don't what happened
with the cameras, but he seems to be heading towards the west side of the museum."

The Doctor's brow darkened. "Why would he do that?"

"I'm going to have a look now," the voice added.

"Tony?" said Miss Shaw worriedly, but it was no use. The radio wheezed,
and she dropped her arm in defeat.

Jaz had quite forgotten the presence of anyone else, but was rudely reminded of it by the young voice from earlier. "Why are we still waiting?" the
boy whined. He sounded as though he were chastising a waiter at a posh restau-
rant. The middle-aged woman, presumably his nanny, looked like she would rather be anywhere else but beside him.

"I don't know," she answered weakly and, in a poor attempt at optimism,
"but I expect we can move on soon."

"Indeed," said the Doctor, overhearing the exchange. "From what I hear, I
live to do some remarkable things. Like go fishing and cook an omelet."

Jaz could tell he was trying to distract the little boy, but the mention of
food was a bad idea.

"I want an ice cream," he demanded. "I want one now!"

Mrs. Carnegie seemed to summon every ounce of patience she had ever
possessed. "Write something in that new book you got," she suggested.

Moodily, the boy pulled out a Future Museum diary and began scribbling,
and Jaz luxuriated in a moment of silence.

The Doctor, meanwhile, had turned to the curator with a renewed interest.
"So, our man is heading west, hmm? Well, I doubt he's interested in the Domestic Room. It's full of high-dry machines and renewable carpets, and I shouldn't
think he wants an anti-gravity nap either. Could he, per chance, be heading for
the Military Room?"

"You mean…?"

He shrugged philosophically. "It was bound to happen one day."

"What is it?" asked Jaz, but the pair wouldn't be drawn. She stared at them
with injured virtue. She had come across such condescension before. At work,
for instance, whenever a snooty customer wanted to book a trip to the Aosta
Valley and didn't expect her to know where it was.

The Doctor gave in. *Death Knell* is in the Military Room," he revealed.
"Stupid decision, really."

Behind them, the boy was arguing again and they had to talk louder themselves.

"Oh yes?" said Miss Shaw, sounding like one of those serenely snobbish types in a Barbara Pym novel. "If you remember, the board enjoyed a robust exchange of views, and it was decided to host the exhibit by a vote of seven to five. Besides," she lifted a chin, all poise and stubborn self-belief, "our attendance rose by fourteen per cent in the first calendar year alone."

But Doctor Omega was unfazed by facts, or how vigorously one might massage them. He moved to the door and Jaz joined him, a tingle of anticipation between her shoulders. Looking out, she expected to see Fantômas in his penguin suit with a gun in his grip, but there was nobody there. Just a corridor, like any other. Narrow, long and eerily empty.

Miss Shaw produced a square device with an earbud.

Jaz smiled. "What's that? An iPod?"

"It's a Babble Booster," she said. "Amplifies sound, especially close conversations."

The Doctor took it cheerfully. "I think our young man may like this," he said with oily kindness and turned to offer it to Percy. But the boy wasn't there.

Jaz threw a panicked glance across the auditorium. The woman was missing too.

"Where are they?" she asked, but the Doctor was already alarmed.

He stepped into the corridor, listening intently through the device. Jaz kept behind him—feeling, with frustration, as though she were cowering, but she had to stay close to the wall or risk being seen.

Turning a tight corner, the old man came to an abrupt halt.

Jaz opened her mouth instinctively, but then remembered not to speak. Instead, she followed his gaze and found a figure at their feet.

It was a middle-aged woman with curly hair. Mrs. Carnegie. Jaz fought back the impulse to cry out. The Doctor bent down, pressed his fingers to her pulse. Faint red marks encircled her neck. Someone, it seemed, had squeezed her dead.

With an effort, Jaz lifted her eyes and stared, squinting, down the corridor. All she could see were thick stretches of shadow. She moved forward, listening hard, her ears almost aching with the effort. Perhaps, she wondered, Fantômas had already taken the boy. He might even be dead, and they could tumble over his corpse right now. A restless desperation suddenly seized her and, before she even realized it, Jaz was running. Her footsteps were fast and heavy and she no longer cared about noise. At any moment, she knew, the intruder could curl around the corner and block her path. They might even collide. Despite this, she felt quite removed from the danger. Her concern for the boy—however wretched he was—had somehow numbed any inhibiting fear.

Finally, she halted, hesitant and breathless. If the boy had remained in the corridor, she would have passed him by now. He had to be somewhere else. Jaz ducked into the Culture Room and glanced anxiously around. A light bulb, small and sickly yellow, glimmered weakly from the back. This room, she noticed, had a much homelier design: a couple of bright red sofas and a coffee table with a commemorative coronation mug of King George IX. Facing it, a television was screening *No Kids Allowed*, a popular sitcom from the 2060s, and a tall curtain draped over the wall where the window should have been. The kind of place, perhaps, where a boy might feel safe.

Jaz considered calling out his name, but it was no use. The sound system was playing a new song by The Beatles, created through the technological manipulation of melodies, lyrics and chord progressions from the band's back catalogue, and she couldn't compete. Confidently, knowing her footsteps would not be heard, Jaz peered over exhibits and peeked under tables. She imagined the boy fiddling with a do-it-yourself face-lifting kit or trying to administer a motion-tattoo but, frustratingly, he didn't seem to be anywhere. With this defeat, Jaz felt her chest tighten and, for the first time, realized that she was lost as well.

The song faded and the room fell to silence. Even the television program had finished. She came to a bookcase stacked with post-apocalyptic survival sagas—best-sellers as humanity hoped to outlast a nuclear war—and paused. She had treaded on something. A diary, with the museum's logo embossed across the front. Like the boy's.

Jaz picked it up and flitted through the pages, her anxious eyes scanning the words. Yes, it *was* his; all scribbled notes about the thief and the weapon and the strange old man who was supposed to save them. If he had dropped this, she realized, then he must have been here, and Fantômas must have snatched him. Which meant that the thief was close.

With a rasping whine, the door opened, and she jerked back beside the bookcase. Of course, she didn't move, but she saw something that did. A long, thin shadow, sliding slickly across the floor like a black snake. It was slow in that elegant way of all predators, and merged smoothly into the darkness surrounding it. Jaz had stopped breathing and didn't dare start again. The way things were going, she wouldn't get another chance, anyway. She heard a crunch of glass and the light bulb blinked out. Jaz tensed, and waited to feel hot breath against her face and a blade across her throat.

But it didn't happen. Instead, there was a gentle tapping towards the door and the rustle of clothes as someone passed through it. Fantômas, it seemed, had left.

Though a natural cynic, Jaz felt a stir of hope rise up inside her and sucked in soft air. Maybe, she told herself, it was going to be all right. The thief had been alone, so he couldn't have found the boy yet either. She could continue her own search and find a way out of the museum as well.

Jaz stepped confidently forward and was about to move further when something gripped her arm.

And she gasped.

"I was wondering where you had got to."

A thin torchlight appeared and, behind it, the wizened face of the Doctor.

Jaz started. "Where were you?" she said, noticing the boy beside him, wearing a coat with built-in heating sensors.

"Behind the curtains," said the boy—and, just as casually, "A man in black killed Mrs. Carnegie."

It occurred to Jaz that he may have been in shock. Or maybe he was just callous.

"You dropped this," she said damply, and handed him his book.

"And I was outside," said the Doctor, "though it's just as well I came in here, it's really quite interesting in its own way." He flashed the light idly on something behind Jaz. It was a newspaper, pinned to the wall, with a photograph of armed soldiers strutting through Downing Street.

Jaz noticed it and blanched. "What's this?" she asked, and began reading the article with earnest absorption.

It was dated 2007, and reported that the Prime Minister would order the killing of the American president and no less than ten percent of the world's population. She wondered, disbelievingly, whether this was a practical joke arranged by the staff of the museum. The Doctor, however, was also awed, and she knew it was true.

"There will be a resistance movement," she said with weak hope, but she couldn't even soothe herself. Her insides had twisted savagely with nausea.

The Dark Ages, it seemed, were coming again. A civilization which wasn't even worth the word. Her mind filled with images of people, weak and submissive and constitutionally scared. No democracy, no hope and no escape. She had to do something. She had to help them.

"Come on," said the old scientist quietly. "Things are bleak as it is. I found the security man—or, I should say, his body."

Even more bad news. With a heavy heart, Jaz followed the pair into the corridor. It was silent – though, of course, if the best thief in history was roaming around the place, would he really make that much noise?

She wished they could be in the auditorium again, before this had even happened, and continue staring incredulously at the exhibits. Come to that, she wanted to be back in her garden on Chesterton Road, putting the washing out. It was dull, yes, but refreshingly free of world slavery and time-traveling criminals.

"Why do you have a funny name?" the boy was asking Doctor Omega.

The old man seemed offended. "Why ever not? I chose it in tribute to someone very important."

Jaz waved a hand for silence. "What do we do now?"

"We keep safe," was his simple answer. "By now, Fantômas should've reached the Military Room and may even have accessed the vault. But he shall need to carry it back. It's heavy, so he will walk slowly." A finger pointed eastwards. "That's where the camera caught him. I'm going to block these corridors so he will be trapped between them."

"Blocked?"

"With a solidification spray."

Jaz smiled resignedly. "I'm not even going to ask this time."

The boy, however, was not so proud. "I want to know!" he demanded and, despite the trauma he had so recently endured, did seem interested.

"It's a sort of wall that's made from steam," the Doctor explained, and fished a hand in his pocket. "I snatched some from the Industry Room. Come the 2130s, all the builders will be using this." He revealed a slim, metal can and handed it to the boy. "Point it away from your face."

The boy studied the object cautiously, as one would observe a new bottle of insect repellent. Finally, he lifted it high, squeezed his eyes shut and pressed his finger purposefully on the nozzle. A jet of grey steam charged out of the can, discoloring the air and hanging languidly like a pea soup fog. They watched with playful astonishment as the steam thickened into something stranger and more substantial. It reminded her of a rain-soaked window or a bathroom mirror after she had showered.

The Doctor reached forward. Instead of his fingers passing through and onto the other side, a faint clink was heard, as though he were touching a sheet of glass. He murmured amusement, and tapped out a brief staccato rhythm. It was hard as brick. Jaz smiled at this crotchety old man in a frock coat. Inside, she concluded, he was young in that whimsical, curious and eagerly joyful way that actual children weren't anymore. He was like Alice and Peter Pan and Jim Hawkins, but with a dash of Ebenezer Scrooge and the Wizard of Oz.

"Now, he can't pass," the old scientist declared with the satisfaction of someone who had just put up a shelf. Jaz certainly believed him. It was as though a wall, made entirely of ice, had been erected in the middle of the corridor. He turned towards the other direction, brows swooped determinedly together. "Right, let's head to the next corridor. With any luck, we won't even meet him."

But no sooner had he said this than the old man came to a jerking halt. And listened. Jaz did too, looking back into the gloom. Yes, there *was* something...

The sound of wheels. A trolley, perhaps. The weapon must indeed have been heavy. It was moving, however, with a restless urgency, as though the thief was eager to escape.

Jaz stiffened in anticipation. She could almost feel the rumble beneath her feet, like an oncoming express train hurtling along a track. She glanced at the boy reassuringly. "It will be okay," she said with a confidence she could not feel.

Why did people always say that? Had anyone ever believed it?

With a tap of footsteps and a rustling squeak, the trolley careered through the darkness. It was now uncomfortably close. For a moment, Jaz thought the wall had somehow dissolved and it hadn't stopped Fantômas at all. But then, as something scraped discordantly, it happened. The trolley slammed into the wall, lurched awkwardly to one side, and cast off its briefcase.

Which, as it lay flat on the floor, began to make noises of its own.

The thief paused grimly, heard its ominous hum. Wheels tinkling, he straightened the trolley again and thrust it into the wall. This time, with such force behind it, the wall broke in two and a slab smacked exhaustedly onto the other side.

The darkness seemed thinner now, and Jaz could make out a hand. It reached through the gap and grabbed a greedy hold of the Doctor's collar.

"Leave him!" she shrilled.

The man in black stepped forward, his mask hiding all emotion. Even more disconcertingly, his hand trailed to a pocket. With a clink of cold metal, he pulled out a gun.

The old scientist, however, was unruffled. "Now, look here, young man," he began, but the weapon raised itself towards him. His old eyes flashed indignantly, as if he had just heard a teenager swear. "You won't get anywhere waving that thing around."

Jaz couldn't restrain herself. "Yeah, I bet you're nothing without the gun!"

This was not quite true, of course. He had the suitcase, and it was now ringing out a series of slow, assertive chimes.

"That's the *Death Knell*," said the Doctor gravely. "You've triggered it, you fool!" He paused, helpless. "We must find somewhere quiet, where the sound can't kill us. Now!"

Their captor, however, seemed to luxuriate in the sound of Armageddon. Indeed, it had a strangely languid elegance, like church bells in the countryside, evoking a peace it would soon destroy.

The Doctor was forthright. "We're all going to die if we don't move."

"Not all of us," was the bland reply.

Jaz wished she hadn't heard that. "You're going to kill us?" she pursued. "Even the kid?"

Despite the mask, the man's confusion was clear to see. "What kid?"

The other two could have asked themselves the same question. No one, they realized, was lurking behind them. For the second time that day, the boy had vanished.

Jaz felt as though her very soul had been sucked out. The odds of finding the boy and hiding them all in time were precisely none.

But then, impossibly, he was there again—leaping from the side, and the ruins of the wall, brandishing the solidification spray. He aimed it high, pressed it hard, and spurted steam into the man's eyes. Even the mask was no use against it.

The thief stepped back, dazed. But the boy didn't stop there. He pushed himself forward, hands waving, fighting for the gun—which, unfortunately, was too much, as it cracked conclusively through the corridor.

Jaz froze, the breath caught in her throat.

The gunman stiffened. Blood began seeping from his right shoulder, his hand pressed stickily against it. Panting softly and, it seemed, with bitter incredulity, he sank to his knees and onto his side.

Jaz crept closer, cautious but concerned, and fumbled for his pulse.

"What happened?" asked a woman's voice. "What's going on?"

It was Miss Shaw.

"Quickly," instructed Doctor Omega. "Get the boy somewhere quiet."

The curator snatched his hand. "Come on!" she cried.

But the boy was having none of it. He pulled himself free and ran off down the corridor.

Jaz was bent over the body. With a flourish, she pulled off the mask. But the man underneath it was not who she had expected to see.

"What's wrong?" came the Doctor's voice.

She hesitated. "Give me your coat. We need to stop the bleeding."

The Doctor drew level, saw the thief's face.

"Do it!" Jaz commanded. "It doesn't matter who he is."

She wanted to believe this, but it was much too hard. The man lying before them was not the thief they had seen in the image earlier. This, she realized with a cold shock, was their next Prime Minister.

Jaz took the Doctor's coat, pressed it against the wound, and wondered how many breaths he had left. Her mind was reeling. This had been an accident, obviously, but would the court agree? The boy was young and innocent and had fought in self-defense. But then, who knew what laws existed in this place? She wasn't even sure it existed itself. With horror and desperation, Jaz kept on pressing the wound. She should have acted fasted, she realized, tormented. Things should not have ended this way.

The chimes echoed on, but she could barely hear them now. The image of the man's face seemed to have been burned onto her retina, and all she could feel was a cold hand on her shoulder as the Doctor lifted her up.

"We need to get him somewhere too," she said.

"No," said the Doctor gently. "We can't help people like him."

In her weakened state, Jaz didn't question his piety, but allowed herself to be led away. They entered a room where a large, square vault stood grandly in the middle. The chimes were slower now, merging into one another to make a long, weary groan. It was as though a clock was ticking down towards their doom.

The door was ajar and the Doctor pulled it wide. Jaz wasn't expecting to see anyone else and jerked with surprise when she peered inside. A tall man was sitting, hunched, in the vault. He was wearing a sack suit and a Raglan overcoat and, without the mask, was only recognizable from his general height and shape. It was Fantômas, certainly, and he seemed just as anxious as they were.

The Doctor's face was lit with a friendly smile. "May we join you?" he asked politely and, without waiting for an answer, clambered inside. "Glad to meet you at last. I'm afraid we had to hide when you were wandering around the Culture Room earlier."

Jaz pulled the door heavily closed and turned to face Fantômas. She was so weary, by this point, that she couldn't summon the energy to be scared. "That was you?"

"I couldn't find this vault," he admitted despondently. "Once I did, and got that suitcase, my so-called partner insisted we go back separately. I don't think he trusted me with it, as a criminal." The thief smiled weakly, as though only now embarrassed by his profession, despite being its very finest exponent.

"And I'm guessing, to avert our attention, he dressed himself in your clothes while you broke into the vault?"

Fantômas nodded and Jaz, sitting back against the wall, blew out an exhausted sigh. Maybe it was the shock of seeing someone shot, or maybe it was this approximation of a nuclear warning, but Jaz felt weak and her head was heavy. It was like she was five years-old again and had stayed up passed her bedtime. Her mum was always letting her do that. Jaz had thought it was a reward for being a good girl. She later learned it was because her mum could not be bothered to take her upstairs and read her a story. Perhaps she was there again, on the couch, and had fallen asleep in front of the television, and this whole day was a surreal dream.

A hard object hit the roof of the vault and she jerked upright in alarm. She remembered, with something like surprise, that they were still underground. Above them, twenty meters of stone and dirt was being unsettled. Jaz tried to focus on something which didn't involve being trapped in a vault with a notorious criminal and buried under a small rock quarry.

"I hope Liz is all right," the Doctor murmured, ignoring the noise.

Jaz could tell he was worried. "I'm sure she will be," she said, still staring at the ceiling. "After all, she survived her travels with you."

The old man, however, was uneasy. "Just about," he said. "She saw things, you see. Traumatic things. Changed her, really, seeing what becomes of the world, as it would with any human."

Jaz could certainly understand that. She could still see that newspaper now.

"Running this place is how she copes with it," he went on. "She has her own version of the future here."

Jaz looked at him levelly. She had forgotten Fantômas was even there. "And how do *you* cope with it?"

The Doctor suddenly sounded vague. "I'm not sure I do," he confessed. "By helping people, I suppose."

"You always try to do that?"

"I could ask you the same thing," he said with wry amusement. "You care for your father; you tried to help me in the hangar; the boy, too, and that fellow out there. You even want to be a paramedic."

Jaz could have asked him how he knew this, but decided weirder things had happened already.

"I think," he reflected, "we like to feel needed."

"We're certainly needed now," she agreed. "I just wish we knew what it was about."

This spiked the old scientist's interest. "Well, it might have something to do with that political upheaval we read about. I haven't known of it till now, you see. Though how time-travel got to be involved, I don't know. Yet."

Outside, the bells had ceased, but the rocks still fell. The vault was half-buried and soil covered the linoleum like carpet. Doctor Omega passed stiffly through the room, somehow managing to avoid being hit. He seemed tired, crestfallen, and Jaz remembered that he had founded the museum. This will not have been his favorite visit. The ceiling rumbled again and the three of them raised their heads with bleak anticipation. It was even more frightening than the chimes.

Jaz searched the corridor. The Prime Minister's recumbent figure was no-where to be seen. She wondered whether he had found shelter or if the siren had caught him out.

The Doctor appeared behind her. In the lines of his forehead, she read his next few words. "I've found Liz... Miss Shaw," he said quietly. In the distance, there came a crash, as another ceiling fell fatally through. "Her knees were scuffed, as though she had fallen." His voice was hard, unemotional. "She had been made to hear the bells."

"Murder?"

Jaz did not know what to say. The usual platitudes seemed somehow un-suitable. Cracks cut through the ceiling, and the scientist moved off with the purposefulness men had in those old British war films she had watched with her dad. It looked comically absurd, though it really shouldn't have been at all.

"Wait!" she called and, with a bound, drew alongside him. "We need to find the boy."

More rocks dropped, closer now.

"I haven't seen him. He must be somewhere under this mess." Jaz was shocked at his dismissiveness. "All that's bothering me now is my ship."

"Ship?" Jaz echoed. She had forgotten it completely. "What's the matter with it?"

"It's gone." They turned down another corridor, passing rooms of rubble.

"If the boy's gone," she argued, trying to stay calm, "and so is the *Cosmos*, then maybe the two left together."

Reluctantly, the Doctor agreed that this was a possibility. "He may have gone in there to hide," he allowed. "The ship's sensors could have detected him entering and automatically dematerialized."

As he spoke, Jaz realized something. Miss Shaw had been pushed to the ground, but the Prime Minister couldn't have done it. Even if he was still alive, he was too weak. Similarly, Fantômas had been in the vault. Both men, then, had alibis. The only other person...

"This way!" cried Fantômas, gliding ahead, and they followed him through another corridor.

At the corner, they stopped, and a look of surprise came into the old man's eyes.

It was the *Cosmos*.

"How did it get here?" Jaz asked bewilderedly.

But they didn't have time for such questions while the roof was falling asunder.

"Quickly!" instructed Doctor Omega and, as rocks crashed around them, they ran into the ship.

The lights welcomed them warmly. Jaz had never been so pleased to see anything in her whole life. The Doctor got up to the bridge and tapped the dashboard affectionately, as one might pat a dog.

"So, the boy didn't take this ship," said Jaz, relieved. "We were wrong."

The Doctor, however, was looking grim. "Oh, he took it, all right," he said. "Think about it." He turned abruptly and Jaz was reminded of her old headmaster at Coal Hill. "Three people have been killed, and we thought the man in black had done it. The boy even said so. But, if you recall, he had heard me mention Fantômas, and how he was wearing black. He knew, then, just what to say."

Jaz had begun to wonder the same thing. "The boy was responsible," she said, her voice hollow. Out loud, it sounded outrageous. He was, after all, just a boy.

"The siren went off," the Doctor continued, "and he fled in this ship. As you would expect, over time, he ruminated on his crimes, and began to see himself as a ruthless murderer. And so he became one. With no more humanity holding him back, he went on to do even more evil things. Eventually, he became the very man he had killed."

"The Prime Minister?" said Jaz, her mind clouding with doubt. "That's who that boy grows up to be?"

"That isn't the least of it," Omega lamented. "He wanted to keep his power, but needed to defeat a resistance which had been mounted against him. He was also in the room, you will recall, when I mentioned the *Death Knell*."

Despite her own misgivings, things were becoming clearer to Jaz. "He made notes," she said, remembering the boy's boredom, "in that diary of his. I saw them myself."

"Quite. Well, as an adult, and still in possession of this ship, he collected Fantômas and brought him here to steal the weapon to use against the rebels. This spot here is where they landed."

He looked fondly at his home, now it was centuries older than the last time he had seen it.

Jaz turned to Fantômas thoughtfully. "Is this true?"

"I only know that he found me, and he was a most curious man."

"He was indeed," said the Doctor, rubbing his brow sorrowfully. "If it wasn't for the Automatic Memory Mangle, I would have recognized him immediately. You see, he and I grew up together. More often than not, he goes by the name of The Master. We are, I'm afraid, old enemies."

The young woman stared at him in shock. "That's… news," she managed.

"Of course," continued the Doctor, "his younger self left in such a hurry, he hadn't noted in his diary the part where such a person was killed. Nor did he realize the urgency to do so. The instinct to kill, of course, would leave its own mark."

Jaz was earnest. "Earlier, you said how two minds can become one, or something, when you meet your other self. You reckon, then, that the presence of the older Percy could have caused the younger one to adopt the same homicidal tendencies?"

"Certainly I do," said the Doctor, and his voice was one of frustration and regret.

Fantômas joined in. "You mean to say, Doctor, he was murderous, because his older self was murderous, and that was only because his younger self was murderous?"

"Hmm."

"But why push Miss Shaw and force her to hear the siren?"

"To test the weapon. He understood what his older self was up to. And the guard was killed because he was about to search the museum and would have noticed there were two identical ships here. He did the same to his nanny because…"

"Because," finished Jaz heavily, "she wouldn't fetch him an ice cream." She paused, disgusted by such a trivial motive. "I thought, at first, the shot had been accidental, but it couldn't have been."

"It was fate *and* fatal," said the Doctor wryly. "Quite literally, he had himself killed. What we call in time travel a rookie mistake."

Jaz looked away uncomfortably. The old man could be ruthless himself, and it wasn't something she appreciated. She paused again, this time in memory of those who had passed. Despite what that memory widget would do, Jaz didn't think she could forget such an extraordinary day.

It was Fantômas who spoke first. Being a killer himself, he may not even have understood the idea of respectful silences.

"Doctor," he said, "can I go home? On this occasion, at least, I have not succeeded in a robbery, which wasn't even my idea."

Jaz did not approve, and she was about to say so, but the Doctor accepted the request without persuasion. Perhaps he suspected how vigorous it might be. "For better or worse," he said, "I try to avoid changing history, and you have a little more of it left to see." He turned to Jaz and his eyes glimmered shrewdly. "And while we're in early twentieth century Paris, we could have a look around ourselves. You always did want to visit the place, and I can get you back home to your father before you even left. What could be better than seeing the City of Light in the Belle Époque, its golden age? With Moulin Rouge, the Ritz Paris and Art Nouveau?"

"Nothing," Jaz agreed but, despite her eagerness to see the place, something was bothering her. "What with everything that's happened here, though, would it be right, do you think? Enjoying ourselves like that?"

The Doctor seemed astonished, and she wondered how a human could be so thoughtless. But then, she realized, she wasn't certain he even *was* human. Few things would surprise her at this point. He looked at her, however, with a delicacy and understanding which seemed to confirm what he had said in the vault. This old man—alien or not—did indeed want to help others. He just hadn't got the hang of it yet.

"The Master tries to ruin lives," he said quietly, "and even ends some to achieve that. The best thing we can do, in response, is live our own."

Jaz nodded philosophically and decided she would light a candle at the nearest church for everyone she had met that day. "Will we have time to visit Notre-Dame?" she asked.

The Doctor smiled. "My dear, with this ship, we have time for everything."

And, with a wheezing, groaning sound, they left the Future Museum behind.

Brian Gallagher continues to chronicle the adventures of Marie Nizet's Captain Liatoukine—from her ground-breaking 1879 novel Captain Vampire, Black Coat Press, ISBN 978-1-934543-01-6)—*moving forward in time. While each story can be read independently, the sequence is most impressive, starting with "City of the Nosferatu (Vol. 10), "The Trial of Van Helsing" (Vol. 11), "The Stake and the Sickle" (Vol. 12), "The Berlin Vampire" (Vol. 13) and "The Death of Von Bork"(Vol. 14). Here is the latest installment...*

Brian Gallagher: *The Skull of Boris Liatoukine*

Moscow, July 1998

The luxury helicopter shook with the force of the rocket-propelled grenade hitting it. The pilot had somehow maneuvered the aircraft to take a glancing blow. However, it was still going down, hard. The helicopter's sole passenger—and owner—was pleased that his investment into on board security measures, including hiring a top ex-military pilot, had been worthwhile. He was less pleased that the ground was coming up fast.

The pilot struggled with the controls. The helicopter crashed and skidded along a road by the Moskva River. The passenger dragged himself out of the wreckage and collapsed. Most of his bones were broken, but he could feel them regenerating already. He looked behind him—the pilot was dead, no doubt about that. Probably instantaneously. Most unfortunate. Such skilled operatives were much in demand. It would be easier to replace the helicopter—an augmented Eurocopter Dauphin. The road they had crashed on was closed for works. Whether the pilot had realized that or not, he did not know.

The passenger lay waiting. He could see half a dozen members of the public running down towards the wreckage and himself. The emergency services would soon be here. However, he was waiting for neither them, or the members of the public. Sure enough, a group of three burly men came from nowhere, armed with pistols. The assassination team had come to finish the job. The few members of the public who had reached the scene backed away swiftly—they did not want to be involved in any mafia business.

The three assassins ran toward the body of the passenger. He got up. All three men fired their pistols—Soviet Makarovs, the passenger noted—into him and looked dumbfounded when their target simply jerked around but remained standing. He grabbed the nearest attacker by the throat and took his weapon; then, he shot the other two in the legs, disabling them.

"Who sent you?" he asked of the first man.

The assassin swiftly replied with a name. More bullets slammed into the passenger—the injured men on the ground had resumed firing. Then their bullets ran out.

"You seek my attention?" their target said in mock delight. "Then you have it!"

He broke the arm of the man he was holding and threw him to the ground. He went over to the terrified men and stared at them.

"Are you all there is? One of you fired the grenade?"

One nodded and then pointed at the first man. Boris Liatoukine promptly shot the man who had not responded in the heart. He then resumed his questioning, as if nothing had occurred.

"Please also tell me who supplied the weapons, my movements, and so on."

He got the answers he wanted and shot the man dead. He went over to the first man—who, by now, was under no illusions as to his fate. Liatoukine gazed into the eyes of the assassin. This man was terrified—he knew he was dealing with the very devil himself. He felt as if all his energy was being sucked out of him—which in fact it was. And the last thing he thought was how like the eyes of a cat his killer's were.

Liatoukine did not take all his victim's energy. Just enough to help him regenerate further. He then stood back and shot the dead man in the heart. For appearances.

He could hear sirens. Within seconds, Moscow's finest were surrounding him. It was fortunate he had already dropped the weapon.

"On the ground, now!" one of them shouted.

"Officers, I am so grateful you have arrived!" he responded. "I am Boris Liatoukine, a businessman of some repute and a friend to many of your superiors. I was forced to defend myself against criminals who killed my pilot and tried to murder me. Truly, it is a miracle I live!"

Liatoukine could see that the officers knew well enough not to make him kneel down with his hands behind his head. How much had they seen? It mattered not. He had enough wealth and FSB[2] influence to ensure that a heroic story of surviving an assassination attempt and killing his would-be assassins would prevail. The publicity would be unwelcome. Perhaps his old nickname—whispered during his time in the KGB and far further back in time—would be used again? Yes, references to *Captain Vampire* could well instill fear into his enemies.

The caretaker closed up the museum. It was a small place in Moscow, linked with a similar establishment in St. Petersburg with a number of items of

---

[2] Federal Security Service of the Russian Federation, the main successor of the KGB.

not much interest to the populace. It had been open for a number of years, even during the communist era, but then it had been billed as a "museum of the bizarre." It did not do good business, on account of its artifacts being clearly fake and uninteresting. It had been too insignificant for the Communists to close it. The caretaker was grateful, however, because it had provided him with a steady job, and was close to his home. Since the end of communism, it had been privatized and rebranded as a "museum of the supernatural." It had duly taken a few more paying visitors—not that the caretaker cared. He had not been paid in months now. He preferred the old regime. He did not care much for this capitalism. The Gulags did not affect him, so he did not care about such things. Increasingly, he could not be bothered to lock the doors properly. And tonight was one such night.

After he had gone, a slim, feminine figure bounded up to the doors. Dressed in a black catsuit, she walked in. She was unmasked, and was clearly a beautiful woman of Chinese origin. She looked around the small hall. That is all it was—the front door led straight into a hall. She was here to steal something and wanted to be seen doing so. But there were no cameras.

Irritated, she went straight over to a exhibit marked "Facsimile of Vampire Skull" in Cyrillic. It would have to be fake—a place like this would not be permitted to contain real human remains.

"Are you real then?" she asked it.

Indeed I am, Irma Vep, said a voice in her head. *Permit me to introduce myself. I am Boris Liatoukine.*

In Surrey, England, a full-bodied Boris Liatoukine had just concluded a business agreement with a notorious Russian oligarch who had made England his home. The vampire and his solicitor looked out of window of the mansion they were in, overlooking the large grounds, complete with helipad and Liatoukine's helicopter on it.

"A fine agreement, sir," the solicitor said. "All the outstanding business issues have been dealt with in your favor—and it was good of him to accept your suggestion to come back to his home to celebrate."

"Yes," replied Liatoukine, smiling. "I suspect the elimination of every single person involved in the attempt to liquidate me—from the assassins to those who supplied the weapons—helped him in being reasonable. I must thank you, Mr. Tepes, for your discretion and skill in this matter."

"My firm has been dealing with your people for generations, sir. Count Dracula was one of our first clients."

Liatoukine and the Count were not the same nationality, but that was not what Mr. Tepes meant. He also knew that the lawyer's firm—despite effectively taking Vlad the Impaler's name—never had Dracula as a client. Even now, there were those who sought a link with Dracula's name for commercial gain.

The Russian vampire pondered for a moment. The Count had seen something in this country, but had been undone by few determined individuals. Often, in dealing with vampires, that is simply what it took. Over the years, Liatoukine had learned not to underestimate the living. He had learned from his own mistakes—and more especially those of others. Despite this country's record in firmly dealing with the supernatural, there were still those who would serve vampires—for the appropriate financial recompense. Using mesmerism, he had discerned from the solicitor that, barring torture, the man would be discreet. Providing, of course, he was handsomely paid.

"I think I would like to have residency here in this country. Many of my countrymen have moved their money here, and I would like to do the same," Liatoukine said to the solicitor.

Mr. Tepes was eager for further commission. "There is a scheme which the previous government instituted. Such rights are given for an appropriate financial investment in the UK. The current New Labor government is keenly carrying on with the same policy."

"What about my previous record with the KGB?" the vampire asked.

"A matter of little interest, sir. It is the financial benefit to this country that is important. As to the publicity you have recently received, due to the attempt on your life and your conflict with our late friend here, I see few barriers being erected—none that cannot be dealt with by investing a bit extra."

They looked down to where their *late friend* was. A pile of white dust they were standing in.

"Most fascinating sir, to see you drain him of energy like that—I understand it is usually blood with your people."

"Yes," Liatoukine said. "My way is more energy efficient. And it certainly helps with the cleaning bills—provided I don't get too much of the dust on me. We should leave soon. We can leave his maid to deal with this." He knocked over an ashtray. "Perhaps they will think he knocked over his ashtray?" They laughed uproariously. "I could have killed him in London, I suppose, but I did want to see where he lived. Everything was set up well—he left our meeting and no one knows where he went. My powers and your employees have done well."

Mr. Tepes bowed slightly. Yes, Liatoukine thought, a foothold in London would greatly help in his business affairs, provided he did not overreach himself.

Back in her Monaco mansion, Irma Vep sat down in her luxury chair and looked at the Skull on the table before her. It looked human, with two fake fangs stuck on. She snapped them off. The real Liatoukine did not manifest fangs—not having much need for them. She addressed the Skull:

"So, 'Boris Liatoukine,' now that we have arrived back safely, perhaps you can finally explain to me why you wanted me to steal you. The messages put about to my contacts of a genuine vampire skull—with great powers—were clearly directed at me rather than just general rumor."

I see little gets past you, Polly Bird, the Skull replied in her head.

Vep's posture moved a little bit more upright. How could it know that? She had her fake public identity as one Mrs. Irene Adler, a wealthy Monaco widow, and then she had her favorite fake identity as the criminal Irma Vep—the cat-suited thief who had stolen so many valuables over the years.

Of course, I know who you are, although I know you much prefer to use the Irma Vep identity much of the time. You are vampire, like myself. Although blood is more your thing. Surely you remember our adventures—remember all that business of the trial of Van Helsing in the Vampire City?

"How..." she started.

I was one of the duplicates of Boris Liatoukine. Of course, you know of his power to create short-lived duplicates of himself? It helped confuse many of his enemies.

Polly was indeed aware of this.

He created me almost twenty years ago, sending me to Afghanistan to confuse those in the KGB who were trying to eliminate him. Spetnaz troops managed to destroy me, and I disintegrated—but my skull remained intact. One of the soldiers took it as a trophy. It would appear that the circumstances of what happened to me permits my consciousness to live on inside it. Such are the ways of the supernatural. I was able to influence the soldier a little and got myself sold to more interesting parties. Liatoukine has no awareness of me—or rather, the times he has been nearby, he has sensed something, but never considered it could be me.

"Why were you in that museum in Moscow, and the other one in St. Petersburg for years before that?" Polly asked.

I see you are well informed. I have been gathering information—from the local aether, shall we say? It helps me to calculate what—or who—may be important in the future. I tend to travel sometimes to find out.

She sensed she would get little more from the Skull on that.

"Why did you want me to steal you? The messages you placed on the grapevine indicated you were valuable—but I know very well that they were directed at me."

Indeed, indeed. We have a common interest. It is but a matter of time before Boris Liatoukine destroys you. Or worse, place you under his control. He has not forgotten his last encounter with you, in which you were enemies. Your being a former ally only makes things worse. I want him dead also—but only in the sense that I should have developed enough power to integrate myself into him—taking over his body and destroying his mind, rather than the opposite, when his duplicates have no more function.

"How can I trust you? You can still be a threat to me yourself?"

I have all his memories, but I am not him. He created me simply to do his bidding, and I was expendable. He may effectively be my creator, but believe me, I feel I owe him nothing, and see no reason to carry his grudges. I have felt his displeasure towards you, but you and I have no quarrel. Help me to take over his body—which will give me all his wealth and power—and I will be grateful. You are an international thief, and provided you do not steal from me, I have no interest in you.

The fake Irma Vep pondered for a moment. She did not trust this Skull. However, the elimination of Boris Liatoukine would certainly benefit her. In 1979, she had told him that they had no real quarrel left after the death of his superior, KGB spymaster Von Bork. However, only minutes earlier, she had turned Von Bork into a vampire in order to kill Liatoukine, and the Russian Vampire was not likely to have forgotten that. He would come for her at some point. If the Skull were to become an enemy, then she would not be worse off than before. The risk was worth taking, and she would take whatever precautions she could.

"Very well. What do you have in mind?"

Excellent. As Irma Vep, you have made one or two thefts in London. That experience will be useful. It seems that Liatoukine is establishing a base for himself in that city.

A few days later, Boris Liatoukine was dining at one of London's finer establishments. He was pleased with how things were going. He had purchased a home in central London. His young wife, Magda, was especially pleased—she had been keen to see many of her friends in London and was delighted to be in close proximity to them—and to Harrods. Boris liked Magda. She was unconcerned regarding the mysteries around him and did not care about his various lovers. Liatoukine had been married many times before, murdering a number of his wives in order to obtain their wealth. That would not be necessary with Magda. He was the wealthy one, and she would most likely be amenable to an amicable divorce when the time came for her to leave his side.

His dinner companion arrived. This was an Englishman in his late 50s. He sat in front of Liatoukine. Harker was a former MI6 officer. He had been suborned by another a vampire in the 1950s. After she'd died, Liatoukine had been able to mesmerize him easily, given that he was already susceptible to vampiric influence. He used him as a private asset, rather than KGB one —the Russian vampire had told no one about him, and kept no records. He was only interested in information of direct interest. He did not ask Harker for major information regarding spy matters. In this way, the Englishman was never suspected of anything, and thus never caught. He'd left MI6 after a successful career and established a private security firm for wealthy clients. Liatoukine made himself one of them. This was rather ironic, thought the Russian vampire. This man was the descendent of those who had destroyed Dracula, and his family may yet be unamused to find out about David Harker's treachery.

"Good evening, Mr. Harker. I understand you have something for me. Please order whatever you desire."

Harker ordered his meal, and then reported to the vampire.

"I have some information for you. The woman you wished my firm to keep an eye on, Mrs. Adler? She arrived in London earlier today. She is staying in a hotel in Kensington. My sources at Heathrow Airport were able to X-ray her baggage. This one is of great interest."

He handed Liatoukine a small palm held computer. The central feature of what appeared to be a hatbox was not what one would usually expect to see. It was a skull. Liatoukine felt like he was looking into a mirror—an unusual sensation for a vampire, even one that was able to create artificial reflections to avoid detection such as he.

"We have no idea how she was able to get through security at Nice and Heathrow Airports. We can only surmise that the agents were bribed," Harker added.

Liatoukine knew better. Polly Bird would have used her vampiric powers of influence to get through all the security checks. But why had she come to London? And what was the significance of that skull, which evoked such strange feelings in him? He had every intention of finding out. Besides, it was past time to deal with Polly Bird—or Irma Vep, since that seemed to be her favorite identity.

"We need to intercept her," he told Harker. "As you know, I consider her to be part of the Vampires gang. The current Irma Vep—the one of Chinese appearance—also needs to be intercepted if she appears, as she well might."

He, of course, knew very well that Vep, Adler and Polly Bird were one and the same, but no need to tell Harker that. Liatoukine proceeded to outline to Harker what he required of his company. However, he was not the only one with an interest in Mrs. Adler.

The Countess Irina Petrovski looked across the London skyline from her hired office in one of London's newest office buildings. She could see St. Paul's Cathedral, and various other skyscrapers in the process of being erected. She liked London. She had many friends and contacts here. She caught a reflection of herself in the window. She was nearing 50, but looked still in her 30s. Her long, luxurious red hair looked as healthy as ever. She knew she was fortunate—her wealth, being from an old aristocratic Polish family, did her no harm. However, she felt that her life as an adventurer had helped keep her young. The battles against communism had gone rather well. As indeed had her sideline as part of a network dealing with the threat of the supernatural. However, there was more work to be done.

Her mobile rang. Such instruments were still relatively new. She liked technology and made sure she had the latest model.

"Ah, Karl, you have arrived? Just introduce yourself at reception, and you will be shown up."

A couple of minutes later, a short bald man entered dressed in a smart suit.

"Karl!" beamed the Countess. "It is so good to see you my friend. Please sit down."

"And you are as beautiful as ever—moreso," he replied.

He came to her, took her hand and kissed it. She was delighted.

"It is good to see old courtesies observed," she replied.

"And I like to practice them," he replied.

They laughed and sat down.

"Well, Countess, it seems something is indeed going on. Boris Liatoukine and Irma Vep are both in London. Not a coincidence, I think."

"The messages on the international criminal grapevine to Irma Vep telling her to steal a skull in Moscow were clearly directed to her—but of course, we have our sources listening out for such things."

"Quite," responded Karl. "My superiors at the BND[3] are only interested, and to a limited extent, in the possible political aspects of Vep's criminal activity—international incidents and so on. The supernatural aspects would be disbelieved, and I would be soon out of a job. But you know all this."

"To think, there used to be whole departments and government organizations that dealt with vampires and so on," sighed the Countess. "Now, with most of the supernatural gone with the modern age, the forces against them have dissipated and it's barely believed they exist. Only a few years ago, you would not have had to be so circumspect with your employer. Even what remains in the archives do not seem to be persuasive." It was an old conversation, and the Countess turned to current matters. "Do you have some information on Boris Liatoukine's wealth for me?"

Karl smiled and produced a folder from his briefcase.

"There, I can produce a lot more that my superiors are interested in. We know he is a former KGB officer. From what we can ascertain, his department went the way all supernatural departments did. With the collapse of communism, seeing where things were going, he wrapped up his own Special Logistics Directorate and left the KGB—or FSB as it would be now—taking some personnel with him. We also suspect he moved his archives, or at least copies of them, into his own custody.

"To build his wealth, he had his own cooperative based on Gorbachev's reforms—these included restaurants and kiosks selling chocolates. Then he took full advantage of the government's voucher scheme. Like the other oligarchs, he manipulated it to gain stakes in state assets. He was one of those who helped Yeltsin get re-elected in 1994 by the 'loans for shares' scheme. This involved a loan to help plug the government's deficit in return for shares in export firms. The loans were not repaid and these people took control of these firms for next to nothing. And, of course, money went into Yeltsin's re-election campaign. He is certainly what we would now call an oligarch. He did all this through mid-

---

[3] The German Federal Intelligence Service.

dlemen, more than the others. Politically, we think he would prefer someone who deals more strongly with the West, for his support for Yeltsin is based purely on his self-interest and holding onto his money."

"Yes," interjected the Countess. "I certainly think his long life and the changes of government in Russia have made him cautious and indeed flexible. He was a Tsarist at some point, fighting the Reds as a White Army officer."

"He must meet with your approval on that point," interrupted Karl smiling.

She wagged a finger at him playfully and then continued:

"...and then, he switched to working for the Communists when they hunted him down in Paris in the 1920s. He eventually took over the department that had tracked him down. Now, he appears to have adjusted rather well to post-Communism. Too well, in fact. He may well be the wealthiest vampire in the world—and thus a threat. Although perhaps someone else has tried to get to him before us?"

Karl nodded and produced another a file and gave it to the Countess.

"As a known ally—albeit in the private sector—of the BND, you can have sight of this material."

The Countess could see it was in regards to the oligarch who had recently vanished off the face of the Earth, after allegedly trying to assassinate Liatoukine.

"The intelligence community believed he tried to kill Liatoukine over some dispute on the selling of shares in an energy company," Karl went on. "Liatoukine appears to have had everyone involved killed, and there is little doubt he is behind the disappearance. There is no hard proof however. He does seem to have taken a liking to London, and unfortunately, it does seem that the British authorities are going to indulge him—not least due to his apparent intent to provide significant investment here."

The Countess shook her head in near disbelief.

"It looks like we need to deal with him then."

Karl smiled and gave her something else from his briefcase. Again, the Countess was delighted with him.

"A Walter P5 Compact pistol—with silver bullets! How considerate of you!" Then her face hardened and she touched the large silver crucifix around her neck. "Vep and Liatoukine are amongst the last remnants of an old threat to humanity. God will guide us in putting an end to their activities."

Night was falling over London. In her hotel room, booked under yet another false identity, Irma Vep was having a conversation with the Skull. She had changed her form into the current iteration of Irma Vep and was sitting in a luxury chair, dressed in her catsuit, with only her head uncovered. She was expecting action that night.

Tell me, the Skull asked, *Why have you taken the form of a Chinese woman?*

"To confuse the police looking for me," she replied. "For some years I used the form of the original Irma Vep. They now think that this version of Irma Vep appearing means there is a gang, which the press have dubbed *The Vampires*, after the original criminal group from 1916. All quite effective."

She thought it best not to mention that she enjoyed watching Hong Kong action films that had actually given her the inspiration. Liatoukine was a snob, and no doubt that went for his duplicate Skull.

Most ingenious. Little wonder no one has failed to capture you. Now, we must move. I am aware that Liatoukine is in London. This hotel was selected as it is close to his Kensington apartment. I sense he is nearby. He must be at home. The plan is very simple. Simply get me into his home, and I will do the rest. Within the hour Liatoukine will be eliminated and I will take all that he has.

"You will get your revenge for Afghanistan and I will be rid of an enemy."

Yes, but please, do be careful in your carrying of me.

Vep picked up the Skull and placed it into a dark, padded shoulder bag. She proceeded towards the window. London was busy at night; she might be seen at some point, although her garb was probably more acceptable in public than it would have been in previous years. She opened a window to the back streets.

"I look forward to seeing how you re-absorb yourself back into dear Boris's body," she said.

"*I look forward to seeing how you re-absorb yourself back into dear Boris's body*," said the voice over the speaker.

"She's mad," said Harker, "she is talking to herself."

Sitting next to him in the back of the private surveillance van was Boris Liatoukine. The references to Afghanistan and reabsorption and his familiarity with the Skull all came together. He did not how this could happen, or the full details of it, but the Skull had to be dealt with at once, regardless of any embarrassment.

"Send your men in now, Harker. Kill her and smash the skull. The ammunition I have provided them will be sufficient."

Ordinarily, Harker would not have done anything like this, but Liatoukine held a mystical hold over him—and the rather large personal commission from the Russian also helped him move beyond his split second of doubt.

In her hotel room, Irma Vep tensed. She could hear footsteps outside.

The door was smashed open and three men with silencers burst in. One took direct aim at her at fired. The bullet flew out of the weapon and towards the vampire. But Vep was already moving. The bullet missed her—silver, she noted—and smashed into the wall.

She grabbed the shooter and broke his neck effortlessly, using him as a shield against the others. She then grabbed a dagger she kept in her boot for such eventualities. She threw the body against one of the other two assailants. He fell back, but regained his balance, and raised his gun.

In a split second it took for him to fire, however, Vep had slit the throat of the other man and he saw something coming towards his head. Her knife embedded itself hard in his forehead and he fell back on the floor, dead.

Vep moved fast. She hurled the bodies fully into the room, grabbed the bag and was out of the window and scaling down the wall into an alley. She always ensured a room with such a view. What was key to getting away was to physically escape before other assailants—or the authorities—came to confront her.

Out of the gloom of the alley appeared two figures.

"Hello again, Polly. Or should that be Irma Vep or Mrs. Adler, or..?" asked Boris Liatoukine, Harker next to him.

Both had pistols aimed at her. She dived, rolled and fired at them. Liatoukine moved swiftly out of the way, but one of the bullets hit Harker and he was flung back down, his bulletproof vest, however, saving his life. Without pausing, Vep was on her feet and out of the alley.

Parked right outside was a Porsche. She made eye contact with the driver and recognized her—Countess Petrovski. They knew each other of old, and even had worked together once, in a fashion. She smashed the passenger window, opened the door and leaped into the car.

"Drive!" she ordered, pointing the gun at the Countess.

The Polish aristocrat turned towards Vep—her silver crucifix seemingly blazing. Instinctively, Vep recoiled, and the Countess shoved her back. Vep fell out of the car and on the road. And she saw her holdall in the outstretched hand of the Countess.

The car sped off. Vep chased it at speed—witnesses be damned! —but despite her efforts, could not keep up with the car. She slowed down and wandered swiftly into a street side.

Boris Liatoukine was less than pleased with the night's events. He had failed to eliminate the threat of the Skull, or indeed deal with Vep. His bravado in talking to her—rather than just shooting her with silver bullets immediately—could have cost him the opportunity to deal with matters at once. Furthermore, Special Branch had become involved. They wanted to know his whereabouts. Vep had no doubt tipped them off. He cursed himself again—he had hesitated to go after Vep due to fear of being recognized by the public, or spotted by cameras. The CCTV that had picked him and Harker up were too indistinct. The others, Harker had deactivated through various means. He was able to give the police an explanation of course—he had one of his duplicates be seen at a public event at the same time. However, the attention was unwelcome, and could damage his presence in London.

A bleep went off. This was his satellite phone with a secure link to Moscow. He picked it up.

"Good morning" said a voice on the other end, in French. It was one of his trusted contacts in the FSB. "We know of the events in London, and that you are perhaps somehow connected. The Kremlin is not pleased. There is an important meeting in London taking place today. The International Monetary Fund is discussing our country."

Liatoukine knew this very well. Russia had been suffering severe financial problems.

"I am aware of this. This incident you speak of saw three British mercenaries killed, not Russians."

The voice at the other end cut him off.

"The international media have been tipped off that this was an incident in which Irma Vep was involved in a deal with Russians which went wrong—and their hired British mercenaries paid the price. The last thing the Kremlin wants is Russian-related violence in London at this moment. What is more, you know that we are not the power we once were. And Yeltsin may even be appointing a new FSB head. Our position is sensitive. The view here is that you should return at once to Moscow—or at least leave the United Kingdom."

Liatoukine understood the sensitivities. It was in his interested that Russia was bailed out and that the new FSB head not be someone who would work against him. However, it was more in his interest to stay in London and destroy the Skull.

"Very well. I will return to Moscow today."

"Excellent," said the voice at the other end, and the call was terminated.

Liatoukine turned around. A figure materialized in front of him. A duplicate of himself. He had reabsorbed the duplicate he had used the previous night, and this was a new one. Given what he had learnt about the Skull, this one had less consciousness than previous versions. He ordered it to go to Moscow and stand in for him. He would stay in London and deal with the Skull.

In her London residence, the Countess had the Skull on a table. She walked around it. Karl was with her.

"Were the police satisfied with your explanation?" he asked.

"Yes," she replied. "I told them that I was looking out for Irma Vep—which was completely true—when everything happened. They know me of old, and we still have one or two contacts in Scotland Yard. They don't like 'vigilantes,' but they had no reason to hold me. It helped that I went to them at once, rather than waiting for them to spot my car's license plate on CCTV. Of course, I gave them Vep's holdall that had some burglary tools in, but I retained our friend here. Our contacts would not be in a position to deal with their colleagues if I did hand it over."

The Skull listened to the conversation. He was also able to absorb some of what these people were about. He knew that they would want to destroy him. They—especially the Countess—were resourceful. It would only be a matter of time before they worked out what he was, of that he was sure. And then, they would destroy him. He had plans for the future—his powers had developed to be able to not quite predict the future, but to know what would become important, and he would not let this Countess stop that. He had to act immediately. A risk, but it had to be taken.

Permit me to introduce myself, the Skull said, startling the Countess and Karl. *I am Boris Liatoukine.*

The Countess reflected later on what the Skull had said. He had been a duplicate of Boris Liatoukine, and been destroyed in his service, only his Skull remaining. Such an existence tormented it, and it wanted to die, but only along with Boris Liatoukine. The Skull wanted revenge. That was why he was here with Irma Vep. Separated from Vep, he now offered the Countess the opportunity. She did not believe the Skull. However, it was too good a chance to destroy the notorious "Captain Vampire." She started to make plans.

Irma Vep left Scotland Yard and was out into the sun. She despised the daylight; it sapped much of her power. She rarely used her original Polly Bird form these days, but it was not likely to be recognized by anyone in the Metropolitan Police. She was tall, raven-haired and, of course, beautiful. It always felt like a special treat to wear this form. She had gained the power of shape-changing decades ago. Suddenly, she gave a start. Next to the revolving New Scotland Yard sign outside the building stood Boris Liatoukine. She could sense that there were others—no doubt, British mercenaries. Would he really make a scene here? He must know he would surely be on a camera. But he put up his hands.

"Peace, my dear Polly. A truce. I am hardly likely to attempt anything here, am I? Let us walk, and discuss matters. Surely we can come to some... arrangement?"

They turned a corner and walked together down Victoria Street, towards the Houses of Parliament.

"How did you know where I was?" Polly asked.

"My servants retain certain connections with the authorities," he replied. "It suddenly came up that someone was inquiring with the police about the whereabouts of Countess Petrovski. We were on the look out for any such inquiries. No doubt you had simply walked in and used your powers of mesmerism. Quite a feat, given our limited powers during the day."

She nodded. He was indeed correct.

"What now?" she asked.

"Tell me about the Skull's plans. Then we shall see."

She thought she could run—she could probably escape. However, there may be something here she had not accounted for. Things had already gone wrong. There may yet be a way to turn things to her advantage. So she explained the Skull's plan. They had reached Parliament Square by this point. They came to a halt by the statue of Winston Churchill. Liatoukine looked over at the Palace of Westminster, and up at St. Stephen's tower that housed the bell of Big Ben.

"Dracula himself came here, you know," he said.

"Much good it did him," Polly replied. "Van Helsing, Mina Harker and the others chased him out from here across Europe and destroyed him in his own homeland."

"Indeed," replied the Russian, "He did effectively try to invade this country. Had he kept a low profile—and spent a lot of money at the same time—perhaps he would still alive today. I often consider that he was the first real casualty of the forces of modernity. Rather than swim inconspicuously with the new age, he thought he could dominate it. We certainly had power before, but we never had total control. Humanity determined its own history, and now their science and intelligence have reduced our numbers. The decline of religion in the West has not helped in the way one might have thought. Worse, the revival of religion in Russia and in the ex-communist sphere has aggravated matters."

Polly was not that concerned about Liatoukine's musings, but thought it best to humor him.

"Yes, perhaps that is why the few of us that remain should stick together."

Liatoukine could see that she may be open to a deal.

"This Skull is not one of us really. It is an upstart entity, nothing more. Help me destroy it and I offer you the same deal: a permanent truce providing you stay out of my affairs. To help you decide, please bear in mind how long I have lived and how I have survived even communism. This Skull is not likely to get the better of me."

That made sense to Polly.

"Very well," she said.

"Excellent," he replied. "We know the Countess's whereabouts, and we should pay her a visit. She will be expecting us, of course. Just as I have contacts here, so does she. It may not be an easy task dealing with her, especially if she has made some kind of alliance with the Skull." Something else occurred to the Russian vampire. "One thing. Why did the Skull stay in St. Petersburg for so long?"

Polly thought for a moment.

"It said it was monitoring something. It claimed it could sense where power would be in the future and wanted to absorb as much information as possible. It claimed it was a slow process, but that this ability eventually told him where power would lie, but could not specifically predict the future. The Skull could be quite boastful, but it did not reveal any details. My personal suspicion is that St.

Petersburg will become the capital again, or that some long-lost descendent of the Romanoffs will be found and the throne restored. I put that to the Skull, but it did not confirm or deny it."

"How interesting," said Liatoukine, intrigued. "There are no Romanoffs left with a claim to the throne. Lenin and his barbarian Bolsheviks made sure of that. However, I think that St. Petersburg could be made the capital instead of Moscow. With that drunkard Yeltsin, such things are certainly possible."

At that point, Liatoukine's mobile phone started ringing. He answered it, and spoke briefly. When the call finished he turned to Polly.

"That was Countess Petrovski. She wants to meet us tonight. St. Paul's Cathedral. Midnight."

Polly looked surprised.

"She has friends in the Church of England, it seems," he continued. "She says she wants to destroy the Skull, but it is impervious to her efforts, even on church grounds. She thinks only I can deal with it by reabsorbing it, which may be true, but I think that physical destruction is best. I do not believe her claim of imperviousness. Our time in the Cathedral will be limited; our powers will be reduced and to stay too long would result in our deaths. During the Tsarist era, I was able to enter churches for long enough to ensure the 'Captain Vampire' stories remained just rumors. I assume you can do the same?"

"I can," she replied.

"It is a trap. We will reconnoiter the area as best we can with my hirelings. We can always not enter. However, if the Skull is there, and we can see what the trap is, we will destroy it—and the Countess."

It was approaching midnight. Liatoukine and Irma Vep were approaching the steps of St. Paul's Cathedral. They came to a halt at the foot of the steps.

"We've reconnoitered and found nothing," he said to Vep. "One of Harker's men was able to stay behind in the Cathedral after it had closed. He was found by a man with a German accent and politely asked to leave. He reported that the only people there was this German and the Countess. Not even any security staff. And outside, there appears to be no threat. The City of London police are simply doing their routine patrols, although, of course, they could approach in significant armed numbers at very short notice."

"I've been scaling along the rooftops," said Vep. "I, too, detected nothing."

The Russian vampire gave her a glance.

"Oh, don't worry Boris. I know very well how to elude security cameras—when I want to."

Liatoukine knew that she liked to be caught on camera occasionally. Her guises as Irma Vep—looking like the original French criminal and now as a Chinese woman—not only confused the police, but also provided her with the entertainment of seeing herself all over the media.

"Or perhaps the police have been told not to respond to any sightings?" he said. "Harker says they are patrolling slightly less tonight. The Countess and her network have their own contacts."

They both looked around. Just a few people out late, mostly tourists, including a couple sitting on the steps. Their enhanced vampiric powers could see no giveaways that any of them were anything but what they appeared to be. Not impossible that they were undercover agents working for the Countess, but they would certainly have to be very good, thought Liatoukine. He looked at his companion's garments.

"Did you have to dress like that? I know you like attention, but..." Liatoukine was referring to Vep's catsuit, which covered her body bar her face.

"Dear Boris, it is my trademark, and I find it rather practical. Which is more than what can be said for your cheap suit."

The Russian did not rise to that. His suit was a rather expensive affair from Saville Row. Vep was originally an English farmer's daughter with a ridiculous name—little more than a peasant in his view. Despite her minor wealth, what would she know of matters of taste and style?

"It's a minute to midnight. I suggest we enter."

They went up the steps and knocked on the doors. They felt tired just going up them. Churches were not conducive to vampires. Prolonged exposure led to death. Neither wished to show or mention the effects of the consecrated ground to their enemies—and more especially each other.

A short bald man opened the door. Liatoukine sensed this was the German Harker's man had seen earlier. He gestured for them to walk down the aisle. They did so. Liatoukine walked down, feeling weaker with every step. The Countess was no fool, making them come here. However, he was confident that he would be able to have enough strength to deal with both her and the Skull. The Skull itself would presumably also be underpowered.

The two vampires could see ahead of them. In the center of the Cathedral, under its iconic dome, stood the Countess, Walther P5 Compact in hand. And next to her, on a stool, was the Skull.

They stopped a couple of feet from them, in front of the chairs that surrounded the inner circle under the dome. Quite apart from the power of the Cathedral, the Countess was wearing her silver crucifix. Some distance was necessary.

Greetings, Captain Vampire, the Skull announced in their heads.

Liatoukine ignored the Skull; it was clearly trying to unsettle him by using his nickname. He spoke to the Countess, pointing at the Skull.

"May I do what apparently you cannot, and destroy this thing?"

"Please proceed," the Countess said, smiling.

He looked at the Skull and began the process of reabsorption. Nothing happened. The Skull laughed manically.

You are too weak, Captain Vampire—this cathedral is taking its toll.

The Countess had expected things would go wrong. She swung her revolver straight over to the Skull and fired. Eliminate the Skull and she and Karl would deal with the vampires themselves. Silver bullets came out of the gun and simply hovered in the air in front of the Skull. Then they fell to the ground.

The Skull rose up from its stool and hovered mid-air. Vep, Liatoukine and the Countess could feel pressure on their minds. They were in agony. The Countess's firearm was flung by the Skull's power well out of anyone's reach. By the doors, Karl, too, was under attack. The Skull ranted in their minds.

Fools! Over the years, I have acquired great power simply by absorbing the psychic powers of people who came to see me in the various museums where I was on display. There were even some genuine supernatural artifacts from which I was able to draw psychic strength. A strange vampiric variant—not blood or energy, but psychic power in my case. How little you know of your own biology, Captain Vampire, and what it has begat. I will now absorb myself into you, take your body and happily crush your mind. These others will be my first meal—if they survive my restraining of them.

You lack ambition, Captain Vampire. You mere wish for power and influence—but on human terms. I will use your position to create new vampires. Many, many of them. I will restore the supernatural. And I will use that to control the world. Finally, vampires will control history, not humanity!

Liatoukine decided to play for time.

"The humans cannot be defeated. Their science and numbers will see to that," he gasped.

He was about to go on, but stopped. Why was the Skull spilling out its ridiculous plans? Why not just get on with destroying him? Reabsorption takes seconds—and if the Skull was that powerful, why had it not done so? Of course! The Cathedral was affecting it as well! There was huge power there—the power of the British nation, its people, its warriors. Was not Wellington and Nelson buried beneath it? This nation had seen off Dracula, after all... His theory was correct; it was what the Skull was thinking as well. There was still a link between them.

Liatoukine sensed fear from the Skull. However, time was short. The Skull was still crushing them down. He was the main focus of its efforts. He looked at Vep. She was on her knees, struggling simply to stand. He looked at the Countess. She was on her feet, her face full of anger and fury, her hands on her crucifix raising it towards the Skull. Her will was stronger than Vep's! She was the answer. The Russian vampire concentrated on the Skull, trying again to reabsorb it. He knew he could not do it, but just a minor effort could be enough to relieve some of the pressure from the others, and the Countess might be able to attack.

They made eye contact. She understood he was trying something. He concentrated what was left of his energy into the attempt. He knew this act itself could destroy him.

Too late, Captain Vampire! Too late! the Skull screamed.

However, both Vep and the Countess felt a slight lessening of pressure. Vep simply fell forward. Seizing the moment, the Countess ripped the crucifix off her neck and smashed it down on top of the Skull fracturing it.

"In the name of God!" she shouted, "I expel you from this Earth!"

She smashed the crucifix down again and again, pushing the Skull back onto the stool it had been on. It started to scream—a disturbing, unearthly sound. Bits of it flew around under the assault, bone and teeth crashing to the floor. Its power was shattered. And then, the power of the Cathedral exerted its full wrath—what was left of it disintegrated into powder.

The Countess stared at her handiwork. She looked at her hand, a little bruised and bloodied from where it had hit the Skull, but still gripping the crucifix. Some of it had broken off—it was fortunate that she had it constructed with steel reinforcement within.

She turned to the vampires. Now it as their turn. She saw Vep already halfway down the aisle, holding up Liatoukine. She shoved a disorientated Karl out of the way, a shot from his firearm going off wildly. And then they were out.

The Countess was too weak to chase them. She looked back at what remained of the Skull. Its powdered remains were blowing away in the mysterious wind that traditionally disposed of many vampire remains. She liked tradition. Vep and Liatoukine would keep for now. Karl staggered up to her.

"They've gone," he said. "Disappeared."

"They'll keep," the Countess replied. "We have scored a victory for God and humanity this night. The Skull had intended to unleash vampirism on a scale not seen before. I shall pray to thank the Lord for His help this night."

She promptly went to her knees. Karl would have preferred to leave at once and do the praying later. However, he knew it would be unwise to suggest this. He sat down on one of the chairs and waited for her to finish.

Liatoukine and Vep had been picked up by Harker in one of his company's vehicles and swiftly spirited away. Both vampires started to feel some energy returning, having left the Cathedral behind.

"I take it we are now on good terms?" Vep asked.

"Yes," said Liatoukine. "Provided you stay out of my way, you have nothing to fear from me."

Liatoukine was in any event too weak for another fight. Regardless, he wanted to be seen as someone who kept his word—to serious people at least—and there was always the possibility he may need her again as an ally.

"Very well. Drop me off here," she said to Harker.

He complied and she disappeared into the night.

It took Boris Liatoukine a few days to regain much of his energy. It had gone well. The threat of the Skull had gone. He was already being more cautious with the creation of new duplicates. Nothing had come out of the incident in the

Cathedral. The Countess and her network clearly still had some influence, but not enough for the authorities to come after him. The current disbelief in vampires was working in his favor. He would still need to tread carefully. The power of the Cathedral was a reminder that he, too, could be vulnerable.

He turned to the newspapers. He was catching up with world affairs, and went to his favorite first, the *International Herald-Tribune*.

And there was an article that effectively revealed what—or rather who— the Skull had been monitoring for years in St. Petersburg—a person it believed would be important in the future.

Boris Yeltsin had sacked the current head of the FSB, Nikolai Kovalev, and replaced him with someone who, until two years ago, was an official in St. Petersburg, and before that, a KGB man—the very organization the Russian vampire had worked for himself.

Like the Skull, he intuited that more change was on the way.

Yes, thought Boris Liatoukine. *This Vladimir Putin would be a man to watch.*

For several years now, Martin Gately has been building a corpus of stories centered around Gaston Leroux' journalist sleuth, Joseph Rouletabille. Each story can be read independently, but this new tale is an early one in a chronological sequence that includes "Rouletabille Rides the Horror Express" (TOTS 13, 1906), "Rouletabille at the Old Bailey" (TOTS 14, 1909), "Leviathan Creek" (TOTS 8, 1916), "Rouletabille and The New World Order" (TOTS 11, 1926), "Rouletabille vs. The Cat" (TOTS 10, ditto), and "Rouletabille on Mysterious Island" (TOTS 12, 1927).

Martin Gately: *Rouletabille in the House of Despair*

London, 1909

Harry Dickson was in the most marvelous mood. The past month had brought him even greater success—and success is the best form of advertizing. More and more clients had been arriving at his recently rented Baker Street rooms. If it carried on like this, he would have to consider employing some sort of permanent assistant, or at least a secretary, to schedule his appointments and manage his diary. As it was, he was spending far too much time tied to Baker Street, taking notes of his meetings with those in need of his help when he really should have been abroad in London, gathering evidence and bringing villains to justice. That was his very meat and drink, the thing which gave him the greatest possible thrill. His instinct was that he would never tire of it.

Yet, perhaps the strangest thing for the neophyte consulting detective was how he had been taken under the collective wing of the *Great Men of Baker Street*—Holmes, Blake, Begg and Drago. He was never short of advice, for it was most freely given. He had been told the correct tailor to visit, the right attire to wear for town and when visiting the country, the best place to purchase a revolver (and which make), how much ammunition to carry, how to swiftly apply disguises, how to fight with a sword stick. He was also given a list of local dog owners who were prepared to loan their dogs to consulting detectives for the right price. Dickson was also taught various mnemonics to enable him to memorize the geography of London, street by street—almost building by building.

Perhaps most generously of all, he had been introduced to incredibly useful contacts within Scotland Yard, Whitehall, and various foreign embassies. Indeed, so much new information had been imparted to Dickson recently that, in the back of his mind, he had started to develop the odd feeling that he had forgotten to do something. It was a nagging doubt which never seemed to coalesce into a fully coherent thought. He had the vague sense that he had forgotten to turn up for an appointment or take a minor exam. Whatever it was, he comforted himself that it couldn't have been anything too important.

Dickson had been taken aback by how much the *Great Men* socialized together and enjoyed themselves when not working on cases. It was an unexpected strand to his new existence, and he fully relished it. The older consulting detectives took great pride in knowing obscure and secret watering holes, restaurants and clubs. It was on one of these outings that the young American first encountered the beauteous Judith Fraser, who had been dining with her aunt and cousin. The *Great Men* nodded to each other and winked furtively as Dickson sought to strike up a conversation with the young woman at the adjoining table.

At first the somewhat fiery aunt was appalled by this contravention of social norms, but only moments later the detective's earnest colonial charm and easy manner had started to win her over. Of course, Miss Judith herself had been smitten from long before the American first spoke. The nominal purpose of that particular evening had been to introduce Harry Dickson to the Praed Street Detective, Solar Pons.

Over liqueurs, Pons had confidentially whispered to Dickson:

"Don't let that girl get away! I have a feeling you may be spending the rest of your life with her."

And so, his single-minded pursuit of Miss Judith began, to the exclusion of all personal interests excepting his detective casework. He was completely intoxicated by her. At the very start, her Aunt Josette played the chaperone, but she approved of young Dickson so strongly that it was not long before the girl was allowed to take walks alone with her suitor in London's lovely royal parks.

It was odd, but these open public parks seemed to foster an unaccustomed anxiety within Dickson. Some sort of submerged half-memory sometimes seemed to cry out from the back of his mind. And there was an unbidden visualization, of sorts. In his mind's eye, Dickson saw himself crawling along the ground through thick grass towards a bearded and dangerous man. The bearded man was drawing something in a small notebook. Dickson had to find out what was in the notebook, even at the risk of his own life—quite why he could never fathom. Essential linkages in his chain of logical thought seemed to have been smashed beyond repair. The more he tried to focus on it, the more it eluded him. Concentration on the issue brought only anxiety, and when he opened his heart to Miss Judith about the matter, the suggestion came that there should be no more walks in parks. They would meet at the Ritz or the Café Royal instead. To her, avoidance of the problem seemed paramount—ignore it and it will go away was her philosophy.

The romance continued, and the things Dickson could not remember, whatever they were, took on less and less of an importance in his life. Had it not, he would almost certainly have mentioned it to one of his mentors. They might have known people, mesmerists perhaps, who could have unlocked his memory. But why bother? Why should he allow this minor unease to sabotage his happiness? Things were going so well for him. He was in love. His career was burgeoning. Some of the greatest men in London held him in the highest regard. His future looked entirely rosy. Yes, Harry Dickson was in the most marvelous mood.

The Journal of Dr. Rupert Grierson - Leytonstone House Asylum, 30th June 1909

The usual problems persist with the women inmates. One common factor for all of them is the overwhelming desire to do themselves extreme harm. One might be forgiven for thinking that all of their intellectual energy, such as it is, must be given over to this end. Nevertheless, the ingenuity that they do display is alarming. Last week, Nancy Pearce, managed to secrete a piece of stale bread upon her person—her previous feigned good behavior meant that she had been allowed to eat in the communal dining hall. To the layman, an additional piece of bread in the hands of a mental patient might not have been thought to be a matter of concern, but over time the bread hardened. Before long it could be sharpened until it had a reasonably effective cutting edge. After a few trial strokes on her upper arms to test the implement, Pearce slashed open both of her wrists. Fortunately, she was discovered before she bled to death, and medical aid was administered.

However, this was not the case with Rosemary Andrews. Andrews was a baby farmer convicted of killing nineteen of her charges, but saved from the hangman's noose by virtue of her insanity. Andrews repetitively and determinedly injures herself with whatever comes to hand. She was to be fully restrained in a straitjacket and strapped to a table, for when she is confined in a padded cell, she strikes her head repeatedly against the wall with sufficient force to damage her neck vertebrae, irrespective of the padding. This means that she is often restrained for a week or more at a time. When she pleads and offers that her behavior will improve, ultimately my staff have little choice but to allow her out of the straitjacket for a probationary period. After all, she could not be restrained in that fashion on a permanent basis. As this pattern played itself out recently, Andrews was released from restraint, but, within a few hours, had torn apart her teddy bear and pushed a handful of its stuffing into her trachea in an effort to asphyxiate herself. She was saved from death by medical staff, but before she could be placed back in restraints, she ripped out her own eyes. Treatment was quickly given, but she remains in agony, and will be for some time since I have ordered minimal analgesics. Let pain be her tutor for a while—it may break down the mental barriers that reason and therapy cannot.

I therefore move onto the male inmates, the most remarkable of these is *JJ*. He may be the most extraordinary mental patient that I have ever encountered. He was brought here by the Metropolitan Police in a highly agitated and psychotic state only a couple of weeks ago. He is devious, highly intelligent and extremely violent. Four orderlies were badly injured on the first day when they placed him within his cell. The patient would not give his name, and he seemed terrified of me. Some of his clothing was marked with the initials *JJ-* and so that is what I decided to call him.

JJ seems to be willing to speak to some of the more junior staff, but his ravings merely reveal severe and grandiose delusions of the most serious nature. He is, by turns, a famous journalist, the world's greatest detective, and possibly some sort of secret agent. A monolithic conspiracy operates against him; he is the victim of attempted assassination and actual poisonings. He says it was after he was poisoned that he was found half-naked on the streets of Bethnal Green. However, the arresting officer told me he was delusional and foaming at the mouth, to the extent that one younger constable wondered if the man had rabies.

He claims to be French, though I am not certain of this. He has not spoken in French to any of my staff. I have read of cases where psychotics will affect a foreign accent, and some stroke victims also speak with an unaccustomed accent during recovery. While being taken to a room for a medical assessment, *JJ* broke away from his escort and was at large within the main asylum building for something like four minutes. When recaptured, the orderly searching him discovered secreted on his person an asylum door master key and a pair of scissors. I have ordered him to be temporarily placed in a straitjacket. I am not particularly given to prescient feelings, but in the back of my mind is the notion that he will find some way to escape again. His orderly reported to me that while being placed back in his cell, *JJ* announced that he was the "King of the Locked Room." No doubt his gibberish is meaningless, but still it fills me with an odd disquiet.

I have given some consideration to possible treatment for this patient, and I have decided that, after a brief period to allow him to acclimatize to life in the asylum, I will commence with intramuscular injections of camphor. The pain from these will be severe, but nevertheless cathartic; it may allow for the re-emergence of his original personality, which I strongly suspect is not that of a French journalist or detective. I will follow up the camphor injections with cold water immersion hydrotherapy. In the most severe of cases, this can be quite successful at resetting the brain's normal functions. But there is the likelihood of the side effect of amnesia. In this case, I hope the unpleasant delusions of persecution will also be erased. I will have freed his mind, and in that I will take great pleasure.

It was the third time little Alfie had made a delivery to the asylum since the strange man had started appearing at the window. Alfie's father had explained to him all about the sort of people who were locked up in asylums. There were two sorts: lunatics and imbeciles. Imbeciles were none too bright, and lunatics were dangerous—or, at least, that was how his father had explained it to him. The strange man seemed clever, though he spoke with quite a thick foreign accent, therefore Alfie deduced that he was a lunatic, and likely to be dangerous.

"Little boy, do not be afraid. I mean you no harm," said the strange man to the rotund boy wheeling the bicycle.

The strange man was high up at a barred window on the second floor of the asylum. The wire reinforced glass of the window had been flung wide by one of the man's keepers to ventilate the cell during this hot spell. Alfie did not see how the strange man could possibly harm him from so far away, so it seemed an odd thing to say, and as the boy drew nearer he could see the man's arms were enveloped in some sort of binding of tough canvas which kept them tight against his torso.

"Just come a little nearer... a little nearer," said the strange man. "I need to tell you something."

"I can't stop to talk. I need to deliver the groceries in my basket to the kitchen," said Alfie, who knew, because once again his father had told him, that the high quality fruit and vegetables from his family's grocers down on Leytonstone High Road were destined not for the consumption of inmates but rather for the table of the Director of the asylum, Dr. Grierson.

"It will only take a moment," said the strange man. "Take out your pencil and notebook."

Alfie looked up at the man with narrowed and suspicious eyes. How had he known he always carried writing materials on him? Most boys did not. Could the man be some sort of mind-reader? Had he somehow been locked up because he was a mind-reader? Alfie decided to stand his bicycle carefully against the asylum wall and take out the notebook and stub of pencil from his apron pocket.

"Write this down: *To Harry Dickson, Baker Street. I have been captured by Grierson and placed in his asylum. I am being tortured. Effect rescue immediately. Yours in despair, Rouletabille*," commanded the strange man.

The strange man had to go through the message twice more before Alfie had all the words down and the spelling correct.

"But what am I supposed to do with it now?" asked Alfie. "I can't ride all the way to Baker Street."

The strange man seemed to consider for a few seconds.

"Then take it to the nearest police station, or give it to your parents," he said.

Alfie shrugged and went back to pushing his bicycle towards the kitchen delivery door just around the corner. The boy had something of a suspicion of policemen which the strange man obviously did not share. He very much wondered how much weight they would place on a note from a madman in a cell in the local asylum.

When the doorbell rang, Harry Dickson leapt up from his desk in anticipation. His own housekeeper was on holiday in the Highlands of Scotland, and so he had Mrs. Bardell on loan from Blake, since Blake was out of town on a case.

He could hear voices from the floor beneath, and as he had expected, Miss Judith had now arrived.

"You just keep on with your knitting, Mrs. Bardell," the girl was saying. "I am quite capable of making a tray of tea and carrying it up to Harry."

"Oh, Miss Fraser! What a fine wife you will make for him, and not before too long, I hope," said the housekeeper.

The American continued to listen, and a few moments later, it was plain that Mrs. Bardell had withdrawn to her parlor and shut the door. Dickson therefore drifted downstairs with a view to surprising her in the scullery. As he rounded the corner, he saw that she already had the kettle on and the best bone china cups and saucers on the tray, but he was surprised to see that her delicate fingers were dropping a tiny soluble white tablet into one of the cups.

"What are you putting in my tea, darling? Not bromide, I hope," joked Dickson.

"Hardly," said Miss Judith. "But you've been looking so run down lately. I thought you might need some kind of tonic to just pep you up a little."

"Why, Mrs. Bardell is right, you are going to make a fabulous wife," said the detective.

"Is that a proposal of marriage, Harry," laughed the girl.

"Well, I guess it is at that—but let me try it again properly. Judith Fraser, will you marry me?"

"Of course, I will. But being a gentleman, you'd better get permission from my Uncle Rupert. You remember how I told you he was my legal guardian until I came of age last year?"

The two of them went upstairs to the sitting room, and once the tea had time to steep they drank it and each other in. To Dickson, she seemed to be more than merely beautiful—she was transfigured, as if lit from behind by some great arc light. The radiance seemed to emanate from beneath her skin, to pass through her being. He was captured by her gaze like a specimen impaled on a pin in a display case. Her burnished copper hair framed her face like a ruddy halo. Her eyes were sea green, but with flashes of sudden fire deep within.

The girl gestured at something on the carpet.

"I've dropped my sapphire earring on the floor, Harry. Would you mind picking it up for me?" asked the girl.

"I… I can't move," said Dickson.

He strained as if at invisible bonds, but could not get up from his chair. '

With a sinuous movement, she reached down to retrieve the item of jewelry and then knelt in front of him.

"It is a beautiful stone isn't it?" she asked, not waiting for, nor seemingly wanting a reply. "It was a gift from my Uncle Rupert. Look deeply into the sapphire. You'll see that it is starting to glow."

The gem did indeed start to glow. At first, it seemed to be little more than the light which might be cast by a firefly, but after a few moments, the intense brightness outshone even the illumination that the transfigured girl seemed to generate. It was like a welding torch was being fired into his brain, His optic nerve overloaded, all was blank whiteness. To think the simplest thought was to marshal an effort akin to shoveling coal.

"You have never previously met my uncle," the girl insisted. "Have you?"

"I have never met your uncle," agreed Dickson, after doing his best to search his memory.

"And the name Joseph Rouletabille is unknown to you. You have never had any association with Joseph Rouletabille."

"I have never had any association with Joseph Rouletabille," the American intoned mindlessly.

"That is excellent," said Judith Fraser.

She stood up now and sloughed off her dress, undid her corset and pulled down her cami-knickers. Moving closer, she put her right nipple to his lips. He latched onto it. She fumbled with his clothes and then sat astride him on the chair. The reward for forgetfulness would be ecstasy. And yes, she thought to herself, she would make a good wife just as she'd made a good whore.

"If the message is from some loony Frenchman, why is it in your handwriting?" said Alfie's father.

"He had to tell me what to write. His arms wuz all bundled up in some kind of canvas," said Alfie.

"Oh? In a straitjacket was he?" Alfie's father asked, somewhat rhetorically. "They save that for the worst of 'em. But I'm still not sure I believe you. You can be a right little liar when you put your mind to it."

"He wants this message sent to a man in Baker Street, where all the detectives live. This Frenchie must be a detective himself, or maybe even a secret agent. Baker Street is too far for me to go on my bicycle. Will you take it for me in your van?" asked Alfie.

"You must be joking. I'm not trotting off on a wild goose chase as a result of one of your lies. It was bad enough when you told me you'd seen a woman with a butcher's knife hiding in our bathroom, and I spent an age searching the house and backyard for her," said Alfie's father.

"Oh, please Dad. Take the message round to Mr. Dickson, or the French detective might be angry next time he sees me."

"I need to take you round to Sergeant Arbogast at the nick," said the greengrocer. "If he puts you in one of his cells for an hour or two, perhaps you will learn to tell the truth."

This was a common threat from Alfie's father who was good friends with the desk sergeant at the nearby police station on Leytonstone High Road. But this time it seemed as if he really meant it.

"Quickly finish off loading those sacks of potatoes then we can be off down the station," said Alfie's father.

The two orderlies were large, burly men and they handled the weakened Rouletabille with great ease. The French detective was propelled down the stark corridor with his feet barely touching the floor. He did not bother to struggle; he needed to preserve what strength he had. Within moments they arrived at the white-tiled hydrotherapy room. The enamel bathtub in the center of the room was far larger than its domestic equivalent, and had already been filled with water and chunks of ice. Almost surreptitiously, Rouletabille began to take deep and rapid breaths in an effort to oxygenate his blood. He did not really know what good it would do. His fear at this point was drowning. He thought that the orderlies would be forcefully holding his head beneath the water until his lungs cried out for air. Instead, they pulled off his pajama bottoms and physically hurled him, legs first, into the great tub.

The shock of the extreme cold hit him like a shotgun blast. He was instantly numb and vested with a lethargy that bordered on paralysis. His arms were still tightly bound in the straitjacket, but his legs and head seemed to be beyond his ability to control. His mind retreated out of his body, as if observing the whole scene from a distance. The body, which no longer seemed to be his, was lifted out of the tub then plunged back into it a second time. Then a third, then with random repetitions that he ceased to be able to count; his brain merely registered their tediousness.

Before long, but he could no longer judge time—so it might have been hours—the water started to seem pleasantly warm. The rock-hard ice was starting to soften at the edges. He held this to be the most important secret he had ever known. He continued to wince and grimace each time he was dropped back into the water. He must give no sign to the orderlies that the shock of the freezing water had abated. At one point, he caught a glimpse of his bare legs, they were blue with cyanosis. The "warmth" of the water in the tub was obviously a relative thing. Maybe it had only risen in temperature a couple of degrees while he was being tortured. Then, he was overcome by a kind of drunkenness, and his body seemed burningly hot rather than cold. It was all he could do in these circumstances to hang onto his identity, to stop his coherent sense of self from fracturing. But from somewhere in the depths of closed-off mind, a single word burrowed its way through the permafrost to the surface: hypothermia. His organs were starting to shut down. Then it all stopped. It seemed to him that the orderlies were carrying him back to his cell just before he would have died.

In his cell, the orderlies gave him a cursory rub dry with a rough towel. The towel had been left on a radiator and was quite warm to the touch. What bliss! As they dressed him, Rouletabille thought what splendid fellows the orderlies were. He wondered for a moment why their kindness seemed to be the only human interaction he had known in his life, and then he realized. He had no recollection of how he had come to be in this situation. No clue of what had happened earlier in time. The cold water had washed away his life. That seemed absurd. There was surely no former life to remember. He had always been here.

Alfie had expected his father to come into the station with him; instead he waited outside and gave him a note to take in to Sergeant Arbogast. Alfie walked under the station's blue lamp and up the steps into its most forbidding interior. The station was as quiet as a lending library, and the desk sergeant was sitting studiously examining something in the immense leather incident ledger which was spread open across the countertop.

Arbogast raised his head revealing his rather florid, mutton chop bewhiskered face.

"Yes, young man? How may I assist you?" asked the sergeant.

Alfie felt that if he tried to speak he would simply be sick, so opted to stand on tiptoes and offer up the scrunched up note his father had written to Arbogast.

"It says here that you are a very naughty little boy who likes telling lies and needs to be taught a lesson," stated Arbogast. "Is that right?"

The urge to vomit had subsided slightly within only to be replaced by a feeling that he would very shortly lose all bladder and bowel control. So, in answer to the question, he merely nodded the affirmative.

"Come with me, then."

Arbogast came around from the far side of the counter and led the rotund boy down the white tiled corridor towards the cells. The officer removed a ring of keys from his belt and unlocked a cell door.

"In you go then, sonny. I'll let you out in the morning."

To Alfie, the six by ten foot cell seemed little bigger than a coffin. He had never experienced claustrophobia before, but it hit him now with the force of a ruptured water main. His consciousness refused to dwell within him, and he found himself looking down at his quivering form as if from the ceiling. He felt considerable sympathy now for the Frenchman locked in his cell up at the Leytonstone House Insane Asylum—they were almost kindred spirits. Nevertheless, he would never again risk his liberty to assist someone, and he would never, ever, trust a policeman. A permanent change had taken place in the boy as a result of this harsh and disproportionate punishment. He would never be the same again.

It had all come back to Rouletabille fairly slowly. The details of his past gradually took on more and more solid form. And though some of the recollections caused him to doubt his own sanity—such as his experiences just a few years ago aboard the Trans-Siberian Express—he could not doubt that these must be real memories. He'd had an existence prior to his incarceration. He was both a detective and a journalist, and he's been tracking down a German spy ring operating in East London. The spies had been trying to steal secrets relating the development of an experimental armed tri-plane which was being tested by the British government on the Wanstead Flatlands between the built-up sprawl of Leytonstone and Epping Forest. And he had not been working on this case alone, there was Harry Dickson too, the young detective he had met at the Old Bailey during the Schellenberger trial.

Dickson's success in the case had caused the neophyte detective to be accepted by the fabled *Great Men of Baker Street* and inducted into their number. Following the aforementioned induction, there was supposed be a short break from the espionage case while Dickson wound up his other outstanding cases. But Dickson had not kept his rendezvous with Rouletabille in Bethnal Green and the Frenchman had been left trying to follow up various leads on his own. This had been a disaster, for while questioning a woman in the *Salmon and Ball* public house, it had become apparent that she was a member of the spy ring. But the woman had already poisoned his drink with some sort of hallucinogen.

When he'd come to his senses, he was incarcerated in the asylum run by Dr. Rupert Grierson—the very man Dickson and Rouletabille strongly suspected of being the leader of the spies; the man who had effected the release of Schellenberger from the condemned cell at Newgate by means of an explosive device.

Now, Rouletabille's memory had come back. But if the ice water immersion treatments continued. day after day. how long could his recollections realistically survive? He was felt pessimistic. His instinct was that it might take only one or two more treatments to fracture his mind completely. Then the thought struck him: could he really be sure this was the first ice water treatment? Could he trust his own memories?

He heard the cell door unlock and then swing open. From his prone position on the floor, he turned his head and saw Grierson enter the room. Rouletabille expected to be mocked, humiliated, or insulted by the doctor. Instead, he was almost entirely silent. The detective had neither the strength nor the will to resist. He saw that Grierson had a syringe and a bottle of yellowish liquid. The doctor opened the bottle and filled the syringe with its syrupy contents. The liquid in the bottle gave off a pungent aroma, which stung Rouletabille's eyes. He could not initially place this rather acrid smell... then it came to him. It was camphor!

Without further preamble, he was injected in one thigh and then the other. Within moments, he was wracked by convulsions, his body jackknifed again and again, fitting and spasming with exquisite pain. All of his nerves seemed to be on fire. After several minutes, the intensity of the pain started to diminish, and he was able to re-establish some sort of control over his muscles. Stillness brought him no comfort. He found that the only way to keep his mind off the pain was to keep hurling himself around the cell, weeping, screaming and babbling. He prayed that his rescuers would not arrive now, for if they saw him now, they could draw no possible conclusion other than that he had become a madman.

"It's such a pity that Mr. Dickson has been so ill recently," said Mrs. Bardell. "Nevertheless, I'm sure that, between us, we will be able to nurse him back to health."

"There really is no need for you to bother yourself with this, Mrs. Bardell," said Judith Fraser. "You know I have picked up more than a little knowledge of nursing from my time as a volunteer auxiliary nurse at the Royal London Hospital in Whitechapel."

"Funny that you should mention Whitechapel," said Mrs. Bardell. "I never told you my husband was a sergeant in the City of London Police before he retired the other year. He saw you leaving here the yesterday when he came to pick me up. He told me he knows you by a different name, 'Vinegar Judy'—the dirtiest tuppenny tart operating on the London Road."

"What! What did you call me?" stammered Judith Fraser.

"Vinegar Judy," said Mrs. Bardell, fixing the girl with a white-hot, Medusa-like, glare.

Without another word, Judith Fraser leapt at the older woman and gripped her throat in an attempt to strangle her. But Mrs. Bardell was surprisingly strong. With some ease, she broke the stranglehold and punched Dickson's lover square on the nose with a right cross that would have made a Bethnal Green prizefighter proud. She staggered back across the scullery with blood flowing freely from her nostrils. Mrs. Bardell lashed out with a sweeping kick which took Judith Fraser's legs from beneath her. The girl crashed to the floor and lay still, blood trickling from the back of her head.

Mrs. Bardell went over to the counter and tipped into the sink the milk from the china cup intended for Dickson upstairs in his sick room—the hot tea had not yet been poured into the cup. In the cup was just the evidence she had been looking for, a partially dissolved tablet. Her regular employer would know how to analyze it upon his return. She anticipated that, without being intermittently drugged, young Mr. Dickson would soon start to make a full recovery.

As Mrs. Bardell thought back, she realized that she had been suspicious of Judith Fraser almost from the very beginning—irrespective of her husband's revelations. The girl had seemed too good to be true. And, inevitably, anything that appears to be over-endowed with goodness will be hollow, false and poisonous—like a perfect white chocolate Easter egg stuffed with putrescence and maggots.

Then Mrs. Bardell heard the sound of footsteps on the stairs. They were light, quiet, almost tentative, something like those of a small child. She rushed out into the hall and saw ascending the stairs a dwarfish, baldheaded figure dressed in a smart dark suit.

"Judith? It is your Uncle," called the little man.

Mrs. Bardell stepped briskly back into the scullery and inadvertently allowed the door to slam behind her. She had only seconds now to find a weapon. Her instincts told her and both she and Dickson would be in great danger when the "uncle" would discover the current condition of his "niece."

She wrestled a butcher knife out from the drawer, and grabbed unconscious Judith by the hair before kicking back open the scullery door.

The little man was now almost back at the bottom of the stairs, having come to investigate the noise from the scullery. A look of shock played momentarily across his face at the sight of the bloodied girl in the hands of the ferocious looking knife-wielding woman. Mrs. Bardell was a strong woman ordinarily, but right now, a substantial amount of adrenaline was fizzing through her system. She dragged Judith along behind her as if she weighed little more than a mannequin, and then threw her along hall to land on the carpet near the feet of the dwarf, only a yard from the front door. The girl moaned, as if coming around, and rolled onto her back.

"Get out of here!" commanded Mrs. Bardell. "And take this unfortunate baggage with you!"

In response, the little man swiftly removed from his jacket pocket a powerful-looking repeating air pistol, and shot Judith Fraser once in each eye. Mrs. Bardell considered hurling her butcher knife directly at the man, but there was a moment of hesitancy, during which he calmly opened the door and stepped out onto Baker Street—re-pocketing his weapon as he did so.

Mrs. Bardell stepped over Judith's body and watched the killer saunter off down Baker Street with a strange, undulating gait. She looked down at the girl and found that she pitied her. What chance had she had in life? Yet someone had picked her off the street and removed her from a life of debasement, only to turn her into a weapon against the forces of good.

She knew that she needed to notify Scotland Yard straightaway, but they could hardly be relied upon to actually catch the dwarfish killer. But to whom should she now turn for help? She took the opportunity to run upstairs and check on Harry Dickson. Yes, he would doubtless recover in time, but for now, he was still lethargic and feverish. Her own employer was unlikely to be back before the end of the week. That left perhaps three of the *Great Men of Baker Street* available to answer her call for help. And if all of them were otherwise engaged, then she would just have to deal with matters herself.

Of course everyone knows that, in order to escape from a straitjacket, you have to dislocate your shoulder. The question is, what do you do once you've got your shoulder out of its socket? Rouletabille had bashed his right shoulder against the wall perhaps only four or five times when there came a crunching sensation, followed by the feeling that the interior of the joint had been packed with broken glass. Nauseous from the pain, he stood stock, still considering what to do next.

After a few minutes he experimentally moved his arm and discovered the higher he moved his arm up his chest within the straitjacket, the greater the slack, the greater his field of movement. Nevertheless, it was excruciating. Fortunately, his arms had only been crossed rather than folded. He doubted he'd have been able to withstand the agony of unfolding them, since this would've involved pulling his arm across his torso laterally rather than just pushing it up. Oddly perhaps, as he forced his right arm over his head, the pain eased. He realized that this was because his shoulder joint was close to going back into position, but he couldn't allow that to happen, he still needed the slack to continue working himself to freedom.

Getting his head through the tight gap formed by the crook of his arm felt like threading a camel through the eye of a needle, but once that was achieved the tightness and restriction seemed to go out of the jacket completely. Rouletabille dropped to his knees, exhausted and in a cold sweat. His arms were still within the canvas of the straitjacket, and his hands were firmly buckled together, but he was able to move his arms quite freely now. A series of swift pendulum-type movements loosened the tongue of the buckle sufficiently that he was able to work at it with his teeth. Then, in an ecstasy of flailing, he was able to free himself completely from the straitjacket, only to collapse exhausted to the floor before losing consciousness completely.

Rouletabille awoke ready to put into action the next phase of his improvised plan: escaping from his cell. And then, he screamed. And then, he fought to stifle the sobs which emanated from him so uncontrollably, for while he had been unconscious, the orderlies had discovered him, forced his shoulder back into position, and put on a fresh straitjacket that was tighter than ever. This time, his arms were closely folded, and it would be much more difficult to get free.

Summoning up the final vestiges of his resolve and his stoicism, he started to beat his shoulder against the wall once more.

Since his time in the police cell, Little Alfie had visited the grounds of the asylum twice. Neither of these visits had been part of his duties as a delivery boy. His father had sent him everywhere in the vicinity except Leytonstone House. He'd therefore developed a spurious excuse for his presence in the grounds of the mental hospital—which were extremely extensive and heavily overgrown. His concocted excuse was that he had taken a fancy to building dens, as he was given to understand some boys did. So far, he had not come close to being caught, but if he was, he'd most likely be let off with a light warning or a cuff round the ear—nothing so imaginative as his incarceration in the police station at the hands of Sergeant Arbogast.

And so, against both his interests and his instincts, he constructed not one, but two dens, concealed within the grounds. Since he was a large and rotund boy, the dens themselves were generously sized, put together from skeletal frames of fallen branches and covered with bracken and evergreen fronds. Purely by the virtue of being assembled from these materials, in combination with the neglect and overgrowth of the grounds, the dens were invisible, unless being deliberately searched for. The second of the dens was in the shadow of an old beech tree, and the interior was actually quite cozy. The grounds were seldom patrolled, and the view from this particular den—through a small aperture he had created, which somehow reminded him of a feature a birdwatcher's hide was likely to have—allowed him to see the drive leading up to the asylum and two of the main pathways leading through the grounds. Most importantly, he could also see the barred window of the strange Frenchman. Little Alfie munched on his chocolate bar, swigged his lemonade, and wondered if the absent Frenchman would ever appear at the window again.

The boy's mind wandered back to what had happened when he was released from the police cell. There had been three men in the police station that he had never seen before. A man in the sort of hat one might wear for shooting in the country; he had one of those mid-length tweedy capes on too; a fellow who seemed to be a doctor, who sported a droopy moustache, and finally a grey-haired man so fat he seemed to have trouble walking.

They had questioned him quite briefly after having spoken to the sergeant, and seemed quite accepting of the information he gave about the Frenchman, so much so that they gave him a shilling. And the boy had been left wondering why he had been punished for lying, when some grownups thought he was telling the truth.

On his way out of the police station, he paused. He was just out of sight, so they carried on talking in loud voices. Devoid of any context, he had to interpret what they were saying as best he could. Spies. There were German spies operating in the area. The Germans were seeking information about the trials of a military tri-plane which was being tested very nearby on the Wanstead Flatlands. The Frenchman was apparently some ally of the British, and they would now seek get him released, since he was most assuredly not a madman.

Later on, he had watched from a distance as the men left, after having visited the asylum. The three of them walked out of the gates without the Frenchman. So where was he?

There was an odd conflict within Little Alfie. His new philosophy of life forbade him from assisting others if it meant that his own liberty might be curtailed. On the other hand, he could not properly know peace of mind until the Frenchman was freed. The boy's eyes continued to scan the grounds and the paths to the asylum building. The three men from the police station had left empty-handed the other day, and as far as he knew, they had not bothered to come back. He looked again at the barred window for some sign of movement. Nothing. But the Frenchman had said he was being tortured. Perhaps they had gone too far and killed him.

Suddenly, an ice-cold hand snaked around Little Alfie from behind and clamped over his mouth. His first thought was that he had been grabbed by some kind of monster, something that had clawed its way out of a grave. Twisting his head, he found himself looking into the vacant, glassy eyes of the Frenchman. His face was milky-white, fatigue and pain had scraped the life from his features.

"It was Hell, but I have escaped," said Rouletabille, before collapsing onto the floor of the den.

For half an hour, Little Alfie crouched over Rouletabille, wondering how to wake him up. His mum was always saying sugar was reviving, so after much thought, he gently opened the Frenchman's mouth and poured in some of his own lemonade. Rouletabille spluttered, but then opened his eyes widely. The boy looked at the man's right shoulder, and it was immediately apparent that it was badly dislocated—high and contorted, like a badly designed marionette.

Little Alfie did not want to see the Frenchman recaptured, he had decided. His principles on this point seemed to have become as pliable as India rubber. He no longer feared the loss of his own liberty because the real authorities wanted to free the injured man. It seemed to him that he stood on the threshold of vindication. He had not lied; he had never lied; and he would soon be in a position to prove this to Sergeant Arbogast, and his father; his father most of all since he seemed to think so very little of him.

He wished he had one of those moving picture cameras in order to record all that was happening around him so he could and make his father see and understand. Perhaps, one day, he would be able to get the whole world to see things from his point of view, to understand his fears and preoccupations.

"We need to get you away from here," said the boy. "They aren't looking for you yet... There's no-one searching the grounds. But I need to get home before it is dark."

"My shoulder is agony... I won't be able to climb the walls. Doubtless they will find me soon, but the pain of the escape was worth for even an hour or so of respite from those torturers," said Rouletabille.

"You won't need to climb. I still have the key to the kitchen delivery gate from when I bring up food. Once we're through that, we're almost home free. There's a bit of loose masonry under the metal railings of the boundary wall. I get in by moving the bricks and then putting them back. There'll be plenty of room for you to squeeze through. Come on!"

Harry Dickson was waking from his drugged and hypnotized state, like a man coming around from years in a coma. Mrs. Bardell ministered to him most effectively, giving him sips of milk and spoons of pureed food as if he were an infant.

There was a period of feverishness and sweating as he suffered withdrawal from whatever addictive filth Judith Fraser had been slipping to him, but just as soon as he was able to vocalize a coherent thought, he started ask about Rouletabille.

The elusive, nagging, forgotten thing from the back of his mind was now at the forefront. He had promised the French detective that he would spend a couple of weeks concluding the cases currently on his desk, and then collaborate with him on the German spy ring case. To have "forgotten" such a commitment was mortifying. Yet, he had not simply forgotten; he had been drugged and subjected to some sort of sinister mesmerism—worse, this had been done by a woman he had believed to be the love of his life. The most horrifying realization was that Rouletabille never turned up to chide him for not coming to his assistance. Where had the Frenchman been all these weeks? Who had him?

"Where is Rouletabille?" screamed Dickson in despair, suddenly sitting bolt upright in his bed.

"Do not concern yourself, Mr. Dickson," said Mrs. Bardell. "The *Great Men* are looking for him. They will find him, and they will save him. So don't you fret."

As he heard those words, he sank back onto his bed, and before long, had returned to a fitful sleep.

It was dusk now out on the Wanstead Flatlands, and Rouletabille had parted company with Little Alfie. He had turned down an offer to be taken to meet the boy's father. His instincts told him to keep away from the streets. There would be too many people, and he was not sure he could tell friend from foe. Once he had recovered slightly, he wanted to see if he could force his shoulder joint back into position.

Somewhere in the air above him, he could hear a droning sound—as if from a far off angry hornet. It was an aircraft engine. Of course! He was walking through the proving grounds of the very aero-plane that the German spies had sought to obtain information about. He could see it now, a delicate yellow and black tri-plane, circling high above him like a buzzard. He could not judge the precise altitude, but it looked to be spiraling lower. Then an inspiration struck him. The plane must be coming in to land. If he simply followed it, he would arrive at a section of the flatlands designated as an airstrip. At the landing site there would be military, and perhaps police representatives, and engineers from the AVRO Company. If he made himself known to them, they would doubtless assist him.

The yellow plane continued to lose altitude; as it did so, the sound of its engine grew more and more and more insistent. The plane was coming nearer and nearer, lower and lower, directly towards him. And yet, there was no landing site in view. The Frenchman had expected the plane to start making towards the horizon, but it did not. On the horizon was a stand of trees, and he had reasoned that these must be blocking his view of the airstrip. The descent of the tri-plane was now accompanied by a kind of screeching or whistling. He had never before heard quite such a sound. It was haunting, almost banshee-like. The plane was entering a dive. Something just behind the propeller started to flare and glow. Searing phosphorescent streaks traversed the hundreds of feet between the plane and the ground upon which Rouletabille stood in just the blink of an eye. There were little explosions of dust and dirt all around him as the machine-gun bullets struck the earth. Only now did he hear the dreadful, repetitive staccato sound of the weapon itself. He ran as best he could, but his attempts at sprinting provided no greater speed than that of a staggering drunkard.

He dropped to the ground as the plane passed overhead, perhaps no more than ninety feet above him. At this point, the firing ceased and the pilot started to execute a turn in order to make another pass at the pathetic stumbling figure below him. Ignoring the lightning bolts of pain in his shoulder, as well as the way that the limb flailed uselessly behind him as he moved, Rouletabille got up and soldiered on. He was gradually nearing the line of trees. Now, he was close enough to see that they were oaks. He kept going, daring to sneak a look back.

The plane had turned and decreased in altitude even more. Now it was perhaps only sixty feet above the ground, but flying straight and level. Coming in for the kill. In the dusky twilight, he was finally able to make out what was beyond the trees. It was a small area of water, much too small to really be called a lake, more of an oversized pond—albeit one with little islands where he could see waterfowl starting to hunker down for the night.

Just as the Frenchman started to reach the shelter of the trees, the machine-gun struck up again. He could hear bullets hitting the bark of the tree trunks, but this time, he did not dare to look back. Instead, he flung himself headlong into the water of the pond. Too late he realized that the water was far colder than he had expected it to be. He had accidentally recreated the cold water torture given to him by the orderlies. He cursed his bad luck as his mind started to unravel into the black incoherence of a fugue state. It was as if he could actually feel his ego leaving his body, being pushed sideways to somewhere else completely, leaving only fragments… crumbs… where his original identity had resided. He clung to those remaining morsels, more precious to him than any diamond: Rouletabille. French. Journalist. Detective. Room. Something about a locked room. The rest was lost now.

From his position of concealment in the undergrowth on the far side of the flatlands, Little Alfie had seen a surprising amount of what had transpired. He really hoped that the Frenchman had gotten away, but perhaps even more than that, he really, really, wished he had a moving picture camera.

The yellow plane came around for one last pass, zeroing in now on the water of the pond where the pilot guessed that Rouletabille was. The pilot was an instant away from ratcheting down the lever that would start the machine-gun spraying death when the presence of the plane startled the geese and other wildfowl on the little island, causing them to erupt into the air in a confused mass of flailing wings and snaking necks.

The frightened birds were so dense that they formed a sudden and danger-ous barrier in the air. The pilot dragged back hard on the joystick to avoid them and plane soared away with its engine whining in protest. The plane did not at-tempt to fire on Rouletabille again. Instead, it headed back to its landing site. The sun had set, and darkness had spilt across the flatlands like a bottle of ink carelessly tipped over on a blotter.

Later, a bedraggled Rouletabille walked in circles across the grass and woodland, devoid of purpose, deep in his fugue state—a wary somnambulist. He came close to the plane landing site and heard voices speaking a language he did not properly understand. Although he did not consciously realize the peril he was in, some submerged instinct urged him away from these men. And yet, he needed some refuge, some sanctuary.

In the moonlight, he saw a grandiose building, almost like a palace, and wondered if it was some sort of mirage. It was not; it was Snarebrook Crown Court, the suburban sister to the Old Bailey which nestles unexpectedly, almost surreally, in the woodland on the edge of London.

Again, his most primal instincts directed him away from the great sightless windows of this darkened edifice. His peregrinations continued and he saw a more modest dwelling. On the periphery of its grounds were a group of men with bulls-eye lanterns. He moved nearer. They appeared to be looking for something, and he wondered what. He could see the nearest of the men was dressed in a deerstalker hat and some sort of mid-length Scottish style cape. Rouletabille had absolutely no idea who the man was.

The house was Theydon Grange, part of the Lord Chancellor's estate, and used as a lodging place for judges conducting cases at Snaresbrook Crown Court. Yes, the French detective had been found by one of the *Great Men of Baker Street,* just as Mrs. Bardell had predicted. And medical attention was swiftly administered. Indeed, it was Dr. Watson himself who reset Rouletabille's shoulder. The injured and amnesic detective was given quarters in a small cot-tage in the grounds of Theydon Grange called the Gatekeeper's Lodge, and Mrs. Bardell was moved in to minister to him with her other charge, Harry Dickson, who was by now greatly improved and free of the pernicious withdrawal symp-toms from which he had been suffering.

Rouletabille was fed with Mrs. Bardell's warming broth and provided with soothing poultices for his still swollen shoulder. But there was an urgency and impatience about the many visitors who came to check on the recovering Frenchman over the next few days. And although they did not pester Rouletabille himself, the question was whispered in hushed tones to Harry Dick-son again and again: "When will Joseph Rouletabille recover his memory?"

The question was a weight pressing on Dickson's shoulders. It swirled around the American's mind day and night. How can memory be recovered?

How can memory be evoked? Particularly when Watson had said the young Frenchman was too mentally delicate to undergo hypnosis. Yet, within Rouletabille's mind would be a myriad of clues to crack this case. Perhaps even the whole solution to this labyrinthine conundrum.

The little sitting room at the cottage had small display cases of mounted butterflies. Rouletabille found these relaxing to look at and would sit in his chair for hours with one of the cases on his lap scrutinizing the multi-colored wings of the insects. Late one morning, Dickson bit the bullet and decided to start questioning his friend.

"Can you remember anything about your time in the asylum? How did they torture you?" he asked.

"Some things are starting to come back. I remember being plunged in cold water. I remember painful injections... of camphor," said Rouletabille.

"Camphor?" repeated Dickson with furrowed brow. And an idea began to take shape swiftly in his mind. "Mrs. Bardell! Could you please light the fire here in the sitting room?" he cried with an odd desperation in his voice.

"Whatever for, young man? It is the height of summer, and really quite hot enough already,"

Then Mrs. Bardell saw the grim set of Dickson's face and realized that there was more to this than some idle request. She hurriedly collected kindling, old newspapers and matches from the kitchen, then commenced to lay the foundations of the fire over the hearth grate. Without another word, Dickson rushed upstairs and they could hear him rooting about in drawers and opening the squeaky doors of wardrobes. In the end, he found what he was looking for. Whatever he had found, he kept secretly in the palm of one closed hand. As Mrs. Bardell decamped to the kitchen to prepare lunch, Dickson put down on the hearth directly in front of the fire a couple of crumbling crystalline spheres. Rouletabille watched with interest.

"What have you got there, my friend? *Boules de naphtaline?* Mothballs?" asked Rouletabille.

"Yes, and mothballs contain camphor..."

The American paused. The heat from the fire was already causing the mothballs to soften, and a sickly, somewhat irritating, aroma was starting to pervade the atmosphere of the room and tickle the back of his throat.

"...and what is more evocative of lost and forgotten memories than something which stimulates the sense of smell?"

Rouletabille breathed deeply, and the disrupted connections within his brain started to re-establish themselves – neurons fired and ganglia pulsed with the fresh flow of information.

"You are right. It is coming back to me in a deluge," said Rouletabille. "And, by God, I will have my revenge on Dr. Grierson."

To be concluded in our next volume...

126

Travis Hiltz has made a specialty of finding and using eccentric characters from little known French fiction in his stories. In his year's offering, he used the heroes of Théo Varlet's 1923 novel Time Slip Troopers *(Black Coat Press ISBN 978-1-61227-078-4), in which a squadron of World War I soldiers from the Trenches is transported back to the Spanish town of Valencia in the 14th century, where they ally themselves with the Moors to fight the Spanish Inquisition. While it is one of several French novels inspired by H. G. Wells'* The Time Machine—*purporting, in fact, to be its sequel—an unsung literary crossover—it has more in common with Mark Twain's* A Connecticut Yankee in the Court of King Arthur, *in that its "timeslipped" protagonists set out to use the advantages of modern civilization, but eventually cannot prevail against the Dark Ages, unlike, say, Sprague de Camp's wily hero in the classic SF novel* Lest Darkness Fall. *And now, for Travis' own sequel to* Timeslip Troopers...*

Travis Hiltz: *The Robots of Valencia*

Spain, 1346

Being an expat was, at best, a daunting. Uprooting yourself from your country; needing to learn a new language, new customs; connecting with a new community... Adding time travel into that formula only increased the stresses and concerns.

A soldier in the French army, Monoclard to his friends, due to a weak eye that had led him to wearing a monocle, had found himself "expatriated" to medieval Spain. Matters of politics, culture, and his own personal beliefs, had made him try to build a life for himself in 14th century Valencia, determined to bring the teachings of modern-day intellectual enlightenment to the people of the Dark Ages. But the Holy Inquisition had disapproved and he and his students had found themselves, if not outright fugitives, at best, cultural nomads.

When his military comrades had fled back to the relative safety of 1913, Monoclard and his students had been left to their own devices. His pale complexion and unruly blonde hair rendered his attempts to disappear into the local population impractical. So he had sent most of his students away, for their own safety, and taken up the life of a hermit.

Now Monoclard sat on the stone sea wall, looking without seeing the unruly waves, while sipping a clay mug of vinegary wine. He had found this little coastal village, and settled down with his few remaining books and supplies from the future, in a ramshackle hut, down at the rocky end of the beach. He had recruited a few students in the village, and attempted to clandestinely keep up their studies.

Monoclard had, of late, grown despondent. His efforts seemed no more effectual then spitting at a raging bonfire. Very soon, he knew, the plague would start its deadly march across Europe. He did not have the heart to stomp on his students' enthusiasm for learning, but he also could not tell them their plans to travel to spread their learning and philosophy were most likely doomed.

Where could they go that the Black Death would not touch? What haven was there where he was not risking exposing them to a horrible, lingering death?

Monoclard sighed, took another gulp of wine, grimaced and dumped out the remainder. He stood up and began walking down the beach to his home. He wore a long robe of rough, brown material, belted at the waist with a length of rope. It gave him a monkish appearance and concealed his French army boots. He had had to abandon most of his modern possessions, fleeing the Inquisition, but refused to part with sturdy footwear.

He tucked his clay mug into a bag made of the same cloth as his robe, slung across his shoulder. It rattled as he walked. He trudged along, his shoulders hunched as if his very thoughts were weighing him down.

It was only his moping posture that allowed him to catch the glint of metal when his booted toe nudged something half-buried in the sand.

His forehead wrinkled as he squatted down and picked up the object and brushed the sand off it. It was a bolt, or a screw of some kind, roughly the size of his pinky finger.

"Odd?" Monoclard muttered, looking up and down the beach.

He paced around for several minutes, poking at stones with his foot. Finding no other bits of metal, he tossed the bolt into his sack and thoughtfully continued on his way.

Night found Monoclard sitting at a crude wooden table, peering thoughtfully at the bolt through his namesake eyepiece, over the questionable light of a single candle.

His ponderings were interrupted by a soft, discreet knock on the door.

Young Alejandro de la Vega was the wayward youngest son of a moderately wealthy noble family. Whether foolhardy or certain that his family's wealth and position would shield him, he was was Monoclard's most loyal student.

"What's that?" he asked, pulling up the only other piece of furniture in the shack, a rickety driftwood stool.

He took from a sack some bread and a bottle of wine.

"A puzzle," Monoclard replied, placing it down the table and tearing off a hunk of bread. "I'm not sure where it came from. Metalwork like this... isn't... isn't done. Not here, not now..."

"Some of your comrades, perhaps?" the Spanish youth asked.

He had heard the stories of Monoclard's arrival in Spain, with a strange group of soldiers from a far-away land, but like most of the students, believed the stories of their magical method of travel was but a fanciful tale, concealing some deep secret on why they had had to flee their home country.

" I don't know," Monoclard muttered, between chews. "We separated under... difficult circumstances. I have no idea who went where, or who even survived... I grabbed what I could and assumed the Inquisition destroyed whatever it got its hands on..."

He shrugged.

"Well, " Alejandro said. "I will have a word with some of the others. We can search the beach where you found that, as well as catch any gossip that might provide us with some clues."

Despite lacking his young friend's enthusiasm, Monoclard had to smile, appreciating his loyalty.

The rest of the night was spent with a meager meal and study from the few books from the twentieth century that Monoclard still possessed.

Days passed and Monoclard became too busy, clandestinely meeting with students and scrounging a meager living, to give much thought to the bolt. Hiking back from a session, he traveled by night along a thin, sandy stretch of coastline at low tide. Once the water began to lap at his boots, he scaled an embankment. He pulled himself up over the top by grabbing handfuls of tall, dried grass and sat on the edge, listening to the surf wash ever closer.

The moon was a fat crescent, which gave him just enough light to see the young woman walking further down the cliff top. It may have been the moonlight, or the wine he'd shared with his students, but she had a faint, ethereal aura about her. There was a hypnotic quality to how her thin, white dress fluttered in the breeze from the water.

"Mademoiselle!" Monoclard called, getting to his feet.

He jogged, unsteadily along, the combination of sand and stone causing him to stumble several times. He had come within mere yards from the young woman when she seemed to flicker, like an image from a moving picture, and was gone. In her place stood an armored figure, like a medieval knight.

It turned around, noticing the ragged time traveler, and began striding towards him. Scrambling backwards, in surprise, Monoclard tumbled over the edge and slid down the wall, landing, thankfully on a sandy patch.

He ran the rest of the way to his hut, not risking the higher ground, and was soaked and exhausted by the time he tumbled onto his thin straw mat of a bed.

The next morning found him anxiously huddled in his shack. Alejandro and the other students were quite concerned at their teachers' anxiety. The young man had come to update him on their efforts at finding other evidence of time travelers. Monoclard waved that away, said he felt unwell and would be unable to continue their studies that day.

The next few days passed uneventfully, Monoclard saw no other apparitions, but that might have been due to his reluctance to venture onto the beach after dark. His students brought him several items they thought might be connected to the bolt. But they turned out to be sea glass, and a cheap silver ring.

Then, one of his students was attacked while on "night patrol," and Monoclard realized he could no longer hide while letting young men play at detective on his behalf. Uneasy and unsure of what he could do, he made his way at the house of Alejandro's family.

He waited in the bushes by the back wall of the house, having passed a message to one of the servants. He leaned against the grey wall, watching as servants went back and forth through the back gate, until the young noble appeared. Glancing about anxiously, he approached his teacher.

"What happened to Pedro?" Monoclard asked, without any preliminary greetings.

"He volunteered to search the beach that night," Alejandro shrugged. "He says he was struck from behind, but the nearly empty wine jug we found with him gives me doubts concerning his story."

"I do not like this. I will not have any of you hurt. Tell the students to stop. Whatever may be going on requires a plan, not adolescent notions of heroism."

Monoclard, crossed his arms and chewed at his lip in anxious thought.

"What do you suggest?" Alejandro asked, feeling both chagrined at the older man's reproach, yet intrigued that recent events were moving his teacher to action.

"We need information," Monoclard muttered. "We need to think, rather than rushing to act. What I saw... the young *mademoiselle* and the... the knight... does that sound familiar? Are there any stories that it reminds you of? Any local tales or legends?"

Alejandro shook his head.

"We're a coastal village... there are a dozen stories about the ghosts of forlorn women, mourning lost lovers..." he said, shrugging.

"Nothing about a knight?"

Alejandro shook his head.

Monoclard slid down the stonewall.

"I don't know," he muttered, running a hand through his hair. "I can't do this by myself... I need help..."

"Tall Isaac is coming," a low, creaking voice said, startling both men.

Monoclard peered at what he had originally believed to be a pile of discarded rags, but was now revealed as an ancient woman, clad in a shapeless grey dress, and working on a pile of mending. She turned a face like a dried apple at Monoclard and Alejandro.

"Who?" Monoclard breathed, astounded at the sight.

"It's Old Maria," Alejandro muttered. "She's served the family for so long that people think we just built the house around her."

"Seek out Tall Isaac," Maria nodded to herself, focusing on her knitting, rather than the two men.

"Who is she talking about?" Monoclard asked, his brow furrowing.

Alejandro gestured for him to join him as they strolled past the old woman and the back gate of the house. Around the corner of the wall was a strand of trees and a wooden bench. The young student sat.

"Maria has a lot of, er, common wisdom, but she also tells tales," he said with a shrug. "Tall Isaac is a, er, children's story. He's an angel, or a wizard. Once every generation, he walks the land, protecting children, fighting monsters, rescuing princesses... things of that sort..."

Monoclard nodded, resigned.

"So, we've gone in a circle," he muttered, picking at his lower lip in sullen thought. After several quiet minutes, he glanced over at his student.

"Tell the others to stay home," he said, sternly.

That night found Monoclard on a sandy ridge above a lonely stretch of beach. He lay on his stomach, peering through the dried grass, at the moon-lit stretch below. He watched, idly picking at a stale heel of bread.

Hours passed with the time-slipped scholar spotting nothing more threatening than a stray dog and an amorous couple seeking a discreet location.

The night grew chill and Monoclard found it a struggle to keep from dozing.

"What are you looking for?" a quiet voice asked, startling him, causing him to roll away.

In the moonlight, he saw a young child, a girl standing amongst the dry grass. Monoclard blinked and rubbed his eyes to ensure he was actually seeing her.

"Who...?" he began.

"Are you lost?" She asked, matter-of-factly, leaning in to better study him. "You feel lost."

"Um... No, not really," Monoclard stuttered, sitting up. "I... uh... live near here. I am watching for a... Well, a ghost... Are you a ghost?"

"No," the child replied with a shake of her head. "And neither is the lady on the beach. My father is coming. He will help you."

"What?" he exclaimed; but the child was gone. "Where did she... Am I losing my mind?"

Monoclard sighed and ran a hand through his disheveled hair. Then he sat down, arms resting on his knees. That was when he saw the ghostly woman again. She moved along with tentative purpose. Her gestures had a flighty quality, almost as if she was performing some kind of dance while she walked. He watched her progress for several minutes; then, as stealthily as possible on loose sand, he slid down the dune and started to follow her.

Monoclard hiked his monk's robe up to his knee to avoid getting soaked by the slowly incoming tide, but was forced to risk his boots in the salt water, as the ground became too rocky for bare feet. He scuttled from shadow to dune, using the scant cover to remain hidden.

The strange woman floated along the beach, eventually coming to a rocky stretch that ended in a mass of brush. It poked out through the rocky ground and even climbed up the cliff face. Packed, so close together, it seemed almost like one prickly mass. With the thick shadows, it seemed foreboding and near impenetrable.

Monoclard stumbled to a halt, as the spectral woman had vanished!

"How...?" he breathed, giving up on stealth and jogging over to the expanse of vegetation.

He peered around for several confused moments before spotting the narrow gap. The lanky scholar squeezed into the opening, for once thankful for the rough, heavy cloth of his robe. Shielded from the scratching, and grasping brambles and branches, he pushed along, struggling to keep from cursing as gnarled branches batted him. He squeezed into a space that provided barely enough room to breathe, but gave him an opportunity to look around.

Monoclard was on the verge giving up and admitting that the woman had actually faded away like smoke, when he noticed a crack running down the face of the cliff. It seemed to grow wider as it approached the ground. This unfortunately distracted him from faint movement amongst the vegetation.

He realized his error seconds before he felt the heavy blow to his temple.

Monoclard awoke, lying on his back on the sand. He could hear the nearby surf and, as he blinked, he saw the sky beginning to lighten. He turned his head, wincing slightly. There was a small driftwood fire nearby and a large leather flask wedged into the sand nearby. As well as his damp boots.

He sat up. A threadbare cloak had been draped over him as a blanket. He looked around as he pulled on his boots. They were still a bit clammy. He studied the flask with faint suspicion, but the chill and the dull throb in his head outvoted his cautious concern, and he took a few healthy swallows. He smacked his lips appreciatively and slowly got to his feet.

He ran a hand through his hair, tentatively probing the tender spot where he'd been struck. He then made sure his namesake eyepiece still hung from its bit of string around his neck. Glancing down, he noticed that it had been his satchel that had served as his pillow. He kneeled down, giving it a quick rummage to make sure all his belongings were still there. Finding they were, he scooped the bag up and got to his feet.

A figure was striding down the beach towards him—an extraordinary figure. From a distance, he seemed remarkably tall and only seemed to grow taller as he drew closer. He leaned on a staff of gnarled wood, appropriately tall to fit his remarkable size. It was difficult to make out what he was wearing, as the man sported a snow-white beard that billowed down nearly to his knees.

"Tall Isaac!" Monoclard breathed, astounded.

The tall old man slowed his pace but continued to stroll around the open-mouthed time traveler in a wide circle.

"Señor Monoclard, I presume?" the tall wanderer said, a small smile struggling to fight its way through his beard.

"I… uh…" Monoclard began, before deciding to just nod.

"You seem to have fallen prey to some mischief," the Tall man said, slowing, but still continuing to pace a circle around the other man.

"Yes, I… appreciate your help… um… Could you possibly stop? You're making me dizzy," Monoclard asked, struggling to keep the ever-moving man in sight.

"I'm afraid not. Perhaps it would be best if you walked with me," the bearded man replied. "I'll see you home."

Monoclard gave a puzzled frown, but nodded in agreement. He kicked sand over the fire and gathered up the flask and the worn cloak.

"I assume these are yours?" he asked as they walked down the beach.

The older man nodded and accepted his possessions back.

"You are a long way from home, Señor Monoclard," he said, with quiet thoughtfulness.

"Well, yes, I'm from France," Monoclard replied, cautiously.

"I do not speak of miles," the bearded man said. "I can smell the time winds upon you."

"What?"

"Did you believe you were the only time traveler I have ever encountered?" Tall Isaac asked with a chuckle. "I have come across stranger things in my travels. My daughter tells me you are hunting a ghost?"

"I don't quite know what I'm hunting," Monoclard replied.

He felt odd about how nonplussed Isaac's reaction was to his unusual status. He felt relieved there was no need to be on guard when talking to the strange wanderer, yet a bit off put contemplating his new companion's fanciful origins.

"Tell me," the bearded man simply said.

Monoclard told of finding the bolt and beginning his investigation, believing perhaps he might find one of his comrades who had also stayed behind, or returned to the past, but now was unsure what sort of mystery he was pursuing.

Tall Isaac nodded thoughtfully, as Monoclard talked.

"Curious," he said, stroking his beard. "The woman and the knight seem connected, but does the knight stalk or is he protecting her?"

"I truly don't know," the time-slipped scholar shrugged. "It's all so odd. These… spirits don't seem threatening… The attacks seem very minor… Some bruising… I suppose I expected ghosts to be more threatening…"

Isaac chuckled again.

"Some ghosts are dire and vengeful," He explained. "Others have a task from life they wish to accomplish, while others still seek to be left alone... It would seem you have stumbled upon one of the latter."

They eventually came within sight of Monoclard's shack. Isaac nodded and then patted the scholar on the shoulder.

"I need to walk and think," he said. "I will return tonight and we shall look for your ghost."

"It's not my..." Monoclard began, stopping.

The bearded wanderer never paused. He kept walking and soon was out of sight. Monoclard sighed.

He spent the rest of the day aimlessly, drifting about his hovel and the gravel beach around it. He gathered driftwood for fire, reorganized his three sparse shelves, contemplated the ocean, dined on his last chunk of hard cheese, all the while, trying to make sense of what he had discovered.

When the sun touched the horizon, Tall Isaac returned. Monoclard had gathered a few items into his shapeless bag and was perched upon his makeshift driftwood bench, waiting and ready.

The ancient wanderer nodded his approval and made a vague gesture for the thin scholar to join him, never breaking his stride.

"I have walked the city," he said, his voice quiet and wistful. "I see young Maria has gained a few grey hairs..."

"How old are you?" Monoclard asked. "Are the stories about you true?"

"Everything you've heard about me is true," Tall Isaac replied with a sly smile, as they walked.

"It's... fantastic!" Monoclard muttered.

"As fantastic as time travel?" Isaac asked, casually.

"What?" Monoclard exclaimed, stumbling on the sand. "How do you...?"

"Oh, scholar Monoclard!" Isaac exclaimed. "As I've said, you are not the first such traveler I have met. You didn't happen to come here with an old gentlemen, a Doctor Omega?"

Monoclard shook his head and, for a brief moment, his memories flooded over him, friends lost, how far he was from home, and the lingering anxiety that he had made the wrong choice in staying.

As the duo walked the beach, Monoclard shared the story of how he and his comrades in the military had stumbled upon the abandoned time machine, their trip to Valencia, and their eventual downfall at the hands of the Inquisition. He spoke of how they'd fled the city, and his worry over who among his friends had returned to the twentieth century, who might have been left behind, and those, like himself, who had stayed in hopes of changing things.

"Valencia," Isaac said, with a sage nod. "I had heard it had been overrun by wizards."

The corner of Monoclard's mouth went up in a flicker of a smile at hearing the people who brought alcohol, the bicycle, and syphilis to medieval Spain described as "wizards."

"So, you are here because of magic," he said. "And I, by science. Which do you think my ghost is?"

"Good, you are a thinker." Isaac nodded. "I was concerned all your knowledge was reciting from books. I do not know. There are aspects that hint it could be either, or neither, or both. The one thing that keeps me going is how the world continuously surprises me."

"I'm glad you're enjoying yourself," Monoclard frowned. "But, people, myself included, have been hurt. This mystery seems small and fanciful, but I cannot shake the feeling there is more going on. Spain, despite its hostility towards me, is my home now."

Isaac nodded approvingly.

They walked in silence along the beach, Monoclard nodded to a few familiar fishermen and for a short period, Tall Isaac gained an entourage of a half dozen local children. He then shooed them away, pointing out to the gathering grey clouds as the reason they should go home.

"On top of everything else," Monoclard grumbled, "we're going to get rained on."

They trudged along until they reached the secluded stretch where the sightings had occurred. Isaac continued to pace along the shoreline, while Monoclard, a hand up to shade his eyes, peered across the beach, towards the mass of bushes where he'd been struck. Seen in daylight, the stretch of beach had lost some of its gothic menace.

"In the light of day, I see how this is a perfect location for smugglers," said Monoclard. "Which might explains the attacks…"

Isaac waved to catch Monoclard's attention, and the scholar jogged over to join him. The old man pointed his staff down at the sand. Monoclard squinted and saw faint footprints, flat heeled and blocky.

"It's doubtful these were made by your ghostly damsel," Isaac said, thoughtfully. "But the knight might have…"

Monoclard nodded

"What of the young lady?" Isaac asked, as they reached the rough foliage, poking at it with his staff. "Prisoner or accomplice?"

Monoclard frowned and shrugged.

Isaac stalked back and forth. Monoclard spotted the narrow gap in the shrubs and pushed his way in. The ground was dryer and the footprints more obvious, as well as bent branches.

"Not that I needed more evidence," Monoclard muttered, rubbing the knot on the back of his head. "But, the knight would seem to be quite solid for a ghost…"

"Careful," Isaac said from outside the shrub barrier.

"I can see the crack in the stone," Monoclard replied. "A person could easily squeeze through it. It must lead somewhere."

"Whether you are about to walk into a tomb or a pirates' den, caution is still advised. My daughter Lotte does not trust this cave."

"Your daughter?" Monoclard asked, turning to face his new ally. "Your ghost is fearful of my ghost?"

He was still pondering that when a pair of hands grabbed his shoulders from behind and pulled him into the opening in the cliff wall. He stumbled backwards, scrapping his scalp on the low entrance. He winced and then blinked, going so quickly from light to shade.

The tunnel was triangular, wider at the bottom and narrowing towards the top. Four stumbling steps left him sprawled on the sandy floor of a larger chamber. He lay on his back for a few seconds before pushing himself up into a sitting position. His eyes grew wide and the indignant protest died on his lips.

Standing, looming over him, were two hulking creatures made of metal. Their bodies were a single barrel of steel, with washtub-like heads bolted on. Their stumpy legs ended in rectangular feet, tube arms ended in crude clamps for hands. A single oval eye and a speaker grill mouth were their only features.

The "ghost girl" stood nearby, her pale features blank, yet wistful, her head cocked slightly to one side, while her body swayed to music only she could hear.

She came nearer to Monoclard, and then bent forward, peering down at him intently.

"Who are you?" he asked, curiosity, winning out over fear.

She stretched her slim hand out, until it was an inch away from his face. She held it there for several heartbeats, then clenched it into a petite fist and straightened up and pointed at him.

One of the metal creatures leaned forward and grabbed Monoclard's arm, yanking him to his feet. He punched at the torso, gaining a handful of bruised knuckles for his effort. He dug his heels in, but the automaton effortlessly dragged him along.

"Excuse me?" a familiar voice asked. "Do you mind if I come in, to be out of the rain?"

Isaac, hunching down, entered the cave. He paced about, taking in the two metal guards with an intent curiosity.

"Not really knights, are they?" he muttered, thoughtfully. "More like iron golems...."

The tall, bearded wanderer sounded as though he was studying exhibits in a museum.

"What're you doing?" Monoclard asked, bewildered by what he assumed was a poorly executed rescue attempt. "Help me!"

"If I did that, we'd never solve your mystery, would we?" Isaac asked, still pacing the chamber. "Ah, that is interesting!"

At the far end of the cave was a massive grey block, nearly the size of Monoclard's humble shack. There were wires trailing from it, up into a crack in the cave ceiling.

The girl and the second metal guard caught up to Isaac. She walked along next to him, and wore the same bland look on her face as when she had studied Monoclard. The clunky machine came up behind the tall man and grabbed hold of his arms, pinning them behind his back, and causing him to drop his staff.

"Truly?" he grumbled, indignantly. "I was being a perfectly reasonable guest."

He offered no resistance, as he and Monoclard were taken around the grey cube to a wide square marked on the ground with a border of metal. Inside the square were four men dressed in the rough clothes of local peasants.

The two newcomers were pushed inside. When Monoclard turned and attempted to step back over the metal border, he felt as if he'd walked into a brick wall. His hands pressed against the empty air, but could not get past the border.

"Magic or science?" Isaac asked, as he began to pace their narrow cage.

"I don't know... Do you have to do that?"

"Yes, I do," Isaac replied, wistfully as he continued to pace.

He peered down at the four men sitting on the ground, looking up at them wide-eyed.

"Do you know them?" asked Isaac.

"Yes, some," Monoclard replied, nodding in greeting to his cellmates. "I believe he serves Alejandro's family; the others work the fishing boats... What is going on here?"

"The guards seem to be contraptions," Isaac replied, running a hand through his beard absently. "Perhaps that large cube is too?"

"There are cables running off it, so most likely," Monoclard added. "But connected to what?"

A section of the cube slid aside, and from the opening a man limped out and over to the prisoners. He as an older man with a shock of white hair; his features were dour. His eyes, shadowed by a heavy brow, were intent with an intelligence bordering on madness. He wore a heavy long coat over a frumpy suit that marked him as having come from the future, possibly after Monoclard's native time.

"What have we here?" the newcomer asked in a heavily accented voice, gesturing disdainfully at the new prisoners with a hand that seemed encased in plastic. "Brigitte tells me one of you shows traces of chronal energy."

Monoclard got hesitantly to his feet and approached the invisible barrier, studying the old man in return.

"Who are you?" he asked. "How did you get here?"

"French, are you?" the other muttered, in reply. "My name would mean nothing to you. I am an inventor, a pioneer denied recognition, tired of my efforts being interfered with... Whether you are allied with Doctor Omega or merely some hapless traveler matters little to me. I'll keep you confined until my work here is done."

"I don't understand," Monoclard continued, unsure if the white-haired man was even listening. "What are you working on? Is that big block your time machine?"

"I'm not a tour guide, nor am I a tutor," the man grumbled. "Why won't your friend stand still?"

Monoclard merely shrugged.

"Are you here to repair your... vessel?" Isaac asked, as he paced.

The two men locked gazes for a second.

"Will these men be released unharmed?" the Tall Man asked.

The other man took a step back, unnerved by looking into the eyes of the bearded wanderer. He had seen something that had managed to crack his shield of arrogant superiority. The young woman glided over to him, and, leaning against the old scientist's shoulder, whispered in his ear.

"What I chose to do with my ship or these... intruders is no concern of yours," he replied with a dismissive wave of his artificial hand.

"So, be it," Isaac said, altering his path.

He stepped over the huddled prisoners and walked towards the invisible wall of their cell. Once he reach the boundary, he walked until he was pressed up against the strange barrier that held them in, and, for the first time since Monoclard had met him, his feet ceased moving.

For several heartbeats, Isaac stood still. Then, he began to tremble up and down the length of his enormous frame, as if the mere act of not walking was taking a herculean effort. He raised one foot, and then forced it back down upon the dirt floor.

Unsure what was occurring, but nevertheless nervous, Monoclard stepped back, urging the other prisoners to move with him.

The air began to hum and then Monoclard felt the walls of their prison shatter!

"Take your toys," Isaac said sternly, as he stepped past the metal strip and away from the cell. "Get in your little ship and be away from this place, this time."

He strode towards the scientist with the wild hair.

"I do not look fairly upon men who mistreat those weaker than themselves, and for all your claims of wisdom and superiority, you are a craven and petty creature."

As he walked, he retrieved his staff from the dirt, brushing it off as he closed in on the time traveler and his feminine ward. Anger and fear struggled in the other man's features. With a sharp gesture, he ordered his bulky metal guards forward to deal with this long-bearded intruder.

Monoclard scrambled to his feet, helped the others up and shoved them towards the cave's entrance. The storm had come and the men ran off into the downpour to freedom. The Frenchman could make out flickers of lightning off in the distance before he turned to offer what little help he could to Tall Isaac.

Swinging his staff, Isaac struck the nearest guard with a clang like a Chinese gong. The metal creature staggered back, bearing a large dent on its chest. The second guard grabbed for Isaac, but the wanderer struck downwards, his staff smashing through the creatures' wrist and leaving it with a sparking stump.

Monoclard raced over, slipping behind the duo of man and girl, and, wrapping one arm around the old scientist's neck, he brought out his service revolver and jammed it into the small of their captor's back.

"Call them off!" he growled at the old man.

"What! Release me!" the savant replied indignantly. "You dare lay hands upon Rotwang!"

"I will dare quite a bit, you overblown, self-absorbed crackpot! Call them off!"

"Release him!" Brigitte said, speaking for the first time. Her voice had an odd, tinny quality, like the speaker of a much-used phonograph. "I said, release him!"

With that, her form began to fade and blur, revealing a familiar, threatening figure.

"Not a knight," Monoclard breathed, wide-eyed. "But another automaton!"

Made entirely of metal, she still retained a distinctly feminine form.

Monoclard raised the revolver, and fired at her. Brigitte staggered back and shook her head, which failed to dislodge the bullet embedded in the center of her domed, metal forehead.

She continued walking towards them, one arm extended. Rotwang pulled free of Monoclard's grasp and hobbled over to the metal maiden. He gently took her head in his hands, examining the wound, and then turned to glare at Monoclard. Whatever he intended to snarl at the scholar was forgotten as the lights in the cave began to flicker.

"The lightning!" he muttered. "I have wasted too much time! Volkites, subdue them!"

The barrel-shaped guards charged ponderously at Isaac, pinning him against the wall of the cave. Rotwang and the metal lady pushed past the startled Monoclard, re-entering the grey cube. He turned to pursue them, but then decided; he'd rather let the demented scientist escape, and be free of him, and moved to help Isaac.

He fired twice more, one bullet lodging in the knee joint of the nearest creature, the other ricocheting off the back of the others' bucket head. When his knee buckled, the Volkite stumbled into his partner, allowing Isaac to catch the two in a bear hug, raising them so their feet were several inches off the floor. He staggered under his burden until he was able to slam them against the side of the strange blocky time machine. Metal buckled and bent, and the grinding of machinery could be heard within the two automatons.

Isaac dropped them to the dirt and turned to rejoin his new friend. Both men became distracted by a strange groaning, wheezing sound. The cave shook, dirt and stone raining down upon the duo.

"I know you are very intent on walking," Monoclard shouted. "But I think we should run!"

They did, and soon found themselves out in the rain, staring up at the stony embankment just as jagged lightning struck some object at the top. Again, the earth shook and the entire cliff collapsed in upon itself like an enormous house of cards.

Once away from the collapse, Isaac slowed to a walk, and Monoclard, shoulders hunched, as his robe grew heavy with rain, hobbled along, trying to keep up.

"So, is he gone, or merely buried under rock and mud?" the wanderer asked.

Monoclard shrugged and ran a hand through his wet hair.

"Do you think he was the one that built the machine that brought you here?"

"Doubtful," Monoclard muttered, taking out his eyepiece and wiping it on his sleeve. "Wondrous as his machine was, he seemed only mildly competent at operating it. Attracting the lightning seemed to be in order to... recharge it somehow, and we saw how that turned out."

"So, we should consider him, not malevolent, but more troublesome," Isaac nodded. "Almost refreshing compared to some I've faced."

"Glad to see the back of him and his tin bullyboys," Monoclard grumbled, hugging himself against the chill rain. "I take it you won't be stopping to rest, even after all that?"

"My day of rest is a ways off yet, young Monoclard," Isaac nodded. "Your mystery is solved and your home is safe. Best be on my way."

"Maybe I should be too," Monoclard sighed. "You and I have attracted a bit of attention... I'm not sure how welcome I'll continue to be, especially if the Inquisition comes to investigate."

"You have a choice to make—to go or to stay," Isaac said, wistfully. "I envy you that. Ah, there's Lotte! I was wondering where she had wandered off to."

Monoclard looked up and, through the rain, could make out the vague form of a child splashing playfully along the beach.

Isaac gave him a brief smile, a clap on the shoulder, and wandered off to collect his daughter and be on his eternal way. Monoclard stood, watching the duo walk off. Then he gave a robust sneeze.

Tomorrow, he could ponder his mysterious new acquaintances, what explanation to give his students, and his own future. But for now, all he wanted to do was take advantage of Alejandro's hospitality, find a quiet corner by the fire and a hot cup of coffee.

*Paul Hugli's latest tale takes place about ten years earlier than the one pub-
lished in our previous volume. This time, it features Honey West's father, Harry
Dickson, and the perennial French superstar, the Nyctalope—plus several other
guest-stars. However, the emphasis is not on Egyptian history and myth, as before, but on the strange death of Edgar Poe, linked here to the notorious "Philadelphia Experiment." Quite a heady cocktail, to be sure, but one knowingly
mixed with brio by Paul in a tale entitled...*

Paul Hugli: *The Night of the Craven Raven*

"To be or not to be, that is the question!" *Hamlet*

Port of Baltimore, October 2, 1949, Pre-Dawn

"Who is John Galt?"

"Just another selfish guy," replied Donovan, waving his Cuban cigar, ashes
flinging, "Like that Howard Roark, who we gave the world to... ah, to design
the new War Department building, in '42. But, no, he wasn't satisfied! He wanted to bring in his own people, dictate funding, and..." He shrugged, taking a
puff of his Havana, bluish smoke billowing lazily to the ceiling of the map
room, then added: "But his idea of a pentagon was genius!"

Henry West, who had asked the question, knew of Howard Roark, and was
not surprised at "Wild Bill" Donovan's reaction; they had worked together in the
OSS during the War, and he knew the CIA's director's mind well. No matter
what else Donovan was, he was a politician of the "Good Old Boys" network:
kickbacks, "favorite son" status, and all the rest that greased the wheels of government. There was no room for mavericks like Roark, and he guessed this Galt
character was made of the same cloth. He repeated his question:

"Who is John Galt?"

"When the experiment we are about to undertake," Donovan said, off a
puff, "was first okayed, we asked Galt to contribute, but he was even more arrogant than Roark. It was all his way or the highway. He put a new meaning to the
'art of selfishness.' In fact, he dropped out of circulation to operate some kind of
commune, called New Atlantis or some such."

"Mr. Galt," Lt. Commander Ian Fleming began, after lighting up a Chesterfield, "had invented an engine which operated on *atmospheric electricity*. It
converted static electricity from the atmosphere into power, without need of fossil fuels, and it was a great deal safer than nuclear energy."

"Wait," West said, scratching his ear, "this sounds a lot like what that Tesla guy, who died a few years back, had invented."

"My father visited Nikola Tesla, while he was performing his electrical experiments in Colorado Springs, toward the end of the last century," said the Frenchman, Leo Saint-Clair, adjusting his filtered goggles. "and witnessed his achievements in wireless transmission of electrical power."[4]

"Yes," West said. "I remember you telling me about that."

"Soon after," the Nyctalope continued, "the inventor—or *discoverer*, as he referred to himself—was placed under contract by J.P. Morgan to build a power-transmitting tower in New Jersey. It did not go well for Tesla, especially when the business tycoon discovered he'd been developing a method to create *free* energy, or at virtually *no* cost. Of course, this did not sit well with Morgan—no profit. Tesla was never the same after that, producing little in the way of new inventions."

"Some say," Harry Dickson, the so-called "American Sherlock Holmes," said as he entered the Map Room, puffing on his pipe, "Tesla was working on the GUT—Grand Unified Theory—something not even Einstein was able to deduce." He joined the other men at the table. "Or was that all smoke and mirrors?"

Donovan stared at Dickson, took a puff on his cigar, then laughed. "Indeed, indeed! Back in '43, we pulled a dupe on the Nazis. We called it *Project Rainbow*, to 'entertain' the U-Boat sitting off the coast of the Philadelphia Naval Yards, snooping. So we gave them a show. Making them believe we had made a ship invisible." After another deep drag on the Cuban he continued: "Damn, how were we to know how close to reality we had come—to what we're about to attempt here, today."

"How does Tesla fit in?" West asked.

West listened as Donovan continued, translating in his head the military jargon and bravo. After Tesla died in April 1943, his apartment had been raided by the FBI. They'd found nothing but cooped-up pigeons and a safe containing nothing more than his American citizenship papers and his 1917 Edison Medal, presented to Tesla by the American Institute of Electrical Engineers. The Feds had also come up empty after searching through scores of barrels, crates and trunks of notes, drawings, monograms at the Office of Alien Property. Tesla's property was eventually released to his nephew's cousin, and taken back to Tesla's native Yugoslavia.

Then, after the War, under *Operation Paperclip*, the United States had split with the Russians the best of the German scientists, engineers and technicians, such as Werner von Braun and his V-2 rocket team. And along with the 1000 scientists or so, the Allies had recovered records and research journals *not* destroyed by the Germans in the final days as Berlin was being stormed. Some of these confiscated documents had dealt with the Nazi's *Wunder-Waffens,* or

---

[4] See *"As Easy as 1, 2, 3..."* in Volume 13.

"Wonder Weapons"—the Allies' own *Wunder-Waffen* was, of course, the A-Bomb.

Among the confiscated Nazi documents and papers were some clearly penned by Nikola Tesla, obviously stolen from the OAP before the inventor's death, thus not there when the Feds had raided the warehouse. In these papers where snippets of ideas for "death-rays," robotics, flying saucers, force-shields, and an invisibility shield."

It appeared the Nazis had had some success with the latter—what the Allies had dubbed *"foo-fighters,"* small fireballs" which seemed to appear out of thin air, buzzing around war planes over Europe, changing through a range of colors, before vanishing. The confiscated Nazi papers had explained these *foo-fighters*.

Coincidentally, the Nazi's experimental crafts had been developed under *Projekt Regen-Beugen*, or *Project Rain-Bow*, based entirely on Tesla's Electromagnetic Wave Modulation Theory: that postulated that, as an engine rotated on its magnetic core, the vibrational frequency increased, while the wavelength decreased... as did its photonic, or "light" energy, causing an object to appear a different color as it turbine raced from low frequencies to higher ones, and higher wave-lengths, thus running through the invisible to the visible to the invisible to the human eye: Ultra-violet, Blue, Green, Yellow, Orange, Red, and Infra-red. Yet, even invisible, the object would carry a heat signature, which could be targeted.

The Germans had stepped up their experiments with Tesla's EM Modulation Device attached to a derelict cruiser anchored in the Baltic. When they had thrown the switch, the ship had gone through a series of color emulations, wavering in and out of visibility, until it had disappeared—completely—only to reappear seconds later.

Everything had seemed fine; the experiment had been assessed as a smashing success. The Nazi scientists had patted each other on the backs, shaken hands and were probably reaching for the champagne, when the recon party had boarded the cruiser. Yet, the celebration had come to an abrupt end as things were no longer so rosy. They had seen horrors—not that they actually cared about the P.O.W. crewmembers—some of them were frozen half-way between bulkheads and the deck, as if it had happened while passing *through* them. While others had gone *nullpunkt*—nothing—zero—just disappeared into thin air.

The Germans never had had a chance to do further work on this project as the War was drawing to an end; though they had had some success with EM Modulation with a large, saucer-shaped, manned vehicle, which a couple of German scientists had perfected, using to escaped at the end of the War. While on a recon mission from Argentina in 1947, something had gone amiss with the saucer and it had crashed outside Roswell, NM. The saucer had shattered into pieces and the two pilots had unfortunately died. They would have made great additions to *Operation Paperclip*.

And now, here, in Baltimore Harbor, aboard the *USS Stockton*, a team was gathered to witness the improvements based on the stolen Tesla papers, and the combined effort of dozens of German and American scientists.

The experiment was scheduled to commence a half-hour later, at 05:00, and Henry West decided he still had time to call his daughter in Bellflower, CA, knowing she'd still be awake at 1:30 a.m. PST, working on her term paper dealing with western birds for her biology class at Long Beach Junior College. She was majoring in—he didn't know—but knowing his daughter, it probably was boys, much to his discomfort. But he'd always given her a free-rein, since she had grown up without a mother. The thoughts of his wife, Honey's mother, still brought a pain to his heart... if only... but wishing things undone was an exercise in futility; he had to keep the truth about her mother from Honey, for her own sake.

West placed the call to California. It rang three times before it was picked up:

"Oh, hi, Daddy."

"You've been a good girl while I've been away?" he asked.

"I've had no complains...so far," Honey replied with a giggle.

"Honeeeeey!"

"Oh, Daddy, be hep. I have protection."

"Honeeeeey!"

"Oh, not like that, Daddy." Honey again giggled. "I meant the pearl-handled .22 you got me for my eighteenth birthday."

Henry West tried to smile, not sure how serious Honey was—she rarely was—and decided to let the subject of biology pass, tapping a book on the table.

"I found a copy of book on birds you needed for your term paper. Oddly, I found it at place called Raven Books."

"Oh, great, Daddy!" Her voice seemed excited over the phone. "That will be the cat's meow, and sure help me in my *bi-ol-lo-gee* class."

"I'll see you in a few days."

"OK! Bye Daddy, and say hi to Uncle Ian."

West hung up just as Lt. Commander Fleming entered to room.

"Just talked to Honey. She said hi."

"She's in college now, right?" Fleming wasn't Honey's blood uncle, but she called him that. He picked up the book on the table.

"Yeah, and a handful!" replied West.

"When did you take up bird-watching, Hank?"

"It's for Honey's biology class."

"Like she needs a biology class."

"Don't remind me, Ian."

144

Fleming laughed, shaking his head, looking at the book in his hand. *Field Guide to Birds of the West Indies*. By some bloke named James Bond... *What a bland name*, he thought. He set the book down. "Time to get this show on the road."

West and Fleming rejoined Dickson, Saint-Clair and Donovan on the observation deck just as binoculars were being passed around, to observe the trial phase of *Project Iris*.

The derelict, *USS Steger*, lay some 200 meters from the *USS Stockton*. The WW II cruiser had been outfitted with a turbine powered by a modification of Tesla's Electromagnetic Modulation Device.

The command was given to engage, and the Navy Brass and civilians raised their binoculars; save Saint-Clair, who required no such optical aid.

A steady hum ensued as the EMD engaged the electromagnetic pulse. Suddenly the hairs on the back of the necks and arms of the volunteer crew on the *Steger* stood on end in the cool pre-dawn as the atmosphere became ionized. Then, through their binoculars, the assembled party on the *Stockton* were treated to a gambit of rainbow colors, blue through red, before a green mist enveloped the *Steger* like dense fog twisting, twirling, tunneling, before quickly dispersing. And in its place was...

Nothing!

"She's gone invisible," one of the Navy Brass exclaimed.

"No," West said, scanning the spot where the *Steger* once was. "There's no displacement in the water, where the hull should be, invisible or not."

"*C'est vrai*," Saint-Clair confirmed. "The *Steger* is no longer here!"

"What?" Donovan exclaimed.

"It's just not there!" West restated. "It's been transported... teleported..."

Suddenly, before any more exclamations could be uttered, the greenish mist returned and quickly burned off as the *Steger* shimmered in reverse order of rainbow colors, from red to blue, and the ship wavered back into view.

Through his binocular Henry West was studying her, noting a crewman who was staggering as if drunk, then just disappeared.

"They're going *Zero!*" West shouted.

And with no hesitation or thought of his own safety, he kicked off his shoes and dove into the water, surfaced, struggled out of his jacket and trousers, then swam a bee-line for the *Steger*, two hundred meters away.

Scrambled up the ladder of the ship, he hopped on deck, where he saw a crewman begin to waver in and out of existence. He immediately placed his hands on the sailor, feeling a tingling surge through his body as the man stiffened and fell to the deck, stunned but alive.

Then West pulled a crewman through a bulkhead as he was about to redematerialize, and continued the "laying of the hands" on other sailors, keeping them whole and in this dimension.

As the rescue men from the *Stockton* arrived and boarded the *Steger*, West yelled out orders and directions on tending to the afflicted seamen, He spotted a staggering figure holding his head. He wasn't a sailor. He as dressed in a black great-coat and black trousers; a very Victorian attire. He appeared to be five-eight, slight built, with black wavy hair and a bushy, but trimmed mustache.

"Someone—see to that man!" yelled West.

Sometime later, Henry West decided the sailors were no longer in danger, though they would have to be isolated and studied for a while, to make sure there were no lasting effects from their experiences.

He took a launch back to the *Stockton*, and joined Leo Saint-Clair on the way to the captain's ready-room, where the strangely-dressed man was being held. A MP was standing guard outside. St. Clair opened the door and discovered an... empty chair!

"Where is he?" Bill Donovan exclaimed, coming up behind them. He got no answer, and turned to the MP, asking: "Where is he?"

"He must've disappeared," the MP stammered.

"Disappeared? Oh, never mind! Did you, at least, get his name, and what he was doing aboard *that* ship?"

"He said..." the M.P. began, then gulped before adding, "...that his name was Edgar A. Poe."

"Poe?" Saint-Clair asked. "Did he say anything else?"

"No, sir. Only that—and nothing more!"

New York, 1955

"Egads!" Manse Everard gasped as he slammed down his empty shot-glass, the scotch having done its job. As an Unattached Agent of the Time Patrol, working for the Office of Spatio-Temporal Anomalies, he was, in other words, a Time Cop. He had no set assignments, though his life was expendable. He was a thirty-year old, stocky-built man, with broad-shoulders, pulling-down the princely sum of $15,000 per annum. For this, his job was to deal with people who messed with the main time-line of reality, following the orders of entities that called themselves the Danellians, a million years in the future, who claimed to be the ultimate descendents of humanity—a race of beings as far above us as we were above the amoeba. Although some claimed there were just Spiders. Or Snakes. No one knew.

Since returning from an adventure in Ancient Egypt, in time of the heretic pharaoh Akhenaten and his beautiful Queen Nefertiti, Everard had just been kicking back, enjoying his vodka.[5] The bottle was half-empty or half-full, depending on how you looked at it. He considered it half-empty.

---

[5] See "*Dream's End*" in Volume 11.

Considering he was "unattached" at the moment, he decided to do a favor for his secretary, and pick up some books for her son's English Literature class. So he wandered across the street to Empire Books. The interior of the bookstore was dimly lit, cluttered, with books stacked every which-way, including loosely resting on shelves, piled on the floor, or on rickety tables.

Everard headed for the stacks, but was side-tracked by a table piled high with old {mostly tattered and dog-eared} "funny books:" *Batman, Superman, Captain Marvel Adventures, Crime & Punishment, Archie, Casper, Little Dot,* and scores more. But what had caught his eye was a stack of *Classic Comics* and *Classic Illustrated* at "two-for-15-cents," as opposed to the other used comics at 5-cents each. He guess it was the cost of education.

Everard began shifting through the stack of *Classics*, figuring his secretary's boy would probably want to do his book report from one of these, rather than from actual books. The pile included *The Three Musketeers, The Count of Monte Cristo, A Tale of Two Cities, Robin Hood, Mocha Dick, Around the World Under the Sea, The Island of Lost Souls, Men on the Moon, When Mars Attacks...* He scratched his head as he had never heard of the last five titles. Plus there were others he was strangely unfamiliar with.

Then his belt buzzer vibrated. It was from the Masters of the Time Patrol.

Baltimore, October 3, 1949, 9 a.m.

Horns, horns, horns, horns, horns, horns—from the honking and clattering of the horns...

This is what greeted Edgar A. Poe as he came out of the netherworld of the *Zero State*, remembering only patches of recent events: being in a rowboat in the bay... roaming the deck of a strange ship... sitting in a chair... then here. But where was *here*?

The honking of the automobile horns caused him to cover his ears, to block the noise. The pungent and noxious vapors of the Fords, Chevys, DeSotos, Studebakers, GMs, Hudsons, and everything in between, including Yellow Cabs, invaded his nose, with somewhat of a sweet smell, altogether preferable to the horse manure which covered the streets of his day. Poe was convinced he had been projected into the future—somehow.

How distant was a future filled with hundreds of horseless carriers and overhead large metal birds? He didn't know, but here he stood, on the sidewalk of a busy thoroughfare, scratching his head in wonderment and awe. But he was getting a headache from the honking horns and exhaust fumes, and thought it best to seek shelter, then try to reason out if this was reality—or some nightmarish hallucination.

In the Ready-Room aboard the *USS Stockton*, Henry West and Leo Saint-Clair were discussing the mystery *and* missing man who had claimed to be Edgar Allan Poe.

"Poe was born in the same year as Lincoln and Darwin, it can't be him, can it?" West pondered aloud, sipping a beer. "Perhaps, he's just one of those Poe look-alikes who gather at this time of the year, here in Baltimore, who somehow wandered aboard." Of course he realized how impossible that was, especially during a military exercise or experiment. "Whoever he was, he appeared dazed and confused before he disappeared—went *Zero*—suggesting he was somehow, in some way, connected to the experiment."

"I agree," Saint-Clair said, "I also believe that our experiment created a temporal rift in the fabric of time, and in some way transported Poe to our time."

"Is this really possible?" West asked, setting down his beer. "You have told me some amazing things during our undercover adventures in the War. But *time travel* !"

"Temporal fluxes are not as common as you may think. They occur when certain events coincide—usually in conjunction with solar activity—combined with a strong electromagnetic event..."

"Like the one produced during our experiment?"

"*Exactement*. Yet, we have a problem here, Henry. Most *controlled* time travel is accomplished via some sort of machine, or ship, which shields the traveler or travelers from Deadly Orgone Energy, or DOE."

"That sounds like a female deer," West quipped, but was ignored.

"All living things—trees, plants, animals, us—are composed of beneficial Orgone Energy, or OE, and this energy deteriorates over the course of one's life, slowly replaced with DOE, until you eventually die. Orgone Energy is quite similar to radio-carbon's chemical properties and half-lives. But that's the rub! If this man is in reality the Poe of a hundred years ago, he's traveled through time without first being processed—a very scientific procedure I will spare you."

"Thanks," West said with a smile.

"Traveling through time in a machine or a ship is safe because men need not be prepared, or processed, because DOE is inert to *non*-organic materials most time-vessels are composed of."

"OK. But how does this..."

"I am getting there, West. If Poe traveled through time without proper preparation, the degradation of his OE by the DOE will be accelerated to a point that, within seventy-two hours, unless we return him to his own time—which will halt the degradation—he will disintegrate into, literally, *nothingness*... into some type of twilight or phantom zone... of which we know nothing about."

"Then we must find him, and find a way to return him to his own time." West pounded back his beer. "That should be no more than a walk in the park."

"If this temporal flux is typical," said the Nyctalope, "Poe would have been plucked from exactly one-hundred years in the past. And, if I remember my history correctly, he will die within a couple days from the day he was taken and to which we must return him."

"But we must try. So he can die like a man; not just dissolve away into nothingness."

"You are correct, *mon ami*."

Poe found himself a stranger in a strange land, an archaism, a man with the sense and sensibilities of a mid-19th century Southern Gentleman thrust into a Brave New World, that of the mid-20th century's hustle and bustle. It was confusing to the man of a hundred years ago, a man out-of-time in more ways than one. He proceeded down the street, trying not to gawk and gasp at his surroundings, some familiar, others fantastical. He held his head down, hands cuffed to his ears, as he moved through the pedestrian traffic. Yet, the infernal honking would not subside. It was not just the cultural shock than buzzed his head.

Poe tried not to stare at the press of people he was passing through, especially the women, shamelessly showing not only their ankles and calves, but some even mid-thigh! *Like wanton harlots on the streets! Scandalous!* The women dressed in trousers, however, didn't really faze him—he'd seen many similarly dressed among the literati of the salons, whom sexuality he had questioned. One can only imagine his thoughts about the bikini which was, er, unveiled that year.

Poe was also intrigued by the *amalgamation* of the races, the "integration" of "colored folks." This future was, indeed, forward thinking!

From the automobiles the radios blazed the latest tunes: *Some Enchanted Evening, Honey Bun, You've Got a Lovely Bunch of Coconuts, Mule Train...* To add to his confusion, he had no idea where the music—if it could be called music!—was coming from; it became just a blurring together of various tunes into a loud, atonal mess.

Broadsheets plastered on the walls were one-sheets for movies, some recent, others in second runs: *I was a Male Order Bride, Samson and Delilah, 12 O'Clock High, On the Town...* Poe had no idea what a motion picture was and decided they were adverts for some type of interactive plays.

He turned a corner and came upon the half-block long Bond St. Books and Magazine newsstand, filled with a bright array of colorful magazines, pulps and comic books, either displayed on shelves, or in cubby holes, or hanging from wires held by clothes' pins. All the standards were prominently displayed: *Life* (with a cover featuring Robert Oppenheimer), *Look, Saturday Evening Post, Time, Newsweek, Reader's Digest, Popular Science*, and a score others. An inside room, watched over by the newsdealer-cum-teller, offered paperbacks and more esoteric publication, including *Titter, Glamour Parade, Peek-a-Boo, Sexology* and *Science and Health*.

Out front, a newsboy hawked the latest issue of *The Daily Bugle*, waving it, handing issues out, collecting the nickels, all the while yelling: "Read all about it! Chuck Yeager breaks the sound barrier! Goes more than 650 miles-per-hour in a Bell X-1! Read all about it!"

Poe was amazed: *650 miles-per-hour? Impossible! All the air would have been sucked away!* Then he noticed the date on the paper: *October 3rd, 1949.* He now knew he was one-hundred years in the future.

But his eyes could help but be drawn to the colorful, even gaudy, covers of the numerous pulps: *All-Story, Big-Book Western, Forbidden Adventures, Her Story, The Masked Rider,* and scores of other westerns, romance, detective, sports, adventure and other pulps, including *Astounding Science Fiction* and *Amazing Stories,* the latter's cover featuring a scantily-clad, large-breasted blonde being ravished by a big-eyed, green space alien, with a helmeted space-man coming to her rescue, ray-gun a-zapping, and a phallic spaceship in the background. And nearby hung a copy of *Superman Comic,* with Orson Welles, dressed in Victorian clothing, signaling that the Martians were invading, with Superman flying in for the rescue.

It was all so confusing to Poe. *Has man advanced so far in only a hundred years? Space craft? Flying men?* Then he noticed a copy of *Star-Spangled Comic featuring Tomahawk,* and a smile came to his face. He had been dubbed "the Tomahawk Man" for his acidity, cutting reviews of books he detested for their mediocrity. If Poe was one thing, he was an elitist.

Then something dawned on him. His clothing. They were definitely out-of-date, yet no one even gave him a second glance. As if they saw an Edwardian gentleman every day.

Poe walked away from the newsstand, turned the corner and discovered why he had drawn scant attention.

Henry West and Leo Saint-Clair, wearing a pair of dark aviator glasses, hit the bricks in search of the displaced writer. In his hand, the Frenchman held a portable chrono-monitor, which—as he had explained to the Long Beach P.I. —tracked the chronal energy associated with time-traveling, which—unlike Orgone Energy—was emitted by both organic and inorganic matter in temporal trans-flux. The device's needle, directed down the thoroughfare, passed Bond St. newsstand, and West spotted a dark-haired man in a black great coat.

"There he is!"

They rushed after him, turned the corner, closing in on Poe, when another "Poe" crossed past them. Then another. And another. And suddenly, they were everywhere: short versions, tall ones, fat, thin, even a female, a black and an Oriental version of the *Master of the Macabre.*

The gumshoes were confused until they notice the banner stretched across the street. The same banner which had greeted Poe, himself: *Edgar Allan Poe Week – Look-a-like Contest – October 4th – Revival Theatre.*

Poe had been astonished by the banner and the many *faux-doppelgangers* of him. For the first time since his arrival in in this strange future land, he was beginning to get an inkling that he was somewhat famous, appreciated—more so than he was in his own time—with fame coming to him only a few years back, with the publication of *The Raven*—when he had become the toast of the salons. Children would rush up to him and yell: *Raven! Raven! Raven!* And he, in turn, dressed in black, would turn slowly, tip his Panama hat, wave his silver cane at them, wink and reply: "*Nevermore!*" The kids would get a kick out of this and wander off, having been "spooked" by *The Raven*.

But that fame was too little and way too late. Though well-known and re-spected—mainly for his poems and essays—he'd only managed to pull down $6000 in over 25 years as "America's first professional writer" —as opposed to others who wrote as side-lines and on a lark. And the great bulk of that $6000 had come from his various essays and editorial jobs, not his poems and tales. Yet, here, in 1949, his image was everywhere—but was not lining his pockets.

What he saw next convinced him that his legacy was not his poems, save *The Raven,* but his tales of the macabre—what he referred to as *grotesques* (melodramas of crime and insanity), and others referred to as "horror" and "ter-ror." It was a Halloween candy display.

The window display of Kay's Candies had all the traditional trapping of Halloween: large grayish-white tombstone, surrounded by carved jack-o-lanterns, plastic skulls, bales of hay, cob-webs, Indian corn, and a stuffed Raven astride a scarecrow's shoulder. At the foot of the tombstone was a multitude of wicker-baskets filled to the brims with boxes of various colored candy-coated licorice. Etched in the tombstone was:

Don't be caught in a Midnight Dreary, pouring over some forgotten lore; don't be a-napping when the Ghouls, Ghosts & Goblins come rapping, tapping at your chamber door. Don't suffer a trick, give a treat... treat them to a box of Poe-mmms: *Red Hearts, White Mummies, Black Cats, Brown Coffins, Gray Sphinxes, and Green Frogs.*

Issuing from the Raven's mouth was: "*Give them Poe-MMMS—only the best, and nothing more!*"

All for the outrageous sum of five-cents per box!

Poe shook his head at the absurdity, and his stomach growled, He needed some substance. Yet he barely had any real money on his person, even less than when he'd left West Point and traveled to Boston under a couple false names: Henry Leonard (after his brother, William Henry Leonard Poe) and a slightly altered version of Henri Le Rennet.

Next to the candy confectionary shop was Bobby Rose's Costumery, whose display window was decorated in orange and black crepe ribbons—under the theme of *Frighten Up Some Treats!*—and exhibited strangely attired manne-quins: a witch, a mummy, a devil, a ghost (something called Casper), a pirate, a ballet-dancer, Superman, and an Edwardian-dressed mannequin, with a black, curly wig and fake mustache, and a small plastic raven perched on its shoulder, with a sign at its feet reading: *"Mad Man & His Raven."*.

Poe was taken aback: *this future world believes me a mad man? Why?* At the moment, he had no answer for this question, though he soon would. Nor did he know what "trick or treat" was. He knew of *All Hallows' Eve*, the time when spirits supposedly rose from the dead, in preparation for the following *All-Saints' Day*, celebrating the Church's many saints and martyrs, but this unholy commercialization was something new to him.

Who would pay the princely sum of $1.68 for a red-and-blue costume of this, er, Superman? And one may wonder what this mid-18th century man might think of the return to the paganism and the commercialization of the two High Holy Days of Christianity: Easter and Christmas!

His stomach rumbled and growled, again reminding he hadn't eaten in… what? A hundred year, it seemed, but was in reality some twenty hours. But how—short of thievery? Everything was so expensive. he thought, as he stared into the window of Kent's General Store, posters of so-called sales plastered across the glass: Fountain pen (95c), typewriter (whatever that was, at $19.49), Kodak box camera (huh? At $2.00), something called Silly Putty at 49c. And the prices for food items were just outrageous: bacon (25c/lb), eggs (49c/dozen), sirloin steak (30c/lb), butter (30c/lb), bread (10c/loaf), and coffee (20c/lb).

The money in his pockets consisted of a 1849 half-cent, a 1849 five-cent piece, and a 1846 silver dollar; the non-princely sum of 56 cents. Perhaps they might have some collector's value, if there were numismatists in era,? Surely there were still practicing that trade, and 100 year-old-coins might realize more than face value; though how much more, Poe hadn't the foggiest idea.

He patted the pocket of his great-coat, felt the bulge, then shrugged. Perhaps he could get some spending capital for *this*? He needed spending money if he was to survive the inflationary prices of this *land beyond time,* and find a way home.

He hurried across the street, dodging honking horn and slurred questions about his legitimacy, usually accomplished by a one-finger salute. The noise was giving him a headache, but he mustered on towards the shops across the way.

He stopped in front of Destiny Books & Things, the window displaying occult literature, crystal balls, *oui-ja* boards, tarot cards and other numerous paraphernalia for contacting the Spirit World. A neatly printed sign read: *Futures & Fortunes Told! Wednesday & Thursday –1-3 p.m. – 50 cents.*

This was right up Poe's alley, as he was more than a "tourist" when it came to occult and mystic arcana. He had attended many *séances,* believed in phrenology (he's had the bumps on his head "read" a few time; got good scalp massages), spiritualism, mesmerism, palmistry, and anything of the supernatural bent, which had influenced his stories and poems. But, alas, it wasn't Wednesday or Thursday, so the reading of his future and fortunes would have to wait— though he hoped both would be realized at his next stop.

Then it appeared before him like an omen: a bookstore named *The Raven— Books... and Nothing More.*

Walking through the door Poe was greeted by a neatly maintained, though crammed, bookstore. The lighting was slightly dimmed, and there was a claustrophobic feeling to the closely placed bookshelves running some forty feet to the rear of the store, labeled with various genre of fiction: *Mystery, Detective, Western, Adventure, Romance, Science Fiction & Horror*, et al. And of non-fiction: *Science & Technology, Economics, .Self-Help, Politics, History & Government*, et al.

Up front was a series of oaken tables piled high with second-hand magazines: *Boy's Life, Blue Book, Esquire, Popular Detective, Liberty, McCall's, Saturday Evening Post, True, Argosy*, and a score others , as well as pulps: *Amazing Stories, Astounding, Unknown, Marvel Science Fiction, Barb Western, Crime Detective, the Shadow, Doc Savage, Justice, Inc., Startling Tales, Thrilling Wonder Stories, Captain Future, Lone Ranger, Phantom Detective, Real Romance*, and dozens more. These could be had for 10 cents each, or 3/25 cents.

On the next table, equally piled high, were "funny books" —*5c each or 6 for 25c*. All the usual suspects were present: *Superman, Batman, Wonder Woman, Green Lantern, Flash, Human Torch, Captain America, Sub-Marnier, Blackhawk, Plastic Man, Captain Marvel, Sheena, Planet, Crime Does Not Pay, Adventures into the Unknown*, and dozens more in all categories, including Western and Romance.

It all confused Poe: *How could a society be as technological advanced as this one seemed to be, and yet this* pap *appears to pass for literature*?

Then he eyed a box stuffed with *Classic Comics* and began leafing through them, flipping through the pages of a few, noting the lackluster art, gaudy colors and cheap paper, again wondering: *Could this be what passes for literature*?

He quickly surmised these were illustrated version of "classic" novels, some he'd never heard of, nor of their authors: Dumas, Scott, Stevenson, Pyle, Hugo, Defoe, Doyle, Verne, and Wells. Though he knew of Charles Dickens, he'd never heard of *A Tale of Two Cities.*

In 1842, Dickens had come to America on a tour of the salons and book stories, promoting himself and his serialized stories, and paid a visit to Poe, who had been the only one to correctly guess the ending of Barnaby Rudge. *They spent a day discussing literature, and Poe had told him of the demoralizing two weeks he'd clerked in his foster day's "counting house," of the drudgery & indentured servitude & complete lack of creativity. And he'd often wondered if Dickens had based his Bob Cratchit character on him. They exchanged letters for a while, Poe trying to get Dickens to submit something to* Graham's Magazine, *which he edited; and Dickens shad aid he'd try to get a publisher interest-*

ed in *Poe's* Grotesque and Arabesque Tales. *But nothing had come of either promise.*

Continuing through the *Classic Comics* he passed Shelly's *Frankenstein*, which he was familiar with, and found interesting, if a tad melodramatic, before he came upon number #40: *Mysteries: The Pit and the Pendulum, Adventure of Hans Pym, The Fall of the House of Usher.*

His jaw dropped at the bastardization of his tales on the comic's tattered, soiled pages.

Edgar A. Poe wept a tear.

"Hey, you, *Pooooooe*," a voice yelled, interrupting Poe's pain, "this ain't a library! No reading the funny books. Either pick a few, buy them... or hit the bricks!"

Turning to the voice after hearing his name, Poe quickly deduced the man had mistaken him for one of those *doppelganger* wandering the streets. Behind a glass display case stood a rather chubby man, shaggy haired and bearded, dressed in tee-shirt ["You Can't Spell *Poet* Without *Poe*"] and faded green pants, setting face-down his gin-rummy hand. His seated gin-partner was clean-shaven, dressed neatly in white dress shirt and black slacks.

Poe approached the display-case/sales counter, noting on the top shelf a rather tattered copy of *Action*, with that Superman fellow on the cover, with a green automobile lifted over his head, priced at a tightly sum of $2.00; twenty-times its cover price! Next to it was some rare books and coins, and other odds and ends. On the counter-top was an assortment of Poe items: key chains, bookmarkers, mugs—all bearing the so-called *Ultima Thule* of the daguerreotype of Poe, taken a few days after he almost overdosed on laudanum: the weary, haunted look that continues to be used on everything from tee-shirts to dust jackets.

Also, on the counter, were two small book stands featuring the 1948 and 1949 winners of the Edgar Award from Mystery Writers of America: *The Room Upstairs* and *Call Northwest 777*. Each was bookended by a bronze bust of Poe.

"I am short on funds," Poe said, digging into his pocket, trying not to stare at the busts of himself. He set his three coins on the glass counter-top. "Might these coins have some numismatic value beyond face?"

"Well, you're in luck," said Jack, the chubby bookseller, indicating his gin partner. "I happen to have a numismatist, here. Hey, Larry, want to take a look as these tokens?"

Larry gave the coins a brief glance, then did a double-take, digging out his loupe, and picked up each coin, in turn, between his thumb and forefinger, studying the obverse and reverse. They were in almost mint-state, and the coin dealer did a quick calculation in his head: 1849 *Half-Cent* ($500), *Braided-Hair, Seated-Liberty* 1846 Silver Dollar ($25) and a 1846 *5-Cent Coronet* ($500-600} —or around a $1,000 or so, together. He looked up at Poe, the loupe still in his eye. "You have any more?"

"No," Poe said with a slight shake of his head. "Only those."

"And nothing more?" Jack concluded with a laugh.

Poe gave him a mercy smile, then to Larry: "You interested?"

Mathematical equations flashed before the numismatist's eyes, but only dollar-signs seemed to register. "How does, oh, two-hundred dollars sound?"

"Fine," Poe said, after swallowing in disbelief. His 55 &1/2 cents had grown by almost $150.

"You sure you don't have anything else?" Jack asked.

"As a fact," Poe said, reaching into the pocket of his great coat and withdrew a 40-page book with tan-leaf cover, placing it on the counter, "I have this."

Bookseller Jack sighed: *Probably just another guy who found something in his attic who thinks he's found another* Guttenberg Bible. Then, taking a look at the book, he stared, put on his bifocals, and gingerly picked up the book: *Could this be real?*

Tamerlane and Other Poems by a Bostonian—the rarest, most sought after 19th century American book, this side of the Audubon bird folios. Only twelve known copies existed, locked away in museums, libraries and personal collection. *If this is genuine... it would be lucky thirteen! And, for some reason, thirteen seems appropriate for Poe*, Jack thought, *I have to have it... if it's real!*

Jack gingerly opened the cover and saw writing on the title page, with appeared rather too dark black to be over hundred years old. He turned to Larry, to borrow his loupe, and in that time the deadly orgone energy emulating from Poe's body had attacked the organic compounds of the ink, turning it a light brownish-tan.

"I thought..." Jack said, adjusting the loupe. "Oh, never mind."

The inscription read: *To Helen—the Glory that was Greece and the grandeur that was Rome,* (signed) *Edgar A. Poe.*

Studying the signature, Jack compared it with a sample on hand; it appeared authentic; boosted by the fact a forger would probably had signed it *Edgar Allan Poe.* Poe never used his middle name, always signed *E. A. Poe, Edgar A. Poe,* or just *Edgar Poe,* out of distain for his foster father, John Allan, who he never got along with, who was rich beyond Midas, but had treated Poe like he was a second-class citizen, and had refused to pay his ward's gambling debts.

Jack removed the loupe and said, "Where did you get this?"

"Ah, like the coins," Poe said, thinking fast, "from my deceased aunt." He paused before adding: "It's been in the family... for ages."

"This 'Helen' can't be the first 'Helen' Poe idolized," Jack intoned, "that was Jane Stith Stanard, the mother of one of his schoolmates, who no doubt reminded him of his own mother, Eliza, who died when he was only a few years old. She showed interest in Poe and his potential. After his mother, this was the second woman who 'deserted' him. He was fifteen years-old and he mourned her conspicuously—this, his ideal woman. But she died three years before *Tamerlane* was published. So it couldn't be her."

"You don't know that," Larry said with a chuckle. "After all, he was the *Master of the Macabre*..."

"Yeah," Jack said without much humor, "so it must be the second 'Helen,' Sarah Helen Whitman, who he had asked to marry him, after his wife died. She lived in Providence, Rhode Island, and she ran a literary salon. But she was a 45-year-old widow, and *The Raven*—as Poe was by then known as—was six-years younger. And she refused his proposal more for *his* reputation, that anything else. They were both into all that occult nonsense. And, more than anything, the meddlesome gossip did their relationship in."

Poe just stared in disbelief: *How does he know so much about my life. This book, indeed, was meant for Sarah Helen Whitman... but I never got the chance...*

"Where did you get this?" the book-seller asked of the strangely-dressed man before the counter. If it was an *associative copy*, one dedicated to a known person, the price could double, especially if *this* Helen was, indeed, Whitman.

"Ah," Poe said, hesitating, and for him the uneasy sensation of being at lost for words.

"Sir..." Jack said.

"Ah," Poe repeated himself, then said: "I inherited them from a deceased aunt. The book has been in the family for years. The Whitman family."

"You have any documentation of pedigree, of prior ownership?"

"Ah, yes, I can provide it."

"OK," the bookseller said, then almost choked on his next words—like most booksellers, he really hatred spending a dime more than he had to: "I can give you five-hundred dollars, and double that if you can provide proof of association."

Poe's mouth quivered—*That much?*—and the bookseller misinterpreted the man's reaction and said: "OK, seven-hundred-and-fifty! And another seven-fifty for the proof of association."

"And I'll toss in one-fifty for the coins," Jerry kicked in.

Poe just nodded.

Jack went into his office to raid his safe, dollar-signs dancing before his eyes. As the Poe book sat, it was worth, at the least, $5,000 at auction; and, perhaps, twice or even four times that for the autograph, and who knows how much more if he could document its association to Sarah Helen Whitman. Plus, it would look great in his display case, giving him bragging rights; people would come from all around to see it and gasp in awe. Thousands of dollars in profits—it was so damn tempting...

The book-dealer and coin-dealer pooled their money together on the counter; fortunately, Larry had a wad, for later in the day, he planned attending a local bi-monthly coin show.

As the money was counted out on the glass counter Poe studied the odd-looking *specie* colored green and about six-inches long, which he guessed

156

passed for money. Then were stacks of ones, fives, tens and twenties—he recognized Washington, Jackson and Hamilton, but had no idea who this Abraham Lincoln gent was.

As the money was being counted out, some change hit the counter-top and Poe spied a Thomas Jefferson nickel. And Poe flashbacked to 1824, at the age of fifteen:

He had just been getting over the death of his first "Helen" when he had begun serving as a Lieutenant in the Junior Morgan's Rifleman Club of Richmond, Virginia, a boys' volunteer company, which had acted as honorary escort for American Revolutionary hero, General Marquis de Lafayette, who had been instrumental in the defeat of Lord Cornwallis at Richmond, in 1781. And now, nearly 45 years later, President Monroe had invited the Frenchman to tour the 24 states of the Union, including a parade in New York City. When the Marquis had reached Richmond, the JMRC had escorted him to Poe's grandfather's grave, where Lafayette had placed a wreath on the grave of War Hero "General" Poe, calling him a "noble heart." This was when Poe began to realize his own heritage, beyond his actress mother and his deserting actor dad.

Later in the day, the JMRC had escorted Lafayette to Monticello, and for the first time, he had met the "Great Man" himself: Thomas Jefferson. They shook hands, but Jefferson hand was weak, with only a hint of the strength it had once possessed.

Around this time, Poe had been 17-years-old, and secretly "engaged" to his neighbor, 15-year-old Sarah Elmira Royster, an engagement that had been quickly cut off by her parents, who didn't think much of their intelligent and athletic neighbor, and had quickly married her off to a more appropriate suitor, Alexander Shelton. After this, Poe had entered "Jefferson's University"—the University of Virginia—where he had excelled at languages and math. He had been two-years younger than the rest of the class of 123 students of mainly plantation gentry, educated in philosophy, languages, law, science and history.

Then the "Great Man" had died on July 4, 1926—fifty years after the "official" signing of the Declaration of Independence—and Poe had attended the memorial service at Monticello, and had stood off from the grieving family and friends, his eyes darting from them to the obelisk inscribed: Here was burned Thomas Jefferson, author of the Declaration of America's Independence, of the Statute of Virginia for Religious Freedom, and Father of the University of Virginia. *He had noted that Jefferson had mentioned none of his public offices: Governor of Virginia, first Secretary of State, second Vice President and third President of the United States.*

Poe had glanced at Jefferson's grieving daughter—his only surviving *daughter—Martha "Patsy" Jefferson Randolph, who was sneaking glances at a light-skinned darkie he knew was the "Dazzlin' Sally" Hemmings of campaign rumors. But was there more...*

"OK, that's seven hundred and fifty smackaroos," the bookseller said, snapping Poe from his memories.

"Thank you," Poe said, stuffing the bills in his coat pockets. "Now... am I at liberty to browse your shelves?"

"Ah... ah... yeah," Jack said, absently waving his hand about, never taking his eyes off the "treasure" in his hands, "feel free..."

Poe wandered back to the "funny books," flipping through the various *Classic Comic* magazines, when it hit him: *I have almost a thousand dollars in my pockets, almost one-sixth of the amount I have earned in my entire twenty-years of literary endeavors as editor, poet, reciter of "grotesques" and essayist. I have endeavored to support myself and my family as a writer, usually a diversionary hobby of the idle rich. Perhaps if I became a novelist I could realize enough to finance my dream project,* The Stylist, *presenting only the elite of the literary world. If I had just churned out a series of novels...*

Based on the *Classic Comic* adaptations he searched the book store for copies of various novels, concentrating mostly in the science fiction and horror sections. Flipping through H. G. Wells' *Outline of History* and the five volumes of *The Pictorial History of the 20th Century*, he was astounded by all the bloodshed, especially the American Civil War—*So that's who that Lincoln gent on the five dollar bill was*—and the two World Wars.

With an armful of comics and books—Wells, Verne, Stevenson, Doyle and, even, Melville—Poe toted the volumes to the glass counter, gingerly setting them down. As the bookseller totaled the books, Poe glanced at the bottom shelf and noted a late edition of *Memoir of the Author*—part of the three volumes of *The Works of the Late Edgar Allan Poe* by Rufus Wilmont Griswold. *Griswold,* Poe almost choked at the name. *How did he come to represent me?*

Poe added that book to his stack, and the book seller, perhaps feeling some sense of remorse at undercutting the man dressed as Poe (or maybe not), said:

"I need forty-bucks for the *Memoir*, but I'll toss the rest in free, as a good-will token toward receiving the authenticity documents."

And he tossed the volumes and comics into a duffle bag.

Poe left.

Saint-Clair strolled out of the Baltimore General Post Office, descending the steps to the sidewalk, where Henry West was waiting.

"What was that all about?" West asked. "Run out of penny postcards?"

"Just dropping a letter... to a friend."

"What's next?" West said with a shrug.

"Just a moment," Saint-Clair said, holding up his left hand. With the right he studied the screen of his chrono-monitor. "Good... good..."

"Good?" West repeated.

"*Oui.* I am receiving a second temporal reading."

"And that's good?"

"Bien sûr!"

New York, 1955

"Perhaps you can help me," Manse Everard said, placing the unfamiliar *Classic Comics* and *Classic Illustrated* on the sales counter, next to an over-flowing ash-tray and mug ("Brooklyn in 1956") of spiked coffee. (Everard thought it was rum). "I'm rather well versed in literature..." Then he truthfully added: "...But I never heard of these titles, or authors."

The bookseller looked down his nose, adjusting his glasses, a cigarette shifting from one side of his mouth to the other, a blue smoke cloud blotting out his features, and looked at the comic books.

"Henry Leonard... Henri Le Renne? Where did you get your education?" He shrugged. "Ha, probably from comic books, ha-ha-ha."

"Forget the Joker impersonation, and clue me in!"

"They are pseudonyms of Edgar A. Poe."

"Edgar Allan Poe?"

"Yep—him and no one else. Ha-ha-ha! But Poe never used his middle name. Something to do with a falling out with his foster father, or some such."

"Where can I find these books by Leonard and Le Rennet?"

"Ah, well, my guess would be," the bookseller said with a wave of his hand toward the back of the dusty, cluttered store. cigarette ashes flicking about, "back there... on the Poe shelves. Ha-ha-ha!"

Smart-ass, Everard thought, but kept it to himself, and ambled to the back of the store, finding three shelves weigh-down by volumes of books by Poe and his two *nom-de plumes*. Among the fiction were some biographical books: *The Rise and Fall of the House of Poe*, *Poe: Man in a Flux*, *Poe-Tastic!*, *The Death of Poe-Try!*, and others. Flipping through the first bio, Manse began to under-stand the change in the time-line.

He flipped through *Mocha Dick* by Henry Leonard: it followed the long, boring *Moby Dick* rather loosely, with cosmetic changes, such as it opened with "Call me Azrael" and the captain was named Israel, with a pet parrot, which on-ly said: "...ashore... ashore..."

Reading the preface, Everard discovered the book was based on the ex-ploits of Jeremiah Reynolds, who failed to obtain funding for an expedition to the South Pole, to verify the Hollow Earth Theory; though in 1824 he did sail to South America and found nothing but impenetrable ice, and reported on a great white whale, *Mocha Dick*, who sank ships. His South Seas adventures inspired this book and Poe's short-story: *The Narration of Arthur Pym of Nantucket*.

With his handy-dandy Absbro-Read, he downloaded a couple bios and some novels. And back at his office Manse sat back at his desk, plugging the Absbro-Read into the Hypnotic-Conditioner, and downloaded the data into his brain.

159

It appeared that in October 1849, Poe had disappeared for a few days, and when he had resurfaced in Baltimore, he was a changed man, not as morbid in his writings as before. He had married the sweetheart of his adolescence, the recently widowed Sarah Elmira Royster Shelton, and began branching out from short stories to book-length novels, including a series as Henri Le Rennet, featuring adventurer René Deveroux, a thinly disguised version of his Auguste Dupin, full of what Poe called *ratiocination* or deductive reasoning, with what the book's author called *scientifiction elements*; including: *Around the World Under the Sea, The Island of Lost Souls, Men on the Moon, When Mars Attacks, Warlord of the Sky,* and *Land Unknown.* Everard recognized the plots, rewritten and extensions of the various concepts of *20,000 Leagues Under the Sea, The Island of Dr. Moreau, First Men in the Moon, War of the World, Robur the Conqueror* and *Lost World.*

Poe's non-series written as Henry Lennard, included: *Mocha Dick, The Enemy Within, Awake the Sleeper, The Temporal Device,* and *The Transparent Man.* Or in Manse's own time-line: *Moby Dick, The Strange Case of Dr. Jekyll and Mr. Hyde, When the Sleeper Wakes, The Time Machine* and *The Invisible Man.*

According to *The Rise and Fall of the House of Poe,* Poe had just cranked out these novels, without the literary beauty of his poems and pre-disappearance short-stories. They were hack work, to help finance his prestige publication of elitism: *The Stylus.* He spent $40,000 to print 20,000 copies of the 128-page pamphlet. He charged $5.00 per copy, and few people had $5 to throw away on an elitist magazine, not even the wealthy *literati* of 1870. Thus Poe was forced to keep cranking out more hack work to pay off the printing bill for *The Stylus,* until he died in 1890, at age 81, a bitter, broken man. But now known as "The Originator of the Detective Short Story," "The Pioneer of Scientifiction," foreseeing television, radio, motion pictures, atomic submarines, airplanes, automobiles and, even, accurate descriptions of dinosaurs, and "The Master of the Serial Character."

"Ravenous Ravens!" Everard exclaimed, removing the knowledge helmet.

Basically, the time-line had changed because Poe had written all of Wells' best-sellers, leaving the British author with *The Outline of History, Divorce As I See It, The War and Socialism* and a score of others, in Everard's own time-line. In this alternate time-line ,Wells hadn't written his most popular novels—Poe had—so he had concentrated of a highly-influential series of essays and books, like *Peace in Our Time, God in the Machine, The Last Shall be First, More Common Sense,* and many more of a pacifist nature.

Wells' books had inspired a NYC social worker, manager of a skid-row soap-kitchen, named Edith Keeler, whose PIP (Peace, Isolation, Prosperity) Movement had delayed the United States' entry into the Second World War, allowing the Nazis time to develop their V-2 through V-5 intercontinental missiles, laying waste to London and other European cities, killing millions with atomic bombs they developed from their heavy-water experiments; plus they had had time to prefect Kammler's anti-gravity-powered flying saucer.

Yet Everard remembered—from his own time-line—that Edith Keeler had died in an automobile accident in the early 1930s, during the height of the Depression. And somehow in *this* alternate time-line, she had avoided that accident and gone on to start the PIP Movement.

The "buzz" from the Danellians he had received in the bookstore read: *Edith Keeler MUST die.* That was all: nice and neat.

There was a knock at his door and Everard's blonde assistant entered, dropping off a stack of mail for him, and left. He flipped through the mail, tossing ads and other junk mail into the circular file as his focus locked on one letter, soiled with age. He knifed it open and removed a short missive. A smile came to his face.

"*Mais oui*, old friend," he muttered.

This missive gave him a possible out, so that he wouldn't be responsible for Edith Keeler's death, and, yet, still mend the time-line: by going back to the causal event and returning Poe to his own time, *without* the works of Wells, Verne, Doyle, Stevenson and Melville. Thus Wells would again write his science fiction, and his political works would come too late in his life to affect anyone. He picked up the newspaper;, the headline read: *Prez Dewey to Meet with the Fuhrer!*

Everard heard a whining outside his tenth store office and went to the window, and saw a slow moving 50-foot diameter saucer passing by. On its up-right tail-stabilizer was a black swastika, in a circle of white, framed in a red square, being escorted by four 15-foot saucers flanking it, each carrying the Stars & Stripes, and marked *USAF-+*.

Manse Everard just shook his head.

Baltimore, October 3, 1949

Poe approached the Hotel Baltimore, entering it to find a relatively opulently appointed lobby, with people hustling about here and there, and others in no particular hurry. He walked to the registration desk and was greeted by a thin man dressed in a black suit and tie.

"May I help you, sir?"

"I require a room."

"Excellent," the manager said, rotating the guest book to Poe, handing him a pen. "Please sign in."

"Ah..." Poe shuttered, looking for an ink well, before the manager took the pen from him and clicked the ball into action, handing it back. Poe studied the pen, struggled, and signed: *Arthur Pym.*

"Very good," the manager said, "Mister…er, Pym." He snapped his fingers and a pimple-faced teenage bell-boy came running. Handing the boy a key he said, "Show Mr. Pym to Room 212."

"Yes, sir!" Then to Poe, "Let me carry that for you, sir."

After a brief hesitation Poe handed over the duffle-bag to the boy, who hunched over at it weight. "Hey, mister, what's ya got in here… a dead body?"

"Only that," Poe said with a smile, "and nothing more."

The bell-boy smiled at the guy dressed like Poe, and lunged the duffle toward the elevator, with the man-out-of-time following behind.

Poe was sweating as they rose in the creaking, jerky elevator, his eyes forced on the sign. *Who was Otis?* he wondered. After an eternity, the elevator jerked to a stop and the doors slid open. The bell-hop led the way down the hall. Poe followed, sweating and pale, still repeating a mantra to a God he did not believe in.

The boy keyed the door, opening it, waving Poe in, following him in. tossing the duffle on the bed, sighing with relief. The room was dark and Poe glanced about, looking for gas lamps to turn up, when the bell-boy flipped the wall switch, illuminating the room with diffused lighting.

"Hmmm," was all Poe could manage.

"Well…" the boy said, palm out, "…anything else."

"Yes, of course," Poe said, searching his pockets, snagging a quarter, dropping it in the boy's palm, hoping it was a significant compensation.

At the steep price of $2-a-day for the room, he had to watch his money. But the tip seemed significant as the boy flipped the quarter in the air, catching it, pocketing it.

"I could do with some coffee, a steak and potato, and a salad… ah, and a slice of apple pie."

"You got it… and thank you, sir," the boy said enthusiastically, "If you need anything else, just ask for Johnny."

Poe nodded and closed the door as Johnny left. Now was time for him to educate himself on the wonders of this strange new world. Emptying the duffle on the bed, he sorted out the comic books, hardbacks, a few paperback and pulps. And then he noticed at the bottom of the bag was a set of clothes, which he guessed probably belonged to the coin-dealer, based on the size.

He ate his meal and savored every bit—especially at the outrageous price of $2.57!—as he skimmed through Victor's *Science and Invention,* which gave a history of inventions: gas light, kerosene, electric, the "Electricity Battle" between Tesla/Westinghouse's Alternate Current and Edison's Direct Current; horse-and-carriages to gasoline-powered automobiles; balloons to airplanes; telegraphy through the telephone; various ships and submarines; the daguerreotype, 35mm, Polaroid, motion pictures (first silent, then talkies}, and other technological and scientific wonders,

Next, he scanned through *When Dinosaurs Ruled the Earth* by William Nichols, and was thoroughly enthralled by these "terrible lizards." He had read Baron Georges Cuvier's 1826 *Research on Fossil Remains* and knew of the English discovery, in 1824, of the *Meglasaurus* ("big lizard"); and he had seen the full skeleton of a mastodon at Rembrandt Peale's Philadelphia Museum.

Though the word *dinosauria* ("terrible lizard" in Greek) was coined by Sir Richard Owen, the *real dinosaurs*—brontosaurs, triceratops, stegosaurs, and the rest—were not unearthed until almost two decades after Poe's death by Cope and March in America's mid-West; and it was not until the early 20th century that P.T. Barnum had extracted the first T-rex from the Montana Badlands. The paintings and drawing in Nichols' book just transfixed Poe...

It reminded him of *The Conchologist's First Book*, which he had rewritten in 1839 for Thomas Wyatt, livingly up the boring tome on sea shells that it was, adding an introduction, and translating works of European experts, including Georges Cuvier. Poe had received a flat $50 for the job. The book had gone through many editions in his lifetime; the only work by him that could claim more than a first printing in his lifetime.

He next pondered *Memoir of the Author* by Rufus Wilmot Griswold, picking it up, studying it, as distasteful memories firing the synapses in his brain. *How did this ol' humbug come to write* my *memoirs? We were cordial, at best, bitter adversaries, at worst. The only thing we had in common was the willingness to work at low pay. Alas, he was Salieri to my Mozart*!

With trepidation, Poe opened the volume and was immediately struck by the raft of letters of testimonial to Griswold, from Poe's friends, editors and fellow writers. Especially interesting were the glowing praise of Griswold by Poe, himself.

Eh, Poe thought, *I never wrote any of these letters, and never would have! I expect the other lauding praise by the others were also, likewise, fictitious. "Rufe" or "Gris" was universally disliked by everyone; never a writer of stories, but willing to work as an editor for the same slave wages as I.*

He was, from the first time I met him, in 1841, filled with professional suspicion. He was willing to put on the façade of cordialness if he had something to gain. At the time of that meeting I was already dubbed The Tomahawk, *for my, er, honest reviews. He was a failed Methodist minister, turned editor, and considered himself my social, moral superior. He aligned himself with the Northern clique of literati, and born into prosperity, he thought me a poor Southern boy with an unimpressive education and an* acid pen *for trying to make myself the literary conscience of America. A man who, I have no doubt, owed his career— if one wished to call it such—to social intercourse and exchange of favors, and who fell into the species referred to as "toady."*

Lies! Damnable lies!" Poe hissed out as he continued to read "his" *Memoir*, which first edition had hit the bookstore just three months after his death. The untruths were piled one on top another: that he had been expelled from the

University of Virginia and West Point on charges of "conduct unbecoming," while he was actually honorably discharged; that he had tried to seduce John Allen's second wife, a woman Poe had detested, who in no uncertain terms had informed him he was not welcome in her "new family," and had sealed any thought of inheritance of any of Allen's $13 million estate; that he had been the illegitimate father of married Fanny Osgood's third child, a woman Griswold himself had tried to seduce, but she had preferred Poe; and other half-truths and outright lies.

In disgust, Poe tossed the book on the bed, and picked up Arthur H. Quinn's *Poe: A Critical Biography* (1941) and scanned it. And he was pleased with what he read. Though this was not the first scholarly work attempting to rehabilitate Griswold's picture of Poe as a perverted addict, madman and womanizer, it was one of the best. Poe was elated to see that Sarah Helen Whitman had written *Edgar Poe and his Critics*—which praised his works, and answered the multitude of rumors, the gossip of the meddling *literati* of the mostly Northern salons.

Poe also learned in Quinn's book how Griswold had come to be his executor: via some surely unethical arrangement with Maria Clemm, Poe's mother-in-law, when the rights to his estate, legally, should have fallen to his blood sister, Rosalie. No doubt, Maria "Muddy" Clemm had been unaware of the antagonism between Poe and Griswold, and may have approached him, knowing he had published some of Poe's works in his *Poems and Poetry of America.* Maria Clemm had received no money—something she could definitely have used—but six sets of the volumes to do with as she pleased. Griswold had kept *all* the original manuscripts she had provided him, easily worth many times more than any monies she might have realized from the sales of the six sets!

Yet, any try at the rehabilitation of Poe's life never really held; the rambling masses liked the morbid aspects of Poe's works, and the picture Rufus Griswold had painted of him—*Mad Man—Addict—Pervert—Womanizer*—kept resurfacing. Griswold had been the *executioner* as well as the *executor* of Poe's life and works; and had forever stuck the poet with the middle name of "Allan" —which Poe had grown to detest.

Pervert? Poe whispered aloud. *Yes, I wept, I collapsed after the death of dear Sissy, my wife, and sunk into a month-long melancholy; yet I never even contemplated—physically—the morbidity that Gris fell into, and the closest I ever attempted that was in* The Premature Burial. *I will not deny many of my poems and stories revolve around an idealized woman who dies and is lost to me, like Lenora and Annabel Lee. Yet, I never went as far as Gris!*

When Rufus Wilmont Griswold first wife, Caroline, had died, three days after given birth to their third child, a son, he had sat alongside her coffin, refusing for thirty hours to give up his post. Friends urged him to get some sleep, and he replied by kissing her wife's dead, cold lips, while embracing her. He had to literally be removed from her tomb. And forty days later, he had returned to her vault, cut off a lock of her wilting locks, kissed her lips and forehead, weeping several hours at her side, before his friends had found him thirty hours later.

Griswold's poetry was trivial at best, banal at worse, Poe thought, *like his* Happy Hour of Death, On the Death of a Young Girl, *and* The Slumber of Death—*all similar to the Transcendentalists: seeking some Truth in verse, while the sole purpose of a poem is Beauty. Yet, is there no Truth in Beauty? Or Beauty in Truth?*

Poe's head ached. Everything was so mind-boggling. Soon the strain of the day and the caloric contents of his meal accumulated, causing him to doze off, having nightmares of black cats, mummies, supermen, rocket ships, oblong boxes, Griswold on a black horse, a screaming raven-haired Sissy in his meaty arm, like something out of a Washing Irving tale. Then, a giant raven swooped down, its wings flapping, smothering until everything went black... And there was nothing more.

"You dirty ol' French bastard!" Leo Saint-Clair heard from behind him as he adjusted a dial of his *chrono-meter*, and turned to face the source of the voice, which added: "Long ways from Lyon, huh?"

"As are you," the Frenchman replied, "in time *and* space."

They embraced, air-kissed each other's cheeks, and manly shook hands. Then Saint-Clair turned to his companion and said: "Henry West, this is the man I spoke of, Manse Everard. He's from, er, the future."

"A time-traveler?" West said, shaking his head. "Will the wonders never cease?"

"Yes. He has a *Time-Hopper* with which he can return Poe to his proper time and place."

"Once we find him," West two-cented.

"*Naturellement,*" Saint-Clair said, scanning his meter. It was now registering two bleeps of chronometric displacement. "Let us narrow the field."

Saint-Clair ran the device up and down Everard's body, jabbed a few buttons, and turned it towards West. "Observe: now there is only one chrono-signature."

"I see two," West said.

"What?"

"Suffering Sappho," Everard exclaimed, "the private dick is right!"

Baltimore – October 4, 1949

Poe had awoken earlier, his naked body covered in sweat, the nightmares just fading. A shower had helped clear his mind, refreshing his body. After toweling off, he forewent his old clothes—in case he was, indeed, being stalked—and dressed in the clothing that had been in the bottom of the duffel bag: a rather sleazy coat of thin alpaca, pants half-worn and barely fitting with any snugness, and coarse material boots.

Leaving the duffle and his book in the hotel room he ventured outside, breathing in the intoxicating flumes of the morning traffic. And he sensed he was, once again, being followed. *Am I being paranoid or are they really men tracking me, and, if so, for what purpose?*

Poe decided to see if he was being followed and ducked under the marquee of the Nu-Bel Theatre, and around the ticket booth, studying the one-sheets, lobby cards and photographs of *Coming Attractions* during *Poe's Week of Thrills & Terror:*

The Gold Bug (1910), *The Bells* (1913), *The Murders in the Rue Morgue* (1914 & 1936), *The Raven* (1915 & 1936), *The Tell-Tale Heart* (1928 & 1941), *The Fall of the House of Usher* (1928), *The Black Cat* (1934), *The Pre-Mature Burial (1936)*, and now showing, displayed on a one-sheet poster, *The Loves of Edgar Allan Poe,* starring Linda Darnell and John Sheppard.

After recovering from the shock of seeing the poster of a biographical film based on himself, he wondered why this Linda Darnell received top billing over the actor playing himself. Because the title read *The Loves of...???* Opposite in a glass display window, was a gaudy three-sheet in primary colors of basically red and blue, advertising: "*Coming Soon... Atom Man vs Superman.* Again Poe wondered on the ubiquitous presence of this *Superman*, though he'd only seen this poster, a costume in a display window, and the comic books. He was unaware of the newspaper strip, radio plays, cartoons, toys, dolls and a plethora of other merchandizing and endorsements featuring the Man of Steel.

He paid his 25 cents—*twenty-five-cents!*—at the ticket booth, gave the ticket to the doorman, who tore it in halves, handing one back to Poe, wishing that he'd enjoy the flick—*flick?* In the lobby, his stomach began to grumble, reminding the time-traveler he needed to attend to it.

At the concession stand, with it varied smells of cooking meat and popping corn, Poe scanned the candies on display: *Baby Ruth, Butterfinger, Poe-mmms* and other goodies dropped into those Halloween bags he had seen in the store windows. *How could any working man afford to 'treat' children at 25 cents each as marked in the display case?*

Then with *ratiocination* which would have made Dupin proud, Poe deduced that the inflated cost was due to servicing a captive audience, who had already paid their admission and had nowhere else to go. Thus foods selling for a nickel on the outside were a shiny quarter inside. His grumbling stomach forced him to make a selection, which he paid for. Then, he entered though the gaudy-red curtains into the almost pitch-dark theater, the only light being dim bulbs on the ceiling and amber-red lights on the aisle sides of the cushioned seats.

Poe took a seat in the center of the back row, under the projection booth, trying to get comfortable and remember what he'd read in Victor's *Science and*

Invention about motion pictures, but he had difficulty trying to concentrate as his stomach protested the empty calories being dumped it to it: the "hot dog," which Poe figured was some type of sausage, but was something else entirely, of some unknown meat, warm, hard, barely digestible; the "butter popcorn," which was soaked in something resembling butter and very salty, which made him happy that he brought an "ice-cold, refreshing" sugary Coke.

Absently he munched on some Poe-mmms—candy-coated, licorice centered, dyed various colors and roughly in the shape of black cats, white skeletons, gray mummies, etc. And his mind drifted to the film's title: *The Loves of Edgar Allan Poe*—just how many "loves" had there been? And just what was *Love*? How does one count the ways? And where to begin, and his mathematically-inclined mind decided to number them from the beginning:

1) Eliza "Liz" (Hopkins) Poe, his mother who had died when he was but three;

2) Francis Allan, his "foster" mother (Poe was never officially adopted); who never financially endowed Poe;

3) Jane Smith Stith Stanard, his first "Helen," the mother of a school mate, a classical beauty, who, no doubt, had reminded him of his mother;

4) Sarah Elmira Royster, with whom a 17-year old Poe had fallen head-over-heels in love, but who has been married off to a more suitable man;

5) Martha "Muddy" Clemm, another "mother figure" who had supported Poe's ambitions and paid attention to his needs;

6) Virginia Eliza "Sissy" Clemm, Muddy's only child, and thirteen years younger than Poe; whom he had married in a secret ceremony in 1835, then again, publicly, two years later;

7) Frances Sargent "Fanny" Osgood, with her blond hair and expressive eyes, married to the well-known portrait-painter, Samuel Stillman Osgood, who had become a close friend;

8) Maria "Loui" Louise Shaw, a generous, giving, devoted neighbor, who, with Muddy, had helped "nurse" him out of his depression after the death of Sissy;

9) Nancy Locke Heywood Richmond—Annie to Poe—whom he had met in 1848, but who was already married;

10) Sarah Helen Whitman, his second "Helen", a 45 years-old widow and poetess living in Providence, but gossip had strained their relationship;

11) Sarah Elmira Royster Shelton—now a widow—and he had come full-circle, back to his youthful sweetheart; the final woman in his life.

If Poe's analytical—and often egotistical—brain would have given way for a moment to his tell-take heart, he might have understood the almost Oedipal nature of his relationships. But he wasn't musing on any of this as the lights dimmed and the curtains opened, revealing the 15' x 25' reflective screen, and a flash of light. Then a title: *News of the Week*, promoting things called suburbs, shopping malls and Baby-Boomers.

After the initial shock—and, indeed, awe—of the talking, moving picture had washed over Poe, he settled back, munched a red heart and black cat as the newsreel reported on yesterday's happening in Boston Harbor: reports of colored lights and a mist, of disappearing and reappearing ships. The Navy and Air Force had released a joint statement: the phenomenon was caused by an inverse layer of cold and warm air in the atmosphere, and the rising sun refracting the various colors like a prism.

Poe sat up straight, spitting out a white skeleton. *Is that it? I was in the row boat, oaring towards the shore—then colors flashed through the skies—and then it was all blank, until I woke groggy, confused, wandering about, on what appeared to be a iron war ship. I was led to an officer's quarter and seated in a chair... Then there was nothing... Until I found myself on the thoroughfare with the congestion of horseless, er, automobiles, and the sweet odor of.., er, carbon monoxide... This is how I got* here, *it must hold the secret of my way back...*

Then a mountain surrounded by stars and the word *Paramount* appeared on the screen, followed by a seven-minute animated feature starring Superman. Poe marveled at the cartoon of muted primary colors, as Superman battled *The Mummy's Curse*, reminding him of his own story: *Some Words with a Mummy,* minus the killing and rampage.

Finally the main feature began: *The Loves of Edgar Allan Poe,* and again Poe cringed at the use of "Allan," watching in amazement, astonishment, disbelief and disgust as the sixty-seven-minute film butchered his life story.

Based loosely on his life, it touched all the bases, but otherwise massacred his life with too many errors to count. But especially egregious was the fiction that he was unable to find a publisher for *The Raven,* when in fact he was paid $24.00, and its publication had made him famous, especially at the salons and on the lecture circuit' also, also making him a target of the literati idle and not so idle's gossip.

As the lights came up, Poe just sat there, pondering what he had just seen. According to Quinn's book his *last word* was *not* that of his wife, Virginia; though his *actual* last word was a common surname, especially in the South, he knew of nobody who might be on his mind at the time of his death, surely not the exploder looking for the Hollow Earth nor Alexander Hamilton's mistress

Yet, in his tell-tale heart, he wished his last word had been that of his dear Sissy. Poe didn't know why. *What could have been... No, what could still be!*

Poe knew there was no way he could save Sissy's life, even if he managed to return to his own time—but he could marry his childhood sweetheart, Sarah, and work toward his opus: *The Stylus.* And he would never think of using his new wife's money to finance his venture; it just wasn't gentlemanly. And with logic than Dupin would deplore, the "Champion of Copyrights" would allow himself to be "influenced" by the books and comics in his duffle, back in the hotel room. And since the books, in his time and era, had not been published yet, there were no copyrights to violate.

The deadly orgone energy was getting to his brain—or was it?

"One of the blips is near," Saint-Clair said, scanning his hand-held device.

"There he is!" West exclaimed, pointing at the man leaving the theater. "Or, I think it's him. Did he change his clothes?"

"He did! The monitor agrees."

"Hey, you!" Everard yelled out. "We need to talk to you!"

Wrong move! Poe rabbited! Running with the superior athleticism he had possessed twenty years ago in school, Poe dashed across the street, dodging and weaving through the honking of traffic, and jumped in the rear of a Yellow Cab.

"Where to, Mac?" the cabbie said over his shoulder.

"It's Edgar," Poe said, matter-of-factly.

"Of course, it is," the cabbie replied, looking in his rear-view mirror. *Another of them-there Poe-sters that come out-of-the-woodwork at this time-a-year.* "I repeat, whether to, Mac?"

"Ah," Poe said, looking out the rear window, scoping the three men giving chase as they rounded the corner, running straight toward him. Turning back around to the cabbie he said, pointing out the windshield: "That away!"

"OK, Mac," the cabbie replied, pulling down the lever on his meter-box, and entered the flow of traffic, cutting off a Packard, which answered with some choice-words and a one-finger salute.

After glancing back and seeing the ensuing trio shrinking in the distance, Poe let out a breath, and settled back for the ride, absently looking out the window, then about the cab. He saw a leaflet someone had left behind: *Grand Opening: Historic Edgar Allan Poe House & Museum.* He held it up: "Take me there."

"Of course, Mac," the cabbie said, eyeing the upheld flyer in his rear-view mirror.

The cabbie pulled up to 203 Amity Street. Poe paid his $1.25 fare (including tip) and stepped out. The cabbie thanked him, and left Poe stranded on the curb, studying the house. When he had lived was now No. 3 Amity Street. The house had been set in a wooden area; now, the woods were gone and other structures crowded the once quaint duplex. It has undergone many alterations over the last century: the top left had been raised at some point, providing a full room on the third floor; it now had a flat roof and not a peaked one as before. The left half of the duplex had also been removed.

With trepidation, Poe entered the house, paying 25 cents to a lady costumed in mid-19th century garb, and slowly took in the entry parlor, with kitchen at the rear. Poe felt a weird sensation standing there; the right side of the once duplex had been his home with the Clemms, from 1833 to 1835. But *now* it felt to Poe as only a *house*, not a *home.* He had shared this residence with matriarch Maria "Muddy" Clemm, her ailing mother, Elizabeth Clemm Poe, her daughter. Virginia Eliza Clemm and cousin Henry Clemm, who would soon die at sea. Someone once said: *You can't go home again*. And that was how Poe felt: it was a house, but not the cozy, crowded *home* he once knew. It had been completely renovated: walls, ceiling and mantle were off-white, and all the wood painted brown. And some carpeting had been added.

Poe took it all in as his eyes were drawn to the framed picture above the fireplace mantle: a painting of Boston Harbor. It was the same painting his mother had willed him, to remind him of his birth city. A tear formed in Poe's eye: *At least something can go home again.*

He wandered through the house, studying the various displays, and realized *none* of it had belonged to him, or the Clemms, including a telescope, traveling desk, Winsor chairs, glassware and china, and other period furniture.

Yet this house had witnessed some of the best of times: a crowded, often chaotic home, but a loving one; the first really *true* home he had felt he belonged, with walks in the near woods in peace and solitude, just a place to think; a caring home… a developing love…. of longing… of creativity….

Poe walked through the second-floor bedroom (Muddy's) and climbed the small, winding stairs to the attic room, which had been young Virginia's. There was a vanity, bed, chair and table, and the claustrophobic nature of the close ceiling evoked many of Poe's tales.

As Poe was leaving the house, he noted a flyer on the table near the door, featuring the tombs of Poe, Muddy and Sissy. Poe wanted to visit them, pay his respects, but he knew his time was limited, and people were still trailing him. He hailed a cab and headed back to his hotel.

He grabbed his duffle-bag of books, comics and clothes, and tipped the bell-boy a Franklin to tell anybody who came looking that he was heading for New York City. Then he hit the bricks, the duffle hung over his shoulder.

Saint-Clair's chrono-meter continued to show two blips—two time-travelers seemingly on a collision course.

It was near noon. Beneath a series of electrical derricks and snapping, surging power lines stood an abandoned warehouse, its windows broken by local hoodlums, its red brick walls covered by an odd growth of moss and ivy. The red-on-blue name of the business, now peeling, chipping, was barely legible: *Adams' Art Supplies.*

Poe approached the seemingly abandoned warehouse, glancing up at the high-tension wires and transformers. Their electrical coronas were playing havoc on the depleting orgone energy in his head as the DOE continued to replace it, driving him to more and more paranoiac thoughts. But in this case, his paranoia was reality.

He snuck into the warehouse through an unlocked door as his trio of pursuers rounded the far corner coming straight toward him. The dusty, cobwebbed warehouse was as dark and forlorn as a haunted house. Poe was becoming too wary to even ponder the many boxes of forgotten wares. Hearing two men talking further in the warehouse, he ducked behind a stack of old shipping crates: *More of them?*

Outside, the Nyctalope re-checked the chrono-meter in his palm and shrugged: The chrono-images were beginning to merge. Then the feed was lost.

"The high-tension power lines?" Everard questioned.

"He must be inside," West said, pointing at the warehouse.

"Shazam!" Everard exclaimed. "You're probably right, West."

"*Oui*," Saint-Clair concurred.

From his hiding place, Poe listened and studied as a white-haired gentleman with a rebellious lock of hair, dressed in a greasy white lab-coat, was discussing some technical business with a hulkish man with a black beard.

"Put this on, Fred. It'll help cut-down on the EM and DOE radiation," said the older man, handing the bigger man a metallic-looking cap.

As the big man donned his cap, Poe spotted a similar shiny cap on the crate behind which he was hiding. He grabbed it and put it on and immediately felt a calmness that he hadn't experienced in a long while: the cap was soothing, blocking the EM emulations and, apparently, some of the effects of the OE/DOE conversion. Absently, Poe pulled a length of fold from a box, tearing it off, noting the shiny surface on one side, the matte-finish on the other. He crinkled it, and was amazed when he was able to straighten it back out flat, So amazed by the foil he almost didn't hear his three pursuers enter the warehouse. He placed a crumpled piece of the Reynolds aluminum foil in his pants' pocket, and ducked back down behind the crate, to listen and observe as the trio shadowing him entered the warehouse.

They cautiously made their way through the darkness, though Saint-Clair had no trouble navigating through the waste-cluttered warehouse, until they saw a glimmer of light at the rear of the building. They stepped into the aura of light being emitted by a floating, glowing hole in space, some fifteen feet across, with the edges running through a rainbow of colors.

Off to the side was what looked like a giant cannon shell with a door and portholes all around it.

"This explains a lot," Everard whispered to his companions.

"Indeed, it dies," said the Nyctalope.

"Huh?" Henry West muttered.

"It's Doctor Omega?" explained the Time Patrol agent.

"Who?"

"No, Omega," Everard corrected. "Another time-traveler."

Oh, great! West thought, *I'm surrounded by people out of some H. G. Wells' novel—first this Manse Everard character, now this old geezer. Hell, for all I know, Saint-Clair might be one too; though we've worked together during the War, and have known him since the late Twenties/early Thirties, there is really little I actually know of him.*

Unbeknownst to Henry West, he had met *another* time-traveler two decades before; but, alas, that's another story.

"A *chronoteer* like myself," Everard continued, "but independent of any agency, and somewhat eccentric. The gorilla next to him is Fred, his current companion and bodyguard." Then in a shout: "Hey, Doctor O, you ol' space-time hound! How they hangin'?"

Doctor Omega looked up abruptly, squinting, shielding his eyes as he took a step forward.

"That you, Manse, my boy? Yes, yes, it is!"

The two time-travelers hugged and slapped each other on the back, and began discussing their most recent adventures, including both visiting Ancient Egypt during the reign of Akhenaten.[6] They were getting along fabulously when they were interrupted.

"Ah, guys...," West said, shifting from one foot to the next.

"Of course, of course," Everard said.

The Nyctalope stepped forward, shook the Doctor's and Fred's hands, and filled them in, up to the arrival of Edgar Allan Poe and their predicament of having to return him to his own time.

From his hiding place behind the crates, Poe was surprised by their knowledge of who he was, even if they continued to use the "bastard" Allan when referring to him. He had tried for close to two decades to distance himself from his foster father's name and legacy; yet it stuck, thanks to that bastardized *Memoir* he had never authorized.

Saint-Clair, West and Manse stared into the rippling, whirling maelstrom of orgone energy and deadly orgone energy, colliding, annihilating one another as the portal continued to collapse in upon itself. Doctor Omega explained, pointing out a rowboat in the water at the other end of the portal:

"This was created by your Naval experiment in the Baltimore Harbor and shifted here due to gravitational forces and the static electricity of the power lines around us. But the portal is depleting the static electricity, causing it to shrink. It will soon disappear entirely."

"Then, if we find Poe, we won't be able to send him back," Henry West said, yanking a thumb over his shoulder at the rainbowing portal.

"But either Manse of Doctor Omega can perform that task," said Saint-Clair.

As Poe listened to the foursome discussing him, words from *Hamlet* flashed through his mind: *To be or not to be, that is the question...* But there was no question here—it was TO BE! He did not wish to be reduced to suba-

---

[6] See "*As Time Goes By*" in Volume 9.

tomic particles as the last of the OE and DOE annihilated one another, reducing him to ionized plasma, then *nothingness.*

"To be!" Poe yelled as he jumped from behind the crates, rushing toward the shrinking portal, the duffle bag slung over his back. "Like the shadow on the floor, I shall be lifted evermore!"

As Poe rushed toward the portal, Henry West tried to tackle him, but came up only with the duffle, the aluminum foil hat, and nothing else, as Poe sailed through the portal.

The four men in 1949 watched as Poe shot through the air, over-shooting the rowboat by inches, banging his head on the side, going under. But seconds later, he resurfaced and managed to crawl aboard the boat, before passing-out, unconscious.

Then, the portal completely collapsed with a loud *pop*, then a sizzle as the last of the OE and DOE were annihilated, leaving only a slight smell of ozone in the air.

"You know," West said, getting to his feet, hefting the duffle bag and foil hat, "Poe overshot the boat and hit his head, which was probably the ultimate cause of his death. But if he still had had that duffle bag when he went through, it might have slowed his trajectory and he would've landed in the boat. So, in a way, we—I—am responsible for his death."

"It was *kismet*, ol' man," Everard said to West. "He had to die the way he did in order to save mankind from a horrible future fate."

"I guess so…"

"Jumpin' Jupiter!" Everard exclaimed, snapping up a discarded newspaper from a year before, reading aloud the headline:

"Dewey Won! We failed!"

Henry West laughed as he handed Everard the newspaper with the front-cover photo of Truman holding up the earlier edition.

Manse Everard went back to his Nazi-free mid-fifties New York. Doctor Omega and Fred continued their travels through space and time. Henry West and Leo Saint-Clair returned to Naval Intelligence, to be debriefed on the Experiment, before returning to their own separate lives.

As for Edgar Allan Poe? On October 3, 1849, his long-time friend, Joseph Snodgrass, received a message from a local Baltimore printer who had recognized the noted poet in the Fourth Ward, lying on two planks.

By the time Snodgrass arrived he discovered Poe in a local tavern, Gunner's Hall, sitting stupefied in an armchair, his clothes dirty, stained, ill-fitting.

The delirious Poe was taken to College Hospital and admitted into the care of Dr. John Moran, who described the poet as "haggard and dirty," yet not under the influence of any "intoxicating drink."

At 5:00 a.m. on Sunday morning, October 7th, when Poe's delirium had subsided, he managed to say:

"Lord, help my poor soul..."

Then he passed into wherever Lenore, Annabel Lee, his mother, Sissy, and all the rest had gone. Or, at least, one can hope so.

The only witness to his death was Dr. Moran, who recorded that in his delirium, Poe kept repeating a name over and over:

"My head... Reynolds... Reynolds... Reynolds..."

Most believe he was referring to Jeremiah Reynolds, the seeker of the "Hollow Earth," whose travels were reworked by Poe in his *Adventures of Arthur Pym of Nantucket.*

Yet Dr. Moran left a few things from his final report on the death of Edgar Allan Poe—perhaps to protect the poet's already tarnished reputation: why was he traveling with such strange currency (obviously counterfeit), made of some kind of cotton-paper, green and about six inches-long. He recognized Washington, Jefferson, Jackson, Franklin... but who was Lincoln? For what purpose was this obviously fake money to be used?

And what of that a strip of what appeared metallic, shiny on one surface, matte on the other. What was this, and where did Poe get it? Was this connected to fake money?

Dr. Moran would never find an answer to his questions.

Nine months before the events recorded above, on January 19, 1949, a cloaked figure paid a midnight visit to Poe's grave. He placed a rose on each of the graves of Poe, Maria/Muddy and Virginia/Sissy, and a bottle of cognac for the three. This man dressed in black cloak, scarf, black fedora and silver-tipped cane, became known as the "Poe Toaster," returning for many years later on Poe's birthday.

Our heroes had managed to correct the time-lines by returning Edgar Allan Poe to his own destiny. In yet another time-line, one where he had not interfered with future literary history, Edith Keeler would receive her inspiration to begin her "peace movement" which would stall the USA's entry into the Second World War from books other than those written by Herbert George Wells,

So Edith Keeler still had to die! But that's a different story, and a different trio of time-travelers.

From time to time, we like to publish a story that breaks the mold. This societal allegory by French author Gulzar Joby, which stars Chief-Inspector Ganimard and his eternal nemesis Arsène Lupin, is one such tale...

Gulzar Joby: *Science outraged, Science murdered!*

What are the police doing? "screamed" the headlines.

"Go get some air, Ganimard. A little squalor will take your mind off the run of bad luck you've been having," said the Prefect of Police.

He gave a hand-written note to Chief-Inspector Ganimard whose head was still reeling from the case of nine mansions robbed in a single night. The second robbery of the Crédit Lyonnais Bank was still hard to swallow, and he could not put up with one more failure. He had to find at least one or two stolen paintings or trinkets to avoid being reassigned to the vice squad.

"A body dug up in Ivry?" said the Chief-Inspector. "That's all you have, Monsieur le Préfet?"

"It's not just any old corpse," said the Prefect. It's a national glory. It's France itself that's been insulted."

So, Chief-Inspector Ganimard put on his coat, did not forget his hat, and hailed a cab, heading toward Ivry. Luckily, he found a pulp magazine left on the seat—something to read. Inside was an outrageous episode of the adventures of Machefer the Alsatian, this time pitted against the Giant Boche. Exactly what he needed—something entertaining with pictures, trying to be scary without quite getting there. When Ganimard arrived in Ivry, he paid the fare, asked for a receipt and went off with the magazine in his pocket. A police officer was waiting for him at the entrance to the cemetery.

"Good morning, Chief-Inspector."

"You look upset, Durand. Haven't you ever seen a corpse before?"

"Oh, sure. Prostitutes, a guy from the outskirts stabbed to death, even children. That's the worst. But this one…"

Ganimard followed the policeman, who closed the cemetery gates behind them. They hurried down a few aisles and found themselves at the crime scene—because a crime had been committed.

The headstone had been knocked over and the grave pillaged, literally gutted, with insane rage. The coffin's old wood and the marble statue had been smashed to pieces, scattered around the soil; someone had even vomited onto the other graves, which had not been spared. Vases were lying on the ground, spewing their dead flowers. The defiled hole inevitably attracted all attention. It looked as if the grave had been blown up. That was the only explanation. However, although the Chief-Inspector believed the policeman's story, no one in the neighborhood had heard any explosions the night before.

"Since it's an old grave, we're probably not dealing with grave robbers," said Ganimard. "Besides, where's the body? Did they take it away?"

"No, Chief-Inspector, unfortunately…"

Ganimard turned around. The scene was even more gruesome. The bones of the skeleton had been scattered over the other graves as if some rabid dog had gotten to them.

"Who could have committed such a sacrilege?"

"That's just what the guard said. He's in the local café, having a drink, trying to pull himself together."

"Oh! That skull is full of excrement!"

"Horse dung, to be exact."

The policeman was right. It was insane. Ganimard stood up and wiped his hands with a handkerchief. He was having a hard time realizing that he was holding the skull of Sadi Carnot, a man who had died too soon, but who had had time to give to France—and humanity—the second law of thermodynamics.[7]

"What madness! Who could have it in so bad for the man of entropy and the second law?"

"Didn't he invent some kind of velocipede?"

"Not at all," replied Ganimard. "He worked on steam and gas engines—as far as I know. He was a true genius."

"I didn't know that. The cemetery guard found him, just like that. I'm sorry, Chief Inspector, but he had time to show the scene to some visitors and reporters."

"Don't apologize. It's OK as long as they didn't remove anything."

"The only thing they took were photographs. I couldn't do anything. I'm alone on duty on Sundays."

"Photos, eh? Hmm. That's more of a problem. The government won't like publicity. But then, they don't like anything much these days."

"What about the deceased?"

"His bones and coffin will be taken away for examination. We'll find some trace of explosives, perhaps some fingerprints, but I doubt it. The cemetery can reopen tomorrow."

While the policeman went to talk to the guard, Ganimard spotted a small envelop that had no markings lying on the ground a few paces away. He took it, opened it, and pulled out a card that had a typewritten message on it; it was a dire warning: *First the dead. Then will come the living. Let progress die.*

The press had one thing over the police: it was faster in breaking bad news.

Chief-Inspector Ganimard only had to skim through the foreign press to learn that the outrage committed against Sadi Carnot was not an isolated inci-

---

[7] Marie François Sadi Carnot (1837-1894), French statesman scientist, who served as the President of France from 1887 until his assassination in 1894.

dent. The easiest thing to do had been to visit the café located next to the Paris Bourse. Many foreigners were regulars there. It was no problem to get a few of the headlines from foreign papers translated, and even entire article when necessary. Thus he learned of the details of other attacks perpetrated upon the graves of illustrious scientists before the official channels.

In England, Newton's tomb had been pulverized by a bomb that had reduced the nave of Westminster Abbey to rubble. Lord Kelvin's grave had been hit, his bones strewn before Parliament during the night, ban act deemed to be beyond all human decency. Similar crimes had been carried out in Japan. Germany, Italy and Belgium. Only the USA had been spared for the moment.

Suspicions had therefore arisen. Despite its fervent denials, had America conspired against the rest of the world to insure its total control over Science and Industry? Ganimard did not think so. It was better to kidnap a scientist and make him work for you than to make such a mess digging up the dead. Moreover, until recently, America had had no great scientists, except for Benjamin Franklin. But the Europeans were bitterly surprised to see his tomb intact, when the graves of Volta, Galileo, Torricelli and Avogadro had been blown up.

France, too, was cruelly hit. Over the next few weeks, the entire police force was mobilized to watch the cemeteries—but in vain. At the Chambre des Députés, the leaders of the opposition were demanding the heads of the cabinet—and they got it.

But nothing seemed to halt the mad desecration campaign against the servants of Science. The tombs of Nicolas Appert, Charles Dallery, Joseph Marie Jacquard, Barthélémy Thimonnier, Gustave Trouvé, even the Montgolfier brothers and the illustrious Denis Papin, were reduced to rubble. The government did not even dare to publicly rebury them, and instead kept their remains well hidden.

The government now feared the worst, the ultimate humiliation—Louis Pasteur's tomb! The coffin was moved by the Army to a secret location and was guarded night and day. But people laughed at the motorized brigades launched by Clemenceau, completely useless. Emboldened, the most fervent worshippers of the Word of God now demanded laws against wicked "Jewish Science." They advocated the return to ignorance, the state of nature, the only thing that could guarantee happiness on Earth.

Ganimard, as a sensible man, was far from such thoughts. He wanted nothing more than to do his duty. The files were piling up. The affair was becoming so important that he was forced to file away the many exploits of Arsène Lupin in a dark metal cabinet, unworthy of the man. He had been summoned by the Interior Ministry, where Aristide Briand had complained that the investigation was getting nowhere, and demanded quick progress.

But the bombs were ordinary, just like the envelopes. The clues led nowhere. Potential suspects had been arrested by the dozens, then released. The systematic presence of horse dung at the sites of the desecrations could not be explained. Ganimard ended up chalking it to just one more proof of the perpetrator's hatred of science. As a theory, the work of a madman was plausible—but a madman who traveled around the world? One had never seen such a case of international madness before. There were instances of small groups out for revenge, from anarchists to conservative Catholics, fighting against materialism and women's right to vote. But none of them were taken seriously.

That morning, while having breakfast on the terrace of the Grand Colbert café, Ganimard saw what had been bound to happen. He did not even have to get his copy of *L'Osservatore Romano* translated.

A famous chemist from Milan had been found murdered, a meat cleaver stuck in his skull.

Ganimard sighed. "This time, it is war."

At the next table, a friendly man with a strong Auvergnat accent put down his cup of coffee. "What did you say?" he inquired.

"I said, it is war—the confrontation between civilization and a criminal organization such as the world has never seen before."

"You're right. We've got to shoot all these Marxists, one by one! I'm a retailer, and I can tell you that the threat of collectivism terrifies me. If we continue to leave these bastards free rein, they'll start a war between France and Germany. See, one of these days, they're going to get hold of a country and enslave its population. You may laugh, yes, monsieur, but war is possible! And who will be its first victims?"

"Soldiers, likely?"

"No! Retailers! Yes, monsieur, war profits only to the big industrialists, the cosmopolitan elites, the capitalists, the bankers and the generals on their horses! Business should be sacred, safe from the turmoils of the world. Why do you think we invented writing? To write poems? Not at all! To do business! To make lists of goods and draw up contracts! But what kind of criminal organization are you talking about?"

"The papers now call them the *Flat Earth Fanatics*."

"Good name! All the same, it's pretty nasty to dig up the dead. Even if I don't trust scientists myself. The swine would kill their own mother for a new discovery."

Ganimard returned home very late after one last inspection tour of Paris. The "Dung Government," as the opposition press had called it, had now fallen. But the new one was faring no better in the throes of a growing panic.

The Institute, like all places that sheltered Science and scientists, had been turned into a fortress. France had had seven scientists murdered—a heavy loss for the nation. The police no longer worried about protecting property. Businessmen and bourgeois came every day to protest loudly. The Parliament was still meeting, but for how long? Elections were scheduled for the following spring and the various "leagues" associated with antiscientists were putting up candidates everywhere. The papers were screaming about German conspiracies and calling for a good skinning of Kaiser Wilhelm II.

The Chief-Inspector turned the key in the lock, entered his modest apartment, closed the door, and took off his hat and coat, which he left in the narrow entryway. Then Inspector Ganimard went into the living room without fixing dinner. He had eaten at a cheap café with some of his men. The deputy-prefect had excused himself, because he had to take a train that night to Compiègne, in order to finalize that city's defenses, since it was planned to become the last refuge, the impregnable citadel of French Science. A fort would have been preferable—the Brest Arsenal, the Charenton Fort, or that of Montrouge, near Paris. The Ajaccio Citadel had been considered for a while because of its remote location on Corsica, but being far from the continent would have made it tough for supplies and the materials necessary for the scientists to continue their research. So, in order to protect the great men effectively, Compiègne had been deemed the ideal choice, far from Germany and the British Channel. From now on, it would be secured by over a hundred military posts, but life would go on as usual inside, with its shops, its crowded Imperial Theater, its bookstores suddenly filled with customers much more demanding than their normal bourgeois or schoolteachers clientele.

The bottle of wine was out of place. Ganimard stiffened up. A man was sitting casually in his armchair.

"Who are you? He asked."

"Your friend. Easy with that revolver, Ganimard. You might hurt yourself."

"You!"

Arsène Lupin had invited himself over! Lupin was drinking from his bottle of Jura wine, which he liked to sip a little before going to bed—his only pleasure in life.

"Don't just stand there, Ganimard, sit down. Make yourself at home!"

"That's very kind of you. What do you want?"

"I'm worried about you, Ganimard, truly. There are dirty dishes in the sink and your laundry hasn't been done in ages. Where's your wife? Is she OK?"

Ganimard dropped in a chair. At least, he looked taller than Lupin in his armchair. Would he have time to get the jump on him and slap on the handcuffs? Probably not.

"She divorced me. Fr years I abused my health while chasing you! I neglected her. So, she left."

"I'm truly sorry. But, come on! For you to want to lock me up at all costs is absurd. What harm have I really caused to society? Now, I've come to help you."

"How so?"

"You're brave, but you're struggling. I have to tell you that I don't like this grave-digging business."

Ganimard understood. It was an insane proposal!

"Help me? But who will be helping me? Vicomte Raoul d'Andrésy, Maxime Bermond, Comte Bernard d'Andrésy, Horace Velmont, Colonel Beauvel, Jacques d'Emboise, Jean Dubreuil, Etienne de Vaudreix, Louis Valméras, Sauvinoux, Prince Paul Sernine, Jim Barnett, Raoul d'Avenac, Baron Jean d'Enneris, Don Luis Perenna..."

"Stop the recital! Tonight there's only a friend of France."

"I don't want your help. Get out!"

"I have powerful means at my disposal, unknown to the government, as you well know. You can't refuse my offer. I'll let you have the glory—that doesn't matter to me. In this instance, I prefer discretion—the sweet feeling of accomplishing one's duty."

Lupin poured himself the last glass of Jura wine and dropped the bottle on the floor.

"I propose a truce, for the time it takes to find who's been murdering these hapless scientists—ours and overseas. Progress can't be stopped! In the name of our old friendship, I will find out before the end of the month."

"We are not friends—and that leaves you only twelve days."

"That's plenty. So, on the last Thursday of this month, go to the public square across from the Academie des Sciences at the time the evening papers come out. I would be really grateful if you come alone, Ganimard."

"And you'll hand me the guilty parties?"

"Of course! You have my word. I must go now, off to meet a woman who's about to leave the Opera. You made me miss the performance tonight."

Lupin left, opening the door as if it hadn't been locked.

More annoyed than angry, Ganimard picked up the empty bottle and had no choice but go into the kitchen and drink a glass of water. Obviously, the lunatic reveled in puzzles. An open box was sitting on the kitchen table. Ganimard leaned over. What new trick was Lupin now playing on him? In the box were six bottles of excellent Jura wine, and a little note that read: *To comfort a loyal servant of order.*

On the last day of the month, a Thursday, Chief-Inspector Ganimard stood in the public square across from the Academies des Sciences. He was not trying to keep his appointment; he even believed that he had forgotten it. Moreover, he had not written it down anywhere. But all of a sudden, he had left the police HQ, walked through the streets and found himself in front of the Academie.

The weather was nice, so nothing was more natural than to have a stroll in the square, find an empty bench, and sit down to smoke a cigarette—even if the mysterious foe was slaughtering a scientist every week and the Bourgeoisie were scared witless—for who, now, would invent new ways of getting rich?

A kid passed by the bench and sold him a newspaper with a terrifying headline: *Murder of Louis and Maurice Blériot. Investigation flounders. Are engineers next?*

An English Lord—to judge by his clothes==sat down next to him.

"Can I borrow your newspaper?" he asked.

"Here. There's nothing but bad news."

Now feeling crowded, Ganimard wanted to change benches, but he recognized the other man and became angry.

"Damnation! It's you?"

"Of course, it's me. Congratulations, my friend! You're getting quicker to unmask me. And you came alone. Good! You want to know, right?"

Ganimard clenched his teeth. Of course, he wanted to know. Still, he would not give Lupin the pleasure of seeing him beg. Stoically, he flicked his cigarette to the ground and crushed it with his shoe.

"If you have something to say to me, say it. Otherwise, I'm leaving."

"The guilty party is a little old man."

"What?"

"Really. A little old man. You see, Ganimard, I saw right away the absurdity of digging up the dead and then killing the living. And the different police forces weren't collaborating. They weren't sharing what little they knew. Each operated on his own. What's really sad is that good people are no longer adequately protected today."

"I don't care about your opinion, talk!"

"No border stops me. What puzzled me the most was the horse dung. But that was the key! It had to be either either a false clue, left on purpose to mislead the investigation, or the act of a madman. Hatred, Ganimard, hatred! I've rarely seen such rage, such desire to destroy, except in governments and arms dealers. To tell you the truth, it wasn't very hard to pick up his trail. I can't explain how Scotland Yard wasn't able to arrest him. All these scientists were murdered by a single man—a former coach driver who had become a tycoon of London coaches, gnawed away by greed and a desire to succeed, which, I confess, warrants some respect. Except that the automobile got in his way! The horse-driven carriages were conquered by the combustion engine and caused him one of those shocks that one never get over. That's your man, in the grips of an obsessive hatred against those responsible—not the car manufacturers, who were just pawns in his sick mind, but the scientists, Science itself! He could have simply replaced his coaches with cars, but no, he chose to sell everything and nurse his vengeance. He sacrificed his family, his reputation, and ultimately his fortune. He went mad, seeing himself as the righter of wrongs, the protector of the horse. So, he set off to destroy Science, starting with the dead."

"That's unbelievable! How could he do it all alone?"

"London is full of desperate people ready to do anything for money. Our little old man never moved an inch. Don't forget that he is a skillful manager of other men. He knows how to organize a business. His savvy turned him into criminal genius. I have to say that he did a great job at setting up an organization."

"So where is he, your little old man?"

"Right here."

"Where? Where, Lupin? You're joking!"

"Not at all. You know how much I like to win. I love triumph. Your man is sitting on the bench across from us. I wasn't going to leave him to the Crown of England, anyway. It was child's play getting him across the Channel quietly."

It was not possible. The vagrant was already there when he had arrived at the rendezvous. The international assassin, the nefarious grave robber, could not be this poor beggar with shaggy hair!

Ganimard jumped up. The old man looked groggy. He must have been drugged. The Chief-Inspector unbuttoned his coat and searched his pockets. He pulled out a notebook with lists of names and places, as well as official papers in English. He knew that they were deeds and bills of sale. Behind him, Lupin was talking away, as usual.

"You see, Ganimard, I always deliver. The French police will now be able to grab all the credit, thanks to me, Arsène Lupin, the savior of France, the rescuer of the Future, the protector of the Arts and Sciences. The government ought to erect a statue in my honor."

Ganimard's hands were shaking. The papers might be fake. Lupin could have plotted everything, masterminded the whole thing! But Lupin did not kill. Lupin fought for money, fame and women. But he could have found some tramp crawling around London, drugged him, and brought him back to Paris to mock the police.

Ganimard came to his senses. No, the man on the bench had to be guilty, he had to be the instigator of the hideous crimes against Science. It could be no one else. Lupin was never wrong, never failed. He had already given the government the plans of a revolutionary submarine. A prank of that kind would be in a terrible taste—he would end up a laughingstock, at Lupin could not stand being ridiculed, scorned, made the subject of unflattering conversations. The disappearance of Science was frightening and disturbing. An eternal optimist, Lupin could not contribute to chaos. He was an enemy of society, but he did not want it to disappear. The guilty party was certainly this little old man.

Ganimard didn't thank his benefactor. That was a bridge too far for him. He would not even shake hands. But he had to show a little gratitude, say something. The phenomenal man whom he had tried, in vain, to put in prison for years, whom he thought he had caught ten times already, had just saved lives by this action. Ganimard turned around. But Lupin had already disappeared. In his place, on the bench, was an old lady feeding cookies to her dog.

As soon as the little old man was in prison, the murders stopped. The world could breathe freely again. The Englishman was more than willingly to talk, even if he seemed to have lost his mind. It did not matter. There was incontestable proof. They found plans in his home in Knightsbridge, stacks of notebooks, receipts, plus three cases of explosives in a Dublin storehouse. The old coachman had managed his terrible vengeance very well.

What was bound to happen, happened. London and Paris argued over the most wanted criminal in the world. English justice demanded him, but France refused to extradite him. By its ingenuity, French police had stopped the insane crime wave and saved progress. The scientists could again work in peace. Polar expeditions set off after a month. Submarines took to the sea. Industrial manufacturing resumed. Department stores filled up their inventory. In Berlin, the new 105mm German cannon made Kaiser Wilhelm II proud.

Making an infernal racket, Ganimard was typing off the physicist's statement as the man groaned in the chair across from him. The veterans of the police force rightfully missed the silence of the pen.

"So, you state that an individual entered your home to steal the contents of your bookshelf and desk."

"I don't know. I found no sign of a break-in. I'd gone out to dinner with some colleagues, and when I got back, my home office was empty—totally empty! No books, no papers, nothing! My life's work, my notes, my mail, my most intimate mathematical thoughts, my boldest theories!"

"Do you suspect anyone?"

"Chief-Inspector, there are not even ten of us in the world who might understand the secrets of the atom. Even we have trouble glimpsing them. It's unimaginable that one of my colleagues would commit such a crime."

"Even a German?"

"Even a German. It might sound idealistic, but Science has nothing to do with chauvinism. What was stolen was priceless to me, but completely worthless to the common man."

"Vengeance? A jealous woman? A disgruntled servant?"

"My old mother takes care of the house—talk to her. But don't bother with our maid; she's got nothing to do with it. She's in shock too, and didn't see or hear anything."

"Can't you just rewrite your formulas?"

The physicist laughed long and nervously.

"Are you joking? I've been working on the structure of the atom and its components for more than twenty years. I've discovered unimaginable possibilities! We'll extract fantastic forces that will be controlled like we dam rivers too. Have you ever got dizzy just thinking about these two questions: What is matter? And what is energy?"

"As a matter of fact, no."

"That's your loss. Everything is there, what the universe is composed of...
I forgot." The mathematician rifled through his pockets. "I found this note on
my desk. I don't know what to think. It's quite absurd. But you, Chief-Inspector,
might be able to make some sense of it."

Ganimard took the paper and read:

*I declare that you scientists, are debasing yourselves by working for gov-
ernments and industry like servile slaves groveling before your masters. I refuse
to tolerate such mediocrity. I have grandiose plans for Humanity. Science is a
source of infinite power, and deserves a master worthy of it. Certain knowledge
should not be left in the hands of children. So, take notice: from now on, I will
keep the most advanced knowledge for myself alone.*

Fantômas

Translation: Michael Shreve & Jean-Marc Lofficier.

Bob Morane is a perennial French YA hero. He was created by Belgian writer Henri Vernes and his literary career began in 1953 at Belgian publisher Marabout. The series—which new authors continue today—totals more than 200 volumes. While a sliding timeline has made it possible for Bob and his sidekicks, burly Scotsman Bill Ballantine and fearless newswoman Sophia Paramount, not to age, the character originally served in the RAF during World War II. This is the period of Bob's life in which French SF author Vincent Jounieaux chose to locate his tale...

Vincent Jounieaux: *The Necropolis of Silence*

Egypt, August 1942

The man was tired. He had not slept in more than 24 hours and he was pacing nervously along the runway, constantly scanning the sky. To the east the night was fading into the first signs of dawn. His rangers had made a road in the sand, a line of lamps with flickering flames that marked out a flat zone next to the oasis. In his arms he was holding a leather satchel with a round flap and hugging it close despite the strap around his shoulder.

He stopped for a second, let go of his bundle and shook his hands to get the blood circulating. Instinctively, he scratched his budding beard and tipped back his Stetson. The poor, lumpy hat had turned every which color but the man could not part with it! Out of attachment or superstition. The wait was getting the better of his patience, so he headed for the Berber tribe that had brought him to the meeting point. The chief was kneeling on a rug, watching over his camels.

"Sinber, you're sure they're coming to get me?" he asked in French with a strong American accent.

"Yes," the nomad answered. "The sun won't have risen before you're gone."

"Well, they better hurry. I'd rather travel at night... It attracts less attention. Do you know the pilots?"

"No, Dr. Jones. A single pilot. From the Royal Air Force. Just you and him, no one else."

"Punctuality is the mark of kings. All is lost! His Majesty's officers are not what they used to be. It's not these kind of monkeys that are going to win this damn war for us. Huh? What did you say?"

The Bedouin chief stood up slowly, adjusted his *chèche* and pointed to the darkened west. No sound could be heard.

"I said that the RAF keeps its promises and what you're carrying must be very precious for you to be so agitated. Maybe it'd be better for it to stay on Egyptian soil. What do you say, Dr. Jones?"

The plane tilted over to line up with the runway—a fighter jet with English colors that Jones had never seen before. The machine looked like the famous Spitfire but its aerodynamic lines were slimmer, more streamlined. It landed smoothly, turned around at the end of the runway and rolled up to them. The engine cut, the propeller slowed and the cockpit was opened by a young pilot. Without hesitating he jumped down and took off his leather helmet. Around twenty years-old, with a crew cut, gray, sparkling eyes, he held out his hand to the famous archeologist.

"Dr. Jones, allow me to introduce myself: Second Lieutenant Robert Morane," he said in English with a heavy French accent.

"Delighted. I was afraid for a minute that the British had forgotten me."

"Sorry. My superiors figured this mission would be a good opportunity to test this prototype." Morane indicated the engine cooling down behind him.

Sinber shook the Frenchman's hand warmly. "Major Bob, what kind of beautiful bird is this?" the Bedouin asked.

"It's the latest in English research, the Martin-Baker MB3. It's got six 20mm guns. A good plane but the Napier Sabre engine's been giving us some problems."

With these words Jones stepped back and gripped his satchel tighter. "What kind of problems?" he muttered.

"Its designer, my friend Captain Baker, lost his life last week after an unexplained breakdown during takeoff."

"It's out of the question that I'm getting into a flying coffin," Jones spit out. "What I'm carrying is too valuable."

The pilot considered the leather satchel with round flaps and raised his eyebrows, "Come on, Dr. Jones, flying the plane isn't rocket science. This prototype is the cream of the crop and I give you my word that it'll get us there safe and sound. Besides, 150 miles is a stroll in the park."

The archaeologist studied the situation silently. It was certainly riskier for him to stay here and wait for another means of transport than to fly in the prototype. He gave in and let the Frenchman help him climb into the MB3.

The first rays of the sun were kissing the dunes when the fighter jet sped off to the north away from the disapproving gaze of the Bedouin.

Sitting behind the second lieutenant, Indiana Jones relaxed. He had to admit that the young Frenchman was an ace pilot and he felt completely safe. The archeologist sighed with relief. The last few days had been pumped full of adrenaline and the pressure from being on guard constantly was starting to release. The treasure he was carrying would soon be safe, far from the hands of the Afrika Korps.

The plane was flying over the desert and the rising sun skimmed over the infinite expanse of sandy hills. The sight combined with the hypnotic hum of the engine overcame his vigilance.

Morane's voice pulled him out of his drowsiness. The Frenchman had not seen him dozing off. How long had he slept?

Indiana grumbled, "Sorry, I was taking a little rest. What did you say?"

He was afraid the officer might ask him about the nature of the "package" he was transporting. Jones had said nothing about it so far. He could not afford to trust anyone and he was hoping the young pilot would not be angry, given the stereotype of the French as excessively proud.

"Do you know Jacques Tourneur?" Morane repeated.

The harmless question relieved the archeologist as he muttered, "Vaguely. He's the Frenchy who made a fortune in Hollywood, right?"

"Yes. I'm looking forward to his next big film, *Cat People*. We'd say *La Féline* in French. I love horror films."

"You know, I don't have time to go to the movies today, but I loved them when I was younger... around your age."

"It's true that I lied a little about my birthday to get into England and join the Air Force."

"My God, what did your parents say?"

"They don't say anything—I'm an orphan. It's my uncle who urged me to leave France. I needed some action."

"Bloody Frogs!"

The second lieutenant laughed, "I don't eat frog's legs, it's a matter of principle with me."

"Me, I'd kiss my principles goodbye if I were starving," Jones replied.

Both of them laughed but their good mood did not last long. Bob Morane stiffened up and turned around, pointing to the sky behind the cockpit.

"Messerschmitts!"

Coming from the west a squad of six planes was heading their way.

"I could put some some distance between us," Morane explained, "but the engine's showed signs of power loss. It might explode if I push it too hard."

Behind them the Messerschmitts were gaining ground, so to speak. They were catching up to the Martin-Baker quickly. Strangely, however, they were not attacking, just surrounding it, two in front and two behind with one on each side. Through the cockpit the German officer to the port side signaled to them to follow. The planes veered off to the west, toward Libya.

Morane turned to the American, "Sorry, Dr. Jones, but I have no intention of delivering this treat to Rommel on a silver platter. We don't have a lot of choice: if you want to stay alive, we'll have to jump with the parachutes and let the plane crash. OK?"

"If the Luftwaffe hasn't shot us down like rabbits," the archaeologist answered, "it's not because of your prototype but because of what I'm carrying! They want to get their hands on it."

"Well, you should've said so sooner."

And Morane went into action. Arming the guns he machine-gunned the two fighters in front while opening the throttle and slamming the stick. Before him the tails of the Messerschmitts vaporized in the bullets. The planes pitched to either side, then plummeted as they exploded in a huge ball of fire. With engines screaming the Martin-Baker shot up through the clouds of black smoke. The attack surprised the other pilots, giving Morane time to complete his loop and set down in their wake, ready to fire. The 20mm guns spit again, crisscrossing the air with trails of white smoke that vanished above the Messerschmitt targets. Morane adjusted for altitude and fired again. This time the bullets riddled one of the German planes, which instantly dropped into a fatal spiral.

"Three down!"

"I'm liking you more and more, little Bob."

The three remaining Messerschmitts regrouped to face the MB3, letting loose harmless bursts of gunfire. Morane did not blink an eye and kept straight at them. He was arming his weapons for another pass when the propeller started spluttering. He did not stop but fired blind. The planes flew by, almost touching wings. The MB3 engine coughed a few more times but they got through them. Indiana Jones turned around. One of the Messerschmitts was diving toward the ground and its pilot was swinging at the end of a parachute.

"Four down!" he shouted.

As soon as he spoke the propeller suddenly froze and the jolt made the plane shudder. In a peculiar silence the Martin-Baker started drifting and losing altitude.

"Dr. Jones, our trip ends here! We have to jump. You're lucky, you're going to be the first one to test the ejection seat that Martin designed. Check the straps on the harness. I'll see you down below!"

Jones had no time to argue before the pilot pushed the ejector. The cockpit glass flew off in the wind that was howling around the plane. His seat went shooting into the air, taking his breath with it. Below him he caught a worried look from the French pilot. Another jolt, less violent this time, and the parachute in the seat unfurled its crown above him.

Indiana Jones gripped his satchel more tightly. The last two Messerschmitts surged out of a white cloud and rumbled around him. The pilots were eyeing him, making sure that he still had the precious cargo—in his present situation, it was hardly possible to hide it! Furious, he pulled out his Colt and fired at the closest plane. One of the shots hit the target and the Luftwaffe pilot's head exploded, spraying the cockpit with blood. The German collapsed on the instrument panel and his plane nosedived to the ground, crashing in a blast of fire and sand.

"Bob!" Jones yelled on seeing the last fighter jet closing in on the paralyzed British plane.

Morane did his best to dodge the gunfire, but the MB3 was not an agile glider. The enemy bullets tore up his left wing. The plane tipped over and he barely had time to eject before the machine turned into a deadly torch. Jones touched down first and the Frenchman a few hundred feet above him was soon at his side. In the distance the last Messerschmitt had disappeared.

The two men were waiting for a rescue squad under the blazing sun, burned by the glare from the sand. To protect themselves in this furnace they had fashioned up tunics out of the parachutes but their meager supply of water did little to quench the fire that was consuming them with every breath. Indiana had twisted an ankle on landing and was using a cane made from the wreckage of a Messerschmitt.

"We won't last long," Jones rasped through cracked lips. "I warned the base on the radio before jumping. They know our position. They'll send a team to pick us up as soon as possible. Anyway, I'm sure the Germans are already on their way... and not to save our hides."

Bob did not respond. He felt like he was sitting on a bed of hot coals.

"And you're a funny young man. They send you on a secret mission to get me out of Egypt. The Afrika Korps dispatches a squad to get their hands on this package here, we bring down five out of six, almost break our necks with those goddamn ejection seats and you, you say nothing, not one question to ask!"

Bob raised his gray eyes peeking through the improvised *djellaba*. "If you don't talk about it, I guess it's because you don't want to."

"If I say nothing, it's to protect you. What I'm carrying can change the outcome of the war! You're young and I don't want to shorten your life by putting my trust in you. Understand?"

"Perfectly. My mission is to bring you back safely so you can get back to your leaders. Who knows, maybe what you've got there will keep me from joining Operation Lightfoot, which Commander Montgomery has been planning. Churchill appointed him to drive Rommel out of Egypt but it's looking a lot harder than anyone could imagine."

The endless wait resumed, silent and monotonous. Indiana Jones had no idea how long they had waited because the heat of the sun had fried his perceptions. Finally, the rumble of an engine could be heard in the distance. He stood up, shooting a flash of pain through his ankle. The sun was balanced slightly to the west.

"A Spitfire! I could recognize that sound a mile off," the Frenchman ripped off his tunic and waved it in the air with all the strength that was left in him.

Jones did the same and waved his Stetson for the pilot as well. Soon the British fighter roared over them, rolling from one wing to the other to show that he had seen them. Strangely, he headed east, toward enemy lines where it disappeared.

The repeated staccato of machine guns followed by a thunder of bombs suddenly filled the desert void. The concert of gunfire ended with one dull explosion, then a column of black smoke rose on the horizon.

The two men stood frozen to the spot. It was useless to run. There was nowhere to hide. Soon a mobile unit of the Afrika Korps appeared, composed of two Kübelwagons, two half-tracks armed with heavy machine guns and a lightly armored vehicle topped with a cannon. The reconnaissance group, which had obviously just survived a serious skirmish, surrounded them, pointing all weapons in their direction.

A German accent ordered, "Gentlemen, give up! The ride is over. Dr. Jones, be kind enough to hand over the chest of Manasseh."

They had been caught by Oberst Benedikt Dietrich whose soldiers had tied them up right away and thrown them into the back of one of the half-tracks. Jones' precious cargo had passed into enemy hands. The American had tried hard to resist but he got a swift, hard punch in the ribs for his effort.

The vehicles rode single file over the dunes, lurching on the trail. At one moment they saw a squad of Spitfires but it stayed out of firing range and vanished over the horizon. Bob Morane was not about to kid himself: if the jets were not engaging in battle, it was not for the sake of their pretty eyes but for that famous chest. What did it contain? Dietrich had mentioned the name Manasseh. Was he talking about Yehonatan Manasseh, son of Moses? Entirely possible. After all, hadn't he picked up Jones around Mount Sinai? Whatever it was, its loss had plunged the archaeologist into deep despair. He did not move, did not speak, completely indifferent to the jeers of the Afrika Korps soldiers. Sometimes he looked up at the Frenchman with eyes that flashed a faint ray of hope as if his partner in misfortune might be able to turn the situation around. Bob was a realist and knew that their enemies left nothing to chance, that their days were numbered. In fact, he was surprised to still be alive now that the Axis possessed the chest. Why were they keeping them alive? Morane saw only one answer to this question: Dietrich was going to use them for something.

The heat had let up a little when the division slowed down near an oasis where a tribe of Bedouin was resting. The camels were drinking from the source while the men were drawing water from a well.

Morane heard Dietrich's voice over the sound of the engines: "Stop! Form a circle. You, set up the tent in the middle and put the prisoners under guard. Roderich, take some men and get water and you, Gerhard, send a cable to General von Värst to tell him we're setting up. Get to it!"

The soldiers obeyed without saying a word and threw Jones and Morane, still bound, into a canvas tent.

Colonel Dietrich made a brief speech to them, "Gentlemen, you can relax. We're waiting for General von Värst. He's the only one authorized to question you."

He patted Jones' satchel, opened it and took out the object wrapped in faded, frayed cloth. Carefully, he unfolded the tissue and revealed a little chest, inlaid and dusty. He examined it in the light of a lamp. The box was apparently made from one single block of wood. There was no lock, no opening, no cover.

"Magnificent! Thank you, Dr. Jones," the German officer sneered.

He wrapped it up again, slipped it into the satchel and hung it around his shoulder.

"Gentlemen, have a rest. I'm going to get a good long drink before the General arrives."

With that he left the tent, leaving the prisoners to their own unquenchable thirst.

Bob Morane tried to wriggle free but the ropes had been tied by a professional and all his twisting did nothing but rattle the chair. Jones had the same result, so the two men gave up.

The tent was empty. The guard had taken away every sharp object. Things were off to a bad start and looked worse for the future. This conclusion depressed the Frenchman. With a knot in this throat he admitted that his short life was about to end here, in the middle of nowhere, in the dunes of Libya. He had climbed up the ranks of the Royal Air Force for nothing. His enthusiasm and charisma had been recognized in high places while he battled body and soul to defend the values of freedom that the Axis powers denied... but destiny had decided otherwise when his mission to pick up an American ally turned into this fiasco. Goodbye to dreams of knighthood in the service of the people, defending widows and orphans! He wanted so much to protect the victims in life, to spare the children from the terrible trials that he himself had gone through! An old saying crept up in his mind: as long as there's life, there's hope.

Chasing away these morbid thoughts, he sat up straight and broke the silence that was unsettling his soul. "Dr. Jones, I guess they figure they'll force you to talk by torturing me. The idea doesn't thrill me at all."

"Me neither, Bob," Jones had come to the same conclusion.

"So," Morane continued, "my curiosity's got the better of me: I'd like to know what's at stake. What's in this chest that everyone's so hot to get their hands on?"

Indiana Jones spoke so passionately that Morane forgot about their tragic situation.

"Yehonatan Manasseh was the grandson of Moses," the American began. "This chest didn't really belong to him but it holds his confession engraved on a golden sheet. In truth we don't know much about this relic, like everything else about the Old Testament. I can tell you that there's no archeological proof that Moses existed... all we have are his writings. According to the book of Judges, Yehonatan was the son of Gershom, therefore the grandson of Moses. What's interesting is that the Masoretic text makes him the son of Manasseh because at the time the Masoretic scribes were scandalized by the attitude of the Moses' grandson as he opposed his grandfather's doctrine. Yehonatan Manasseh and his tribe of Dan was struck with apostasy. The situation got so bad that certain Church Fathers suggested that the Antichrist would come from this heretical tribe of Israel. In short, for my sponsors, this papyrus might overturn all the philosophical, theological and cosmological beliefs we hold today."

"Sorry, Jones, but it's all Hebrew to me."

Indiana stared at the Frenchman for a minute without uttering a word, then he broke out laughing.

"Ha, ha! You're priceless, Bob! Let's just say that Manasseh was one of the disciples of Seth, the third son of Adam and Eve. They thought they were the enlightened humanity. They worshipped the infinite spirit of the universe, the true God of the immortal kingdom of 'Barbelo' and for them this world below, our world, was the realm of an evil, vile creator God called Nebro or sometimes Ialdabaoth... who had deceived Moses."

"What does all this have to do with us?"

"Some members of the Axis see the testament of Manasseh as a way to destroy the Gnostic Jewish tradition on which Rome was founded. Imagine that the manuscript proves the existence of Nebro. Such a revelation would justify, in the eyes of the Germans, the war they're waging against the Euro-American Jewish heritage."

Bob thought about all this before responding to Jones' ideas.

"On the other hand, if the manuscript restores Moses in his role as prophet and destroys the theory of the perverse god Nebro, it would support the American believers who see their country as the new Jerusalem, right?"

"Right," Jones replied. "I'd go even further. If the manuscript is in favor of the heretical theory, it'd be better for the allies if this document doesn't fall into the hands of the Germans and likewise if it supports the traditional Jewish position, it'd be better for the Axis to make it disappear."

"Of course. Whatever the papyrus says, it's going to shake up the world."

In a split second the collateral effects of such a revelation flashed through the mind of the Frenchman: on one side an Axis victory and the birth of the an Enlightened Church worshipping Nebro; on the other side an Allied victory with the triumph of monotheistic religions and the installation of the new Jerusalem in the USA.

The voice of the American shook him out of his reverie, "That's why the mystery has been so well guarded!"

The discussion between the two prisoners was interrupted by a blast of wind that rattled the tent violently, almost tearing it off the ground. A shrill scream accompanied the gusts, drilling into their ears. Through the slit in the tent Bob Morane watched, fascinated, the vertical landing of a German fighter jet.

"Incredible! They've managed to build the famous Triebflügel!" He turned to Indiana Jones, "We've known about this project but still I can't believe my eyes. What an extraordinary machine it must be to pilot!"

Outside, the plane with its rotating wings disappeared behind the circle of armored vehicles. The whistling faded as the turbines slowed down and a desert wind kicked up.

"Our time has come," the archeologist stated.

They did not wait long. Three men bent over as they entered under the canopy. With all the medals hanging on his chest the first must have been General von Värst, followed by Oberst Dietrich and a soldier with a cadaverous face who was carrying a jar. Von Värst dusted off his coat with the back of his glove and stared at the archeologist whose forehead was badly bruised. He paid no attention to the French pilot.

"Dr. Jones, I have no time to lose. Rommel is expecting me in an hour. Talk to me."

"I have nothing to say," the American snapped back.

"Want to play the stubborn child? I don't have a lot of choices: either you talk or we torture you to death, beginning, of course, with your crew member."

Von Värst made a quick sign to his henchman. Emotionless and waxy-faced, the demonic-looking soldier knelt down by Bob and slowly opened the metal cover of the opaque jar. The man appeared to lack all emotions, not a single spark in his eyes. A sharp odor filled the tent.

"Chloroform," Bob thought, trying to see inside the jar.

The skeletal soldier reached into his coat and pulled out long, wooden tongs with the ends wrapped in cotton. He stuck it in the jar and pulled out a yellow scorpion, 4 or 5 inches long. Its big tail tipped by a black telson was curled up for the moment. The man raised his dead eyes to the general, awaiting his orders.

"Let's see if this little desert dweller can loosen your tongue," von Värst nodded to the soldier.

He rolled up Morane's pant leg and laid down the yellow scorpion, shaking it a little with the tongs. The movement woke the animal from its lethargy. Its stinger threatened, poking into the empty air a few times before pricking the Frenchman's calf. Morane winced.

"Don't say a word," he ordered Jones.

"But I don't know anything, I swear," the archaeologist blurted out to the torturers.

Morane withstood the first sting bravely. Except for a little nausea, the venom only burned his leg. The systemic effects of the neurotoxins came with the second attack of the arthropod after the German placed it, stinger at the ready, on the Frenchman's chest. His body was hit with a series of icy waves and a cold sweat ran down his back. His sight blurred and Jones' begging along with von Värst's demands came from a different space, stretched out like in slow motion. The monster was waving the scorpion in front of his eyes with a sadistic grin slashed across his sickly face.

Morane wobbled. He could no longer think straight. He saw everything like through the prism of a wild kaleidoscope: the dancing scorpion, the drop of venom on the tip of its stinger; a soldier coming in to the tent to warn them and dropping to the ground straightaway; Oberst Dietrich pulling out his luger, leaning on the table to stay on his feet.

Outside, yelling and gunfire broke out. Dietrich sniffed the water in the pitcher on the table and fell backwards. Bob smiled: the Germans had been drugged! Von Värst was howling incomprehensible words. The freak soldier whacked Jones on the head with the butt of his Mauser, smashed the oil lamp on the ground and followed the general out of the tent. Their shadows disappeared in the flames like two demons dancing in hell.

Bob felt dizzy. His thick tongue was stuck to the top of his mouth. He was going to die and it did not matter whether it was from poisoning, dehydration or getting burned to death... The light faded. Thick smoke surrounded them. Out of the cloud came a sparkling green vial whose contents were poured down his mouth, a cold elixir working against the effects of the venom. Behind the vial floated the chiseled face of a Bedouin.

"They got away in the half-track," it said. "You're the pilot from the RAF. We have a chance to get the chest of Manasseh. Come on."

"But Dr. Jones?" the Frenchman mumbled, looking over at the American sprawled on the sand.

"Don't worry. We'll take care of him just like you."

Like all the soldiers in the camp, the German pilot was lying unconscious. Near him the Triebflügel stood with its nose pointing at the sky where the first stars were peeking through the indigo twilight.

"You feel up to piloting this thing?" the sand man asked.

"No pain no gain!" Morane said, even though he still felt groggy after the antidote.

They climbed up the ladder into the cockpit and the Frenchman sat down, sorry that he was not in better shape to enjoy the moment. The Berber was trembling with impatience but kept silent, leaving the pilot to get used to the prototype control panel. After a short time that seemed an eternity to the Bedouin, Morane buckled in and asked his companion to do the same. He pulled two starters and the engines roared in unison. The plane, which took off vertically, started shaking. The humming of the two counter-rotating, triple propellers got louder as it churned up a sand storm over the oasis. The plane lifted up, stabilized in the hands of the French pilot, then tilted over to head west toward the Axis territories. The gyroscopic cockpit pivoted and the gloomy rows of dunes under them marched by in the darkening night. Morane figured that the fugitives were 20 to 40 miles ahead of them because not much time had passed between the hasty departure of the general and their takeoff.

"There!" the Bedouin shouted as he scanned the dark horizon.

In the distance, 10 degrees east of their position, two white prongs were bouncing over the desert hills.

"Force them to stop! I'll take care of the rest," the man pulled out a relic that looked a lot like an old revolver.

"Whatever you say," Morane replied.

He steered the plane over the escapees by nose-diving over a wide arc. When they were directly above the half-track, Bob pushed the tail rotor and the Triebflügel fell lower. Although blinded by the maelstrom of sand, the German vehicle kept going, getting closer and closer to the armored truck that maintained its speed, paying no attention to the overhead threats.

"Desperate situations call for drastic measures," Bob sighed as he cut the fuel to the central propeller.

The Triebflügel dropped straight down. Its landing gear struck the front of the half-track, raised on impact, then fell back down. The plane was destabilized and tilted over. Its blades bit into the dunes with a shrill cry. Morane tried to straighten it out but in vain. The twisted propeller could not lift the plane, so it crashed down. The Frenchman tried to raise the nose to lighten the shock as much as possible. When it hit the ground his forehead smashed into the control board. He could do nothing but slip away into unconsciousness.

An oil lamp cast a dim light over the necropolis of the Guardians. With slow and respectful gestures the man laid the mummified corpse of his predecessor in the rocky alcove. The remains joined the thousands of other Guardians of which he had been one of the links in chain, a fragile link since on his watch the chest of Manasseh had fallen into impure hands. It was not the first time a Guardian failed at his mission. But this failure had cost him his life! No inscription was carved over the door of the crypt whose dark color clashed with the countless ruby vaults that were ornamented with the names of the Guardians lying therein.

Luckily, disaster had been averted and the wooden chest was back on its pedestal in the center of the underground city. The time of revelation had not yet come. Many Guardians would come to protect the forbidden temple. How the American archaeologist had managed to break into the stronghold, escape the traps in the maze and outwit the Guardian to get away with the treasure, no member of the Brotherhood was able to explain. Whatever the case, the threat

had passed and the witnesses of the violation had received the ointment of se-
crecy, that preparation concocted by the priests in their isolation to erase the
memories of the undesirables. The actual entrance of the Temple had been destroyed, the maze modified and the new Guardian of the underground city was
alone now, buried hundreds of feet under Mount Sinai. Defending the chest of
Manasseh was his only duty even if the solitude would drive him mad. He
closed the necropolis behind him. The stone door locked with a dull thud that
echoed down the long galleries of dark vaults.

The two men stood before the medical unit on the British base. Their au-
thorization for leave had been delivered by the doctor after a few days hospitali-
zation for a head trauma. That had been the official diagnosis, the result of a
crash they had been in. the two men had been picked up next to the wreck of the
Martin-Baker MB3, the French pilot having suffered two scorpion stings as
well. A miracle they made it out alive! Neither Morane nor Jones remembered
crashing and could not explain to their superiors why their parachutes were
found hundreds of feet away from the burned carcass of the plane, both them
torn to shreds.

"What are you going to do now, Bob?" the American asked as they shook
hands warmly.

"I'll go back to the 23rd Armored Brigade. The doc signed me off because
an important battle is brewing on the coast of El-Anaheim. And you, Dr. Jones?"

"I'll go back to Egypt. My government wants me to find a relic that might
change the course of the war. I don't like the idea of going back empty-handed."

"Well, good luck and maybe one of these days... Indy!"

The American smiled, checked his leather satchel, patted the Colt in his
holster, glanced down at the whip on his hip and turned around, waving goodbye.

Translation by Michael Shreve.

A number of novels by renowned French SF author Pierre Barbet were translated by DAW books in the 1970s—including Games Psyborgs Play *and* The Enchanted Planet, *which feature the character of Setni (his career seems to be told backward as he is an Admiral in the first book of the nine-volume series, a Captain in the next two, and a mere Officer later). Setni is a space-time investigator for the Great Brains of Kalapol who rule the Galactic Confederation from their seat on Beta Geminorum (Pollux) in the far future. This is one of his investigations...*

Jean-Guillaume Lanuque: *Lucretius' Maze*

Rome, 58 B.C.

Gnawed away by clouds, the light of the moon grew dim passing through the narrow windows at the top of the stone wall.

The grandfather clock materialized in the darkness, swaying as the hands above the pendulum marked a time that existed only elsewhere. There was a click and the door opened, a green light coming from inside it.

A dark figure stood in the strange doorway. It was Titus Crow, a specialist in the occult and the secret mysteries of civilizations. Before traveling through the universe in his alien clock, he had undergone a complete body transformation and was now trying to return to his own era.

"I have the feeling I've landed in a more suitable era than that Jurassic beach I had such a hard time getting away from," he said. "Now the question is, where and especially *when* am I?"

Just as he finished voicing this thought, he felt a movement nearby the imposing hieratic statue that he saw through a row of columns. As he got closer to the stone colossus, Titus Crow hailed the person in several languages. The man—a portly specimen dressed in green—froze briefly before taking off, running toward the opposite end of the building.

Titus Crow did not hesitate to run after him, but was blocked by the falling statues that were knocked over by the mysterious individual. The place became filled with the noise of them crashing to the ground, followed by the sound of a door slamming. Thinking that the building would not stay empty for long, Titus Crow quickly went back to his clock under the blind gaze of the two-headed idol.

That was when he saw the open book with crumpled pages on the tile floor at the foot of a column. He stopped and picked it up. He translated the title from the original French: *Guide to Rome in the 1ˢᵗ century before J.-C.* The date of publication was *1936.*

As usual Titus Lucretius Carus was working alone in his home office. Having abandoned the traditional method of dictation to a literate slave, he now preferred to write himself, alone, protected by his bookshelves full of scrolls. The room was cluttered, covered with manuscripts that were so many doors to ideas and knowledge from the past, or countries from the farthest reaches of the earth—the ink and papyrus equivalents of the multiple eyes of Argos.

On the ceiling, a thin line of smoke from the two oil lamps set on the corner of his desk formed a black spiral, cloudy and silent, which he had to waft away as it constantly reappeared. The light was just enough for him to write comfortably, and the furniture remained in the shadows, which was far from displeasing Lucretius, who was thus reminded of all that was still hidden in the darkness of his ignorance.

It must be said that what he was transcribing needed very little encouragement. He was, in fact, laying down, in a coded language of which he alone held the key, the memoirs of his travels: how he had located the last Spartacians and their island utopia, sadly destined to a brutal fall; the expedition he had led unwillingly to the dark realm of the dog-men; his encounter with the glass giants; the way he had managed to discover what was hiding behind the Elusinian mysteries; the humanopaths created in the middle of the desert by a strange exile from the Museum of Alexandria...

Suddenly, it was like the silence between two thunderclaps: the moment before, there was nothing; suddenly, a narrow cabinet, with a door and strange iron rods sticking out of a metal disk at the top, materialized right in front of him. The most astonishing thing was that a man dressed like a barbarian stepped out of it calmly.

"Are you my Nemesis or my Genius?" asked Lucretius.

"Neither," the man spoke in literary Greek. "My name's Titus Crow and I wanted to meet the most famous poet of this century."

"Are you sure you're talking to the right person? And first, could you explain to me how you got into my house?"

"I have come from the past. The thing that you see before you is like my chariot."

"I thought I'd seen all kinds of extraordinary things in my life, but you have succeeded in arousing my curiosity."

"I didn't choose you at random, Titus Lucretius Carus. I know of your rational convictions, and I think you may be the only person in Rome who can help me with my problem."

"In that case, give me some time to talk to my servants and prepare a place that will be more comfortable for us to discuss the matter."

The Roman left to tell his slaves that an unexpected guest had shown up. "I feel increasingly certain," Lucretius said to himself, "that the more I think I understand the world, the more its complexity escapes me."

When Titus Crow was alone, he took the opportunity to decipher the titles of some of the papyrus rolls that were cluttering the room: the writings of Epicurus, of course, that would spark the same desire for good in 20th century truth seekers, and Plato, Aristotle, Eratosthenes, and Pytheas, the peerless explorer... Lucretius' office was a temple of philosophical and scientific knowledge.

The Roman soon returned and led his guest downstairs, to a winter lounge with a glass window that looked out onto an enclosed garden. The two intellectuals stretched out on the benches with some light refreshments on a low table between them.

"Titus Crow, tell me frankly, are you one of those gods whom my master Epicurus places in some distant land, and whom he imagines care not at all about us poor, simple humans?"

"No, I'm just a simple human myself. I'm traveling through time and trying to get back to my own era, which is almost two thousand years in your future. But I've been stifled in my progress by some unidentifiable malfunction originating in your present... What exactly is your present?"

"We've just entered the year 695 since the founding of the City."

"I see. March, 58 B.C., therefore," Titus muttered.

Then he told Lucretius what he had experienced in the temple where he had first stopped.

"You were in the temple of Janus. It's one of the oldest religious buildings in the City, but I don't understand what one of your contemporaries could be looking for there, except maybe for the Sibylline books?"

"Would you be tempted to investigate the matter with me to find out?"

Next to the sanctuary that was Lucretius' home, which was almost frozen in silence and contemplation, the streets of the Subura district were almost a freak show. Marching across the streets, Titus Crow was assaulted by smells and sounds: urine mixed with garum and spices, the scent of rotting meat mixed with that of oil, while the shouts of merchants whizzed by, along with the curses of those he bumped into, and the laughter and the singing of Numidian musicians. Everything was sprawled under a pale sun, shivering in this biting cold. It was a harsh contrast with his memories of his Latin translations, calling up the fragrance of old paper and ink.

Lucretius strolled casually through the dodgy crowd. He was always torn between two emotions when he walked through the shadiest areas of Rome: one, a disgust in seeing to what levels if infamy his contemporaries could sink, but also a deep empathy with respect to how these miserable incarnations of life struggled in the face of such adversity. Like that beggar, stoic, his hood pulled over his face, sitting on the dirty ground that the snow, having turned into black sludge, had only made darker. But a patrician on his litter had just answered his pleas by tossing him a skinless chicken thigh, knocking over his bowl and the few coins it contained.

Lucretius had barely passed by the beggar when the four slaves carrying the litter fell to the ground simultaneously, their master along with them, dirtying and tearing his expensive toga. Furious, he started to swear at them and beat them with his sandals, before being assaulted by the locals who were only too happy to empty the contents of their chamber pots on a noble head. Stained with urine, excrement and waste water, the patrician fled without further ado. What surprised Lucretius the most was that he thought he had seen all his slaves thrown off balance at the same time, tripped up for no apparent reason. He turned to look at the beggar again, but he was gone. Only the empty bowl remained in his spot.

"Your city is full of attractions!" said Titus Crow. "Tell me, are we there yet?"

"The Empty Jug tavern is on the next street to the left."

The two men had to bow down as they entered the semi-underground room through a small door. The tavern was lit only by a few rusty oil lamps hanging on the walls, and its ceiling was blackened with layers of soot. It was only half-full, but already drowned in clamor and the odors of wine more or less digested. Sitting at a table to the side, a man with a bursting belly and a red face called them over with exaggerated movements of his arms. Dressed in a gaudy toga, with mid-length hair, he was busy picking his teeth.

"*Eques* Lucretius! It's always a pleasure to see you and do business with you," he shouted.

Lucretius had preferred to leave his toga with the thin red stripe at home along with his gold ring that made the *equites* recognizable to everyone, but he was dealing with a person who knew him well.

"That's not why I'm here, Ariston. I'd like to ask you about a recent incident in the district."

"Buy me a drink then. It'll loosen my tongue in the absence of a warm, wet woman!"

While the three men were sitting at a dirty, stained table, a one-eyed woman came and set down three wooden cups and a jug.

"Ariston, have you noticed anything a little different or strange lately?" asked Lucretius. "An unidentified presence, or some strange thefts?"

"Some of my girls have indeed spoken of infants who seemed to have disappeared swiftly from the pile of rubbish on which they had been carefully laid. At least, their bodies were never found again… And I have to admit that this is deeply disturbing to me, because my brotherhood is supposed to guarantee order in this seeming chaos, not to mention the fact that babies sell rather well when you can find the right customers. Some have even started to whisper about a new cannibalistic cult from the East. Rumors are spreading, thanks to one of these vile, stinking Orientals, a certain Rael. He swears he saw a Lamia snatch a newborn and carry it off towards the Tiber. Myself, I think that he must have ingested too many of those Asian substances that they think help religious tranc-es."

"Now that you mention it," Lucretius's voice became thin and reedy, "I haven't seen my orphan friends for a few days."

"What are you talking about?" asked Titus Crow.

"You see, Titus, among the babies abandoned in Rome or its suburbs, who are used by... well, in more or less legal circles," Lucretius glanced at Ariston who was pouring another cup of wine, "some of them eventually gain their free-dom by running away. Thus, communities are born, and some of them who live in the underground are in contact with me. I've allowed them to keep their free-dom in exchange for information. They're my immigrants from the *Cloaca Max-ima*, so to speak—my gang from the sewers."

Snow was starting to fall when Lucretius and Titus Crow left the tavern. After going through a few narrow alleys, and coming to a crossroads marked by the traditional public fountain with a votive statue, they noticed, with some sur-prise, that the neighborhood was deadly silent.

Of course, the snow was already muffling some sounds, but such silence at the end of a Roman afternoon was very odd. That was when they saw several men—six in all—armed with sticks coming out of three alleyways to form a cir-cle around them. Strangely, they were not hiding behind hooded cloaks and they stared at them, not even blinking.

"Friend Lucretius, I'm afraid we must resort to the use of force," said Titus Crow.

"Do you think it's necessary to warn me, given this image of a foul philos-opher that you continue to have of me?"

Their enemies rushed them, weapons held high. Titus Crow barely had time to duck the first blow before blocking one of the brigand's kicks and knocking him off balance into the third goon. He still got hit hard on the shoul-der, but while he was falling backward, he used his martial arts skills to grab his attacker around the waist and toss him behind him, directly into the edge of the fountain. He had just enough time to hear a thud and see the water turn red, spiced up with bits of brain., when two more men rushed him with swords.

In the meantime, Lucretius had quickly pulled out his own thin sword that he had been hiding in his belt, and faced off against the other three enemies. When they rushed him, he held off the first two by slicing through the air as he lunged at the third, cutting deep into his thigh, before pushing him back into its two cronies. A sword appeared in one of his adversaries' hand but he managed to block the thrust; however, he could not protect himself against the stick from the second enemy. Bent double, he barely saw the swordsman pounce on him as he lifted his own sword, which cut the man's hand clean off. He was still recov-ering from the attack when he nearly got knocked out by another blow from a stick.

Dizzy and wobbly. his sight turning purple, Lucretius could just make out the face of his enemy right before seeing blood spurting out of his throat; it had just been skewered by a blade.

One of the men threatening Titus Crow had also just been stabbed in the back and had fallen to his knees, while the other, surprised, could no longer avoid being kicked in the head by the time-traveler.

A new figure approached them, sheathing his own sword as he came forward.

"You don't have to thank me. I think we're colleagues in a way, my dear Titus Crow," he said, smiling.

The man had a dark complexion, like an Egyptian, sharp features, and under his cloak, his body seemed strong.

"Can I ask whom we're dealing with?" Titus Crow asked.

"I am Setni—at your service! Like you, I'm only passing through these troubled times. I have been watching you since you walked past me earlier. I was disguised as a beggar."

"Ah! That explains it! Are you a time-traveler, too?" asked Lucretius.

"Yes—but one temporarily in distress. But I'd rather continue this discussion in a more comfortable setting, if you don't mind. In the meantime, we should question your attackers, at least those who are only wounded."

On approaching the men, however, they were surprised to see that they had all died without the slightest expression of pain on their faces. Ripping off one of the men's clothes, Setni found his chest tattooed with ivy vines—the sign of the cult of Cybele, the Great Mother.

For this meal offered to his somewhat forced guests, Lucretius had chosen the smallest but best heated dining room. Rather than being constantly bothered by slaves serving the food, he preferred to break with tradition and leave his guests to pick from the dozen different dishes. Titus Crow was not fooled, however; the attractive cuisine was hiding a real lack of supplies, probably the result of Lucretius' declining fortune.

"Let's say that time is like a maze built by Daedalus," Setni began. "Without a string long enough to guide you, you would surely get lost in eras you don't want to visit, or even into other threads of history. Besides, the god at whose feet Titus Crow landed might perhaps be a remembrance of another traveler, caught forever in a fold of the time continuum."

"You believe in Euhemerism, Setni!" sais Lucretius.

"It just takes one simple change to the past, a *clinamen* as you say, a swerve of atoms, to change the future, and therefore our respective presents."

"By referring to my writings, you're inspiring me to work harder on them, if they're also remembered in your era."

"Only one, but not just any one—a poem on your conception of the world. But I'll stop there. I've already revealed too much."

202

"Tell me more about your reasons for being here. You mentioned some kind of distress…"

"In your past, during the Punic wars against Carthage, I gave in to my desire to help some other time-travelers from my own era change the course of history, and thus revive our own declining race. The attempt failed and I was reconditioned by the Great Brains who sought to test my new-found loyalty by sending me back to your ancient Rome—not without a warning: to control my own sexual impulses, for fear that my love of the fairer sex might push me into making more irrational choices."

"I would have to agree with your, er, Great Brains. A clean body makes a healthy mind," Lucretius commented. "That said, it's a flagrant violation of your free will."

"Yes, but the Great Brains act only for the good of our species—quite different from your own leaders. Nevertheless, I have to admit that this freedom of past eras had had an undeniably intoxicating effect on me. It was like the freedom of a wild animal!"

"And you, Titus Crow," asked Lucretius, "do you have as much experience in time travel as our friend Setni?"

"I traveled much farther back in time, if you can imagine it. And I think the knowledge I have gathered from reading forbidden tomes is unrivaled when it comes to strange phenomena."

"Undoubtedly," said Setni, "but I have visited many strange worlds and met many strange beings throughout the galaxy, and experienced many strange things, in person, not sitting in a library."

"Is not the ideal, my friends, to balance study and adventure, as I am striving humbly to do?" remarked Lucretius.

The Roman's observation left both Setni and Titus Crow speechless. It also managed to relieve some of the tension. The two men from the future proposed a toast to their noble host.

"My dear Lucretius, what drink is this that we're enjoying?" asked Setni.

"It's wine, mixed with some honey and certain spices—a savory little weakness of mine, I admit."

Deep down, Lucretius was more nervous than he showed. His present bliss was just the effect that the liquor normally had on him, but did nothing to resolve the current emergency…

The two Tituses (Crow and Lucretius) walked through the streets of Rome, strangely deserted in the cold morning air. They had left Setni to follow the trail of the Cybele worshippers, and had decided to explore the mystery of the Sibylline books stolen by the time-thief from the temple of Janus.

Getting to know Lucretius better, Titus Crow saw him more and more as an equal to his friend, Henri-Laurent de Marigny.

"The library where I'm taking you has a curious history," explained Lucretius. "Originally it was a network of natural caves discovered under the Quirinal hill. A senator claimed the land after financing the work to transform it into baths. Believe me, the place excites the imagination. It became a special meeting point for high-level friends of Marius. All this happened thirty years ago, during the civil war."

"I don't see the connection with books, unless the baths also served as a haven for reading?"

"Not at all. Except maybe for reading bodies? When Sulla took back control of the City, he instituted proscriptions, and that's when tragedy came into these caves. One day, when the baths were full of their usual customers, trying to forget the gloomy atmosphere of the City, some supporters of Sulla blocked their only exit after bribing the slaves in charge of heating the baths. The fires were lit to maximum intensity and the screams of the poor men boiling inside in the heat went on for many hours, before they finally died out in the steam. No need to say that the place was no longer much visited after that. A scholar, the youngest son of a rich, patrician family, took advantage of the situation to buy it for a few sesterces. That's whom we're going to see. If there's anyone in the City who has a copy of the Sibylline books, as my connections have informed me, it's him!"

The two men came up against a massive double door, the original sculptures of which represented Nereids and Tritons; they had been broken off in several places. After Lucretius banged on the wood with a coded knock, the door cracked open, revealing two furtive eyes, before the lock was released and access allowed. Once the door was closed again, the silent doorman turned around and faced the two men, revealing that that his lips had been sown shut with a thin, golden thread.

The walls of the corridor, once covered with elaborate mosaics, were now stained with grotesque forms, swollen enamels with white blotches, as if the screams of the dying had battered the walls, leaving a veil of silence behind.

On entering the first room, previously reserved for the cold baths, Titus Crow choked back a cry of surprise: before him was a wide basin dug out of the ground, literally overflowing with books, piled on top of one another, forming a tortoise shell of papyrus. As far as the eye could see, the other pools were in the same condition. Almost all the original walls having been knocked down. But even more astonishing, the ceiling was studded with ropes holding wooden platforms and ladders between them, covered with blankets, braziers and veils.

In the middle of this outlandish landscape, a figure suddenly burst out from behind a curtain: a fat, old man with long, white hair, his face clumsily painted with gaudy make-up. He boomed out toward the two newcomers:

"Light, light, have you ever triumphed over the anger of your ancestors? Lucretius, what do you think of my new verse? I've been working on it for one of the tragedies I'm writing, *Helios Dethroned*! But the birds keep bothering me, their cries and the sound of their wings are everywhere! Shoot, my good men, shoot! Don't leave a single one alive!"

In the huge cave sparsely lit by oil lamps, scattered pretty much all over, shapes were writhing silently. Some were moving the volumes, like mixing dyes; others were flexing bow strings without arrows; others again were looming over tables, darkening the leaves. On closer examination, Titus Crow saw a clumsy form slowly poring over several different scrolls. On looking at the scribe, he could not help but stumble back, almost falling down, for the man's eyelids were also sown shut with golden thread.

He looked around and realized that everyone shuffling over the floor was either blind or mute...

"Where are we? Is this the antechamber of Hell? Why are all these men mutilated?"

"It's hard to respond to your understandable surprise," Lucretius whispered. "Cassius says he bought these slaves like this, that they had inflicted this tragic fate on each other after reading certain sacred texts, or that they were servants in this site of debauchery, voyeurs, or forced participants... They also say that these men were the only ones captured from the revolt of Spartacus after escaping crucifixion."

In the meantime, the old man popped up next to them, swinging in a basket that hung from the ceiling.

"Let them decorate their throats with the breath of amethysts! Friend Lucretius, do you persist in the illusion of knowledge as a refuge?"

"In fact, I came with my friend Titus here because I know that you have all the Sibylline books."

"Plataea! Yes, I do! I was there, trampled by the horses of Diomedes. But no, these ancient books do not exist in only one version. I used to have a copy of the most sacred one somewhere in the middle of this maelstrom..."

"I only want to look at it, in Jupiter's name!"

"Oh, orichalcum of the waxing moons, that precious metal that disintegrates in the flame of Neptune... Come on, Sophocles, Socrates, meet me at eight degrees latitude, five feet up," he yelled as he pulled the ropes and moved off toward the rocky firmament.

"What are they doing?" Titus asked.

"Cassius invented a coded geography of this place that is known only to him and his slaves. He's just given an order to find what I asked him for."

"Dive in, the water's rising! Soon the mud will soil all these cheap papyri! Scratch away, golden cockroaches!"

A slave went down into the basin and his head quickly disappeared under the impossible heap of rolls. He came out holding a worn volume in his hand and gave it to Cassius, who handed it to Lucretius.

The Roman perused it, then handed the scroll back to the librarian.

"I'll give it back to you, Cassius. I'm truly disgusted by this work!"

"We're on a stage that doesn't exist, my friend. That's why the meaning escapes you—just like the color."

After a final wave goodbye, Lucretius put his hand on Titus' shoulder and they left the cave, a reflection of the deranged mind of its master.

"In truth, I switched the rolls and gave him back a blank one. It's not the first time I do this. The most incredible thing is that, when I come back, these blank rolls are black and old, as if they'd been there forever. Here, you can read it for yourself."

"It looks like a bunch of incantations," said Titus Crow after perusing the scroll. "Yes, these formulae remind me of some books I have read—unholy, accursed works. See here, the name of the divinity in question: *Shub-Niggurath*, an entity that incarnates both fertility and plague..."

"That name means absolutely nothing to me. What does our enemy think will happen if the incantation actually works and he summons that deity?"

"It's simple: the total destruction of Rome."

Slipping through the aisles of the temple of Idaea Mater, built on the Palatine, Setni was trying to be as unnoticeable as a ghost. Glancing into the *naos*, he caught sight of an odd scene: before a huge, black, shiny stone, no doubt the result of rubbing and cleaning, a group of young men were thrashing each other with branches. They were completely nude, except for a rectangular piece of skin over the genital area, pierced with a tiny circular opening.

"Well, if ever I have to get rid of some of these fanatics, at least I don't have to worry about their future offsprings."

Since the occupants of the temple were clearly busy with their ceremony, Setni could easily visit one room after the other. Although his inspection of the kitchens turned up nothing, the same could not be said for the next room where a well had been dug. He brought up some water in the bucket attached to a rope and analyzed it with his multi-task detector. Fortunately, the Great Brains of Kalapol, even though they had deprived him of his faithful Pentoser, had left him the use of a wide array of technology. The results were unquestionable: the water had been poisoned with a strong, hypnotic drug and, given its consistency, it could only have been poured right into the groundwater table.

The three men were walking through the underground tunnels of the Roman quarries, which they had reached through the sewers of the *Cloaca Maxima*. Despite his wish, Lucretius was guiding them, right behind Setni, holding a torch, while Titus Crow closed the ranks.

"We're really in the bowels of the City, and I'm surprised that they're so empty," the latter said.

"There is a real underground life here, normally, you know," said Lucretius. "But is it a distorted refection of the Mistress of the World above, or the true image of its syphilitic foundations—who knows?"

206

"Lucretius, how did you discover this world that's mostly hidden from the historians of the future that Titus and I have read?"

"The successive projects to enlarge Rome needed tunnels dug to find the best stone, then to drain the swamp, not to mention the underground portions of the hundreds of temples and buildings... Above all, the legends say that the grottoes already existed before the founding of the City, used by forgotten sects. Later, a real underground life found refuge here, from all kinds of people living on the fringes of society: prostitutes wanting to escape their pimps, abandoned children, escaped slaves, all sorts of criminals, Jews, and other believers in banned religions. But I have to admit that I've only mapped a small section of these tunnels."

"With my electronic tracker, we won't have any problem finding our way through this maze," said Setni. "Now all we have to do is find the other time-traveler."

The winding tunnel was starting to get dangerously small, forcing the explorers to crouch down. Just as they reached a crossroads, the air before them became distorted, outlining the contours of a nightmarish creature. Its naked body was like that of a voluptuous, young woman, with firm breasts covered with thin, black hair, but her arms ended in eagle claws, while her face was but an enormous mouth, opening all the way up to her forehead, with several rows of pointy teeth, her red eyes spilling scarlet tears. The monster was floating lightly over the ground, making no noise but slowly approaching Setni. Two shots of his laser gun had no effect on her.

"Get back, quick!" said Setni. "Titus, do you have an incantation to chase that thing away?"

Lucretius marched straight up to the mockery of a woman, close enough to touch her. She dissolved harmlessly.

"Well, well.... How on Earth did you do that?" asked Titus Crow.

"My dear Titus, this sort of being exists only in myths, not in the real world!"

"You sure are confident of yourself."

"For once, it wasn't us," Setni smirked.

Walking toward the spot where the ghostly apparition had materialized, he pointed to a little device stuck in the top of the wall.

"A projector. A simple, miniaturized projector. What worries me is that it's the same kind that my old partners used, except they were all mindwiped by the Great Brains."

"Our intruder from the 20th century has obviously recovered some of their technology."

The group continued their trek through the bowels of the City. It took them another half-hour, crossing other adjacent tunnels, which they did not explore, before they reached their destination. They came out on a peak overlooking a huge cave, in which one could have easily fit another forum. It was barely lit by some kind of spectral glow coming from the depths. Leaning over, they saw a staggering spectacle. Many feet below them, a fence of sculpted stone was surrounding a pit filled with a bright, gelatinous mass that was shaking and jerking. Creatures were taking turns crawling out of it or sinking back into it—unformed humanoids wandering around aimlessly.

"Titus, can you figure out where we are exactly?" asked Setni.

Looking up, the occultist used his rebuilt eyes to try to pierce the semi-darkness that filled the cave, the walls of which curved toward the top.

"There's also a small monument, like an altar with a circular duct that you can barely stick your arm in, that leads straight into that pit."

The three explorers cautiously climbed down and walked towards the temple.

"That pit is the *Umbilicus Urbis*," explained Lucretius. "The supposed center of Rome, and a protected opening because it's believed to lead to the infernal realms. It's a pit that drops into the abyss of time. Some say that it's bottomless and it goes all the way to the center of the world."

"That legend appears to have a modicum of truth," said Setni.

"Wait, I think I found our foe," exclaimed Titus Crow. "Over there!"

He pointed to another tunnel located on the other side of the cave.

"I think I recognize the man I saw in the temple of Janus, or at least its shape," said Titus Crow.

They saw an individual dressed in some kind of green overalls, an open book in his hands, chanting. Abruptly, he looked up from the grimoir, smiled at them, and said in French.

"You got here too late, *mes amis*! Shub-Niggurath has been awakened and is about to spring to the surface to destroy arrogant Rome!"

Setni pulled out his laser weapon and fired, but the man had already sunk back inside the tunnel, out of reach.

"I didn't come here alone, you know," he shouted at them, sure of himself.

The three men suddenly saw a swarm of children run out of the tunnel, some kids holding babies in their arms. Many of the smaller kids held knives, stakes, swords and daggers. Titus Crow stood his ground firmly against the flood, Lucretius safely behind him, Setni , however, was tripped up and fell into the pit, dragging several children with him.

He landed right next to the giant entity, but rolled away immediately. One of the children, however, smashed his skull on the stone next to him. The others were completely swallowed by the colossal creatures which had started surging upward. All kinds of things emerged on its surface: tentacles, nipples, vaginas, mouths by the dozen, like a mad scramble—the fruits of a Bacchanalian cult afflicted with hysteria.

Children continued to run out of the tunnel and toward the pit, and let themselves drop into the body of Shub-Niggurath, which absorbed them immediately.

Titus Crow and Lucretius tried to stop them, but that only triggered more aggressivity. The kids scratched and bit, swung their weapons. Even though Titus Crow felt no pain, thanks to his artificial and now indestructible body, it was a different story for Lucretius, whose wounds were bleeding.

"There's more and more of them!" said the Roman. "We can't kill them all! They're possessed and killing themselves! Titus Crow, hit them with your superhuman strength. That's the only solution."

"Of course, you're right. The spell will be broken."

Doing what he said, Titus Crow controlled the power of his body and delivered blows to the leaders of the mob, aided by Lucretius' club.

At last, after several long minutes, the two men were the only ones standing, in the middle of a pile of tiny bodies.

In the meantime, Setni had not remained idle. He had, at first, been surprised by the creatures popping out of the body of Shub-Niggurath, half-human shapes, as if cut down in the middle, displaying their organs and muscles, barely covered by a veil of transparent skin. They had tried to drag him into their Mother, sticking to him, literally, forcing him to wriggle out of his clothes until he was left wearing only his metallic underwear and boots.

A few shots from his laser gun bought him just enough time to slip away and start digging handholds into the rocky walls of the pit. Then, he climbed up quickly in order to reach the cave, and the tunnel where their enemy was hiding.

When he saw Titus Crow leaning over the edge of the pit, he used his free hand to signal him his intent, then continued on his way.

The occultist pulled out the papyrus taken from the infernal library and started uttering the guttural incantation that would open a portal above Shub-Niggurath's head, and closing the exit that would otherwise land him right in the middle of the Roman forum located above the cave.

As he reached the opening of the tunnel, Setni fired at the ceiling, bringing a rain of stones down upon their green-clad enemy. Then, he jumped in and caught the other man in an arm lock. It was easy enough to do because their foe was wounded and not in a great physical shape.

Once the other time-traveler as securely on the ground, Setni used that opportunity to place him under the influence of his psycho-inductor.

"So, buddy, tell me everything before you die," he asked.

In a flat voice, the dying man droned out his confession:

"My name is Montbrison. I come from 1942 in a time-vest invented a scientist named Noel Essaillon, who was once a client of mine. I was a lawyer in Lyon. I found the blueprints for this vest amongst the papers of his Estate after his death. I had gotten involved in a sordid murder before, and had just been exposed by a skinny P.I. named Nestor Burma. I managed to escape the police, but I had to flee. Thanks to my friend Klaus Barbie, I had discovered the existence of the Great Old Ones. So, I decided to travel to Rome before the the Empire in order to destroy it and let the Gauls, the Celts and the Germans flourish. But to

209

do this, I had to get certain old Sibylline books with their incantations and capture enough children to feed the awakening of Shub-Niggurath. I found them all over, even in Rome itself, where I also subjugated the servants in the temple of Cybele to become my agents... to..."

The time-traveler's head slumped and he was gone forever.

In the cave, Titus Crow had just finished the incantation and Shub-Niggurath's body was slowly vanishing. Just as one of its tentacles was about to reach him, it disappeared completely with a clap of thunder.

A thunderclap was just the thing that struck Setni's back.

In the steamy atmosphere of the baths, he and Lucretius were getting a massage from Numidian slaves, whose arms were twice the size of their thighs, and were slapping them with perhaps too much enthusiasm.

The man from the future, however, was used to this kind of treatment; nothing was better than a massage—if only he had some feminine company! Maïcha's lovely face flashed through his mind...

Setni finally struggled to stand up and, with Lucretius still by his side, went into the inner gardens to have a snack.

"Do you really think, friend Setni, that that creature we chased away was a god? Titus Crow seemed so sure of it before he went back into the folds of time in his strange contraption."

"I'm in favor of an alien entity who washed up here on Earth a long, long time ago. I recorded the thought-waves it emitted and it seems that all the dreams of conquest your countrymen were harboring came partly from its presence under your city, Now that it's left, your desires for expansion won't be so great. If you want my opinion, our friend Titus Crow has a tendency to look at everything through the darkest glass."

"A little like me with Epicurus, I guess."

"Oh, but you are much more of a materialist than him!"

Leaving behind them the heat of the baths, Setni and Lucretius were struck by the cold outside. They hugged briefly, knowing that the moment to say goodbye had arrived. Setni handed a small statuette to Lucretius.

"You see I've chosen the image of your favorite goddess—Venus," he said.

"It's the allegory I like—not the goddess."

"Exactly. It's only a receptacle. When you decide you want to join our, er, organization, you just have to smash it, which shouldn't be a problem for your conscience. You will see a little box inside with a rectangular mirror. You just place your right hand on top of it and you will be transported at my side."

Lucretius and Setni grabbed each other's forearms warmly before the latter vanished into the crowd. The Roman stared at the porcelain statuette. To chose between a future where war was being waged between divinities on a cosmic scale, and another where men (or their descendents) were acting as cruelly and vainly as gods?

Lucretius opened his hand and let the statuette fall to the ground. Immediately, it was crushed by the wooden wheel of a psychopomp chariot carrying corpses to the pyre.

Translation: Michael Shreve & Jean-Marc Lofficier.

Nigel Malcolm's new saga features a dystopian near future where the Nyctalope, once again, and very reluctantly, appears to serve the forces of fascism that have overtaken France. This second chapter follows "Tomorrow Belongs to the Nyctalope," published in our previous volume, and widens the scope of the series, (re)introducing new and old characters...

Nigel Malcolm: *Enemies of the People*

Paris, the near future.

Up in the night sky, an armored police squad descended in a flying van—known as a police spinner wagon. It landed in a neglected street in the south east sector of Paris.

As it almost touched the ground, a ramp dropped and a team of twelve men filed out and ran in two lines of six towards an abandoned bar. The last two officers of each line stayed in front of the bar, and trained their riffles on the boarded-up door and windows. This was where another resistance cell was allegedly meeting in secret.

One line filed down a side-street while the other scaled a low fence and jumped through a small, overgrown garden on the other side. The aim of the two lines was to go around each side of this building to take down any lookouts, and meet at the back entrance to storm the illegal gathering together.

That was when things began to go wrong.

The first of the officers scrambling through the garden had just reached the side of the building when he came face to face with a slouched-hatted figure—a vision from the past.

A moment later, that officer was unconscious with a broken wrist.

And so was the officer behind him.

And the one behind him. Protective head gear made no difference.

Eventually, this vision had overpowered all five officers before any of them had had a chance to raise the alarm. Combat training, self-defense and even tasers were no match for this *Belle Epoque* predator.

Meanwhile, the other line of five had reached the back entrance. The team leader noticed that his comrades hadn't arrived yet. He assumed that they had been held up by something, maybe a look-out. They wouldn't be delayed for long, though. The obstruction would be dealt with quickly. It was much easier just to kill scum like that. Those lives were cheap, and this was for the greater glory of France. The others would join them shortly.

He gestured at his team to get ready to raid the premises. They got into position. They smashed the door in and stormed the place.

"Hands up! Hands where I can see them! I'll shoot you! I'll shoot you!"

For a moment, the rebels were paralyzed with fear.

Then they started looking behind him. The Team Leader realized that he was the only one shouting.

He risked turning round.

He saw Judex punching the fourth of his team unconscious.

The Team Leader immediately swung his gun round at his assailant, but Judex grabbed it from him and rammed the butt into his face.

The Team Leader was unconscious before he hit the ground.

The groups of rebels looked at Judex in awe. The dark-clad man put a finger to his lips to gesture silence.

He paced through the room to the bar's entrance, where he peered out through a gap in the shutters. The last two officers were standing guard, ready to mow down anyone who stepped out. They were still unaware that the rest of the squad had been immobilized.

Judex turned and addressed the rebels:

"Listen, we have very little time. The police and SNIF are on to you. You must get away from here and lay low for a few weeks. Then regroup. Turn left out of the back entrance, turn right into the side-street, and get away from here! Go!"

The rebels filed out of the room. A couple of them nodded or whispered their thanks.

Once they were safely out, Judex approached the front door. It was mostly glass, but with yellowed newspaper taped over much of it. He peered out at where the two remaining officers were standing.

He reached into his utility belt, and pulled out one of two signal flares he was carrying. They were fireworks, but powerful ones.

On his chest was a small electrical device that he switched on. This was a field dampener: It jammed—or rather froze—all CCTV cameras in the area, making it easier for him to get around discreetly in today's surveillance state.

He braced himself, and aimed the signal flare at the door. He fired.

The firework blast smashed through the door. The two officers stumbled backwards in shock, Judex ran through the door and overpowered them quickly before they had a chance to do much.

He then sprinted onwards to the police spinner wagon, just a few yards up the street. His field dampener would have prevented the driver from seeing this assault. He had taken a gamble on him not looking out of the window or hearing the blast and wanting to see what had happened. He thought he was taking bigger and bigger risks these days.

Judex got to the van and leaped in through the ramp entrance. The driver gave him no trouble, and was soon lying senseless on street sidewalk outside.

Judex closed the doors and drove the spinner wagon up into the sky. He got out a pen-stick and plugged it into the onboard computer. This would help him to access and download the latest intel about Government security operations.

As he drove the wagon upwards, he could see the tops of the buildings outside the windows, but the TV screens showed that he was still on the ground. This baffled him until he looked on the rear view monitor and saw the two officers still standing on guard outside an intact bar entrance, and remembered to switch off the field dampener. The screens switched to showing that he was now over Paris's steel and glass skyline.

Judex steered the wagon round into the direction of his rendezvous point with his partner.

Suddenly, every electrical circuit in the cockpit fused and sparked—even his field dampener, which winded him. He glanced around anxiously, trying to work out what was happening.

The wagon crashed onto the top of a building. The driver's seat was designed to absorb the impact. Nevertheless, he was lucky to have dropped onto a high roof rather than crash onto the streets below.

Judex realized that he had been hit by an Electromagnetic Pulse gun—a device that could mimic the blowout of electrical equipment that a nuclear bomb would cause. The police now seemed to carry them as standard equipment, which they were always ready to use. Given that all vehicles relied heavily on electronic components, it was a very heavy-handed and reckless way to deal with suspects driving away. It wasn't just cops and SNIF agents that used them either. Enough criminal and resistance gangs had EMP guns, too. Anyone could have fired at him.

The wagon began to wobble. Judex realized that it was balanced precariously on the edge of the roof. Carefully, he unbuckled his seatbelt and opened the door. Fortunately, he was on the good side of the rooftop. He rolled out and dropped onto the roof.

He looked around. No one was visible. Whoever had shot him must have fired from the ground.

The wagon was about to keel over. Judex considered holding the side and trying to pull it down, but realized that he wouldn't have enough strength and weight to stop it from tipping over.

He couldn't do anything, but he had an obligation to stop harm coming to anyone in the streets below. He pulled out the other signal flare. Fortunately, it didn't rely on any electronics. He fired it into the air. Hopefully it was enough to warn people of the danger.

The spinner tumbled away. Judex was tempted to stay and watch, but he knew he was being hunted, and he had just given away his position. He also didn't have a field dampener now. So he glanced around to get his bearings, and spotted the tip of the recently built BlackSpear Tower. It was about a quarter of a kilometer away, but if he could reach it, he would soon be at the rendezvous point.

Judex ran across the flat roof, dodging between the air vents and chimneys. When he got to the opposite side of the building, aware of the strong winds at this height, he took out his two rope guns. Each could fire wire chord over long distances.

He adjusted the settings on one rope gun to fire hard, and aimed at the top of the BlackSpear Tower. It hit, and a suction pad on the end of the rope attached itself to the building. Judex tugged at it just to make sure. Then he fired the other rope gun on a low setting at the roof he was standing on.

After checking it, he leaped off the roof, pulling the chord of the first rope gun and letting out the chord of the second, sliding swiftly from one building to the other.

He glided into the darkness between the large, fluorescent obelisk he had left, and towards the other. Overhead, there were military spinners, helicopters and the stalks of searchlights. Fortunately, the flying vehicles were all far away enough to let him get across discreetly. There were moving traffic lights and neon hundreds of meters below.

On the minute-long journey, Judex found himself reflecting that just as climate change was beginning to make the weather noticeably warmer in everyday life; for him, the world seemed to be getting colder, because he was now forced to travel so high from the ground.

He arrived on top of the BlackSpear building, and soon unstuck and retracted the chord in both his rope guns. His meeting point was now only another skyscraper away. His arms and legs felt stiff. Fighting the regime was beginning to take its toll on him. And yet he couldn't stop. Stumbling slightly, he started to jog along the rooftop.

But then, another man stepped out in front of him.

He recognized him instantly.

Fantômas.

Despite the many years, the legendary criminal mastermind looked younger and fitter than ever. In fact, Judex thought that he had some sort of glow about him, as if he were only in his twenties. Even his evening attire looked somehow plusher than before.

"In a hurry?" asked Fantômas.

"Yes," replied Judex, "I do not wish to be rude, but please excuse me."

Fantômas laughed. Judex seized his moment. He ran at Fantômas to throw a punch at him, but the other was quick, and side-stepped it, seemingly without effort. He slashed a knife at Judex's guts, but the dark-clad man was wearing a protective bodysuit and so the blade didn't stab him. But the force of the thrust was enough to make him bend over and fall backwards onto the ground.

Fantômas lunged down on Judex, aiming the knife at his face. Judex rolled out of the way with a swiftness that surprised even him. Back on his feet, he poised for the next round.

Fantômas lurched forward with his knife. Judex blocked it with his arm, which was also covered in light armor. Fantômas thrusted at him a few more times in a frenzy. His blows were becoming more powerful.

Judex decided to hold his position until Fantômas would get tired and slow down, but that moment never came. The monster seemed to be preternaturally—maybe even supernaturally—strong and unrelenting.

So Judex went back on the attack. He hoped that the unrelenting stamina was but a deception. With all his speed and strength, he tried to land a punch in Fantômas' face, but the stamina was real. Fantômas grabbed Judex's extended arm and twisted it. The dark-clad avenger shrieked—despite years of training against crying out in pain whenever he was injured.

Judex tried to look Fantômas in the eyes. All he could see was a chilling blankness.

Fantômas swung Judex around two or three times—to Judex, it may have been longer. Then, almost as an act of mercy, he let go, and his opponent went flailing through the air, landing hard at the very edge of the rooftop.

Judex lay there, gasping. He was winded, and his cape was strangling him. With his left hand, he released the cape's pin. It was an encumbrance now, and he was fighting for his very life. He tried to move his right arm, but it was paralyzed. He struggled to get to his feet, but was just flailing against the cape.

Fantômas strolled over, laughing.

"Well, it's been fun." he said, "Very few people have been my equal. It's almost a shame that you weren't one of them." He stood over Judex, fiddling with his knife. "All good things must come to an end—even you. I'll see to that personally."

He raised his dagger and…

…an iron spear pierced his torso.

Judex saw a look of surprised amusement on Fantômas' face in the split second before the force from the spear caused him to stumble forward and fall silently off the side of the building. A look that had suggested that he saw being pierced as an amusing distraction rather than a death.

Judex heard a spinner land a few meters away. He only knew of one vehicle like that which could launch spear—his. He had added the iron rods as a weapon against some of his more supernatural opponents. It had been flown here by his associate, who must have been tired of waiting long enough to know that their plan had gone wrong.

He lay there, trying to breathe and endure the pain. A moment later, she was crouching over him. She also wore a suit of that light body armor, but with a balaclava to conceal her identity, instead of a slouched hat and a cape.

"Can you move?" asked Una Persson.

"Yes… I… think so." said Judex, hoarsely.

Una unraveled his cape and helped him back to his feet.

A few minutes later, they were in the spinner and soon out of the area.

The peaceful darkness of the bedroom was shattered by the screeching alarm of an incoming call on the vid-screen.

"Action stations." muttered Colonel Auguste Pichenet as he woke up.

He struggled out of the duvet covers, switched on the bedside lamp, which nearly blinded him, and stumbled over to the vid-screen.

Hedwige Roche-Verger, a.k.a. "Choupette," who was in the same bed, groaned loudly and pulled the duvet over her head.

Pichenet answered the call, and found himself squinting at the angry face of President Schasch.

"Madame President," said the Colonel croakily. "To what do I owe..."

"What took you so long?" she demanded.

Pichenet was startled and confused for a moment, and he glanced at the time to see if he had overslept and missed an important meeting.

"It's just after 3 a.m.," he said. "What's the emergency?"

"Judex has struck again. This time, he's left a burning police wagon in a street. Fifteen innocent bystanders were killed. *That's* the emergency, Colonel."

"Judex? Don't you mean Fantômas?"

"I mean Judex!" President Schasch almost shouted.

"But Madame President, I know Judex. I even met him a few times. He may be a ruthless vigilante, but he doesn't kill innocent bystanders. In fact, the number of deaths he has prevented must be in the..."

"Officially, Judex's terrorist actions have now led to fifteen innocent deaths. He is a public menace and an enemy of the people," snapped Madame Schasch. "Bring him down, Colonel Pichenet, unless you really want to spend the rest of your career as a border patrol guard."

Pichenet was shocked.

"Yes, Ma'am," he replied. "I will arrest Judex and bring him in as soon as possible."

"No," said Madame Schasch testily. "I want you to unmask him—and then kill him. And I want visual evidence, too, Colonel. I want to see the blood splattered, the unmasked corpse, of the terrorist known as Judex. And I want it on every news site and every billboard."

She terminated the call, and the screen went blank.

Pichenet sat on the edge of the bed for a moment, to let this order sink in. Choupette's rumpled pillow-face emerged from under the duvet.

"She wants Judex's dead body plastered across the media like that? She is a sick woman."

Auguste quickly shushed her.

"It's how we defeat our enemies now, and show the world we've defeated them," he said. "It's very popular with the public, I'm told." he added, quietly.

"They call it death porn, *chéri*."

Auguste stood up and shuffled into his slippers.

"You're not actually going to order your people to kill Judex are you?" she asked.

"I don't have a choice. She is my boss."

"Go back to sleep, Choupette," he said, grimly. "I'll be back in a moment or two."

He picked up the glass of water on his bedside table and sipped it as he walked out of the bedroom and into his study.

As he sat at the desk, waiting for his SNIF-issue computer to come on, he looked around the room at his collection of political memorabilia, including that signed photograph of the Nyctalope standing together with Marshal Pétain.

A few days ago, he had thought that his hero, the Nyctalope, would have appreciated this being a part of his collection, but instead, he had become angry. Obviously, he had controlled his anger in front of his boss, but he had made it quite clear that he was ashamed of that period in his life. This had surprised Pichenet, and he'd found himself thinking a lot about it over the past few days.

A moment later, he had sent out orders to the SNIF night duty officers to find and execute Judex, and bring in his corpse.

Then he looked through his encrypted e-mail and found a report filed by Leo Saint-Clair, stating that the Room inside the Zone had been successfully located and destroyed. This gave Pichenet an idea.

He replied to Saint-Clair's encrypted e-mail, instructing him to report to his office this morning at nine.

"So now I can adopt the identity of Fantômas and become a serial killer!" said Una Persson wryly, as she hung up the costumes onto two mannequins.

Judex was lying exhausted on a gurney in his castle's sick bay area. His arm was in a sling.

"Please don't," he said.

"According to some people, anyway."

"And assuming the current Fantômas is really dead."

Una gave him an bemused glance. "You don't think he's dead? Even after the evening?"

Judex turned his head to look at her. "He is much more powerful than I have ever known. It seems that during times of great evil, Fantômas is at his most powerful. It is as if he *feed*s on the evil of the society around him. The only way to weaken him is to weaken the evil in society."

Una looked skeptical. "Or just stab him with an iron spear and push him off the top of a skyscraper," she replied.

It was just as well that Una had come along to work with Judex. He didn't exactly agree with her politics, but they were both allies fighting a common enemy, and he welcomed her help.

"For an anarchist, you are surprisingly tidy," he said.

"We have to look after our equipment. Keep it in good working order," she replied.

Una picked up the misshapen slouched hat and put it back on the Judex mannequin. She held it for a moment and examined it.

"Having said that, you should get another hat out of storage. And a new cape as well. These are looking quite tattered."

Judex rubbed his arm. Fortunately, it was strained rather than broken, but it was still going to take time to heal.

"They'll last a little longer," he said. "I've become quite good at sewing and mending hats and capes."

Una raised her eyebrows. "You can sow?" she said.

"Oh yes. This life has taught me many skills. Anyway, since my gold mines got bought out two years ago, I've had to make the resources last for as long as possible."

Una's face changed to thoughtful as she absently placed the hat onto the mannequin. "You can't go on like this forever." she said, "We need to consider a new approach."

Judex frowned. "What other approach is there?" he asked, warily.

"Take a few days off. We need to regroup. Form a larger strategy."

"I can't take time off, people are dying. And how can we regroup? There are only two of us."

Una paused. "I could get hold of Zenith." she said, tentatively.

Judex acted exactly the way she had feared. "Out of the question! Zenith is the worst kind of criminal." he scowled.

"But he's an ally against the regime!"

"He doesn't believe in anything. He treats everything as a game! How can I trust someone like that?"

Una paused for a moment. "Alright then," she said, as patiently as she could manage, "I could try and get a message through to Teku Benga. There's a chance that Oswald Bastable isn't lost in the multiverse. He's a former soldier. And straight as a die. You'd get on with him very well…"

"*If* he isn't lost, and assuming he can get through the borders into France."

Una lost her patience. "Look, if you want to carry on alone and get killed, you carry on as you are. Just don't expect me to help you."

She carried on putting away the equipment, her annoyance shown in the occasional banging or slamming of things.

Judex's head sank back onto the pillow. He was too tired to even feel guilty about upsetting one of the few friends he had left.

As the TV news reported on the "latest terrorist outrage from Judex,", Leo Saint-Clair sat in his chrome kitchen in his central Paris apartment, baffled by the claim that the vigilante had massacred fifteen innocent civilians. This was not like the Judex he had known in the past.

219

As he drank his coffee and ate his croissants, he reflected on how he really needed to find a different news source. All the big French news channels were now effectively overseen by the Government, who had enough influence to get over some—what was the expression again?—alternative facts.

So he turned off the TV and had his breakfast in silence. He had just gotten back from the Zone the day before, and sent a report to Colonel Pichenet that he had successfully infiltrated and destroyed the alien artifact known as the Room. He had lied—he hadn't destroyed it at all, but he'd had an epiphany there. It had given him a new focus and a new energy. He was now on a new, bolder, bigger mission: he was going to bring down the Government.

But until he worked out how he was going to do that, he would carry on with his current brief for SNIF—track down and either acquire or neutralize alien technology for the regime. Maybe he could secretly make contacts with others who wanted to overthrow this government.

They also wanted him to become the face of the Regime. But Saint-Clair didn't want to publicly endorse President Schasch. That brought back too many unhappy memories of collaborating with the Vichy Regime, so he was hoping he could carry on retrieving alien artifacts for SNIF for as long as possible.

He finished his breakfast and, with an eye on the time, went into the bathroom to get ready for the day ahead.

In the bathroom, resting on a chair, was an unusual looking undershirt. It had wires and red tubes all over it. Propped up in front of it was an envelope. Leo wondered who had left this here. He had gotten back very late the night before, and this certainly hadn't been there then. And no one could have gotten in in the night without his knowing.

He opened the letter. The letter paper was elegant. He hadn't seen anything like it for years. In a scrawl made by good-quality ink, it just said:

M. Saint-Clair, I advise you in the strongest possible terms to wear this under your usual day clothes. You will thank me—and and yourself—for it quite soon.

There was the Greek symbol *Omega* as a letterhead. So that's why he'd heard that wheezing, groaning sound in the middle of the night! He'd thought he'd dreamed it.

As he showered and shaved, he wondered why the Doctor would leave something like this for him. He had met Doctor Omega a few times, and was familiar with his file at the Kariven Archive. In fact, he got to witness a couple of librarians there debating whether or not to give Doctor Omega an entire section of his own.

Presumably, he would soon be caught up in a series of events involving alien skullduggery here in Paris, and he would be teaming up with the old man again.

Leo put on the undervest, then a suit and tie, and that pungent aftershave. He left his apartment for the underground parking lot, where his SNIF-issue spinner car was parked, ready to fly him to work.

On the way to SNIF HQ in Noisy, Saint-Clair put the spinner on automatic pilot while he checked his encrypted e-mail, including Colonel Pichenet's summons to his office at nine o'clock.

Colonel Pichenet looked like he hadn't slept well. He was also considerably less cheerful than he had been when Saint-Clair had last met him. He was flicking through images on his j-pad, which was connected to the big flatscreen TV on the wall. The pictures were of a crashed police wagon in a street.

"This is all Judex's work. We're saying that fifteen lives were lost because of his activities," he said.

More images scrolled by.

"Judex? You mean Fantômas?" asked Saint-Clair, unaware that his boss had had this very conversation with his superior six hours before.

"No, I mean Judex. Fantômas doesn't exist. But here, we have documentary evidence that the terrorist known as Judex does exist, and is very active. It's here somewhere."

Eventually, Pichenet stopped scrolling through this album of pictures, and the TV screen panned out to display the icons on his j-pad. Then another icon was tapped, and a new selection of pictures flashed up.

"Ah, here we are."

For a brief moment, Leo saw that one of the pictures was of the crashed police wagon, but this time, there were lots of bodies around it, and patches of fire burning on the road and wagon. Often officially released images and documents were carefully edited or severely redacted before being conveyed to the public, but this seemed different. The fire looked odd somehow, and the light on the corpses didn't seem to match up with the light in the rest of the street. Clearly this image had been altered to deliberately stir up public fear. After all, the Colonel had said *we're saying* that fifteen lives had been lost. Saint-Clair knew that this was a lie, and the Colonel did too. Truth was a flexible concept these days.

So Saint-Clair decided to play the innocent, and test how far this lie went. Also, it would look too suspicious if he just accepted these 'facts' without question.

"Colonel, I have met Judex a few times. I have known him to be ruthless, but he has never endangered the public. When I knew him, he was a vigilante, certainly, but not a terrorist."

"When did you last see him?"

Saint-Clair thought for a moment.

"It must be... Thirty years ago now."

"Then it can't be the same person, can it?" said Pichenet, coldly.

"Colonel, that is a question that has baffled the police, SNIF, and conspiracy theorists for decades. Judex might be a succession; a legacy; or even a secret team of people, or is he the same person who started out before the First World War? Nobody has any definitive answers."

"How can it be the same person? He'd be over a hundred and fifty years-old at least!"

"If you remember, Colonel, so am I. In fact, I'm probably older than the original Judex."

Pichenet's bafflement turned to grim determination. "All right then, if he really is the original Judex, then he has clearly gone bad. If he's a new Judex, who started sometime in the last few years, then he's an evil terrorist who is simply using that identity. Either way, the man we're calling Judex is an enemy of the people, and I'm ordering you to find him and bring him here. Dead or alive—is that clear?"

Saint-Clair was stunned for a moment.

"Is that clear?" Pichenet repeated.

"*Oui, Mon Colonel*," Saint-Clair said.

"Dismissed."

Saint-Clair saluted, and left the office, deeply disturbed.

He went to his own office, and sat down at his desk. The room was under-furnished and completely impersonal. The place had only recently been allocated to him, and he had not spent much time there.

Saint-Clair stared at the switched-off computer in front of him. It was so new that it still had its paper cover on it from the factory. He could see a thin layer of dust on top of it.

He didn't know Judex that well, although he had met him a few times. Yet he seemed to be an ally. And Judex could be an ally to him now. He could make Pichenet's order work to his advantage. He would have to be very careful though. Especially here at SNIF HQ.

So he got up and left the building. He flew his spinner back to his apartment. He knew he had an old communicator there, which he had used before to contact the crime fighter. The apartment may be bugged, but Leo decided that if SNIF asked him, he could say that he was using this means to smoke out their so-called *enemy of the people*.

After rummaging through a few cupboards and drawers, he found the communicator. He had to wait for the battery to charge up first, so he made a cup of coffee while he waited.

Then he tuned it to a frequency that he was surprised he could still remember after more than thirty years, and started transmitting.

"Calling Judex. Calling Judex. Are you receiving me? Come in. Calling Judex. Calling Judex..."

He carried on for about twenty minutes, all the time wondering if rebel groups or SNIF could hear him. He occasionally looked over at his front door, half expecting an armed squad to burst in.

He jumped when a voice croaked back:

"This is Judex. Who is calling?"

Leo hesitated for a moment. Then he responded:

"This is the Nyctalope."

There was a pause at the other end.

"Can you repeat that?"

The voice was electronically distorted. Judex was very careful to keep himself anonymous, but something about the intonation made Leo wonder if this was a woman he was talking to. He could have been wrong. Judex might even be a woman now—it was not impossible. The nagging sense that he was walking into a trap lingered, but he had to take this chance.

"This is the Nyctalope. I need to meet up with you, Judex."

There was further silence, and Leo looked in the direction of his front door again.

"Your voice signature confirms that you are indeed the Nyctalope." said the croaky voice. "Get to Fanferlot Villa in Sector 19 at nineteen hundred hours tonight. The code word is the name of the third person who was with us when we last met. Over and out."

"Over and out," said Saint-Clair, realizing that the conversation had already been terminated.

He sat back in his armchair. He knew where Fanferlot Villa was. He had met Judex there once before, though it was not the last time they had met.

That may or may not be Judex. He tried to think if it was the intonation of the Judex he knew. It could be a completely new Judex. And he couldn't quite shake off the notion that it was a woman's voice. Yes, it was very likely to be a trap...

Over the rest of the day, he thought about how he could best prepare for all these scenarios.

Back in Judex's castle, the crime fighter had cleaned himself up and felt more rested, though his strained arm was still in a sling. He was furious with Una Persson, who he had found sitting at the communications desk.

"Are you mad?" he shouted at her after she had reported her conversation to him. "He could be anybody! SNIF are already hunting me down."

Una remained composed, if defensive. "He was using your old radio frequency from thirty years ago!"

"Una, I stopped using that frequency because my enemies were about to find it."

"But that was nearly thirty years ago. It's forgotten. It could only be the Nyctalope."

Judex paced the room pensively.

"He contacted us!" said Una. "His voice matches your voice-recognition software, I've told him to meet us at the Fanferlot villa. So if it is someone pretending to be the Nyctalope, then he is meeting us at a deserted house with nothing to lead him here. It's a risk worth taking."

Judex stopped pacing and looked straight at her. "Even if he really is the Nyctalope, how do I know he's not working for the Government? He collaborated with Vichy, and he now works for SNIF. They may be using him to get to me."

"Well, if he is, then he's not going to stop us, or find your lair."

Una stood up and walked over to the mannequin with her light armored jumpsuit on it, removed it and flung it over her arm. "I will meet up with him, anyway. If he is genuine, I will work with him. You can stay here if you want, but you'll be working alone. And if I'm honest, you probably won't last much longer."

Una walked off to the changing area. Judex watched her go. Even when she was angry, there seemed to be something dignified about her.

He looked at the chair in front of the computer, went over and sat down in it heavily. He rested his elbow on the table, and his face in his hand. He felt so old, so tired, and so lonely.

It was beginning to get dark when Leo Saint-Clair set out in his spinner. He'd installed a jamming device so that if SNIF were tracking his movements, they'd see that the car was still parked in the underground parking lot.

He gained enough height to be inconspicuous to other drivers, as well as the police patrols. Admittedly, he could just give them his name and SNIF I.D. number and they would let him pass. However, it was better if less people noticed him.

He was soon flying at approximately half the height of most skyscrapers. As his spinner weaved between them, Leo could see through the windows as people in suits were either still hunched over computers in their offices, or putting on coats to leave work. Possibly hoping to do some food shopping and get home safely before the curfew.

He wondered if he could detect a sense of tension in some of these ordinary Parisians' movements. Different people behaved differently under occupation. Yes, there were brave people who joined a resistance movement. Though many—for their own sake and the safety of their loved ones—just kept their heads down.

And then, there were some people who, for those reasons and others, collaborated—like he himself had done. But he was working towards his redemption now.

His spinner swooped around another building. They were getting less tall as he headed northwards. Eventually, he left the cluster of skyscrapers and saw only darkness ahead, punctuated by a few searchlights and lines of lights tracing out the streets below.

Saint-Clair descended, following the paper map he had printed out at home earlier. He daren't use the sat-nav as it might have given him away to SNIF, or even Judex. Using that old communicator had been risky enough.

He landed the spinner at the side of a half-abandoned street. He stepped out cautiously onto the cracked sidewalk. Leo glanced around. No one was out here, not even the prostitutes. He surveyed the pot holes on the street and reflected that, while fascism made the trains and buses run on time, it certainly neglected the thoroughfares.

Saint-Clair looked at the Fanferlot villa, Clearly, it had seen better days. He walked up the path through an overgrown garden to the front door.

It was open. Saint-Clair walked cautiously inside.

He stepped into a drawing room. Like the rest of the house, it had been almost stripped bare, except for a few abandoned sticks of furniture. His night-vision could make out two figures, presumably hiding in the shadows. Judex and a woman.

"Who goes there?" demanded the woman, sharply.

"Leo Saint-Clair."

"What's the password?"

"Sexton Blake," Saint-Clair replied, while realizing that the woman's voice and outline looked familiar, "Good evening, Mrs. Persson," he added.

Una seemed to sink a little. She knew she'd been caught out.

"Hello, Leo," she said resignedly, before warmth returned to her voice. "It's been a long time. How are you?" She pulled the balaclava up to reveal her face.

"I'm fine thanks. Never better." He turned to the other figure in the room. "Hello, Judex, you can come out now."

Judex unhunched himself and prowled up to the other two figures.

"Of course, your night-vision," he said. "I know of your abilities. But I also know your weaknesses as well. Don't think I can't destroy you, Nyctalope!"

Saint-Clair rolled his eyes. "I'm sure you can. But if we have to fight this evil regime, we have to leave the macho posturing to one side and start working together."

Judex stepped closer to him. Saint-Clair noticed that his arm seemed stiff.

"You want to fight this regime? But you work for SNIF. And you used to work for Vichy," said the crime-fighter.

"That was a century ago, you idiot!" shouted Saint-Clair, finally losing his temper. "Look, you know me better than that. If you're the same Judex that worked with me and Blake to stop Lord Ruthven from unsheathing that damned sword, then you know who I truly am!"

This outburst seemed to leave Judex taken aback. Una was impressed.

"I wish I had been there to witness *that*!" she said.

"It was much less dramatic than it sounds," said Judex. "Mostly it took place in a supermarket parking lot in Orleans."

"Reims," Saint-Clair corrected him, "A parking lot in Reims. There was a cashier from that supermarket who probably still wonders why her car's battery was completely flat." It then occurred to Saint-Clair that maybe Judex deliberately got the location wrong to test him.

Judex seemed to relax a little.

"All right, Nyctalope, because we have worked together before—and I am learning to trust my associate's judgment and ideas—I will form an alliance with you." He held out his hand.

Leo was a little suspicious that the hoary old crime-fighter was about to fling him across the room. However, he decided to take the risk. He took Judex's proffered hand and shook it.

Una smiled. Saint-Clair shook her hand too.

"Madame Persson, it is a pleasure to work with you again," he said.

"And a pleasure to work with you too," she replied, smiling.

Though having said that, he couldn't tell if this was the same Una Persson he had worked with—even slept with—before, or one of an infinite number of others wandering throughout the Multiverse. But she seemed to know him, unless he was one of an infinite number of other Saint-Clairs. He decided to stop thinking about it. Instead, he returned to the current situation.

"So, who is benefitting from the Schasch regime?" he asked.

"Her party is financed by BlackSpear Holdings," said Una. "Led of course by Colonel Bozzo-Corona."

"I never thought I'd hear that name again," said Saint-Clair. "I thought he'd died years ago."

"So did I," said Judex. "Apparently, he went through several aliases, but it's the same man. The same group of people. I say 'man,' but it is difficult to say what he is."

Leo frowned, and paced the room.

"That's profoundly disturbing," he said. "He will be enormously difficult to defeat."

"He may not be easy to defeat, but we can tip the balance so that the opposite to his Black Coats is in the ascendant." said Judex. "It's a balance between good and evil. I had a fight with Fantômas last night. He is more powerful than ever. We must stop evil being in the ascendant."

While he was saying this, Leo noticed Una looking uncomfortable with this talk of good and evil. She clearly viewed the world in different terms. Order and chaos, he seemed to recall.

"We are all trying to put this into terms we can understand," said Leo, "whether it is political, historical, or metaphysical. But we all agree that if we can damage BlackSpear, we can weaken and damage Madame Schasch enough that she is voted out of office at the next election."

Judex and Una exchanged glances. Then Judex spoke:

"There will be no next election. Haven't you been following the news, Saint-Clair?"

"Admittedly, I have been out of the country—even off the planet—over most of the last twenty years. When did France stop having elections?"

"After Madame Schasch won the last two, and a landslide majority in Parliament," said Una. "Officially, the Chambre des Députés have voted to suspend all elections until the terrorist threat to France had been defeated. Hence the armed police and curfews."

"And the 'terrorist threat' to France is all conveniently vague and open-ended. So elections are suspended indefinitely," murmured Saint-Clair.

Una looked at Leo closely.

"And the most disturbing thing about this set-up?" she said. "That the people willingly voted for this president and her government. Even though the signs were obvious to all."

Pichenet paced around his office in the manner of someone who knew it was time to go home, but still had things to do. Choupette came into the room, to share a car home.

"I'm just waiting for this one e-mail," Auguste explained. Then a moment later, he said to her: "What is it, Choupette? I know when you want to say something to me."

She breathed in tentatively, then she got her j-pad out of her bag.

"Maybe I could show you something on your screen…"

Just then, the door abruptly opened. A massive, hulking figure strode in.

"Haven't you heard of knocking?" said Pichenet, annoyed.

It was the Marchef.

He brushed past Choupette without looking at her, snatching the j-pad out of her hands, and tossed it across the room.

"Shut up," he said, as he walked up to Pichenet. "Speak only to answer my questions. Why the hell did you bring Saint-Clair back into service?"

Pichenet found himself standing to attention. The Marchef was not officially his superior officer, but he came and went from SNIF HQ as if he were in charge, and the colonels and generals were wise enough to treat him with respect and deference. Pichenet tried to justify his decision as if he were standing on the carpet in front of a stern boss.

"Lieutenant Saint-Clair is one of our best officers. He has plenty of experience and…"

"Do you really think he supports us?" shouted the Marchef. "Do you really think he's on our side?"

He grabbed Pichenet by the throat and picked him up, wedging him violently against the glass wall that overlooked the city.

Pichenet instinctively grabbed the Marchef's wrist. He was hanging on by that, rather than his throat. Fortunately, being shorter and slighter than average worked in his favor.

"He believes what we believe!" Pichenet said, sounding less calm than he wanted to.

The Marchef snorted dismissively.

"He sided with Vichy, added Pichenet.

The Marchef dropped him. He fell onto the floor.

The Marchef regarded him as if he was something the brute had just scraped off his shoe. "You idiot. He didn't destroy the Room, he's working against us."

Pichenet looked at him, surprised. The Marchef answered the look.

"No, he didn't," he repeated. "It's a good job BlackSpear got someone to trail him and check up on him. Not like you bunch of useless SNIF amateurs."

Pichenet was about to protest that Saint-Clair had sent him a report to tell him the Room had been destroyed, but instead decided he would just come across as a naive simpleton, so he kept quiet.

The Marchef sat down at Pichenet's computer and pressed a few keys. He ignored the other two people in the room watching him cautiously.

Pichenet looked over at Choupette. He felt a sense of wounded pride at her seeing him like this. She stood there, calmly. She would have intervened, but her training had led to her to stand by, and evaluate the situation. She would have known that this Government-sanctioned thug could easily kill both of them, so taking him on would only be counter-productive.

"This medical report says Saint-Clair recently had a new, modern mechanical heart fitted. Good—an EMP gun can kill him. Looks like by keeping up-to-date records, you've actually done something right for once," said the Marchef, as he stood up to go.

"Please don't kill him," croaked Pichenet, sounding more pleading than he intended.

The Marchef turned round and glowered at him.

"I *will* kill him. Then I'll kill Judex. And if you're lucky, I won't kill you."

He walked towards the door without looking at either Pichenet or Choupette.

She waited until the thug had left the room, and then she hurried over to Pichenet. She helped him up onto the office chair.

"He shouldn't be allowed to treat you like that," she said. "There was a time when being a Colonel in SNIF commanded some respect. Are you alright?"

Pinochet nodded, rubbing his throat.

"I would have come over and done something if he'd gone further," she added. "I should have."

"Yes, my love," said Pichenet, placing his hands on hers, the years of affection showing in one simple gesture.

"You could have overpowered him," she continued. "You'd have been entitled to. It would have been self-defense."

"In my younger days, perhaps, but now, I'm not so sure," Pichenet replied. "BlackSpear is the real power behind the throne. I could no more defy the Marchef than I could the President."

Choupette remembered something. She stood up.

"That reminds me of what I wanted to say to you." She went over to where her j-pad was lying on the floor, and picked it up. Fortunately it hadn't been damaged. As she walked back over to Pichenet, she pressed a few touchscreen keys that linked her photographs to the big screen on the wall. Pichenet turned to see what she wanted to show him.

It was an old picture from years ago. Back when they were both so young. It was him and Choupette standing in front of that blue Midget car he used to drive. He had a blond fringe and wore a black turtleneck sweater. Choupette had long blonde hair and a fresh face. It was a bittersweet image, and it punched him straight in the heart.

"Remember that? Remember *Langelot*? The man who fought villains with powerful schemes? The man who didn't just blindly follow his superiors' orders?"

"Actually, I always followed my superiors' orders," said Pichenet. "Well, nearly always."

"The man I fell in love with! Whatever happened to him?" demanded Choupette.

"He grew up," replied Pichenet, angrily. "He realized he couldn't just run around having adventures anymore. He became aware of the bigger political picture. He understood that times change and that he had to change, too. Especially if he was going to stop the 'villains with powerful schemes.' He saw that the enemies of France were no longer folks like SPHINX or Cordovan, but insidious, anonymous cells of terrorists and cyberterrorists who could come from anywhere and strike at any time. He realized that the only approach was one with a strong president at the top, taking tough decisions."

"And now, our enemies are in charge," said Choupette.

"Our enemies have changed."

"Do you really believe that working for the people we used to fight while shooting at protesters in the street is why you joined SNIF? Is this freedom? Is this really in France's best interest?" she shouted.

Pichenet was outraged. "I could have you arrested for saying that!"

"Is that why you joined SNIF all those years ago?" she repeated.

Pichenet couldn't answer.

"I'll make my own way home tonight." Choupette said, before storming out of the room.

Pichenet sat there. He was losing her. Absently, he stared at his computer. It was Saint-Clair's medical record.

He considered trying to save him. Or at least get a warning to him. But he knew that his communications were being monitored. He'd be executed for treason. He might even end up in the same mass grave as the Nyctalope. And Judex.

He looked round at the big screen. It still had that old picture of him and Choupette. It was like looking at a picture of a beloved relative who had died a long time ago, but who hadn't been mourned. So he clicked the mouse and the picture vanished.

He thumped the table hard. He tried to steady his nerves. Wasn't he expecting that e-mail? He typed a few keys, leaving the medical files and returning to his inbox. The e-mail was there. He read it, but didn't really take it in.

So he switched off the computer and all the equipment in the room and stared at the blank computer screen. He was definitely not the man he used to be. Was that a good thing or a bad thing? People change over time; they develop and grow. Yet he'd overseen the execution of "dissidents," and now he was virtually an eyewitness to the Nyctalope's death. But what could he do?

What could he do?

At the abandoned villa, Saint-Clair; Una Persson and Judex had been talking for a while. Proposing strategies, arguing through possible difficulties. But finally, between them, they became aware of a way to destabilize Madame Schasch's government.

"Well, I can't say that it's a watertight solution, but at least it gives us a fighting chance," said Saint-Clair.

Even Judex looked more relaxed.

"I am used to waiting for my opportunities. Besides, there is nothing like a dictatorship to make people appreciate democracy," he said.

"That's not always true," said Una. "But democracy is better than this."

Saint-Clair put his hands in his jacket pockets.

"So, all I need to do now is find a pretext for going to the United States. There must be an alien artifact there that I can 'investigate' for the state." he said.

"While Judex and I find a corpse, dress it up as Judex, and give them the death porn they want. I've been trying to persuade this one to take a few nights off for a while." said Una, looking at Judex.

"Yes. I'll let my injuries heal," the crimefighter reluctantly agreed. "Then the three of us shall meet again, on this date next month."

"Agreed," said Saint-Clair.

He shook hands with Una and Judex again, and made to leave. As he got to the door, he turned round one last time.

"For France," he said. "The real France."

Saint-Clair left the building, got back to his spinner, and made his way back to his apartment. At least he would get back comfortably before the curfew. He felt happier now that there was a plan. He could tell Una and Judex were too.

He felt good as he parked the spinner, and went upstairs to his apartment.

Then he saw that his front door was wide open, and he stopped feeling good. The splintered doorframe suggested that it had been kicked open by someone or something very powerful.

Saint-Clair stiffened and braced himself. He went inside.

The Marchef was sitting in an armchair, drinking a glass of wine. There was an opened bottle from Saint-Clair's wine rack on a small table to one side of him. There was an EMP gun resting on the chair arm to the other side.

"About time," said the Marchef. "I've been waiting here for over an hour."

Saint-Clair looked at him.

"My apologies. I didn't know you were coming," he replied.

"And your wine tastes like shit," said the Marchef, cockily.

"That's a shame," said Saint-Clair. "I was saving that for a special occasion. It's a Château Margaux—very much a wine for a sophisticated palate."

"Well, this is a special occasion for you—your death. Do you want some?"

Saint-Clair knew all the exits from his living room.

"No thanks. Not now the air has gotten to it," he said.

"Good," said the Marchef. "I'll just get on with killing you then, Nyctalope."

He quickly grabbed the EMP gun and fired it at Saint-Clair.

Leo felt a bolt of electricity shudder through his chest. He was stunned and struggled to breath. He sank to his knees, and saw huge patches of red spread fast over his shirt. He looked up at the Marchef in terror and confusion.

The Marchef just laughed.

"How's that new heart working?" he asked.

Saint-Clair fell face down on to the floor, twitching. Then he became still.

The Marchef stood up and walked over. He prodded Saint-Clair with his foot. Then he casually walked out of the apartment.

Pichenet arrived home, and said good night to his driver.

As he let himself into the house, he found himself feeling afraid. Not of intruders—the security was excellent—but it seemed empty. Maybe Choupette had left him.

"Choupette?" he called out.

No answer.

He jogged up the stairs with an energy he thought he was too tired to have.

"Choupette?" he called out again. More desperate-sounding than he intended.

The silence was fierce.

"I'm in the bath!" called out Choupette, in the distance.

Auguste quickly walked over to the bathroom door, and could see that the light was on inside.

"That's alright. I'll make us some dinner. Come down when you're ready," he said, relieved.

He walked downstairs to the kitchen, feeling much happier. He made a mental note to have a small cryo-freeze chamber installed in the garage, so he could keep flowers in it to give to her at times like this. It would be too late to go out and buy some now that the curfew was almost upon them. He could still have used his status as a SNIF colonel to buy flowers from a merchant, but he didn't like to abuse his position.

In the kitchen, he opened the fridge to see what he could turn into an evening meal, when the TV on the wall started bleeping. It would have been the President calling.

Pichenet signed irritably, and then tried to make himself look pleased to receive a call from her. He answered the call.

"Good evening, Madame President."

Madame Schasch looked much happier than she had eighteen hours ago.

"Good evening, Colonel! I just wanted to congratulate you for the final capture of Judex. SNIF has succeeded where so many others have failed over the years."

This was news to Pichenet, but he decided not to show it.

"Thank you very much," he said.

"It'll be all over the late night news. The people of France will sleep soundly in their beds knowing that SNIF is keeping the nation safe."

"Of course."

"Well, good night, Colonel."

"Good night, Madame President," Pichenet saluted.

The TV went blank. Pichenet was going to contact one of the night-shift officers to hear what had actually happened with Judex. If he was really dead, which he felt rather sad about. Then he had joined the Nyctalope, who surely was dead too, by now. It really was the end of an era.

He had absently been putting some vegetables on a chopping board and getting ready to slice them up, but suddenly, he took the chopping knife and threw it across the room.

It stabbed the plasma screen like a dartboard. He was *still* the man in that photo! Older and wiser, yes, but he did a lot more good back then as a junior officer than he did now as a colonel. What had he become? He had to find his way back.

He thumped the kitchen table, and then burst into loud laughter.

Choupette walked in, wearing an old dressing gown and a towel around her head. And a concerned expression on her face.

"Are you alright?" she asked.

"No," he replied honestly. "But I hope I will be. One day soon."

Later, Pichenet contacted a night duty officer who told him more about Judex's death—he'd been found dead in a small street. It seemed that he'd died of heart failure, which seemed an anti-climactic way for a figure like him to go. Pichenet made a mental note to make more effort to eat healthily and take more exercise.

He was also informed that the Marchef had killed Leo Saint-Clair. This haunted him for the rest of the evening, but he made an effort to talk to Choupette about it.

Then, later still, he was contacted to be informed that Saint-Clair's body had vanished.

When he had been shot by the Marchef's EMP gun, the Nyctalope had been genuinely stunned and winded.

But as he gasped for breath and looked down at the blood patches staining his shirt, he realized that it wasn't him—it was the undershirt Doctor Omega had given him!

Now he understood why everyone seemed to think he'd had a modern heart fitted. The Doctor must have had that piece of fake news planted on his file. He still had the same old mechanical heart he'd been given all those decades ago—which was still working perfectly, and had no electronic components in it. Taking an EMP blast had no effect on him. A gunshot would have been far worse.

Maybe Doctor Omega had changed history by saving Saint-Clair this way? Leo was still alive, and now knew that others were also working against this regime.

So he played along and pretended to die. He lay still until he was sure that the smirking Marchef had left the apartment.

Then he got up, removed his leather jacket, and hurried into the bathroom, where he took off the shirt and undershirt. He was thinking about how to dispose of them both, when he noticed that the undershirt was dissolving into thin air—like an aspirin in water. It had started dissolving since he took it off. Obviously it was something that the Doctor had brought from the future. The blood stains were disappearing from his shirt and torso, too. So he left what remained of the undershirt in the bath to completely disappear, and stuffed the shirt into the laundry basket.

He grabbed some toiletries and hurried into his bedroom, where he put them into a bag, which he put in a rucksack, along with some clothes. He put on a clean shirt, and glanced around the room one last time.

He had bought this place forty years ago, as a convenient place to stay in central Paris. He had several other residences around France and the world, and he was rarely at any of them. This place was still decorated in the same neutral colors it had been when he had bought it. He'd only really added a few personal items, like the framed picture of Sylvie on his bedside table. He quickly stuffed it into his rucksack.

Saint-Clair only paused in the living room to quickly put on his leather jacket again, and then he opened the window that led to the fire escape. An alarm should have gone off, but he had had it disabled in case he had to leave the apartment this way.

Down in the underground parking lot, Saint-Clair could see that the coast was clear. He only had ten minutes to go before the curfew. He got into his spinner and quickly drove out of the exit.

If a patrol stopped him, he'd have to use his SNIF credentials to go on his way, but he hoped it didn't come to that.

He took to the air, and weaved his way around the buildings. He made it out of the city with minutes to spare. Dodging the searchlights, Saint-Clair sped on into the night.

He had to get out of the country. Germany was too far. Britain was nearer, but he doubted he could get over the Channel at night, with border patrols on the French Side, and the so-called Fortress Isle taking pot shots at him on the other.

So he headed for Belgium. He could stop over there, change vehicles, and fly to the US.

Surprisingly, this setback hadn't scuppered the plan at all. He just had to be back in one month, to meet with Una and Judex again.

Christofer Nigro has already spun several tales featuring Paul Féval, fils' crea-tion, Felifax the Tiger-Man (available from Black Coat Press, ISBN 978-1-932983-88-0), as well as his half-brother Felanthus, in "Eye of the Tiger-Man," published in The Shadow of Judex, *then in "The Privilege of Adonis" (*TOTS *Volume 10), "The Noble Freak" (Volume 11), "Justice and the Beast" (Volume 12) and "Kindred Beasts" (Volume 14).. This is a direct sequel to the last in-stallment...*

Christofer Nigro: *The Anti-Adonis Alliance*

Paris, May 1937

Quasimodo looked down from his post atop the towering Notre-Dame ca-thedral, quietly surveying the throngs of normal people going about their daily business. He saw many men dressed proudly in topcoats, neckties, and immacu-late cuffed trousers striding about; on their arms were many attractive women looking gloriously radiant in their pleated skirts and semi-revealing Gatsby dresses. These men had lives which the current incarnation of the Hunchback of Notre-Dame could only dream of, all the while enjoying intimate liaisons with entrancing women that was equally alien to his experience.

The streets themselves were filled with fancy new automobiles churned out by France's native manufacturer, Citroën, each of them exquisite modes of transportation the misshapen secret inhabitant of the world's most famous ca-thedral could never hope to own himself.

And this angered Quasimodo on a level that simmered with the fiery inten-sity of a volcanic eruption.

As these normal people scampered about with excitement on their way to the much-anticipated International Exposition of Arts and Technology (unaware this would be the last such exposition Paris would ever hold), Quasimodo's crooked, yellowed teeth were firmly gritted as rage flowed through his powerful but malformed physique. He would have given up almost anything to be able to wear a double-breasted overcoat with a stylish Ivy cap adorning his head and a shapely woman in a chic Doeuillet-Doucet dress holding his hand as he strode down the boulevard. Such sacrifices would have included his entire sense of probity.

Fate, however, was about to take a decidedly unexpected turn for the Paris-ian who descended from the genetically afflicted lineage that periodically pro-duced one such as Quasimodo. It began with the Hunchback being startled out of his incensed musings by a raspy and unexpected voice which suddenly ad-dressed him from a few feet behind.

"A pity you cannot walk among the rabble and live as they do, *hein, mon ami?*"

Quasimodo turned to behold a tall, lanky individual dressed in a dark cloak and what appeared to be an immaculate ebony suit and tie ensemble. The figure's face was hidden under a porcelain white mask, and the top of his head was covered by a black hat that appeared to be tightly secured with a nylon string. The mask did not, however, conceal the piercing yellowish eyes of this menacing apparition.

"Who are you?" the now thoroughly infuriated Quasimodo demanded. "How did you get up here?"

"To answer your second query first, there is hardly any place in all of Paris from which I am denied ingress," the strange figure replied. "As for your first question, I am one who can readily relate to your plight and place in life. But the latter need not be one so humble and, dare I say, *pathetic.*"

"Get out of my home now! Or, I shall rip you apart with my bare hands!"

Quasimodo raised his arms to reveal his enormous, spade-like hands and muscular fingers to make it clear that his capability of carrying out such a threat matched his willingness. But the darkly dressed figure before him did not so much as flinch.

"Temper, temper, *mon ami.* My name is Erik, and I am here to offer you both friendship and a proposition."

"I told you to get out of here!" the Hunchback reiterated with unbridled fury before charging at the mysterious interloper.

Quasimodo's great size and years of climbing the cathedral's spires, coupled with his mutation, gave him strength rivaling that of any Olympic weightlifter; his charge was therefore a force to be reckoned with for any mortal man. Erik, however, was no mere mortal.

With surprising speed and agility, the Phantom of the Opera side-stepped the Hunchback's attack at the last possible moment. It was a move designed to ensure that Quasimodo's forward momentum caused him to slam into the stone wall directly behind his intended target. The misshapen misfit bounced off it with great force, falling on his lop-sided back.

"Now, as you recover from stunning yourself in such a humiliating fashion," Erik said, "please take the time to listen to my proposal."

However, Quasimodo was quick to display his great resilience by promptly recovering and returning to his feet in mere seconds. The Phantom quietly resolved not to underestimate this one.

"Impressive," Erik conceded aloud. "Though you are not sufficiently dazed, I must again insist that you hear me out before you consider resuming your attack."

But the Hunchback cared nothing for what Erik insisted upon. All he did care about was how much he wanted the brilliant pianist-cum-master-assassin out of his home. And at this point, preferably *in pieces.*

Once more, however, Erik was prepared. The Phantom again side-stepped Quasimodo's rhino-like charge. Only, this time, since he wasn't standing in front of a stone wall, he resorted to an altogether different measure to stop the Hunchback's attack. That took the form of quickly throwing the loop of his dreaded Punjab lasso around Quasimodo's massive neck.

The burly man-monster found himself halted in mid-stride by the extremely painful garroting around his throat. He resisted and pushed against the choking force with all his considerable might, which proved of no use since Erik held fast with an amazing degree of strength that belied his own thin build.

"Can we now speak in civil fashion?" the Phantom asked his gagging opponent. "Or must I carry this through all the way to its unfortunate conclusion?"

Quasimodo continued to gasp and hack at the punishing strangulation before falling to one knee, his resistance greatly diminished.

"Ah, that is good," Erik said, responding in kind by lessening his strangulating pull. "Now, let us put this unpleasantness behind us and get down to the matter at hand…"

Erik's sentence was abruptly cut off as Quasimodo took advantage of the Phantom's relaxed grip by suddenly grasping the rope attached to the loop around his neck and pulling it over his head with all the strength he could muster. That proved enough, as the murderous musician found himself hurled directly over the Hunchback's head, and slammed down on the floor.

This served as another, more painful, reminder that Quasimodo was not to be underestimated. And that Erik, too, could become his victim. Still, the Phantom was nothing if not resilient. He recovered as quickly as the Hunchback had done previously. As a result, when the still gasping and coughing Quasimodo rushed towards the Phantom again, he found his masked adversary on his feet, pointing the business end of a very sharp blade towards his throat.

Since the Hunchback's resistance did not include immunity to stabbing, let alone in the throat, he halted his charge, this time voluntarily.

"I would cease and desist from any further hostilities if I were you, Quasimodo," the Phantom said calmly but firmly.

"You know of me?" the Hunchback queried, as his hands shook from the continued surge of adrenalin through his bloodstream.

"I know of *much*," the Phantom replied. "Including the fact that your wretched ancestor, whose story was recorded but disguised as a work of fiction, much like my own saga, had a name and a role that has now been passed on to you, *mon ami.*"

"Shut up! I have no friends!"

"That need not be so. Understand that your predicament is not entirely unique in this cruel world we share."

"You can't possibly understand my lot in life, masked man!"

"*Oh, non?* Then perhaps I should let you gaze upon what lies beneath this mask."

With a quick movement of his free hand, Erik pulled off his disguise, revealing the hideous skull-like visage beneath. The Hunchback stood glaring, his mouth agape.

"Feast your eyes, Quasimodo! Glut your soul on my accursed ugliness! One that rivals your own!"

The entranced Hunchback covered his gaping mouth as his tortured mind processed the sight he now beheld. Erik gave him the time he needed to do so, and the two outcasts locked eyes for nearly a minute until Quasimodo finally broke the silence.

"I do know you. *Of* you, that is. You are… the assassin. The one known as the Phantom of the Opera."

"None other. One whom you know is not to be trifled with under any circumstances; even when he approaches in the name of friendship. A rare gesture on my part, to be sure, and only extended to a truly kindred soul."

Quasimodo glowered at Erik for several more seconds before slowly and cautiously lowering his arms and unclenching his fists.

"I am listening," he said. "What proposition do you offer?"

Erik smiled, a grin that was anything but pleasant to view.

"Excellent! I recently attended one of the periodic gatherings of those who walk within the, er, *special circle* to which I belong. Where deals are made and handsomely remunerated opportunities to ply our dangerous trade are exchanged. There, my *daroga* led me to a contact he had from India, who in turn passed on a lucrative offer from a wealthy Brahman named Sourina. He is a man of unscrupulous nature who now finds himself in exile, widely believed to be dead, although not separated from the fortune his former position enabled him to acquire. His offer was to apply my unmatched skills at bringing about the bloody demise of one with whom I believe you are acquainted: Rama, the Hindu lord also known as Felifax, the Tiger-Man."

Quasimodo's expression again took on a look of barely controlled fury, albeit not directed at Erik this time.

"Him! The one who invaded the sanctity of my home and, er, quarreled with me during a previous trip of his to Paris!"

"The very one."

"But he doesn't live here! He lives in the jungles of his native India!"

"That is indeed his domain. But Sourina has discovered that Rama will be returning to Paris soon to oversee an art exhibit dedicated to the goddess Kali for the Great Exposition. He will arrive in just a few days' time. He will be traveling with his trusted confidante, Baber, a secret agent of Scotland Yard who operates in Benares. My *daroga* will deal with him. However, Felifax is a more challenging target, even for I. Hence, my reaching out to you for assistance. Accept, and I shall generously reward you, plus you will have the satisfaction of getting revenge against the Tiger-Man. And you will be earning my friendship, which may be worth more than all of the above."

The Hunchback clenched his fists and gritted his crooked teeth once more as he recalled Felifax's handsome features and perfect body, which provided him with a plethora of opportunities cruelly denied to Quasimodo.

"You see, my friend," Erik continued, "though I, unlike you, have not had a personal squabble with Felifax, I take as much pleasure at being the author of his demise as you will. And not solely due to the reward offered. Like you, I have had to endure the torture of watching men blessed with the gift of Adonis strut through life like glorified peacocks, reaping the benefits of the roll of the dice made for them by Fate. They naturally attract opportunities denied to those of us who drew the poorest hand. They enjoy the easy benefits of being winners in every aspect of life, including the attentions of the fair sex, who do naught but recoil in horror at the mere sight of those like you and me.

"They often become beloved heroes, because the side of the angels eagerly opens the pearly gates to welcome them. Those of our lot, on the other hand, must at best exist on the sidelines; or at worst, lurk in the shadows. It then becomes easy for the darkness to overwhelm us, corrupting our psyches with loneliness, bitterness, hatred, and despair. Is it any wonder that what lies within us invariably comes to match our unfortunate exteriors?"

Quasimodo's clenched fists trembled with a growing wrath as the Phantom's words struck deep within his troubled soul. It was not difficult for the Hunchback to make his final decision.

"I accept! Let us prepare for this, friend Erik!"

Two days previous, when Erik had attended the underground meeting where he had been offered the contract he had just described to Quasimodo, there had been a significant detail of which he had been unaware.

All assassins of note, including the Phantom, presumed the underground facilities where they met to conduct their business was unknown to all but those in their circle, and a complete mystery to law-enforcement. Hence, they conducted their mutual business with but a moderate degree of caution.

The Phantom was one of only four assassins allowed to bid for such a lucrative assignment, as this deadly quartet were widely considered to be the absolute best that France had to offer. All four quietly listened to Sourina's agent, who operated as a mole for the powerful Brahman inside the French government. Despite demanding a high price, Erik's bid was ultimately accepted. He received the job, and the other three assassins simply walked away without making a complaint.

That was a form of deference that Erik had grown comfortably accustomed to. What he was not accustomed to, however, was being duped in any fashion. Unbeknownst to the Phantom of the Opera, one of the other three bidding slayers, Armand de Sainte-Croix, was not actually whom he appeared to be.

Upon leaving the hidden facility, the mustachioed killer with the sandy hair and easily recognizable facial scar drove many miles outside of Paris in a very expensive, shiny azure 1936 Bugatti 57SC Atlantic. After carefully determining that he wasn't followed, "Armand de Sainte-Croix" detoured his vehicle into a secluded wooded clearing, where the automobile's true owner kept it secured in a garage cleverly concealed within an artificial thicket.

It was in this safe location that the faux assassin removed his disguise to reveal a face that many in Parisian high society would have recognized as belonging to millionaire socialite Jacques de Trémeuse—the alter-ego of the notorious vigilante Judex, who had long ago secretly dispatched the real de Sainte-Croix and taken over his identity to acquire choice intel from the underworld.

Hence, unknown to both Erik and Quasimodo, Felifax would not have to face the impending threat alone.

In the early evening just after dusk, Felifax and his loyal aide-de-camp Baber were strolling through the decrepit neighborhood of Montreuil just outside Paris. The former was visibly uncomfortable in his overcoat and trousers, and not even his close friend could convince him to adorn himself with a derby or any other fashionable hat for men. He was too used to the freedom of running about in his native jungle with nothing more than a loincloth to cover him.

"What I cannot understand is the need for men in these Western societies to wear such constrictive clothing, even during the warmer months of the year," the Hindu prince griped. "Do these outfits not become soaked through with their perspiration during that time?"

"What *I* cannot understand is your need to walk through this area of urban blight when a first-class hotel was made available to us," Baber countered with a snicker. "This is hardly a section of Paris whose scenery is worth taking in."

"I believe you misunderstand my purpose for visiting here, my friend. 'Urban blight' holds no terror for me. And I would think it shouldn't for you either, considering how many people in India have no choice but to live under similar, or worse, conditions. I wanted to see for myself how the Western nations with their advanced technology still fail to provide adequate living conditions to so many of their citizens. And with no jungle outside for any of them to escape to and live a life more in tune with the natural world, it is little wonder there is so much strife here!"

Baber chuckled at what he considered his friend's naïve sense of equity.

"Rama, that is what the communists in Paris and elsewhere in Europe have been rioting over of late. Unfortunately, their favored prime minister, Mr. Blum, has now been ousted and replaced by Mr. Daladier, and this country will likely go to war against Germany now that that frightful Herr Hitler fellow is running it. Scary people! What will become of India if Herr Hitler should defeat England, I wonder?"

"Many of these leaders are 'scary people,' to me, Baber," Felifax replied as he awkwardly tried to adjust the strangling necktie he was compelled to wear. "I do indeed fear the prospect of a world dominated by the likes of Hitler, but as you know, I equally dislike our nation being colonized by your British masters. A system capable of giving its own people so little is bound to create conflicts and leaders like Hitler, and Stalin… or those of England and France."

"Ha! Perhaps you should spend less time promoting art depicting the savage majesty of Kali and join the next rally of communists wishing to occupy the Citroën factory! Perhaps you will get a free automobile out of the deal!"

"I'd rather not use one of those foul-smelling carriages! Besides, I do not empathize with a company that produces such automated engines of filth, and then has the audacity to display its obscene wealth by placing its glowing logo on the Eiffel Tower."

"Ha! That made the Tower look like a beautiful Christmas tree! I loved it!"

The muscular Indian prince sighed. "I had forgotten that you had adopted the ways of your employers, where worshiping deities has been replaced by the worship of business."

Baber again laughed with amusement at his friend's view of the rapidly changing world of the 20th century. "It has been said by many that the leaders of these nations you find so deplorable are merely practicing their own version of the law of the jungle. Survival of the fittest! Conquest of the weak by the strong! Is this not the code you see the animals, and even the flora, with which you have such a strong bond live by, each and every day? Why should man be any different?"

Felifax pouted as he continued to fiddle with his necktie. "Because man is not a slave to instinct as are the animals. Their motivations, however savage, are always pure. They do not choose how they live. They cannot relate to each other, and to their environment, like humanity does. Unlike us, their primal purity does not include ethics. This bestows man a degree of responsibility in its behavior towards each other, and the world around it, of the kind that we cannot expect from the animal kingdom. Moreover, humanity's unique ability to construct technology, that has the potential to destroy its environment in ways the animals cannot, make him doubly—nay, triply!—responsible for reining in the darker impulses that come with intelligence."

The Tiger-Man quickly found himself so absorbed by his philosophical tirade that he unthinkingly moved several paces ahead of Baber. He pointed to a dilapidated apartment building. Across the street was what appeared to be an abandoned two-story mill.

"Take this building for instance!" he said. "No one appears to be living there. Are people in such an advanced nation expected to live in a series of brick and mortar shacks? Should a civilized country rely on the fluctuations of its paper money to provide for its citizens? Can we at least agree on that much, Baber?"

This time, however, Felifax was greeted with silence. Because it was not like Baber to avoid providing a wry rejoinder to his complaints, the Tiger-Man turned around and discovered that his friend was nowhere in sight.

Since his keen, jungle-honed hearing had picked up no sound, he found the disappearance profoundly distressing.

"Baber! Where are you? Call out to me if you can!"

Hearing no response, Felifax knew that something was seriously amiss. He was well aware of the thieves and ruffians one might encounter in such an urban landscape, but due to his formidable prowess, he had not felt the need to exercise the type of caution that ordinary people who visited this neighborhood would have. Whomever was behind Baber's sudden and utterly silent disappearance was more dangerous than any member of the city's typical criminal element.

Realizing that further verbal beckoning was futile, Felifax began putting his other great senses to use. He sniffed the air around him, attempting to catch any unusual human scent; or even a human-*like* scent, since he had actually encountered a werewolf the last time he had visited Paris. The Hindu prince now began to regret that he hadn't prepared better for his return to the French capital.

As for Baber, he now stood in a hard-to-notice cubbyhole built into the side of the tenement, which aligned with a darkened alleyway off to the side. It provided a vantage point from which anyone within could spy on Felifax frantically searching for signs of his missing friend.

This cubbyhole was only big enough for two people, and two people were indeed inside it. One was Baber, caught in a strong grip by his assailant, a man holding a razor-sharp *borka* blade to his throat. The attacker, who had once held a law-enforcement position in Persia, spoke to him with a Middle Eastern accent.

"Be silent, Baber *sahib*, or I will have to silence you permanently. And I will do that by slicing into the organ that provides you with speech."

It was then that the *daroga*, the latest in a line of steadfast servants and bodyguards to the Phantom of the Opera, felt an unpleasant sensation near his genitals.

"I believe you are now aware that you are not the only one holding a blade to someone's vitals," Baber whispered, just audibly enough so as not to provoke a sudden move on the part of his captor. "If you glance downwards, you will see that the sharp poke you feel in your most precious jewels is the tip of my knife. Should you cut my throat, my muscles will contract, and you will be emasculated in a very bloody manner. If you are lucky, you will promptly bleed out. But if you are not so lucky, well, then I hope you can adjust to spending the rest of your life as a eunuch."

"I understand the precariousness of my situation," the *daroga* interjected. "But yours is equally so. And I will not yield, no matter what part of my anatomy you threaten with your blade."

"Then. it would appear we are both at an impasse, *sahib*. I can only suggest we both watch whatever scenario is about to unfold, involving my friend and whoever your master may be. I am confident as to what the end result shall be."

"As am I, Baber *sahib*. So, let us take your advice and quietly watch what is about to ensue, without taking any part ourselves. If your friend is the victor, I will release you, and you, in turn, will allow me to leave without protest. But if my friend should win, I will cut your throat as instructed, regardless of the unpleasant fate I will be subjected to at the same time. Do we have a deal?"

"It seems fair to me. We do indeed."

Felifax continued to sniff the air and look for signs of Baber. His concentration was such that he was taken unawares when Quasimodo suddenly sprang out of a second story window of the building. As the Hunchback's powerful legs weathered the landing right behind the Tiger-Man, his sinewy arm simultaneously elbowed his adversary with great force.

The jungle lord was immediately brought down to his knees. Quasimodo then grasped the stunned Felifax by the head and hoisted him in the air like a raggedy doll. Before the Hunchback could slam his opponent's face on the filthy street, as intended, the spiritual son of Kali recovered from his daze and grabbed onto Quasimodo's wrists with his equally powerful hands. This enabled him to thrust his legs backwards to deliver a pulverizing double kick to the Hunchback's diaphragm.

The brutal and unexpected blow to Quasimodo's vulnerable lower abdomen forced him to release his grip. Now he was the one down on his knees as he gasped to recoup the air that had been painfully ejected from his lungs.

Meanwhile, Felifax flipped back onto his feet to face his opponent. He stood in a combat ready stance and recognized the twisted man in front of him.

"Quasimodo!" he said, through gnashed teeth. "I see that you still haven't learned the lessons I tried to teach you during our previous encounter—after you had abducted my precious Djina. Well, then be prepared to receive another, even sterner, lesson."

The Tiger-Man generously waited for the Hunchback to cease his tortured inhalations and recover enough breath to get back to his feet, something Quasimodo did with notable celerity. Or perhaps, it was not so generous on Felifax's part, as he wanted his opponent standing and facing him while he delivered the promised lesson.

"You arrogant clod!" Quasimodo screamed just before attacking. "I will take away the beauty that gives you an unfair advantage over me in *almost* every way imaginable! I will make you just like me!"

"You mean, so I can likewise wallow in self-pity and weak-minded hatred, rather than making the best of my lot?" Felifax retorted. "Good luck on that!"

Quasimodo's response was to bellow in rage as he rushed the Tiger-Man. The Hunchback threw a series of rapid-fire blows, all of which Felifax carefully swatted aside thanks to his superior reflexes, knowing it would be very unwise, even for him, to take a single blow from someone as powerful as Quasimodo. Hence, he allowed himself to remain on the defensive for several seconds as he took the full measure of his foe and prepared for his retaliatory offense.

Damn the restrictive clothing these so-called civilized people insist on wearing! he thought.

However, Quasimodo's flurry of strikes did cause him to back up several feet towards the derelict mill on the opposite side of the street. He was unaware that this was part of a plan that had not been orchestrated by the Hunchback alone.

Thus, as soon as Felifax was directly below the factory's open windows, he felt the loop of a Punjab lasso lowering tightly around his neck. A powerful pulling force was applied from above, and the Tiger-Man found himself lifted off the ground to a halfway point between the first and second stories of the mill. He gasped furiously as his life was being choked out of him.

"Hah! Leave a piece of him for me, Erik!" Quasimodo sneered with a waving of his fist. "I must have a piece of him too, remember?"

"Do not fret, *mon ami,*" came the Phantom's voice from window from which the deadly garrote had originated. "I will leave just enough life in our target that he will still feel plenty of pain when I let you finish him off."

Just then, however, Felifax made a startling move, the likes of which Erik had never before witnessed in all his years using the Punjab lasso. The Tiger-Man grasped the rope and swung his feet against the surface of the building. Now, he was no longer choking since he was braced against the outer wall of the mill. Felifax roared as his eyes took on the features of a feline and his incisors began enlarging. The jungle lord called upon the assistance of the dread goddess Kali, and now manifested his primal roots, courtesy of the *Panthera tigris* DNA encoded within his genome.

"Erik!" Quasimodo shouted. "I can't reach him from down here! Do something before he, er, does something else!"

"Worry not, I have the matter in hand!" the Phantom shouted back, but with only a tone of semi-confidence.

Unfortunately, even that limited degree of self-assurance would prove to be unwarranted a minute later when Felifax, still steadied against the wall, tugged onto the lasso with a single mighty heave of his enhanced musculature. This new, unexpected move took Erik off guard and sent him flying out of the window. The now-freed Tiger-Man fell and landed on his feet on the sidewalk below. However, he found himself still unable to remove the tightened loop of the lasso wrapped around his neck.

As for the Phantom, his flight out of the window was halted without injury when Quasimodo rushed forth and caught him before he could hit the ground.

"I got you, Erik! Now, let us finish off this fool together!"

"*Merci,*" the Phantom muttered with sincere gratitude, but barely concealed anger. "Let us do exactly that!"

Now in his primal mode, Felifax tore off his coat and the white dress shirt underneath, leaving only the hanging necktie, and revealing the tiger-like stripes that had now appeared on his skin.

First, get out of these garments! he thought.

The son of Kali then roared and bared his teeth as he ran towards his foes, clearly intending to rip them apart. The Phantom of the Opera, however, was no ordinary adversary.

"Remember the maneuver I showed you!" Erik yelled to his ally as he side-stepped Felifax's attack.

As intended, the Phantom evaded the assault while Quasimodo met it head on. As Erik had hoped, the Hunchback was strong enough to effectively hold the snarling, hissing Felifax in place for the few seconds it took the cloaked assassin to get behind him.

The Tiger-Man then found himself pulled off Quasimodo with surprising strength as Erik grasped the lasso still hanging from his target's neck. He then resumed his act of strangulation, this time on the ground. The Phantom, however, understood that not even he might succeed in choking Felifax to death before the Tiger-Man broke free, so he put the next part of his plan in motion.

Since the *daroga* was otherwise occupied keeping Baber out of the fray, this next part would entirely depend upon Quasimodo.

The Hunchback smiled in ominous anticipation as he raised both of his massive fists in preparation for wading into the choking Felifax and mercilessly pummeling his foe from the front, while the Phantom garroted him from behind.

But this plan was thwarted when a new factor entered the fracas. The Punjab lasso strangling Felifax was suddenly severed by a high-caliber bullet.

Erik turned to see the silhouette of another dark-cloaked figure with a prominent slouch hat standing several meters to the left.

As the newcomer walked into the dim illumination of the street lights, the gun-wielding interloper's identity became chillingly obvious.

"Judex!" Erik exclaimed in a grating tone.

"That is correct, monster," the vigilante said in his usual, sinister monotone voice. "I have long wanted to bring you down. Removing you from this world will be one of the greatest gifts I shall ever deliver into the hands of Lady Justice."

Of course, Judex was not going to let the Phantom know that they had met only recently, when the crime-fighter was operating in the guise of "Armand de Sainte-Croix."

"We shall see which of us is dispatched this night, vigilante," the Phantom said with a jeering grin concealed by the black mask he wore.

With a blur of motion, the Phantom somersaulted to evade a second shot from Judex and dashed into the front entrance of the mill. In a second shadowy

blur, the vigilante followed him, intent on ending the career of the most dangerous assassin in all of France. This left Felifax and Quasimodo to deal with one
another.

As the Tiger-Man coughed and choked on his knees, still recovering from
the Phantom's second garrote attempt, the Hunchback took full advantage of his
foe's momentary weakness.

The large misshapen man rushed forward and grabbed Felifax from behind
in a crushing bear hug, being careful to wrap his mighty limbs around his opponent's upper torso, so that the jungle lord would be unable to bite them. Then, he
squeezed with such force that the Tiger-Man had to exhale, preventing him from
attempting to bite his way out.

"I will crush the life out of you!" Quasimodo decreed as he did his best to
do precisely that.

Felifax gasped and struggled to break free, but the devastating power of the
Hunchback's grip kept him from securing a single breath of much-needed oxy-
gen. The Tiger-Man realized that even his great resilience would eventually fail,
as he began to feel his rib cage and sternum give way to the relentless pressure.
Nevertheless, he was nothing if not a quick thinker, even when subjected to such
massive pain.

Inspired by the Phantom's use of the Punjab lasso, the feline combatant
quickly removed his remaining necktie. He then whipped and twisted it behind
him with both hands to form a makeshift noose which he swung around Quasimodo's neck. The jungle lord prayed to Kali for strength as he pulled the necktie
tightly with all the power he could muster.

Quasimodo began choking, and panic flowed through his malformed body
as he recalled being strangled by Erik's lasso a few days earlier. He initially
tried to maintain his grip on the Tiger-Man, but the latter used his formidable
will and primal power to strengthen his garrote.

Quasimodo's tongue began protruding from his mouth as the strangulation
continued, eventually becoming too severe for him to withstand it. That, combined with his growing panic, finally forced him to release Felifax.

The now-freed Tiger Man growled in a fit of animal ferocity as he turned
himself and his foe around. Then, aided by a mighty surge of adrenalin, he
pulled forward on his makeshift garrote and flipped Quasimodo's massive body
directly over his shoulders. The Hunchback quickly went airborne and smashed
clear through the padlocked wooden door of the building across from the mill.

Felifax took a minute to fully recover from the punishment which had been
delivered to his rib cage, and slowly reverted to his human form. Now thinking
like a man again, he walked over to the tenement and peered through the opening to check on his opponent. The sight of Quasimodo lying unconscious on the
dirty tiled floor, his legs sprawled up and over the bottom of the staircase, reassured him.

The Indian prince then looked down at the ropey cloth in his hand. "It is good that this necktie turned out to be useful for *something.*"

Judex carefully walked through the dinge-infested mill, his keen eyes scanning the darkness as best they could for any signs of his dangerous adversary. The darkly-cloaked vigilante was quite aware of the fact that the genius dispenser of both lovely concertos and horrific murders was one of the deadliest being alive.

Judex considered using the tube-shaped flashlight he kept in a hidden pocket of his cloak to more efficiently make his way through the darkness, but ultimately decided against it. A small, moving orb of illumination would likely reveal his position to the Phantom before it revealed the whereabouts of the latter to him. Hence, his decision was to rely on his own vision alone.

The dark avenger had by now been at this game for a few decades, and he had developed something close to what was sometimes referred to as a "sixth sense." Thus, he was able to move aside quickly enough to avoid having his back perforated by a small but extremely sharp blade hurled from a point directly above him on the rafters.

The metal implement clattered loudly as it hit the floor. In a blur of motion, Judex pointed his firearm in the general direction from which the blade had been thrown and fired. He heard the bullet ricochet off the upper wall, but could not discern whether it had hit a flesh and blood target.

"Do not presume that I am now unarmed, my esteemed adversary," echoed the voice of the Phantom from the shadows above. "I have another, and, in fact, you cannot know how many I have hidden in my own cloak. You are not the sole individual to discover the use of hidden pockets inside a cape."

Judex again let off a shot in the general direction from which the voice emanated. And again, he heard the projectile bounce harmlessly off the wall. The vigilante realized the Phantom may be playing a game to entice him into exhausting his ammo. The skills wielded by this strange assassin were rumored to be legion, with no clear consensus on the limits of his capabilities. Hence, Judex knew such skills may include the ability to "throw" one's voice for the purpose of strategic misdirection. Could he truly trust his own senses in this oppressive darkness against a foe such as the Phantom?

Judex's ruminations distracted him just enough that he wasn't fully able to evade the next hurled blade. His instincts served him just enough to turn so as to prevent the weapon from embedding itself into his sternum, at which it had been aimed. Instead, it sunk halfway into his left leg.

The vigilante was nothing if not resistant to pain, however, and, this time, his senses proved on target. And that target was literally the Phantom, who, in this instance, failed to effectively shield the direction of his whereabouts. Judex's next shot managed to strike Erik in his right shoulder.

The impact sent the assassin crashing through the glass of a second story window, to plummet into the waters of a canal directly adjacent to the other side of the mill.

"*Échec et mat,*" Judex said triumphantly as he carefully removed the blade from his calf and tightly wrapped a binding he had stored in his cloak around the wound. "I can only hope the world has finally seen the last of you."

Erik held onto one of the mooring poles built inside the canal with his one good arm, his body half immersed in the cold waters. It was a difficult situation even for him to escape, and for the moment, all he could do was to hold on.

That moment soon ended when a massive hand grabbed his arm and easily pulled him up. The wounded assassin had been rescued by Quasimodo, who had regained consciousness and escaped under the notice of Felifax.

"Erik! I am glad I found you! You're hurt. We need to get you help."

"I have had worse, *mon ami.* And worry not, I have a special physician on hand for such predicaments. You need only get me back to the Opera House."

"I will help you."

As the two began to walk back towards a nearby hidden cab, Erik could not help but say more to the Hunchback.

"Thank you for coming to my aid. Most others, save perhaps for my *daroga,* would have left me to die."

"I merely did... what friends do, *non?*"

Erik could do naught but smile at the expressed sentiment. He began to feel as if he may have gained something of inestimable value out of this failed venture after all.

As Felifax recovered from the battle, he was delighted to see Baber rush up to him from out of a nearby alley.

"I shall answer your obvious question without your need to ask it first," the British agent said. "I was held at knifepoint by a truly nasty character with a Middle Eastern accent. I suspect him to have been the man known to law agencies as The Persian or The *Daroga.* We watched your battle from our vantage point, and, true to his word, he released me when you proved the victor; and true to my own word, I allowed his retreat to spare both our lives.

"I am nearly certain of his identity, because I believe the one in the dark cloak who was trying to kill you, alongside the Hunchback, was none other than Erik, the so-called 'Phantom of the Opera,' France's deadliest assassin-for-hire."

"So, that's who he was," Felifax said. "And that explains why you vanished with such suddenness."

"Indeed. Considering what you faced, your triumph was impressive. I had no doubt of the outcome, however. Well, maybe just a little. But considering whom you fought tonight, I think you can forgive me for those niggling doubts."

"I do," said Felifax. "Especially as there were a few of what the English refer to as 'close calls' during that battle. But I did not succeed alone. That other cloaked individual who came to my aid... he, too, seemed familiar."

"That would be me," Judex announced as he suddenly appeared behind Felifax and Baber, the limp due to his injured leg barely noticeable when he walked. "I am pleased to see you again, Rama, despite the grim circumstances."

"Judex!" Baber said with his own glimmer of recognition. "You two have met before?"

"We have," said Felifax, with a frown. "He invaded the Indian jungle some years past to steal something from a tribe under my protection."

"It was to save the life of a good man and valued friend," the vigilante said. "And you tried to stop me from that task. I only did what I had to do."

"It was more complicated than that," Felifax rejoined. "But needless to say, you have my gratitude for coming to my aid here. I will not even ask how you knew I would be in need of such assistance."

"I have my ways," Judex replied. "But that is not the only reason I approached you, and why I would have done so even if I had not uncovered the threat to your life. There is something important of which I must inform you. Some months ago, I encountered an even more tiger-like being in the woods of the Bois de Boulogne, who assisted me, and the same friend I mentioned earlier, in dispatching Bertrand Caillet, the dreadful 'Werewolf of Paris.' That being called himself Felanthus, and he said he was your sibling."

"Felanthus!" the Indian prince exclaimed with heavy emotion. "I thought him forever lost to me after our battle with the Monster of Frankenstein!" Felifax grabbed the vigilante by the lapels of his cloak and pulled him closer. "Why did you not contact me at once? Why did you not help him find me?"

"You are a difficult man to locate," Judex coolly replied. "Sending telegrams to one who resides in the jungles of India is no easy task. And your sibling refused my offer of help and fled, because of his mistrust of humanity. Now, kindly remove your hands from me or I shall remove them for you."

Baber made a necessary intervention by grasping Felifax's hands and slowly removing them from Judex's person. "Now, now, Rama, no need to take this out on the gentleman who helped you and delivered this important message. At least now, you know that your brother is alive, so..."

"Yes!" Felifax resounded. "I will move all the stars under Vishnu's gaze to find my brother and bring him back to India with me where he belongs! I will track him down, starting from the wooded locale that Judex mentioned! And I shall not fail him any longer!"

Then, the Tiger-Man dashed off at blinding speed, leaving both Judex and Baber standing behind.

Felifax's quest to find his brother had now begun.

A new story by John Peel is always a treat. This year's tale features the extreme-ly realistic settings and well-researched events of the notorious Jack the Ripper murders; it blend a variety of odd characters to create an even weirder plot. Its protagonist, Carnacki the ghost-finder, investigates a strange conspiracy which may lead him to uncover the real reasons behind the Ripper's killing spree...

John Peel: *The Gutter God*

London, 1888

When my friend Carnacki issues a dinner invitation, none of the recipients would willingly stay away. Only the direst of emergencies would prevent at-tendance. One reason is that Carnacki's feasts are utterly superb—the finest res-taurants in either London or the continent cannot compare to the viands he serves. And yet the food is the least of the reasons we attend. It is the post pran-dial conversation that is the largest lure.

I say "conversation," but it is rare that any of us join in. We simply sit and listen to Carnacki tell us of his latest cases. For he has a somewhat unique occu-pation, one that provides him with thrilling and barely believable anecdotes.

Carnacki is a ghost-finder.

I do not mean to imply that he is a spiritualist or some sort of a psychic medium—though he has some abilities in that field—but that he investigates cases that would appear to involve the supernatural. Most frequently, of course, the so-called hauntings turn out to be fakes—though even those cases frequently have their interesting and entertaining sides—but there are times when he en-counters something genuinely preternatural. The tales he tells of those encoun-ters are frequently chilling, but are always unfailingly fascinating.

At this particular dinner, though, the general conversation, for once, cen-tered about a rather different topic, and Carnacki sat through the discussion of the Whitechapel Murders with a slight smile on his face, but a very different ex-pression in his eyes. When we sat down after the meal to brandy and cigars, we gathered in a semi-circle about him as usual, and waited to see if he could pro-vide a tale one half as interesting as the one we had been discussing.

As ever, he did not fail.

I perceive that you are—understandably—all intrigued with the tales of the events in Whitechapel (he began). This foul stain on humanity who calls himself Jack the Ripper. Allow me to make a prediction that the trail of blood is almost complete, and that the police will not be able to arrest the perpetrator of these dreadful slayings. I can see the look of surprise on your faces, but I assure you that I do know whereof I speak. Allow me to enlighten you.

To understand these events, I shall have to tell you of an encounter I had almost two years ago. To call it difficult to believe would be an understatement; at the first, I was extremely reluctant to accept the truth of it myself, especially since it concerned one of the most degraded and disgusting creatures I have ever encountered.

I was, at the time, involved on a case which is quite immaterial to this tale. Suffice it to say that I had been hired to find a young lady of good breeding who had inexplicably vanished into Whitechapel. Her story has its interesting elements, and I may go further into it at some other date. What matters here, though, is that I was led to the sordid backstreets of one of the poorest and most blighted areas of our otherwise fair city. You can really have little idea of how terrible the conditions are, or how degraded the inhabitants have become. There are public houses on every corner, though I would hesitate to call the liquids that they purvey there as either refined or refreshing. They sell gin, mostly—the coarsest and most potent that they can manage. A pennyworth of that... liquid serves to help blot out the realities of the sordid life in those filthy, inhospitable streets.

The inhabitants of Whitechapel, for the most part, are the dregs even of the lowest layers of our society. It is almost impossible to understand how terrible and neglected their lives are. They lack the basic requirements of food and drink, their clothing is scarcely better than the rags our servants use to clean our floors, their children little more than the savages in either their demeanor or their education. The men take whatever employment they can, without questioning its purpose or legality, and the women... well, their lives are worse. They have very limited avenues of employment, and so many of them turn to selling their somewhat dubious charms to anyone who will pay them. I find it difficult to judge them for this choice—if, indeed, you can call that business a *choice*. It is a degrading and dangerous life, and many find themselves cheated, beaten or worse. The deaths of those poor unfortunates we read about in the newspapers are the rule and not the exception, sad to say. The only reason that these deaths are even remarked upon is because of the sheer brutality involved. The fates of the women who are merely beaten or killed cleanly do not merit a mention.

Obviously, then, my mission to find out why a well-bred woman would venture into such a place was quite urgent, but it also required some care. I could hardly walk among the inhabitants of those wretched streets in evening dress – it would mark me out instantly, and make a target out of me; certainly for robbery, and perhaps even worse. So I went in a careful disguise that made me look like one of them. If you had seen me as I was then, you would have crossed the street to avoid me – or, even, called a constable on me! But my disguise was suitable for where I was heading.

I eventually came upon one of the public houses on a small, grime-laden street that I shall not specify, and there I chanced across the most amazing figure. On the surface, he seemed indistinguishable from the many other wretched souls that filled those streets. His clothing was filthy rags, his body looked riddled with disease and his eyes were blood-shot and rheumy. To every appearance, he was a drunk living out the last of his days imbibing the cheapest, foulest gin that he could purchase.

And, yet—that was not the truth of it.

You cannot live the kind of life that I do without being able to detect notes of the odd or unusual, and this man reeked of both, along with the spirits he had imbibed. As I looked at him, I understood that this was no mere drunk. He was slumped, semi-conscious, against a wall of the public house that seemed barely strong enough to hold him up, let alone the building, but there was a strong sensation of *power* about the figure. I am sure that the very thought of this seems absurd to you, but it is true. And the truth was about to become stretched out of almost all proportion.

I bent over this man, studying him, and his hand shot out and seized me by the throat. His inebriation was not a pose, and his voice was slurred, his sentence structure twisted and difficult to follow. I shall not attempt to reproduce it—if I even could! —but will instead translate what he said into coherent English. But do bear in mind that some of his sentences took several minutes for him to deliver and me to decipher.

"You trying to rob me?" he asked, and then peered myopically into my face. "No... No, you're not simple thief, are you?" He released his grip, allowing me to breathe freely again (though I inhaled more alcoholic fumes than good, clean air). "You can see me, can't you?"

"Of course I can see you," I agreed. "It would be difficult to miss you."

"No," he countered. "You can *see* me. Do you know who I am?"

"No," I replied. "But I know who you are *not*. You're no simple alcoholic, are you?"

"You've the ability to see that much at least," he muttered. He waved a shaking hand. "Go away, and leave me alone—it would be better for your peace of mind." I had a strong feeling that he meant this quite literally.

But you all know me well enough to be able to predict that the last thing I was now able to do was to walk away from this mystery. I bent and examined him again. To the outer eye, he was nothing more than he seemed—another of those helpless drunks, laid out in the streets of our so-called fair city, beyond help and beyond redemption. But to the *inner* eye... he was nothing of the kind. I could feel the tingle of raw power emanating from the man. I have, as you know, in my adventures sometimes encountered the truly supernatural creatures that exist on the fringes of what we term reality. There is no mistaking any of those for what they truly are, and there was likewise no mistaking this pitiful creature as a being of immense—and yet contained—power.

252

"What *are* you?" I asked him. "From which other dimension do you originate?"

He laughed in my face. "Ah, ghost-hunter," he replied, "you have no understanding. I'll repeat myself—walk away, forget you ever saw me and let me get drunk in peace."

"You *know* me?" I asked.

"Never seen you before in my life," he replied. "But you have an unmistakable odor about you."

Considering the foul stench emanating from him, this was an uncalled-for insult, but I allowed it to pass; he could clearly detect my abilities as clearly as I could discern his.

"Explain yourself to me," I demanded.

"You had your chance," he complained. "I told you that you could walk away, but no, you wouldn't." He glared at me. "You consider yourself a truth-seeker, don't you?"

"It is my avocation," I agreed.

He spat on the ground. "*That* for your avocation." (It took him several attempts before he managed to stagger through the word.) "*This* is a truth you won't want to know."

"Try me," I suggested.

"I'm Bacchus."

I glared at him. "You've certainly been indulging in a bacchanalia."

"Bacchanalia?" He laughed, derisively. "You have no idea what you are saying."

I stared at the disgusting apparition before me. "You are Bacchus, the god of wine and drink? You appear to be taking your profession rather too much to heart." I did not—*could not!* —believe what he had said. And yet—there was still that inexplicable aura of true power about the man. If he *was* a man...

"You should be thankful that I'm drunk," he said. "Trust me, you would not dare face me if I were sober. Neither you, nor any other man in this entire blighted city." There was a cold ring of assurance in what he said.

"The gods of the ancient world were merely legends," I reasoned. "The embodiment of a primitive people's fears and desires."

"How terribly Victorian of you," he sneered. "Science rules the world, and superstition is banished to the outer darkness." He laughed. "You, of all people, ghost-finder, should know how narrow-minded that belief is. You've encountered the beings and powers that inhabit other spaces and times than merely this. How can you so blithely dismiss the existence of the gods, then?"

"Can you prove your rather fantastical claim?" I asked him.

"Why should I want to?" he demanded, belligerently? "I've told you who I am and asked you—for the sake of your own sanity—to leave me alone. Be a good little, timid mortal and do precisely that. Let me stay a solitary drunk."

"After what you have said, how can you expect me to do that?" I asked him. "I must know more."

"Of course you must," he sneered. "That's the trouble with you mortals—always trying to increase that meager supply of knowledge that you think encompasses all of reality. I have told you all that it is safe for you to know, so, for once in your life, do the sensible thing and walk away and forget you ever saw me. Go find the woman that you seek. You can find her at..." and he gave me an address.

"I didn't tell you that I was looking for a woman."

"No, you didn't. But I pay attention to what *isn't* said as well as to what is. You should learn to do the same."

"How do you know these things?" I demanded.

He pointed a shaky finger at his wretched self. "Bacchus, remember?"

"If you are indeed the Roman god of debauchery, then why are you here?"

"I'm debauching myself, of course," he said, as if that were the most obvious feature in the world.

"But *why*? And why here, in Whitechapel, of all places?"

"Because *here*, I'm nothing and nobody special," he growled. "To almost everyone who passes, I'm simply another stinking drunk. Even the vermin of society cross on the other side of the street. Here, I am nobody and nothing. Here I am *safe*."

"I shouldn't think you're that safe," I muttered. "If you manage to get inebriated and stay so, then you must have money. Aren't you likely to be manhandled by a passing pickpocket?"

"Money?" He turned over a filthy hand and several golden coins rolled from his feeble clutch. I picked one up, and it was clearly a drachma, with Alexander the Great's head upon it, and apparently freshly minted. I stared at it, and then at him. "You mistake my meaning," he added. "I don't mean that I am safe from other people—I mean that *they* are safe from *me*."

"I don't understand."

"Of course you don't," he agreed, amiably. "That's fine. But what you *really* mean is that you *want* to understand—and that is a dangerous thing, my friend. But I can see I'll get no peace until I reach the point where you can accept no more, so I'll explain. Some." He considered for a moment. "What do you think happens to a god when people stop believing in him? When they stop worshipping him?"

I considered the point. "I should think he would shrivel up and cease to exist. Without worshippers a god is surely nothing."

"Nothing?" He barked a laugh. "You've a lot to learn about the gods, you small-minded creature. You seem like an educated man—haven't you ever read the stories of the gods?"

"Of course," I agreed.

"Then try and remember them," he snapped. "We gods don't *need* mortals. Never have, never will. Our power isn't dependent on some sniveling little jumped-up monkeys putting their faith in us. Our power is inherent—we were born with it, and it is a part of us. What sort of feeble gods would we be if we relied on humanity's beliefs to make us anything?" He eyed me with true disgust. "As if we rely on you arrogant idiots for anything!" He shook his head, which seemed to make him lose focus for a moment.

"Then what *does* happen when people stop believing in you?" I asked him. I realized that, somehow, I had slipped into believing his incredible claim, that I *did* accept this being in the gutter as one of the ancient gods of our world.

"We lose touch," he said promptly. "We lose our—for lack of a better word—our humanity. Recall the myths—how savagely and casually the gods behaved. We turned people into animals for slighting us, or trees, or a breath of wind. We annihilated cities, laid waste to the world. We fought and killed, and raped and maimed. Oh, we had power, and very few restraints. Remember those tales?"

I did indeed, and was somewhat surprised that I had forgotten them. The elder gods were indeed a selfish, arrogant and wretched lot at times.

"It was only our worshippers that kept most of us in line," Bacchus said. "We couldn't go around butchering you all if we had become addicted to your worship and your tasty sacrifices, could we? We were obliged to look after you, to keep feeding our needs. Ah, but once you forgot, once you slipped away from adoring us and burning offerings to us... why, then, we were free to do whatever we wished with you again. No consequences, since you no longer believed in us."

"You're saying that the old gods are still around?" I asked him, astonished.

"Most of us, yes," he said, belching. "Mars is doing pretty well for himself these days. You may not worship *him*, but you serve him well enough. And Venus—that old lecher herself... Even in these Victorian days of hypocrisy, she's doing very good business" He waved his hand to encompass the inhabitants of Whitechapel about him. "Even if they only charge a shilling a time, these women serve her, and the men worship at her altar. As for me—well, there's drink enough to float the fleet that sank Troy, eh?"

"So we're worshipping you without being aware of it, you mean?"

"Something like that, yes."

"It doesn't explain why you're a drunk on the streets of London, though."

"Believe it or not, I actually *like* human beings. Oh, you can be a cantankerous, evil pile of excrement sometimes, but there are some of you who are half-way tolerable." He waved an unsteady hand about. "These... ladies of fallen virtue, for the most part, for example. They're not pretentious or hypocritical about what they do – they sell their bodies in order to remain alive... and have a tipple or two at my altar. They're quite refreshing, unlike the people in power in this benighted country of yours. Those politicians and the wealthy are just as bad as they've been throughout history, and they think that their hands are somehow cleaner because they cloak their evil behind a thin veneer of respectability. But their actions are less honest than those of petty thieves, prostitutes and villains that inhabit these disgusting streets."

I was not about to get into a political discussion with an inebriate—god or not—so I returned to my unanswered question. "But why are you drunk?"

He sighed. "I *told* you—I *like* these people. I'm saving their lives by staying drunk. Drunk, I can't harm them, only myself. But if I ever allow myself to get sober..." He shook his head. "You wouldn't like the consequences."

I confess, this self-proclaimed god intrigued me, and I was tempted to remain and converse with him. But I had a mission, a woman to try and save, and I reluctantly bade Bacchus farewell so that I could continue with my task. "Will I find you here if I come again?" I asked him.

He glared at me darkly. "It would be better for you if you didn't seek me out," he replied. "I rarely overstay my welcome, anyway, so I shall move on. Believe it or not, there are places lower than this that I haven't visited yet."

I left him and hurried to the address he had given me, remaining alert as I did so. It became quite clear to me that there were people guarding that domicile—if such a word could describe the filthy, disreputable place that I finally discovered. The guards were attempting to blend into their surroundings, but they were simple enough for me to identify. There were far too many of them for me to attempt a rescue, even assuming the lady I was seeking was actually ensconced within. I would need help, and that meant the Metropolitan Police.

Fortunately, I had made the acquaintance of a certain Inspector Lestrade—a simple, effective operative, who, perhaps, lacked imagination, but is an efficient and thorough officer of the law. I met him in his office at Scotland Yard—after changing back into my regular clothing, to ensure I wouldn't be arrested when I presented myself at that bastion of respectability! I described my problem to him, and he understood immediately.

"There's a new gang at work," he explained. "Frenchies, for the most part. Call themselves the *Vampires*, probably to throw a scare into the credulous, Mr. Carnacki. Like a lot of businesses these days, they're attempting to expand into the international markets, and they've got a toe-hold in Whitechapel."

"What do they do, Inspector?" I asked.

He shrugged. "Whatever may pay, I'm afraid—plenty of thefts, a bit of common extortion—you name it, they'll have a hand in it somewhere." He sighed. "There's been no ransom note for this missing lady you're after?"

"None."

"Pity; that would have made it simpler. In which case, I suspect she's been snatched as a part of a white slaving ring. She's of good breeding, and there's some who'll pay a good price to—ah—enjoy the favors of such a woman."

"She'd hardly cooperate, Inspector."

"She wouldn't be given a choice, I'm afraid, Mr. Carnacki. Putting it delicately, they have been known to addict their victims to opium or worse, till their poor victims will do anything for more of the drug. Anything..."

I shuddered at the thought. "Is there nothing we can do?"

"Of course there is." He managed a wan smile. "It takes a while for the addiction to take root, and she's only been gone a couple of days, so she's probably only on the periphery. If we manage to get her free, she'll need some medical attention, but probably nothing more."

"And she will be... untouched?"

"I'd say so," he said with conviction. "The... untouched bring a higher price, and these lads prefer their money to their bodily pleasures." That was at least slightly reassuring. "I'll put together a squad of men and we'll raid the house tonight. We'll probably only get the foot soldiers and not the generals, but we should hopefully be in time to save the young lady."

We made arrangements to meet up as close to the house as we thought we could get—considering how difficult it would be to conceal a host of London's finest. Lestrade warned me to come armed. I took my service revolver. Despite their name, the *Vampires* were not truly supernatural creatures, but merely unscrupulous men. True vampires would hardly draw attention to themselves by advertising their nature. This meant that I needed none of my usual equipment, so I could travel lightly.

The raid went off as Lestrade had planned. He's not the most imaginative of men, but he's very efficient when it comes to routine police work. He had the dwelling we sought surrounded, and then led the charge to close the net about the fiends we were after. They fought like the very devils, wounding several of the officers and killing one. A number of the gang were taken alive, but several perished rather than surrender.

Lestrade and I were amongst those who made it into the house. I was forced to use my weapon several times, but I could not wait and see the effect I may have had on those we fought. I hesitate to detail what we discovered when we forced our entry into that sordid dwelling, but we did discover the young lady I was after—and several others also. They were all in drug-induced stupors in foul rooms. Lestrade's assessment of the situation had been precisely on target. As I say, a most efficient officer.

The fighting was soon over. I discovered that I had suffered a very slight graze that I cannot recall receiving, and Lestrade's hat was rather the worse for wear; other than that, as I've said, a number of the police were wounded—mostly lightly—and one killed. But the bulk of the gang was captured. They were transported to the closest police station, and then the medical men came in. One of them, a Doctor John Watson, I knew slightly, and he examined my young lady before instructing her to be taken to a nearby hospital.

"You have been fortunate," he informed me. "The drugs are freshly administered to her, and, though she has been badly affected, I seriously doubt that addiction will have set in. Her family should be able to see her in the morning, and I would recommend a long recuperation, preferably somewhere with a little sunshine."

That was, incidentally, effected. At last report, the young lady is quite recovered from her ordeal. The effects of the drugs she was administered have affected her memory of her time as a captive, and she recalls very little of the horrors that she suffered—thankfully. Some of the other victims were not so fortunate, I am afraid to say, and two of the women had to be committed to an asylum, and there they remain. A foul business, from start to finish.

Rather naively, I had imagined that this was the end of the *Vampires*, but it turned out that it was, in fact, merely the first move in a longer game. We had severed a limb from the gang, but, like a hydra, two more grew back in its place. But it was some two months before my ignorance was completely exposed.

As you may imagine, I was reluctant to abandon the hope that I would find Bacchus once more. The inebriate had intrigued me, and I am ever the student seeking knowledge. I could only dream about what I might be able to learn from such a being. It might sound foolish of me, but I found myself growing more and more inclined to accept his claims of his divinity. Oh, I realize that he had offered me no proof of any of his claims, but he had been instrumental in the rescue. Of course, it was possible that he had simply overheard unguarded conversations between members of the gang who did not worry about some stupefied drunk in the gutter, but somehow I did not think this the case.

As a result, I found myself wandering in disguise whenever I had the time to spare through those wretched streets over and over, seeking out the foulest of public houses and gin-shops, hoping that at one of them I should stumble across Bacchus. For two months, though, I was completely unsuccessful. I examined many drunks—not a very cheering task, I can assure you—and was accosted more than a few times. My revolver saved my life more than once. I cannot count the number of women who offered to sell me the use of their bodies for meager amounts of money. Even had I been inclined to accept their offers, their squalid dress and unhygienic status would have revolted me.

And yet, I pitied them, even the foulest of the women or the most debauched of the men. They have so little, and their prospects are non-existent. They cannot improve their state, and there are but few who will help them. They are like the insects that scurry for cover if you turn over a rock in your garden—repulsive, but seeking only to live their lives. The police, for the most part, do not even venture into those streets, leaving its inhabitants to prey upon one another. There are a few churches that attempt to help, but such aid is so little and so ineffective that it makes not the slightest difference. I am aware that I sound like the most earnest of social reformers, but you could not spend time among these people without either hardening your heart to their misery or else feeling compassion. Fallen as they are, they are as human as the rest of us.

Everywhere that I went, though, I heard talk of the *Vampires*, and it quickly became apparent to me that we had effected but little damage to that criminal organization. Its influence was growing in Whitechapel, and its effects were terrifying.

I spoke with Inspector Lestrade about this, and he regarded me gloomily.

"There's not a lot we can do about it," he said. "The locals view the police force as worse than the gang. Those that won't help us out of fear of reprisals won't do it because they think we're after them. And I suppose we might well be. My friend Mr. Sherlock Holmes speaks often of a mysterious person he calls *The Napoleon of Crime*, but if you ask me, Mr. Carnacki, he's looking in the wrong place. This bunch is the real problem, not some hypothetical master-criminal. Confidentially, Mr. Holmes is a fair detective—almost good enough to be on the force—but he thinks too much, and sees things that aren't there. But, then, we all have our weaknesses, eh?"

I did not mention that I was looking for an ancient Roman god myself in those sordid streets. I am quite certain I know what his response would have been.

And then, as events turned out, Bacchus found me. I was on the hunt for him again when I was accosted by a disreputable middle aged woman of obviously slender to non-existent means.

"Mr. Carnacki?" I had no idea how such a woman would know my name, but I acknowledged that she had identified me correctly. "I've a message from '*im*," she informed me. "'E says as to how you should scarper from 'ere, soonest."

I knew that she could be referring to only one person. "I must see him," I replied.

She rolled her eyes. "'E said you'd say that." She shrugged. "Follow me, then, duckie."

And she set off at a pace I was challenged to match. I'm not entirely certain quite where she led me—the streets there are all alike, and there are many dark and twisting alleys—but our journey terminated, inevitably, before an extremely vile public house. Bacchus was seated in what they refer to as the saloon bar. He looked as blighted as before, but his eyes were no longer bloodshot, and he was clearly not inebriated.

"Carnacki, you damned fool," he said by way of greeting me, "I knew you wouldn't have the sense to listen to my warning." He turned to my companion. "Alright, Polly, you can go now—but be back within the hour—and don't be alone."

"You know me better'n that," she said.

She gave me a wink, and hurried off.

"You picked a poor time to seek me out," Bacchus growled. "I told you that you wouldn't like me if I wasn't drunk."

"And why are you not drunk, then?" I enquired.

"Because I'm off to war, Carnacki, and you have to be stone-cold sober to kill. Or, at least, I do. My army, on the other hand, is better off drunk." He waved a hand at the bar, and I realized something. I had noticed that it was rather full, of course, but now I saw that the occupants were almost all women. There was a barman handing out glasses of milky gin and buckets of foaming beer; there was myself, and there was Bacchus—if he could be called a man. Other than that, the place was filled with women in stages of intoxication. And they were clearly all of them women of little virtue.

"This is your army?" I asked, unbelieving. "And who do you fight?"

"*Les Vampires*, obviously," he growled. "The authorities bleat on about needing evidence to convict while that gang of cutthroats and cutpurses terrorize the area. I told you, Carnacki—I like these people. They're rough and crude, yes, but they are honest – well, as honest as they can be—and they don't pretend to respectability while hiding their vices."

"One of which is obviously drunkenness," I pointed out. "Your... *army* will be in no shape to be able to fight when you require them."

"Carnacki, you blasted fool, I had thought you an educated man. Does that not include a classical education?"

"Of course."

"Then how is it that you've forgotten about the Bacchae?"

The Bacchae... What a fool I was! I had indeed forgotten those stories for the moment. "Then..." I stared in horror at the prostitute brigade.

"Ah, your education returns! Yes—then..." He gestured at the women tossing back gin and beer. "Now do you understand why I ordered you to stay away?"

"I do indeed." I have to confess that a wave of fear washed over me. "Do I have the time to retreat?"

"I'm afraid not." He gave me a rather unpleasant smile, showing pure white teeth in that filthy visage. "Your only chance is to remain very close to my side. Disobey me this time, and even I will not be able to save you."

I really cannot describe the stress of the subsequent hour. As the women became progressively drunker, my fear rose, for they were changing. They were no longer women out to make a shilling or two by selling their dubious favors; they were becoming Bacchae... Worshippers of the god of wine and debauchery. His more than lethal followers...

And then the woman Polly was back, with more of her female friends, and they set to, aiming to get drunk as swiftly as possible. As they did so, I glanced outside. The windows had not been cleaned for a lengthy period, and it was difficult to make details out, but it was clear that the street outside was empty.

Bacchus noticed my gaze. "The word has been sent around, Carnacki," he assured me. "There will be none of my people out there—the only ones who will dare those streets today are the *Vampires*—and these." He nodded at his sodden followers.

I am uncertain how long I sat there, my terrors and imaginings increasing, but the women were growing less and less human and more and more inebriated. There was an unholy smile on the face of Bacchus as he regarded his army, and I realized that he was somehow drawing power and strength from these creatures. Eventually, though, that tortured period ended, and Bacchus clapped his hands once, loudly.

"It is time," he announced. "They come."

I had seen and heard nothing outside, but he clearly had senses that I lacked.

With a roar of rage and fury, the Bacchae began to pour into the deserted streets. Most were unarmed, but some snatched up cudgels or any instrument that came to hand. I was certain I was not imagining it, and that their teeth and nails had grown and become sharper... Their eyes showed none of their humanity, and their entire demeanor was more akin to a rabid dog than anything remotely human.

I remained close beside Bacchus, as he strode outside to commence his war. I knew only too well what would be my fate if I should lose him...

At the end of the grimy street, a second army started to filter in. These were the *Vampires*—well dressed, and well-armed. And—unfortunately for them—virtually entirely male. There was only one woman—elegantly dressed, as if for a promenade in Regents Park. Bacchus saw my surprise.

"She is their leader," he explained, with a sneer. "She is called Corvena Septimus[8]—at least, for the moment..."

"A woman," I breathed. "In command of these wretches?"

"Not merely a woman, but also a mother," Bacchus replied. He smiled. "Prophecy isn't really my gift, but *in vino veritas*, you know. Her daughter will grow to be more than her mother, and she will remember this day as a warning. It is the day she will become an orphan."

There was the crack of pistols as the *Vampires* opened fire. Several of the prostitutes fell, but that did not discourage the rest. Even those wounded screamed and pressed forward.

I cannot describe what followed. It would revolt the mind, and my memory strives within me to blot it out. The Bacchae had but a single thought—to annihilate their enemies. They used whatever weapons they had—primarily teeth and claws—and they simply tore their foes apart. It did not matter how many of the Bacchae fell—the remainder pressed on, overwhelming the intruders and ripping their flesh from their bones. Blood and entrails were everywhere in the nightmare that followed.

I confess, I hid my face from much of what occurred. I have seen much in my days, but this – this was more than I could bear. Men were literally ripped apart, and those transformed women drank the blood that flowed as if it were

---

[8] Yes, like "Irma Vep" (her daughter), her name is an anagram...

their cheap gin. And all of the time that the slaughter went on, Bacchus had a peculiar, unpleasant smile on his wretched face.

This was why he preferred to stay drunk—to avoid this from occurring. But now it was necessary, and he reveled in it. It was the dark side of his divinity, one that he preferred not to indulge. But now that it had come upon him, he drank it in.

Unfortunately, I did see the fate of Corvena Septimus. She had imagined that her followers were capable of dealing with any rabble, and had clearly expected this to be a one-sided battle. It was, of course—simply not the side that she had assumed would win. As she realized that her men were doomed, she turned to flee.

The Bacchae seized her, and showed her no mercy. I heard the screams, which were mercifully not over-long. When the army passed on, there was nothing human about what they left behind.

Eventually, of course, there were no more foes to fight, and the transformed prostitutes searched for further victims. The streets had been emptied of their usual inhabitants, and the only target remaining visible to them was me. I had several moments of near terror, I can confess, but Bacchus was my protector. As the enraged women approached, he seemed to draw from them their drunken fury, and they slowly subside into weary women. They spoke not a word, but passed by, staggering from exhaustion now and not drunkenness. In a very short while, Bacchus and I were left alone as the women sought rest wherever they could find it.

The war was over.

Bacchus regarded me with a savage smile. "I did tell you that you should pray that I remained drunk," he informed me. "Now I do believe you understand. It might be best if you did not seek me out again. I shall be hard to find, in any event, as I shall get gloriously and helplessly inebriated again. And London will be safe once more."

I do not know how I made it home again, but I did, and I slept, thoroughly exhausted myself, for more than a day. And this time I have obeyed the instructions of Bacchus—I have not, up to this moment, sought him out again.

The tale, we thought, was finished. But then Cavanagh spoke up. "You said at the start that this tale of yours relates to the recent Whitechapel Killings and this so-styled Jack the Ripper. Yet I confess I do not see the connection." There were murmurs of agreement with this remark.

Carnacki gave a wan smile. "That is because there is something more that you need to know. The female lieutenant, the messenger to me from Bacchus— the one called Polly. Her full name was Mary Ann Nicols, and she was the first victim of this killer. The subsequent ones have all been major members of that army of Bacchus." He regarded us all with care. "It is clear, then, that the *Vampires* were not all wiped out, as we had imagined. Some survivor is meting out revenge on the slayers of his companions, and utilizing their deaths to create terror amongst the remainder."

"You said that this Jack the Ripper would probably never be found," I reminded him. "And that there would be no more victims."

"Indeed I did," he said, grimly. "For, just this evening, I received a message from *him*—he is sober again, and I am warned to stay far, far from Whitechapel this night... And I would advise you all to do the same."

Frank Schildio]ner's next novel, to be released in early 2019 by Black Coat Press, will feature the iconic character from the Vampires gang, Irma Vep, in a dystopic alternate universe where World War I never happened—Irma Vep and the Great Brain of Mars. *In order to provide us with a teaser of sorts to that new saga, Frank penned the following tale...*

Frank Schildiner: *Irma Vep and the Cottage of Doom*

Irma Vep caught the glint of a knife blade out of the corner of her eye. As she suspected, a team of three dacoits crouched in the handsomely manicured bushes, awaiting her entry. Not good, but not a major concern if she took care.

The Marvel Cottage was typical of West Sussex, a small stone and wood walled structure with a slate roof that looked as if it would cave in with the first heavy rainstorm. A long lush lawn surrounded a cobbled path that led to the red painted wood front door. The elderly lead glass windows sparkled in the last glimmers of sunlight before the coming dusk.

Happily, the property appeared deserted, with the exception of the trained cultist killers imitating garden gnomes. Irma Vep mentally shrugged; there was little else to do except confront the dacoits. Sliding a small razor into her palm, she vaulted the rock wall and headed towards the front door.

Dressed in her black leather cat suit, she knew she made an odd figure. This cottage was on a lonely lane, the closest neighbors a half-mile away. Since even those dwellers were away at the funeral, there was no time better than the present. Additionally, the enemy expected the infamous Irma Vep on this job. Best to provide them with the full experience.

She was just reaching for the doorknob when the dacoits struck in their classic style. As her dear Eidolon had explained, these crazed killer cultists always operated in teams of three. Each man possessed a specific, deadly skill and they trained years perfecting their murderous craft.

A silken cord silently slid across her leather-covered throat. The band, more noose than garrote, tightened instantly upon contact and pulled her body backwards. Irma raised her hand and sliced through it, her razor biting through the cord with ease.

Then, she ducked, hearing the whistle of a heavy club pass over her head. That was the second killer, as important as the rope-thrower. Their job was to strike the head of the target and weaken their struggles. Effective and dangerous, it was a form of attack used for over two thousand years with proven results.

The third man leaped into view before Irma Vep. A short, wide, triangle of steel was gripped tightly in his left hand. With an undulating cry, he stabbed out, aiming for the crouching woman's chest. He was a tall man with olive-colored skin, a slim slice of a nose and a pencil-thin mustache. His clothes were simple drab robes with a thin red cord wrapped loosely around his neck.

To Irma Vep's eyes, this handsome killer resembled the heroic figures that appeared in the films from America. He could perfectly fit in with the Rudolph Valentinos, Ramón Novarros and Rudy Valentines that came from studios like Woltz Pictures.

The crazed look in the man's eyes, not to mention the spittle across his lips, was truly off-putting, even to this most jaded of souls. The man was, like all death cultists, little more than a demon in human form. They craved the death of any who did not yield to their blood-soaked view of existence.

Diving off to her right, Irma Vep sailed over a carefully coiffed shrub and watched as the dagger man plunged his blade deep into the stomach of the lasso holder. Both men stared in shock as a spray of crimson *vitae* covered the knife wielder's arm.

"*Om Krim Kali,*" the dagger man whispered as his compatriot slid backward off his blade.

Rolling to her feet, Irma Vep kicked out, the knife edge of her booted foot striking the dagger man on the side of his head. The impact sounded like a hammer slapping into a side of beef. The assassin dropped to the ground with only the softest moans escaping his lips.

The club-wielding dacoit stared for a second at his fallen friends, and then howled like a wounded wolf. He was tall, almost two meters in height, with broad shoulders, a deep chest and a narrow waist. His face was a larger version of the dagger man's, though possessing the harsher, sharper lines of age. The wooden stick in his huge hand was enormous, longer than his arm and as thick as his barrel-shaped thighs.

Irma Vep smiled as the enraged killer charged forward, his weapon above his head. Reaching into the pouch on her belt, she pulled out a small white object that resembled a bell. With a flick, she hurled the item at her attacker, striking the dacoit's mighty chest without an audible sound. The object exploded on contact, sending a wide plume of pale powder across his face and torso.

The dacoit gagged, choked, coughed, gagged, and wheezed as the fine powder flew into his eyes, nose and mouth. In an instant, he found himself blind and unable to breathe as the miniscule particles overwhelmed his every sense. He dropped his titanic weapon to the ground, pawing at his face with both hands.

Irma Vep stepped behind the assassin and swept him off his feet. The blind and gasping cultist crashed to the cobblestone walk and lay upon the stones, lightly moaning. With a smile and a nod, the cat-suited burglar turned away, returning to the door.

The lock opened with a light snap and the door with a light creak. The cottage was exactly as it appeared from the outside—charming, yet showing the clear deterioration that came from age. The front hallway was a small square, about a yard in length and width. A set of rickety wooden stairs led to the tiny second floor. To the left was a living room, furnished with a matched set of Chesterfield sofas that looked as if they were being held together by dust, cobwebs and prayers.

Irma Vep's trained eye spotted no alarms or other traps—this was a simple job. She merely needed to locate the papers, probably in a locked drawer of some kind, and escape before others arrived. A simple enough proposition in theory.

"I think it is time for Brünnhilde's aria from *Die Götterdämmerung.*" She thought, and softly sang the haunting lyrics of that unpleasant man, Richard Wagner. as she moved through the living room and tested for hiding places.

Music made an unpleasant, dull job, slightly enjoyable.

She found such a hiding place a moment later in the fireplace, a loose brick near the top of the mantle. To the casual thief, this might be a good hiding spot, easily missed in a search of the elderly cottage. But for Irma Vep, a woman raised by the Vampires Gang as a burglar *par excellence*, the location was amusing, at best.

She noticed that the brick was cleaner than the rest of the dirty room. This meant that either someone had specifically cleaned that one brick, or that said item was still in use. Basic reasoning suggested the latter.

Moving aside the brick, Irma Vep removed a small bundle of papers. She glanced at the title and smiled. This was exactly why she was in Iping rather than enjoying the sights, and wealthy idiots that deserved a few less possessions, of distant London.

She had just finished rolling the papers when the front and rear doors exploded inward. Thrusting the papers into her belt pouch, she sighed with audible annoyance.

"Just for once, as a gift, I would enjoy a job that does not end in complete disaster," she said, shaking her head.

The two metal men that entered the cottage seconds later only slightly resembled humanity. Standing about two meters tall, their basic shape was human. They possessed two legs, two arms, and ten fingers. That was where the similarity ended. Made from a silvery metal, their inhuman limbs and torsos shimmered with mirror brightness in the vanishing sunlight. It was as if a pair of powerful, monstrous mirrors had suddenly invaded the crumbling cottage, illuminating the small rooms.

The metal men possessed jeweled eyes that pulsed with a red aura on faces that possessed no discernible human features. No noses or mouths, not even a slit resembling a maw. It was as if their creator, having provided the barest resemblance to humanity, decided against any further connection to that species. These creatures did not even resemble statues, despite their human-styled extremities. These metal monsters had more in common with the steel girders from the vast factory cities encompassing the globe.

266

"Oh, my," Irma Vep said in her musically-accented English. "This is a rather unique development."

"English with French accent," the mechanical being by the front door said.

The voice was human—a strong bass tone with a commanding edge. "Hand over the papers and you will not be harmed."

"I know that voice," Irma Vep said as she rolled her eyes. "Fen-Chu, master of the mechanical men. You always put your voice in each of your toys. Such ego!"

"Irma Vep? Only you would be so bold as to mock Fen-Chu, master of the world. Your death shall be a lesson to all who trifle with my power!" the voice replied.

"*Mon Dieu!*" Irma Vep replied, shaking her head. "Do you ever stop ranting and threatening? Listening to you or your compatriot, Pao Tcheou, is quite insufferable."

"Die!" both machines cried and stomped forward.

The wooden floors creaked and crackled beneath their steel-shod tread, barely supporting their vast weight.

"*Oh, la, la!*" Irma Vep said, stepping back.

Both metal men stood between her and any escape. She had doubts even her Eidolon could survive a battle with two of these monsters—therefore cleverness was the best path.

An idea struck her, one that caused her made-up face to crease in a sardonic grin. This plan was chancy, but if successful, could lead to her successfully escaping. Backing up a step, she glanced at the brick fireplace, grateful the old, filthy place did not possess a wooden mantle.

Waiting until the steel creatures were almost within reach, Irma Vep exploded into action. Leaping up and backwards, her booted feet landed on the fireplace's top. Without pause, she pushed off the mantle top and launched herself forward.

Flying like a human dart, she sailed between both metal men. Their steel arms, unable to grab her, clashed together as they snatched empty air. The clatter of their extremities sounded like the crash of cymbals. The mechanical men then turned around, immediately following her path.

Though the doorway was open, Irma Vep did not head outside. Fen-Chu's creations might be slow on turns and reactions, but they did possess two characteristics that made them deadly: they did not tire and were relentless in their pursuit. She needed to destroy them, or at least incapacitate them before she could flee from the Marvel cottage.

Without pause, Irma Vep ran up the narrow wooden stairs, hearing the wood whine and groan beneath her weight. She stopped at the top of the stairs and looked back, seeing the silvery shapes about to follow her.

"Come and get me, you stupid mechanical *jouets*. I quake with terror at your approach," she called, looking down at her two opponents.

The two metal men did not pause, but began to climb the wooden steps, heading in her direction in a slow walk. The steps creaked and crackled, and the sound of wood splintering filled the air. The stairs shook and shuddered, but somehow allowed the two massive inhuman creatures to progress.

Irma Vep waited, her foot silently tapping impatiently as the silver creatures slowly strode upward. She then sighed as they reached the middle of the stairs, grateful they had finally arrived at a point of no retreat.

Smiling, she set her plan in motion. Leaping forward and down, she struck the steps with her feet just above the first metal men.

With a crack that sounded like a lightning bolt striking a tree, the entire staircase instantly shattered into thousands of splintered shards. The wood, already rickety from age, and barely supporting the weight of the mechanical men, splintered and disintegrated in an instant.

The steel men fell from sight, their heavy bodies crashing straight through the floor beneath into the stone basement. Nearly a ton of wooden, brick and plaster followed their plummeting forms, burying the two mechanical men under its terrible weight.

Irma Vep, her feet and hands splayed out against the walls, stared down at the devastation.

She smiled and began to sing again as she crawled on her hands and feet causing her to resemble a large spider as she moved along the wall towards the door below.

Within minutes, she was out of the cottage and headed towards her rendezvous place, located in one of the few non-industrialized parts of London, Regent's Park.

The park was illuminated by a row of electric lamps, all of which cast odd eldritch shadows across the small expanse. The huge looming towers of the new industrial towers surrounded this last trace of old England like the ramparts of an ancient castle. However, instead of stone and mortar, these spiraling walls and battlements glimmered as moonlight struck their cold metallic walls.

Irma Vep had a meeting, an important one with a unique gentleman. He sat on a bench, a tall hatless figure with fine gray hair and a heavy, long mustache. He possessed the lean build of a former athlete, though his ramrod stiff bearing gave him a vaguely military air.

Irma Vep dropped by his side, her movements as silent and swift as a cat. She grinned at the taller man, impressed as always by his calm control.

"*Bonsoir*, Colonel!" she said. "Have I kept you waiting?"

"No, no, my dear lady. A very good evening to you. I suppose you were successful in your quest for the papers in question?" Colonel March said, rising a few inches and bowing slightly before resuming his seat.

"But of course," Irma replied and handed him the bundle. "Griffin's notes on his invisibility formula. I encountered some competition from Fu Manchu's dacoits and Fen-Chu's metal men, but nothing worthy of notice. Mr. Marvel had not hidden the notes particularly well, either."

Colonel March studied the documents for a few seconds before nodding and placing them in his overcoat pocket.

"Excellent, excellent. Now, I did promise my assistance to you and your friend, the Eidolon. A pardon is, I'm afraid, out of the question—too great a possibility of scandal, you see. However, Sir Henry Merrivale pointed out to me that your service, plus the disappearance of Kathulos of Egypt, supposedly at your hands, did great service to the Empire. As such, we are transferring your case files to a new Inspector, Claud-Eustace Teal. He has exhibited a marked tendency towards gestures of sympathy towards individuals such as yourself. Therefore, you are still a person of interest, but welcome in the Kingdom. Is that acceptable?"

Irma Vep nodded and rose, "Quite acceptable, Colonel. A pleasure doing business with you. Should you require us again, do not hesitate to call. You are far more acceptable to me than Mister Holmes's replacement in the secret service."

"I shall do so," Colonel March said, also rising. "One more request, dear lady?"

Irma raised an eyebrow, "Yes?"

"If you discover a burning desire to steal a set of crown jewels, please consider the French or Russian ones instead of the British? I should find it uncomfortable pursuing you after so successful an operation." Colonel March said, before bowing slightly and disappearing from sight.

Irma Vep laughed as she left the park, then a thought hit her.

How well guarded are the Czar's jewels?

Michel Stephan once more takes over the mantle of the late and regretted André Caroff to craft a short and poignant vignette starring the unforgettable Madame Atomos and one of the best song writers of all times…

Michel Stephan: *Madame Atomos Likes Her Music*

New York, December 1980

The apartment was in a beautiful building, the *Dakota*, located near Central Park in New York. It was an apartment made for a star, which should seem logical since John was very much a star. He was a member of the most famous band of all time. Then his voice had gone silent several years ago. For five years, he had not put out a single record. He vegetated in New York, spending his days with his wife, Yoko, and his son, Sean, moping around inside his gilded cage.

However, things were changing fast now. A few months earlier, John had made another record, a collection of his latest songs, along with some of his wife's.

John had spent hours at his seventh-floor window where he could watch the man wandering around in the crowd. He had spotted him among all the fans who passed by his residence. He had not spoken about this man to Yoko, but she had felt that something in her husband had changed over the past few days. In fact, John was becoming increasingly nervous.

Finally, he made up his mind.

"I have to tell you something," he said to her. "Something really weird is happening. Since the beginning of the week, there's been a guy walking around in front of the building."

"So? What's the problem? What makes him different from any of the others?"

"I don't know. Something tells me he's here to kill me. To tell you the truth, I've always known he would come. I've been fearing this moment for years."

"Come on, John, people don't kill rock stars! Most of them can take care of that themselves, like grown-ups, with an overdose of drugs, legal or not. Of course, you were part of the most important band in rock history, but you never wrote anything but rather harmless songs. They don't kill people for nothing."

"I know they don't kill people for songs! And you know perfectly well what I'm trying to say."

"OK," said Yoko. "But personally, I'd rather we didn't talk about it anymore."

270

John moved away from the window and sat across from his wife in the back of the little kitchen where the steam from the brewing cinnamon tea was starting to spread its fragrance.

"What I mean, Yoko, is that everything I predicted is coming true."

She did not answer, so he went on:

"It was really *her* who we ran into at that party. It was *her* I offended by throwing half my whiskey on her. And it was *her* who told me that one day, she would kill me."

Yoko suddenly looked up.

"Your argument doesn't hold water," she said. "You're crazy, John, and I can prove it. First of all, the party you're talking about was five years ago. If Madame Atomos had really wanted to kill you, you'd have died a long time ago. Plus, you know there were all kinds of Madame Atomoses at those parties. It was a fad at the time; it became a running joke, pretty much expected at every party. And I'm sure the woman you humiliated, and who you've never heard from since, was not that dangerous Japanese once considered public enemy number one in this country. Believe me, if you had disrespected the real Madame Atomos, you wouldn't be here to talk about it."

But John was not listening. He was remembering the party where he had met the woman who had been haunting him all these years. It was after that night that he had become sterile, musically speaking. Once again, the images flashed through his mind.

"It was just after recording *Sergeant Pepper's Lonely Hearts Club Band*. We were thinking about what we were going to put in the liner notes. We'd decided to go one better than the Rolling Stones in provocation. In fact, it was my idea. For the picture, we chose a cliché: the band in front of a flowerbed and behind us a hundred faces, a collage I made myself. Faces of famous men and women, from Gandhi to Brigitte Bardot. And right over Paul's head, I put Madame Atomos. We almost brought out the record like this. But in England, they didn't like it. We were under contract with EMI, and then in the US, they categorically refused. Almost 10,000 liner notes had been printed and we had to make emergency changes to the image at the last minute. And an open hand replaced the face of Madame Atomos over Paul's head. What a waste! It meant nothing anymore. And one evening, during a reception, this woman comes up to me. It was a Japanese woman who was obviously very well informed about the difficulties we'd had with the liner notes—even though nobody was supposed to know about it. She told me something like this: 'My name is Kanoto Yoshimuta and I really like what you did.' It was a comment I thought was really dumb, so I answered, 'Well, not me!' Then I don't know… I guess I threw the rest of my drink on her."

"But it wasn't Madame Atomos, John," Yoko insisted. "There's no way. Besides, the real Madame Atomos has bigger fish to fry than worrying about music and liner notes!"

"And I'm telling you, I know for sure that it was her. I knew it was her right away, from the intense look in her eyes, so intense that I couldn't listen to what she had to say. After I threw my drink on her, she said, 'The day when... I'll kill you.' And then she left."

"That makes no sense, John! 'The day when...' what?"

"The day when you write this, when you do this, when... It could be anything... I don't know, Yoko. I can't remember what she said. There's something I absolutely must not do, and that's why I haven't brought out a bloody record in five years!"

"So now you've cheated fate, John. *Double Fantasy* came out almost a month ago and it's already been a hit!"

"And I fear the consequences for not putting out all my songs. So I mixed them up with yours."

"Come on, John. You don't die for songs."

He stood up and went back to the window.

"You know, this guy outside, there's something I didn't tell you about him. I went to talk to him. His name's Mark Chapman. He's a fan and came here just for me. He's got a nice face. He shook my hand and asked for an autograph. He told me that I was his idol, and he was going to stay around here for a while. I thought he was really nice, quite charming, and yet, I'm sure he's going to kill me because Madame Atomos told him to. Bloody hell, what did I do wrong? What should I have done otherwise?"

"Why not tell the cops?"

"The cops? That's not my thing."

"Well, in that case, keep living a normal life, go down and see him, go talk to him, invite him to dinner. You'll see that it's all in your head."

But John was not listening. Now he was talking to himself.

"As long as I haven't done what I wasn't supposed to do, I'm safe."

"Well, at least that's progress," Yoko sighed.

Their discussion was interrupted by the interphone buzzing. It was the mailman coming to deliver their mail. As usual, the fan letters were bundled up. There were also three official and personal letters, one of which was from their friend, Richard Starkey, and one was from their record company in the US. That was the one Yoko opened first.

"EMI is starting to get impatient and thinks you're putting off the promotion of the album a little too long. We're going to start touring soon and that'll clear up your mind. Come on, John, say something. You're a hit again."

"You're right! I'll go drop by the studio. Downstairs, I'll say hello to my number one fan, Mark Chapman. Here, give me Richard's letter so I can read it on the way."

Yoko handed him the envelope and kissed him before he left the apartment.

Alone now, Yoko looked at the third letter. It was an official letter from Washington DC. She opened the envelope, read the document and her face suddenly lit up with joy.

"There you go!" she smiled brightly. "This time John's going to be in seventh heaven. We've been waiting for this for months. He's finally got his American citizenship!"

Translation by Michael Shreve

A new Tales of the Shadowmen *would not be complete without a story featuring that wonderful rogue, Arsène Lupin, and we can always count on David Vineyard to provide one. The following tale takes place rather late in Lupin's career and manages to bring in several characters from Sax Rohmer's oeuvre...*

David L. Vineyard: *The Theft of the Golden Asp*

Yorkshire, 1938

The house had stood alone and ancient for more years than most of the locals could remember. It rested in the rolling hills of Yorkshire, high on a rise overlooking the green and rocky countryside, a vast estate that had once been home to power and wealth, but now was silent, lonely, isolated.

Locals cut a wide swath from it; even the most audacious poacher avoided the estate. Part of the reason was to be found in the current occupants of Skarr House, named after the family who had built it—strangers, foreigners, some more foreign and far stranger than any of the locals cared to imagine.

Rumors abounded of strange, dark men, curious and dangerous animals roving the great gardens near the house, and, most of all, of the new owner, a man no one had seen, but who all had speculated about; a man said to practice strange rituals in the upper floors of the once-elegant home, alleged to have turned its cellars into dungeons, a man who did not tolerate or welcome visitors, save when necessary repairs had to be effected, as one roofer had recently mentioned.

All anyone knew of him was his name, and only his last name—a "Mr. King" of London and other parts unknown.

Mr. King, formerly of Limehouse, was better known to Scotland Yard and the police of the world as the leader of the Si Fan, the criminal mastermind of a thousand brilliant crimes and brutal murders... Dr. Fu Manchu.

It was early September. A crisp moonless night with low fog hung over the grounds around Skarr House as Fu Manchu, dressed in his traditional gown and lightly stroking the head of his pet marmoset, climbed the stairs to his laboratory located on the top floor of the house. It was occasionally inconvenient to have it there, but practical. The frequently curious odors that wafted from his lair were often poisonous, and rather than having them permeate the rest of the house it was far better to have them confined to the upper story with its great skylight and wide balcony, both easily opened to the soft breezes that usually caressed this hilltop estate.

His mere presence drew enough attention without filling the low vales between the rolling hills with strange and poisonous mists. This was a way station, a literal hideout, a place to gather his forces and gird them for action to come; Not a place to advertize his presence, or risk the curiosity of that meddler Nayland Smith.

This countryside was filled with meddlers, from the Sussex bee-keeper to that saintly rogue with his silly calling card and that jovial bulldog-bred overaged schoolboy and his troop, all too eager to push their Anglo-Saxon noses where they weren't wanted. It seemed at times you couldn't turn around without stirring the interest of some self-appointed guardian of the Western world.

Fu Manchu's mood was curious this night. Recent triumphs should have lifted his soul, but instead, there was a curious anticipation that, somehow, somewhere, his brilliant mind had overlooked some small but vital aspect of his latest plan—the infamous other shoe of Anglo-Saxon parable.

Save that, in the Devil Doctor's business , undropped shoes could all too easily lead to a far different drop, from the gibbet.

His plans, long term, far longer than those of most persons in his situation, were all too easily foiled by some fool incapable of following one tenth of their brilliance and complexity. How else to explain the success of that fool Nayland Smith against him, or his more recent failure in Egypt at the hands of the damned Frenchman, Arsène Lupin.[9]

These thoughts still whirling in his great brain, somewhat distracted, Fu Manchu unlocked the doors to his laboratory and entered.

With a sharp squeal, his pet marmoset leaped from his arms and fled down the hallway behind them. Fu Manchu's fabulously honed reactions hardly let a gasp escape his lips before he had plucked a German Luger from beneath his robes and his long nailed thumb had released its safety. His free hand found the light switch even as he stepped swiftly out of the door frame where he had been silhouetted only seconds before.

The chill that ran up his spine had nothing to do with the unnatural cold in the room.

The layout of the laboratory was such that, near the entrance, was a low couch where he sometimes rested, and an overstuffed straight-back chair, occasionally reserved for his daughter, Fah Lo Suee, who had often soothed her soul there. Beyond, the lab itself was a strange mix of the West and East, lined with cages containing exotic and toxic specimens, both animal and not.

What caught his immediate attention was the figure seated in his daughter's chair. It was Occidental, tall, attractive in the way of the West, dressed somewhat disconcertingly in white tie and tails, with a red and white silk-lined cape, a slender wolf's head walking stick resting against his leg, and a pair of white silk opera gloves folded in his lap.

He had been in disguise the last time Fu Manchu had met him. Now he seemed both younger and more vital, to the point that the Devil Doctor could

---

[9] See "The Third Eye of Osiris" in Volume 14.

imagine that he, too, had access to the *elixir vitae* that was the secret of his fantastic longevity.

"Arsène Lupin," he hissed, the threatening black barrel of the Luger never moving.

The Frenchman merely looked at him, not moving, not speaking. His expression was bored, dismissive, but Fu Manchu sensed the steel spring tension in him.

Fu Manchu was not used to being caught off-guard, but he recovered quickly. Without leaving Lupin's resting figure for long, he quickly scanned the room. Save for the open balcony, the source of the cold air, nothing appeared to have been disturbed—but then it wouldn't be. What Lupin sought was obviously not kept here.

Quickly, keeping Lupin covered, Fu Manchu crossed the room and closed the balcony doors. He then returned to the Gentleman Burglar, who still sat preternaturally still, and turned on the gas in the grate, striking a match and lighting the fire before he seated himself across from the silent Frenchman.

"I find myself at odds, Monsieur," he said. "On the one hand, I should summon my dacoits immediately and have you bound and tortured in the basement below while contemplating your imminent end. On the other, curiosity drives me to inquire what your game is? I know that you have come for the Golden Asp of Cleopatra, but I cannot, for the life of me, fathom your method, however much I admire the mere feat of reaching this house alive. I cannot imagine how you avoided the veritable army of death that surrounds it."

Feeling somewhat more himself as the heat began to suffuse the room, Fu Manchu began to relax.

"All these years, and we have never formally met," he continued. "Yet, I have felt your fine hand in my affairs more than once. There was the business of Hanoi Shan in Saigon so many years ago,[10] and too many times since, but this is the first time we have actually sat opposite each other, adversaries, and yet ones with so much in common that we might well have been the greatest of allies, though I suspect neither of us could stomach being under the orders of the other."

More expansive now, Fu Manchu warmed to his subject.

"I should have known that the Asp would bring you here when I liberated it in Paris. You have always had a particularly personal interest in the treasures of France, even those 'liberated' from other countries—as the little Corsican liberated this from Alexandria during his brief foray into Egypt.

"Of course you know its history... Cleopatra, knowing that her alliance with Antony had led to her ruin, had asp made by the finest jewelers in her kingdom. Filled with venom from the cobra, the arm bracelet had a forked tongue which, when broken off, reveled a crude hypodermic needle delivering

---

[10] See "The Jade Buddha" in Volume 5.

death to anyone it bit. Of course, as it happened, she had no need of the Asp at the end, a real one being at hand, but the Roman soldier who, at Octavian's orders, tried to remove it from her arm perished from its bite.

"The Asp was lost during the long decadence of Rome and its ultimate fall, briefly showing up in the hands of Saladin, and again in those of Suleiman the Magnificent, but then vanishing from history until it was found by one of the artists Napoleon had brought with him to Egypt. Since then, it has rested in the Louvre in Paris, a curiosity of Western imperialism."

Fu Manchu paused, studying Lupin. The latter's absolute stillness was becoming unnerving, as if some latter day sphinx sat across from him, unmoved by his words and unthreatened by his weapon.

"The actual value of the Asp beyond monetary," he continued. "Its very existence had escaped the notice of even the wisest of Western scholars. Knowing nothing of true history, they were unaware of the existence of a cult born in the dying days of Antony and Cleopatra that believed that, one day, the great Queen would return, bringing with her the rebirth of the Egypt of old, driving the Imperial powers out, and returning that Holy Land to its previous greatness. Their symbol was, of course, the Golden Asp that their queen had created for her suicide.

"Having foiled my recent attempt to acquire the Eye of Osiris, you know my interest in Egypt in these troubled days—so great an interest that I do not allow the bracelet out of my presence."

So speaking, Fu Manchu drew back the sleeve of the arm that held the Luger and revealed the delicate golden snake entwined on it, slender as a woman's despite its strength.

Lupin's eyes barely flickered, and still he sat, unmoving.

"Damn your arrogance," Fu Manchu flared. "You'll speak freely enough when the rats begin to gnaw through your Gallic guts. Your game, whatever it is, is up, Lupin. There is no escape, no rescue, no..."

Fu Manchu's green eyes suddenly snapped; he leaped to his feet and walked to the center of the room.

"What is it? A bomb, a gas... you have something up your damned sleeve. Tell me, or I'll kill you where you sit."

His eyes swept the room. What was it? What was the trump card without which the damned Frenchman would not have cared enter his lair? It had to be in this room, and somehow connected with his unnatural stillness.

Fu Manchu's blood ran cold. His eyes quickly scanned the rows of cages on the wall, and very real terror crawled through his spine as he noticed one that had barely been opened, so narrow that only something long and slender and silent as death itself could have escaped unnoticed.

The unwinding green death rushed across the floor at him, its hideous black mouth and fangs bared in anger.

Fu Manchu fired the Luger twice and the black mamba's head exploded under the impact of the shot. The snake writhed in agony at his feet.

In that instant, he caught a glimpse of Lupin, swift as the deadly snake, bringing down his wolf-headed walking stick twice: once smashing his wrist, sending the Luger across the floor, the second blow dropping Fu Manchu to the ground.

The Frenchman moved quickly, bolting the lab doors from the inside, then ripping the cords from the curtains to the balcony to swiftly bind the Devil Doctor's hands and feet on the low couch, before taking a silken handkerchief from his pocket to make a gag, But none of this before carefully removing the Golden Asp and placing it in an especially lined pocket inside his opera cape.

The Gentleman Burglar heard an outcry at the door and the sound of pounding fists. In the same sibilant hiss of the Doctor, he spit out:

"Leave me! Now! Go fools!"

He spoke in perfect Mandarin, his voice an almost exact echo of the Devil Doctor's. The noise outside the door was silenced and he waited as he heard Fu Manchu's servants retreat beneath the threat of their leader's own voice.

Fu Manchu opened his eyes slowly, his anger only tempered by a wave of nausea and the throbbing ache in his head and arm. Lupin was seated across from him, only this time more animated, his eyes and smile sparkling.

"Ah," said the Frenchman, "I wanted to say *adieu* before I took my leave. As you may have guessed by now, I was well aware of the dual nature of the Golden Asp, and equally aware that you would never let it leave your person. With that in mind, I knew I could not hope to recover it without personally bearding the lion in his den, as it were.

"It took me some weeks, and more detective work than I care to recount, to find you, but even the great Fu Manchu must pay for things, and while it it was Vidocq's great rule to look to the woman, my own has always been look to the money.

"Having found you, I then spent some days observing your formidable defenses. A look at the plans for the house, which I found in the old church nearby, and watching you enter this lab and spend long nights with the lights on here, led me to deduce that this would be your personal lair—the one where I could to find you alone. So, when you recently dispatched your daughter on an errand to London, it became clear that it was time to strike."

Lupin rose and nodded at Fu Manchu, whose cold eyes were like daggers.

"I admit the business with the mamba was an improvisation," the Frenchman continued, "but in our line of work, no campaign is complete without some such diversion. I left the balcony windows open when I entered, and waited until the room was quite cold, fearing that you might enter too soon and spoil my plan. Then—and I confess it chilled my very soul to do so—I opened the door to that foul thing's cage, crossed to this chair, and sat frozen, waiting for you to arrive, hoping its cold blood would kept it quiescent.

"If it gives you any comfort, I hoped the creature would not kill you. I do not believe in the waste of lives, not even yours, but considering the blood that might flow if you succeeded, it was a risk I was willing to take.

"Now, I fear I must take my leave. I have no doubt you won't be bound by those ropes for very long, and I do need a few minutes to effect my escape. I won't say *adieu* after all, merely *au revoir*, for I am certain we will meet again. It seems inevitable, and who is to say when we do whether it will be your or my last great play in the game we have chosen. Good night, Doctor."

Lupin bowed, then crossed swiftly to the balcony, disappearing in the darkness as he stepped out of the light.

"No!" I said.

Sitting across from me on a cold October afternoon in the bar of the George V, Lupin looked up, startled, as I slammed down the manuscript he had handed me.

"No?" Lupin said, unused to such passions from his Boswell. "No, what my friend?"

"No," I repeated, "my readers just won't have it. Where is the romance, the bravado, the brilliance? The story, as written, makes no sense; it reveals nothing of how you brought it off, or why. My readers are not interested in seeing the great Lupin ploughing through dusty church records and estate tax records—that is for more mundane adventurers. Where is the passion, the panache?"

"Your readers are tyrants," Lupin commented sipping at his Pernod. "Would they strip Lupin of all of his mystery, his magic?"

"Yes, they would. And I would. They love to read about you, but most of all, they love the idea that they might be you if they had your brains, your gifts, your charm. They don't want to mystified by you; they want to revel in your cleverness. We are not in the business of Houdini."

"I still say your readers are tyrants, but I suppose there is some truth to your observations, and after so many years at this game, I should be a bit more open. So," he leaned back in his chair, "what specifically bothers you about my latest tale?"

"Well, for one, that damned snake."

"The mamba?"

"Yes, the mamba, one of deadliest serpents in the world, and you free it and sit there, blithely hoping it will strike Fu Manchu rather than you. Who would believe the great Lupin could not come up with a better distraction than that? It's cheap melodrama; it's lame"

"Lame? A black mamba, lame? I must say, your readers are demanding, if they find a black mamba lame—but I suppose, it does all seem a bit fantastic.

"Imagine then that Lupin, having learned Fu Manchu kept such a serpent in captivity in his lab, visited a herpetologist in London several days before the events of the story, and then imagine that he purchased from that same herpetologist an African cousin of the mamba, a large non-poisonous snake from the African veldt which, in evolutionary defense, learned to mimic the mamba in coloring and temperament, frightening off would be predators, particularly those who might think twice about swooping down from the sky on a deadly mamba.

"Then, imagine that Lupin carried such a serpent with him when he entered Fu Manchu's lab and, leaving the balcony door open so that the cold air would keep the serpent quiescent, he then used the dog leash and stick provided by Fu Manchu himself to remove the real mamba from its cage and transfer it to another, empty one. Then, he replaced it with the harmless snake and left the door cracked open, planting in Fu Manchu's mind, along with Lupin's strange actions, the idea of the mamba's deadly escape.

"Then, of course, when Fu Manchu became agitated, the faux mamba, still mimicking its deadly cousin, warmed up by the fire that Fu Manchu himself had lit, feigned an attack, allowing Lupin to strike and overcome the good doctor."

"That makes much more sense," I said. "That speaks to the Lupin my audience expects. Now this business about gaining access to the house..."

"My God, man, must your busybody readers strip me of all my secrets?"

I shrugged.

"Oh, very well. Of course, Lupin knew that crossing the open grounds of Fu Manchu's estate would be suicide. Therefore he needed a plan, something simple and audacious, and he saw it in a walk in Hyde Park in London on a Sunday afternoon. Balloons.

"Not fragile children's toys, of course, and neither a giant airbag, too easy a target, but a heavy duty weather balloon, capable of carrying a single man aloft. Of course, the weather patterns would have had to be studied, and thankfully, the Royal Navy provides such records with typical British efficiency. And of course, there would have been test flights in the countryside, and then, with careful planning, the right night would have been chosen, with the correct prevailing winds. Wearing a harness and lifting off from a nearby high hill, Lupin would simply have floated above Fu Manchu's killing ground until he was positioned over the great house, on the roof of which he landed by using a valve to let the helium out. Then, after securing the balloon and producing a rope, Lupin would have climbed down to the balcony.

"After having retrieved the Golden Asp, Lupin climbed back up to the roof, re inflated the balloon with the helium tank waiting there, and repeated the journey, the winds carrying him to a nearby road where a motorbike and leathers waited to convey him some miles away, where a driver and Rolls, replete with waiting champagne, had been exactly positioned for a rendezvous..."

"Wait..."

"What now? Have you tyrannical readers another problem with Lupin's travails?"

He was clearly enjoying the game now, forcing me to drag every carefully planned detail out of him.

"That extra tank of helium..."

"Oh, that! Lupin had left it there when he had visited the house three days earlier to repair the roof and get a lay of the land in daylight..."

"But how...?"

"Good God! But these readers of yours leave me with no mystery at all. Very well, go back some weeks before the crime ,and imagine that Fah Lo Suee, the daughter of Fu Manchu, who has been known to have ambitions of her own, believed she was better equipped to wield the Golden Asp, presenting herself as the reincarnation of Cleopatra and inflaming the passions of a new movement. Imagine that she sought to relieve her father of the Asp and needed a daring burglar, a man with nerves of steel and a brilliant mind.

"Imagine that Lupin, having heard that she was looking for such a man—because, as you know, he always has one ear to the criminal underground—imagine that, with the help of a few friendly rivals whom Fah Lo Suee had already approached, such as Smiler Bunn, Henry Prince, John Mannering, Anthony Trent, and a certain wonder-man named Waldo, led Fah Lo Suee to believe that a Portuguese cracks-man from Brazil, by the name of Boaz de Jao, was just the man for her needs—the Brazilian Bat-Man no less.

"Imagine, too, that the young lady, who has something of a taste for older authority figures—something best explained by Dr. Freud perhaps—became quite taken with the self-same Boaz. Imagine that she provided him with accurate details of the house, the roof, Fu Manchu's draconian security, and even the location of the various poisonous creatures caged in his lab. You might even imagine that the black mamba distraction was her suggestion—the female of the species being far deadlier than the male, as Kipling once suggested.

"You might further imagine that she called for a repairman for the roof, and she aided Lupin in smuggling in the helium tank, and then she arranged for her father to send her on an errand on the night of the crime, but in reality, stayed not too far from Skarr House in order to meet with this Boaz, who greeted her with food and wine—the latter containing a strong sleeping draft so that she spent the night bound and gagged, fuming at her own foolishness much like her father. You might even imagine Lupin lingered long past the time needed so that he could direct Fu Manchu away from any suspicion of his daughter."

"Brilliant!" I exclaimed. "A triumph!"

"A triumph? Moments ago, your readers would have none of it, and now that they have stripped it of all its mystery, you call it a triumph? No, Maurice, not a triumph; indeed far from it."

"How so? You have the Asp, you outwitted both Fu Manchu and his daughter, you escaped with great audacity..."

Lupin dismissed this with a wave of his hand, a weary smile playing on his lips.

"There is some truth in what you say, my friend, but the coda is a most disappointing one. Upon returning to the waiting Rolls-Royce, Lupin discovered that the driver had completely forgotten to chill the champagne. Have you ever tried to celebrate with warm champagne? No, my friend, I tell you, as Fah Lo Suee could certainly attest, it is impossible to get good help these days, the whole night was spoiled."

We were short by a couple of pages for my usual 300-page target for this volume, so I thought I might as well squeeze in this little what if... story I did for our French sister series Les Compagnons de l'Ombre *a few years ago...*

Jean-Marc Lofficier: *Bertie of the Jungle*

"Tally-Ho, Cheetah!" said Tarzan, grabbing the vine.

"Ouk ouk ougl!" exclaimed Cheetah warily—but in vain.

For this "vine" was not actually a vine but rather Histah the boa, who skillfully dodged Tarzan's grip.

The Lord of the Jungle calculated his fall and landed in the grove of doudou plants just below him. Alas, the latter housed Numa the lion who was taking a nap.

Limping and bleeding, Tarzan dragged himself into the shade of the wascian tree, where he sat on Horta the wild boar by mistake.

After a long and exhausting run through the jungle, Tarzan found himself suddenly nose to nose with Gorgo the buffalo, who thought he had recognized a distant cousin in the young man's moccasins.

The agitated discussion ended in Taug the Gorilla's hut, ransacked for the seventh time that month by the "friends" of Tarzan.

A detailed explanation, of the less courteous kind, ensued, at the end of which Tarzan was expelled by the Mangani and had to find shelter with Mbonga the cannibal, who received him with open arms, already licking his lips.

Meanwhile, the ferocious Babaorom tribe had slain Jane Porter, the hunter Koynos had the stuffed head of Jad-bal-ja the lion on the wall of his mansion, and the ivory traffickers had decimated the tribe of Tantor the elephant.

Because, on this world, so close and yet so far from ours, it was not John Clayton, Viscount Greystoke, whose parents had been shipwrecked on the shores of Darkest Africa, but Bertram Wilberforce Wooster's.

ANTICIPATION

FICTION

Pierre BARBET

LA PLANETE ENCHANTÉE

FLEUVE NOIR

Credits

The Vertigo

Starring:	Created by:
Isidore Beautrelet	Maurice Leblanc
Professor Woland	Mikhail Boulgakov
Cagliostro the cat	Tiziano Sclavi
Doctor Morel	Adolfo Bioy Casares
Vorski	Maurice Leblanc
Miss Brunner	Michael Moorcock
Hareton Ironcastle	J.-H. Rosny Aîné
Rachael	Philip K. Dick
Professor Stangerson	Gaston Leroux
Doctor Cinderella	Gustav Meyrinck
Doctor Helfern	Bob Kane & Gardner Fox
M. d'Outremort	Maurice Renard
Doctor Cornelius Kramm	Gustave Le Rouge
Professor Spallanzani	E.T.A. Hoffmann
Co-Starring:	
Oswald Bastable	Michael Moorcock
A.I.M.	Stan Lee & Jack Kirby
Rotwang	Fritz Lang
	& Thea Von Harbou
Also Starring:	
Captain John Flanders	*a.k.a. Jean Ray*
And:	
The Time Machine	H.G. Wells
The Pleasure Machine	Jean-Claude Forest
The *Fulmar*	Jean Ray
The Jewel of Judment	Roger Zelazny
The Eye of the Serpent'	Graeme Morris
Metropolis	Fritz Lang
	& Thea Von Harbou

Daniel ALHADEFF has always alternated phases of profound lethargy with intense hyperactivity. During the latter, he had written mystery, fantasy and science fiction stories, which have twice earned him the ActuSF award He also composes lyrics for several bands and singers. His first short novel was published in the collection *Small Murders in Switzerland*. He tries to play the violin which doesn't make him popular with his neighbors. This is his first contribution to *Tales of the Shadowmen*.

High Noon of the Living Dead

Starring:	Created by:
Jed Puma	Enzo Magni
Tashi	Enzo Magni
Also Starring:	
Doc Holliday	
Billy the Kid	
Jesse James	

Matthew BAUGH lives and works in Albuquerque, NM. He is the pastor of a small church and an editor for Permuted Press. He is also the author of *The Vampire Count of Monte-Cristo*, a mash-up of the classic story of adventure and revenge with vampires, ghosts and Faustian bargains, the co-author, with Win Scott Eckert, of *A Girl and Her Cat*, which continues the adventures of classic TV heroes, Honey West and T.H.E. Cat. He is a regular contributor to *Tales of the Shadowmen*.

A Bug's Life

Starring:	Created by:
Spiridon	André Laurie
Kenneth Williams	Bob Olsen
Mrs. Williams	Bob Olsen
Fryser	Bert I. Gordon & Jack Turley
Hobbs	Saul Bass & Mayo Simon
Joseph van Ee	W.J. Abbott
Robert Parry Renault	Based on Stuart Anthony
	& William Bruckner
	& Robert F. Metzler
Co-Starring:	
Doctor de Villa	Bob Olsen
Gregor Samsa	Franz Kafka
Doctor Francis Ardan	Guy d'Armen
Holroyd	H.G. Wells
Mye-Mye	Árpád Ferenczy
Timothy Thümmel	Árpád Ferenczy
Minunians	Edgar Rice Burroughs
Professor Cavor	H.G. Wells
Doctor Moreau	H.G. Wells

Mortimer Dart	Brian W. Aldiss
And:	
Herakleophorbia	H.G. Wells
Giant Ants	George Worthing Yates
	Ted Sherdeman
	Russell Hughes

Adam Mudman BEZECNY is a graduate from the University of Minnesota Morris. Her previous publications include the novels *Tail of the Lizard King, Deus Mega Therion, Jim Anthony vs. the Mastermind,* and *Kinyonga Tales* as well as the online stories *Dieselworld* and *Words from the Inner Circle.* She is the editor-in-chief of *Odd Tales of Wonder* Magazine, and she also writes movie reviews for the blog Adam Mudman's A-List, which sometimes publishes her fiction (mudmansalist.blogspot.com). He is a regular contributor to *Tales of the Shadowmen.*

A Waltz in Norbury

Starring:	**Created by:**
Edward "Ted" Malone	Arthur Conan Doyle
Professor Challenger	Arthur Conan Doyle
Lord John Roxton	Arthur Conan Doyle
Maxime d'Olbans	Jean de la Hire
Leo Saint-Clair the Nyctalope	Jean de la Hire
Co-Starring:	
Austin	Arthur Conan Doyle
Jessie Challenger	Arthur Conan Doyle
Enid Challenger	Arthur Conan Doyle
Nemor	Arthur Conan Doyle
Sherlock Holmes	Arthur Conan Doyle
Dr. John H. Watson	Arthur Conan Doyle
Lucifer	Jean de la Hire

Thierry BOSCH is the head of the Optoelectronics Group for Embedded Systems at the French scientific institute LAAS-CNRS. His research focuses on the design of laser sensors for measuring distances, vibrations and velocities. He's won the European Mechatronics Award (Research category) in 2010 and the Jean Ebbeni prize awarded by the Optical Measurements Club for the Industry of the French Optics Society in 2011. He's had a number of stories published, in both French and English before. He is currentlyworking on a novel, *Alamud Ahab and the Great White Werewolf.* This is his first contribution to *Tales of the Shadowmen.*

The Crater of the Dead

Starring:	Created by:
Jaydee	Danilo Grossi
Miss Kiss	Giorgio Trevisan
Professor Quanter	Fausto Oneta
Doctor Omega	Arnould Galopin
Co-Starring:	
Professor Bernard Quatermass	Nigel Kneale

Matthew DENNION lives in South Jersey with his beautiful wife and daughters. He currently works as a teacher of students with autism at a Special Services School. Matthew writes giant monster stories for *G-Fan* magazine and he has recently published three giant monster novels, *Chimera: Scourge of the Gods*, *Operation R.O.C.: A Kaiju Thriller* and *Atomic Rex*. He is a regular contributor to *Tales of the Shadowmen*.

Doctor Omega and the Future Museum

Starring:	Created by:
Fantômas	Pierre Souvestre & Marcel Allain
The Master	Barry Letts, Terrance Dicks & Robert Holmes
Jasmine "Jaz" Driscoll	David Friend
Doctor Omega	Arnould Galopin
Liz Shaw	Barry Letts, Terrance Dicks & Robert Holmes
Co-Starring:	
Inspector Juve	Pierre Souvestre & Marcel Allain
The Mechonoids	Terry Nation

David FRIEND lives in Wales, where he divides his time between watching old detective films and thinking about old detective films. He's been scribbling out stories since he was seven years old and hopes, some day, to write something half-decent. Most of what he pens is set in a 1930s world of non-stop adventure with debonair sleuths, kick-ass damsels, criminal masterminds and narrow escapes, and he wishes he could live there. This is his first contribution to *Tales of the Shadowmen*.

The Skull of Boris Liatoukine

Starring:
Boris Liatoukine
Polly Bird
David Harker
Irina Petrovski

Co-Starring:
Irene Adler
Irma Vep
The Vampires

Created by:
Marie Nizet
Paul Féval
based on Bram Stoker
based on Arnaud d'Usseau
& Julian Zimet

Arthur Conan Doyle
Louis Feuillade
Louis Feuillade

Brian GALLAGHER has a BA in Politics and Society and lives in London. He works in the media and for many years has written on the politics, economics and many other aspects of Croatia and has been quoted in Croatian and international media. In relation to that he has written extensively on Croatian-related cases at the International Criminal Tribunal for the Former Yugoslavia. He has always been interested in science fiction, classic horror, comics and is proud to be a lifelong *Doctor Who* fan. He is a regular contributor to *Tales of the Shadowmen*.

Rouletabille and the House of Despair

Starring:
Harry Dickson
Judith Fraser/Vinegar Judy
Joseph Rouletabille
Dr. Rupert Grierson
Mrs. Bardell
Solar Pons
Sherlock Holmes
Sexton Blake
Seaton Begg
Victor Drago
Also Starring:
Alfred Hitchcock

Created by:
Anonymous
Martin Gately
Gaston Leroux
Martin Gately
William Murray Graydon
August Derleth
Arthur Conan Doyle
Harry Blyth
Michael Moorcock
Chris Lowder & Roy Preston

Martin GATELY is the author of the official prequel to Philip José Farmer's first novel, *The Green Odyssey (Samdroo and the Grassman* in *The Worlds of Philip José Farmer 4 – Voyages to Strange Days)*. His writing career commenced in 1988 when he wrote for D C Thomson's legendary *Starblazer* comic book. He is also a contributor to the UK's journal of strange phenomena *Fortean*

Times. For Black Coat Press, he has provided stories for the following anthologies: *Night of the Nyctalope, Harry Dickson Vs. The Spider* and *The Vampire Almanac Vol. 1*. His latest work is an adaptation of Edgar Rice Burroughs' *Pirate Blood* into comic strip form – drawn by Anthony Summey and available on the official Edgar Rice Burroughs website. He is a regular contributor to *Tales of the Shadowmen*.

The Robots of Valencia

Starring:	Created by:
Monoclard	Théo Varlet & André Blandin
Alejandro de la Vega	based on Johnston McCulley
Lotte	Paul Féval
The Wandering Jew	Paul Féval
Brigitte	based on Fritz Lang & Thea Von Harbou
Rotwang	based on Fritz Lang & Thea Von Harbou
The Volkites	Maurice Geraghty & Oliver Drake
Co-Starring:	
Doctor Omega	Arnould Galopin

Travis HILTZ started making up stories at a young age. Years later, he began writing them down. In high school, he discovered that some writers actually got paid and decided to give it a try. He has since gathered a modest collection of rejection letters and had a one-act play produced. Travis lives in the wilds of New Hampshire with his very loving and tolerant wife, two above average children and a staggering amount of comic books and *Doctor Who* novels. He is a regular contributor to *Tales of the Shadowmen*.

The Night of the Craven Raven

Starring:	Created by:
Henry West	G.G. Fickling
Leo Saint-Clair	Jean de La Hire
Harry Dickson	*Anonymous*
Honey West	G.G. Fickling
Manse Everard	Poul Anderson
Doctor Omega	Arnould Galopin
Fred	Arnould Galopin
Co-Starring:	
John Galt	Ayn Rand
Howard Roark	Ayn Rand

The Danellians	Poul Anderson
The Spiders	Fritz Leiber
The Snakes	Fritz Leiber
Edith Keller	Harlan Ellison

Also Starring:
William J. Donovan
Ian Fleming
Nikola Tesla
Edgar Allan Poe (and all other figures pertaining to his life)

Paul HUGLI has a degree in Zoology, and has written for everything from *Cracked* magazine to general interest pamphlets, and for most of the first, second *and* third tier adult magazines. He is the author of three published "adult fantasy" novels, and the acclaimed *Traci Lords Companion*. He has also been employed as a science/math instructor, and as a "Floor Manager" at a local "Gentleman's Club." In addition, he once owned/managed Destiny Bookstore, which dealt in SF, comics and adult "fantasy" magazines, for 30 years. He now has three novels in the works. He is a regular contributor to *Tales of the Shadowmen*.

Science Outraged, Science Murdered!

Starring:	**Created by:**
Ganimard	Maurice Leblanc
Arsène Lupin	Maurice Leblanc
Fantômas	Pierre Souvestre & Marcel Allain

Gulzar JOBY is a French SF writer with degrees in physics and design, His first story was published in 2008. Since then, he has written many more stories and articles on subjects ranging from science fiction to hard science and technology. He has also directed several short features and documentary films and is very fond of photography. He has won prizes in the prestigious ENSTA ParisTech short-story contest in 2010 and 2011. This is his first contribution to *Tales of the Shadowmen*.

The Necropolis of Silence

Starring:	**Created by:**
Indiana Jones	George Lucas, Philip Kaufman & Steven Spielberg
Bob Morane	Henri Vernes

Colonel Dietrich	Vincent Jounieaux
Also Starring:	
General Gustav von Värst	

Vincent **JOUNIEAUX** is a Professor of medicine and the author of many scientific articles. Married, father of four children, he decided at age 51, after writing the story "The Abominable Conspiracy" (published in *The Shadow of Judex*) to embark on a trilogy of SF novels, starting with *The Time of the End*, followed by *Space Requiem*, both published by our French sister imprint, Rivière Blanche. This is his first contribution to *Tales of the Shadowmen*.

Lucretius' Maze

Starring:	**Created by:**
Titus Crow	Brian Lumley
Setni	Pierre Barbet
Shub-Niggurath	H.P. Lovecraft
Montbrison	Léo Malet
Co-Starring:	
Rael	Peter Gabriel
Henri-Laurent de Marigny	Brian Lumley
	based on H.P. Lovecraft
Pentoser	Pierre Barbet
Noël Essaillon	René Barjavel
Nestor Burma	Léo Malet
Maïcha	Pierre Barbet
Also Starring:	
Titus Lucretius Carus	

Jean-Guillaume **LANUQUE** is a teacher by trade, a historian by training, and a writer by passion. He conducts research on French science fiction, and has put together and edited four anthologies published by Rivière Blanche on the theme of the *Merveilleux Scientifique*, revisiting and updating the heritage of pre-1950 SF. He has also written a series of stories featuring "The Marvelous Four," a group of 18th century superheroes, also for Rivière Blanche. This is his first contribution to *Tales of the Shadowmen*.

Enemies of the People

Starring:	**Created by:**
Judex	Arthur Bernède & Louis Feuillade
Fantômas	Pierre Souvestre & Marcel Allain
Una Persson	Michael Moorcock

Auguste "Langelot" Pichenet	Vladimir Volkoff
Hedwige "Choupette" Roche-Verger	Vladimir Volkoff
Madame Schasch	Vladimir Volkoff
Doctor Omega	Arnould Galopin
The Marchef	Paul Féval
Co-Starring :	
Monsieur Zenith	Anthony Skene
Oswald Bastable	Michael Moorcock
Jean Kariven	Jimmy Guieu
Fanferlot	Emile Gaboriau
Sexton Blake	Harry Blyth
Lord Ruthven	John William Polidori
Colonel Bozzo-Corona	Paul Féval
The Black Coats	Paul Féval
BlackSpear	Jean-Marc Lofficier
SPHINX	Vladimir Volkoff
Cordovan	Vladimir Volkoff
Sylvie Mac Dhul	Jean de La Hire
And:	
The Zone	Arkady & Boris Strugatski
Teku Benga	Michael Moorcock

Nigel MALCOLM lives in Kent, England. He works as a teacher of English as a Foreign Language. He is a long-term *Doctor Who*, *Star Trek* and *Prisoner* fan—long before all the new-fangled versions came along. He is still working on that elusive steampunk novel and various short stories. He is a regular contributor to *Tales of the Shadowmen*.

The Anti-Adonis Alliance

Starring:	**Created by:**
Quasimodo	based on Victor Hugo & Sean Todd
Erik	Gaston Leroux
Felifax	Paul Féval, *fils*
Baber	Paul Féval, *fils*
Judex	Arthur Bernède & Louis Feuillade
Co-Starring:	
Sourina	Paul Féval, *fils*
Djina	Paul Féval, *fils*
Bertrand Caillet	Guy Endore
Frankenstein Monster	Mary Shelley

| Felanthus | & Jean-Claude Carrière |
| | Christofer Nigro |

Christofer NIGRO is a writer of both fiction and non-fiction with a strong interest in pulps, comic books and fantastic cinema, and a regular contributor to *Tales of the Shadowmen*. He may be known to some by his websites *The Godzilla Saga* and *The Warrenverse*, as he is an authority on the subject of *dai kaiju eiga* (the sub-genre of cinema specializing in giant monsters), and the characters featured in the comic magazines published by Warren. He has recently revived and expanded Chuck Loridans' classic site MONSTAAH, and has since been published in the anthologies *Aliens Among Us* and *Carnage: After the Fall*. He is a regular contributor to *Tales of the Shadowmen*.

The Gutter God

Starring:	**Created by:**
Carnacki	William Hope Hodgson
Inspector Lestrade	Arthur Conan Doyle
The Vampires	Louis Feuillade
Dr. John H. Watson	Arthur Conan Doyle
Corvena Septimus	John Peel
	based on Louis Feuillade
Cavanagh	William Hope Hodgson
Co-Starring:	
Sherlock Holmes	Arthur Conan Doyle
Irma Vep	Louis Feuillade
Also Starring:	
Bacchus	
"Polly" (Mary-Ann Nicols)	

John PEEL was born in Nottingham, England, and started writing stories at age 10. John moved to the U.S. in 1981 to marry his pen-pal. He, his wife ("Mrs. Peel") and their 13 dogs now live on Long Island, New York. John has written just over 100 books to date, mostly for young adults. He is the only author to have written novels based on both *Doctor Who* and *Star Trek*. His most popular work is *Diadem*, a fantasy series; he has written ten volumes to date. He is a regular contributor to *Tales of the Shadowmen*.

Irma Vep and The Cottage of Doom

Starring:	**Created by:**
Irma Vep	Louis Feuillade
Fen Chu	George Fronval

Colonel March	John Dickson Carr
Co-Starring:	
Thomas Marvel	H.G. Wells
The Eidolon	Frank Schildiner
Rudy Valentine	Gene Wilder
Woltz Pictures	Mario Puzo
Pao Tcheou	Edward Brooker
Griffin	H.G. Wells
Fu Manchu	Sax Rohmer
Sir Henry Merrivale	John Dickson Carr
Kathulos	Robert E. Howard
Claud-Eustace Teal	Leslie Charteris
Mycroft Holmes	Arthur Conan Doyle

Frank **SCHILDINER** has been a pulp fan since a friend gave him a gift of Philip Jose Farmer's *Tarzan Alive*. Since that time he has written *The Quest of Frankenstein, The Triumph of Frankenstein, Napoleon's Vampire Hunters* and *The Devil Plague of Naples* for Black Coat Press. Frank has been published in *The New Adventures of Thunder Jim Wade, Secret Agent X* Volumes 3, 4, 5, *Ravenwood, Stepson of Mystery, The Black Bat Mystery, Pride of the Mohicans, The New Adventures of Richard Knight* and *The Avenger: The Justice Files*. Frank works as a martial arts instructor at Amorosi's Mixed Martial Arts. He resides in New Jersey with his wife Gail who is his top supporter. He is a regular contributor to *Tales of the Shadowmen*.

Madame Atomos Likes Her Music

Starring:	**Created by:**
Madame Atomos	André Caroff
Also Starring:	
John Lennon	
Yoko Ono	

Michel **STEPHAN** was born and lives in Brittany with his wife and two children. He has been a fan of science fiction, fantasy and horror since age 10. He loves Universal monster movies (especially the *Frankenstein* series), sci-fi serials and collects Aurora model kits. He has recently written new *Madame Atomos* novels for Black Coat Press's French sister imprint, Rivière Blanche, and is a regular contributor to *Tales of the Shadowmen*.

The Theft of the Golden Asp

Starring:	Created by:
Doctor Fu Manchu	Sax Rohmer
Arsène Lupin	Maurice Leblanc
Fa Lo Suee	Sax Rohmer
Co-Starring:	
Sir Denis Nayland Smith	Sax Rohmer
Sherlock Holmes	Arthur Conan Doyle
Simon Templar	Leslie Charteris
Bulldog Drummond	H.C. "Sapper"McNeile
John Mannering	John Creasey
Anthony Trent	Wyndham Martin
Henry Prince	Cecil Freeman Gregg
Smiler Bunn	Bertram Atkey
Waldo the Wonderman	E.S. Brooks
Also Starring:	
Maurice Leblanc	

David L. VINEYARD is a fifth generation Texan (named for his gunfighter/Texas Ranger great grand-father) currently living in Oklahoma City, OK, where the tornadoes come sweeping down the plains. He has useless degrees in history, politics, and economics, and is the author of several tales about Buenos Aires private eye Johnny Sleep, two novels, several short stories, some journalism, and various non-fiction. He is currently working on several ideas while battling with a three month old kitten for household dominance and the keyboard of his PC. He is a regular contributor to *Tales of the Shadowmen*.

Bertie of the Jungle

Starring:	Created by:
Tarzan	Edgar Rice Burroughs
Bertie Wooster	P.G. Wodehouse
Also Starring:	
Babaorom	Hergé
Koynos	Jean de La Hire

Jean-Marc & Randy LOFFICIER, the editors of the *Tales of the Shadowmen* series, have also collaborated on five screenplays, a dozen books and numerous translations, including *Arsène Lupin, Doc Ardan, Doctor Omega, The Phantom of the Opera* and *Rouletabille and The Mystery of the Yellow Room*. Their latest novels include *Edgar Allan Poe on Mars* and *The Katrina Protocol*. They have written a number of animation teleplays, including episodes of *Duck Tales* and

The Real Ghostbusters and such popular comic book heroes as *Superman, Doctor Strange* and created the Mayan detective series *Tongue*Lash*. In 1999, in recognition of their distinguished career as comic book writers, editors and translators, they were presented with the Inkpot award for Outstanding Achievement in Comic Arts. Randy is a member of the Writers Guild of America, West and Mystery Writers of America.

WATCH OUT FOR

TALES OF THE
SHADOWMEN
VOLUME 16: VOIR DIRE
TO BE RELEASED DECEMBER 2019

DO NOT MISS THE RETURN OF

IRMA VEP

IN
FRANK SCHILDINER'S

IRMA VEP AND
THE GREAT BRAIN OF MARS